**If you'd like to keep track of the titles
you've read,
Don't mark up our books – mark this
paper instead.**

The
Fisher Boy

The Fisher Boy

Stephen Anable

Poisoned Pen Press

Poisoned
Pen
Press

First Edition 2008

10 9 8 7 6 5 4 3 2 1

Library of Congress Catalog Card Number: 2007940713

ISBN: 978-1-59058-480-4 Hardcover

Poisoned Pen Press
6962 E. First Ave., Ste. 103
Scottsdale, AZ 85251
www.poisonedpenpress.com
info@poisonedpenpress.com

Printed in the United States of America

*For my
family*

Author's Note

The Truro in my book is bigger and more wooded than the real town existing today on Cape Cod. However, the incident in World War I, the shelling of the *Perth Amboy* by a German submarine, actually took place on July 21, 1918, as reported by Mary Heaton Vorse in her wonderful Provincetown memoir, *Time and the Town*.

Chapter One

In Provincetown, I felt enveloped in the shivery skin of a paranoid, all goosebumps and heartbeat. Everyone was a suspect in the brutal murders. Nothing seemed real but a sense of fear, fear as elemental and prevalent as the Cape Cod sand.

Provincetown *is* sand. It's just a sandbar really, washed together by glaciers and billions of tides—and slowly washing apart. Roots hold the whole of Cape Cod together, roots of grasses and shrubbery and trees. What man has done, building windmills and saltbox houses, Coast Guard stations and condominiums, the Pilgrim Monument and Route 6, is all secondary. Provincetown and all of Cape Cod is sand, no more stable than the sandbar at your favorite beach, the one that shifts, seductively, from summer to summer. That evangelist, who intruded into our lives that summer, was right about one thing, about the temporary nature of this coast…

◇◇◇

A ship was the harbinger of disasters to come, a ship the otherworldly white of a piece of the moon, like the *Flying Dutchman* dropped anchor in Provincetown Harbor. But everyone knew this wasn't the ghost vessel of maritime legend, but the Swedish tall ship, the *Vasa*, sailing down the coast from Boston to Annapolis, with a crew of blond cadets with sunburnt ears, dressed in wide-collared, old-fashioned sailors' suits. Everything that happened that hot, dry summer when the rain refused to come, when the drought inflicted a kind of malnutrition on the land, seemed to begin with the presence of that ship on the silvery stillness of Provincetown Harbor.

I teased my friend Arthur about the *Vasa*. "Did you order that ship? Did you order it special for your party?"

And he laughed. "If I'd ordered that ship I'd have ordered the crew to be here *en masse*."

But no one needed an order to attend Arthur Hilliard's parties. In fact, people fought for invitations. Arthur was tall, with wiry gray hair. Big-boned and theatrical, he was as bright as the Gilbert and Sullivan scores he'd sung through college at Yale. Over the years, his body seemed to grow in proportion to the extroversion of his personality. Already, on Memorial Day weekend, he was as tanned as the cordovan of his tassel loafers, and he had donned his standard preppie summer drag, an indigo jacket shot through with yellow and shrimp-pink.

Like me, Arthur was a Bostonian, but it was his summer place in Provincetown that made his reputation. Buttercup-yellow, on the harbor side of Commercial Street, this extended saltbox was one of the most lavish homes in the West End. It all but groaned with antiques: gilt sconces delicate as frost, marble lions looted from pagodas, paintings of clipper ships in seas turbulent as Jacuzzis.

Years later, I'd remember that house not as a series of rooms but as a series of parties. Although Arthur was rich, he was in no sense materialistic and never any kind of collector. He *owned* things, he didn't buy them. Fun as he was, he was never frivolous. His parties—the springs of liquor and tables of food, the tequila and crab cakes, gin and lobster bisque—were always thrown to benefit a cause.

He was a fashionable yet beloved figure, which is often a contradiction in terms. "Think of the word 'colony,' as in 'summer colony,'" he'd say. "What did people do when they colonized a place? Exterminate the indigenous population with a combination of prayers and smallpox, then plunder the natural resources." Arthur worked to ensure we didn't colonize Provincetown, didn't treat the year-rounders as scenery or summer help, then vanish each autumn to forget the place. His parties funded good works for the town, bought computers for its schools, saved a marsh from reincarnation as a strip mall.

I suppose Arthur functioned as my "mentor," a slightly creepy term, I've always thought. We were both alumni of St. Harold's, a second-rate prep school that had expired two summers before in the Berkshires. He was my elder by a good twenty years, so we hadn't crossed paths on the playing fields, but had met much later at a restaurant-of-the-moment in the South End. He'd scrounged up my first job at an advertising agency, where I'd extolled the virtues of software and after-shave and had seemed too earnest to be fired.

But that was over. I'd left my job, paycheck, and health insurance for a sort of bungee jump into show business. Staying in Provincetown for the summer, renting a seedy furnished apartment above a leather store, I'd volunteered to book gigs for our fledgling comedy troupe. We had done ten well-received shows in the basement of a food co-op in Cambridge, and were now trying to crack the Provincetown club circuit. But we were late, pitifully late, because most clubs had booked their acts months before.

Sitting on my host's chintz sofa, I reminded Arthur I was hungry for introductions to the club owners sure to flock to his party. "We just need a break," I said. "We're 'almost there.'"

"I've been 'almost there' for most of my life." Arthur gave me an aquarium-sized gin and tonic. "Don't worry, Mark, all the contacts you need will be here today. Everyone knows I inaugurate the season."

"Roger Morton is especially important." Roger Morton owned Quahog, a restaurant known for its so-so food—flour-filled chowders and "scallops" that might be skate—and top-rate entertainment.

"He'll be here, they'll all be here."

"I've invited our best actor, Roberto Schreiber." I shamelessly added, "He's very attractive."

Strangely, the single Arthur let this remark pass, saying, "I want you to see my newest treasure." Some jade bodhisattva or Staffordshire spaniels a maiden aunt had given him, I assumed. Then this guess imploded when he said, "He's in the kitchen, making the bouillabaisse. I asked you early just so you could meet him."

Arthur led me through the low-ceilinged rooms, most painted a muted pea-green and containing enough nautical artifacts—scrimshaw, engravings of battles involving the *Constitution*—to make me think the treasure could be a sailor shanghaied from some earlier time, complete with pigtail, tarry fingers, and clay pipe.

"This is Edward," Arthur said. "Edward Babineaux."

Edward was short, five-six or so, with buzz-cut, honey-colored hair and the snub nose of a child or a Hummel figurine. His blue eyes matched the shells of the mussels he was cleaning, and the alertness of those eyes fought the sensuality of his other attractions—the muscular column of his neck, his full lips. He was twenty-five at most, half Arthur's age, in one of his host's monogrammed shirts, and, evidently, nothing else. The long, pin-striped expanse of Brooks Brothers cotton just covered the tawny hair of his thighs.

"Mark is a star of the stage, just as you are a star of the kitchen," Arthur told him. Then the doorbell rang and he drew a long slug from his gin and tonic before kissing Edward, then rushing to greet his guests.

A blush stained Edward's face. Was he was ashamed of being kissed by a much older man or by his sparse, borrowed wardrobe? Sometimes I'd worried that Arthur compensated for being single by loving all of society through doing good works. Edward might literally signal a change of heart.

Edward drew the vast abundance of fresh fish toward him over the polished granite counter. Here were clams with shells sturdy as castanets, crab legs, bloody pieces of tuna...It prompted me to remember a story my mother had read me when I was a child about a Chinese boy who swallows the sea, exposing its contents on the ocean floor: whales, shipwrecked junks, corals, and mermaids. When I mentioned my mother and the story, Edward didn't bother glancing in my direction. "My mother wasn't a reader," he said. Clearly, Arthur hadn't chosen him for his conversation.

"…So you're a friend of Mark's," Arthur was booming from the dining room. "He's in the kitchen, talking to my treasure."

Roberto Schreiber cursed the Southeast Expressway in English and Hebrew. San Juan-born, the son of an astrophysicist, he was an actor bristling with a scientist's efficiency. Wearing a T-shirt silkscreened with a pair of kissing lavender dinosaurs, he scrutinized everything: the kitchen, his host, and especially the cook. Since he could meet a person and map their essence—voice, posture, walk, then "do" them—I was dreading that he might do Edward, or, worse, Arthur, but he was civil.

"This is my treasure," Arthur said to Roberto. "Besides being beautiful, Edward is a chef. He's been at the shore all day, harvesting the ingredients of our feast. He's been very careful to remove all the pearls from the oysters, so none of us choke."

"There are no oysters in my bouillabaisse," Edward stated. Arthur certainly hadn't chosen him for his humor either.

"We must let Edward work his witchcraft in peace," Arthur said. "Michelangelo didn't carve the *David* in public."

So Arthur ushered us out into The View: the terrace of gray-blue flagstones, the garden, the water. Here were spiky mauve delphiniums, masses of daisies, irises in varying blues and ivories, and peonies heavy with globular flowers, creamy pinks and whites cool as moons. Interspersed with these were ferns and grasses, and a fishpond with waterlilies and wrestling putti. Shading the garden was an immense silver maple, while beyond stretched the great bowl of Provincetown Harbor, where the tide was out, the dories resting on wet ribs of sand. Off in the distance was the *Vasa*.

Other guests began arriving as we wandered through the garden. Some Siberian irises were in bloom, their flowers so delicate they looked torn. Roberto broke off a blossom and wedged it behind his ear, changing himself from the young Samson into a Polynesian. "What's that ship?" he asked, so I told him, then said, "Remember, we're on a mission. Bookings, bookings, bookings."

We would be breaking a sacred Provincetown taboo. You weren't supposed to network at Arthur's parties. Nobody brought business cards or even carried a pen. It was an unwritten rule that everyone was off-duty. People celebrated the coming summer and surviving the long New England winter.

Guests with drinks were drifting out onto the terrace, twins with moustaches they might have borrowed from one another and the Unitarian minister in her orange dashiki. Somebody was complaining that the *Vasa*'s captain was heterosexist, keeping his crew "quarantined" in Provincetown after giving them liberty in Boston. The twins began spouting statistics about the *Vasa*, how it was a full-rigged ship built in 1930, 253 feet long, with a steel hull, carrying a crew of 80.

"Someone said it was Hermann Goering's yacht. It was impounded after the war."

"Yes, it's considered unlucky. Cursed."

"It ran aground off the Isle of Wight. A cadet died of a ruptured appendix off Madeira."

"But it's so beautiful!"

"Like a mirage!"

From a corner of my eye, I caught sight of Ian Drummond, laughing as he swigged a bottle of beer. "I hope they let visitors on the *Vasa*," one woman was saying as Ian maneuvered past her to punch my arm. "Long time no see!" he said, and immediately I noticed that he'd bulked up, added muscle, lots of muscle.

"Roberto," I said, "I'd like you to meet the man who rescued me from the Atlantic."

Ian laughed, but Roberto wanted the details.

"Nothing dramatic," Ian said. "A childhood adventure gone wrong. Two brats in a rowboat during a storm."

"I thought you'd moved to San Francisco."

"Yes," Ian said. He'd spent "two wasted years out west," involved as the lawyer in some real estate deal. But he decided that San Francisco "wasn't serious," and the geology bothered him. "The earth moved, then so did I."

"Ian and I were at prep school together. At St. Harold's," I told Roberto.

"The late, great St. Harold's," Ian said.

"Late?" Roberto said.

"It closed. It had a rather small endowment. A problem I'm sure none of us share."

"It's a health spa now, isn't it?" I was fighting the image of dowagers in towels sipping carrot juice in our ex-classrooms.

"Something like that." The subject was painful for Ian. Unlike me, he'd always loved the school.

The terrace was now filling with people, a cross section of Cape Cod and Boston, people of all ages and sexualities. A party was taking shape, a warm weather animal with the short intense life of something born in a vernal pool. Already, I was regretting my giant gin and tonic because my thinking felt compromised by the alcohol.

"I saw your troupe on a visit to Cambridge," Ian said. "I didn't have time to come backstage." He took a swig from his Heineken, then swirled it through his mouth, as if rinsing his teeth. "You're quite the performer," he said to me. "You too, Ricardo." He enjoyed sabotaging names, and the way he'd said "performer" was crisp with condescension. Ian had been quite the performer in prep school, quite the ladies' man at dances at St. Harold's, whirling his dates, dipping them low while holding them at the small of their backs.

"So what do you think of Arthur's treasure?" Ian said. "Personally, I've never seen anyone cooking bouillabaisse half-naked and sniffing amyl nitrate!"

"Dinner is served!" our host was calling.

His guests on the terrace, a hundred or so people, chatted and laughed a bit more loudly in anticipation of the food as they began filing into the house, toward the dining room. Edward was now clothed, in a T-shirt tie-dyed like the aurora borealis and gym shorts made of an ice-blue material like Mylar. His "masterpiece," the bouillabaisse, was steaming in three deep pottery tureens painted with squid swimming through garlands of seaweed.

"It smells just like Provence!" somebody remarked.

We helped ourselves, buffet-style, from a candle-lit table in the dining room. People began sawing the fragrant loaves of Portuguese bread and pulling at the mountain of salad—spinach, endive, dandelion—with silver tongs. Soft party sounds rode the warm wind, gossip, the rattle of ice cubes, the scrape of espadrilles and deck shoes along the carpet. Everyone seemed happy—except Arthur.

"Does anyone else think it's too hot for these candles? Aesthetically, they're fine, but it makes me hot just to look at them. Of course without them this room is just so murky…"

Everyone averted their eyes. Our host was known to be bipolar and had just stopped taking his meds cold-turkey. He fidgeted with the candles, shifting them and pinching at the dribblings of hot wax.

Then, seizing the moment, Edward elbowed through the crowd, and, with a dancer's grace and what seemed to be a single elegant gesture, snuffed out the candles and raised the window shades. Quickly, someone applauded, defusing the tension.

"It's just like Edward to let the sun shine in!" Arthur laughed.

"I can't wait to taste this." Ian cut in line to attack the bouillabaisse. He sampled it, then remarked in a loud, distracting tone, the assured voice that is a sure sign that all is not well: "This is absolutely wonderful!" Everyone focused on Edward's masterpiece, Arthur freshened their drinks and we all gradually migrated back onto the terrace.

There, I was embraced by a stately woman with something of the young Vanessa Redgrave in her physique, a kind of hippie majesty. She wore a long paisley dress and amber beads like pieces of butterscotch. This was Arthur's cousin, Miriam Hilliard.

I told Roberto that Miriam made jewelry, beautiful things set with strange stones, not the haphazard Afghan or Tibetan junk, dull as old jackknives, predominant in so many Provincetown shops. Miriam confided that she was already having trouble with customers, this early. "There are so many street kids this year! It's worse than the Summer of Love." In her mid-fifties, Miriam was old enough to have experienced Haight-Ashbury in its prime, but back then she had been at boarding school in Lausanne, a Nixon Republican addicted to skiing, before the Peace Corps, social work, and motherhood altered her views. Miriam had burnt out doing social work, bringing the job home, taking the cases to heart. Making jewelry, dealing with gemstones and precious metals instead of broken lives, was infinitely less burdensome. She reported that Chloe, her three-year-old, was growing like the proverbial weed, spending the day at her shop, where the cashier was doubling as babysitter.

"I see you're enjoying the bouillabaisse," I said to Miriam. She tended toward vegetarianism when not lapsing into chicken or fish, but found the bouillabaisse "heaven." And she had been reluctant to try it. "I got sick eating mussels once, in Barcelona."

"Edward made it," I said.

"So the treasure can cook," Miriam whispered. "Does anyone else know Edward? I mean, he just came in with the tide. Arthur found him sleeping on the beach in back of the house." She reverted to social work jargon, to M.S.W.-speak: "Marginal people can have issues."

So many guests were congregating on the terrace that plants in the garden were being damaged, some impatiens flattened, some hibiscus crushed. On Arthur's silver maple, the leaves, upturned in the wind, looked dusted with metal.

"Oh, there's Roger Morton," Miriam said, as a man as thin as his malacca cane came weaving through the crowd. His bony fingers were crowded with rings, with onyx, black opals, and rectangles of turquoise, and his vest from India was sewn with dozens of tiny, round mirrors.

"Do you know him well? Could you introduce us?" I asked Miriam.

Just then the twins, suddenly sporting strands of pearls, swooped onto Roger and began a conversation which threatened to be long.

"We have this improv troupe," Roberto told Miriam. "We need a break so bad!"

"I think Roger books his acts by March." Sensing our desperation, Miriam had become a little distant, and was also gazing distrustfully at her bouillabaisse.

Then Roger Morton, his cane stabbing the flagstones, nudged the twins, Roberto, and me aside to greet Miriam, saying, "How wonderful to see you! I've refurbished the White Gull from top to bottom. You've got to see it!"

Besides Quahog, Roger Morton owned the White Gull, Provincetown's most elegant guest house, with its deep pillared porches, cobalt-blue hydrangeas, and an iron fountain of Triton blowing a horn of water. Roger recounted the improvements he'd made to the White Gull, then asked Miriam, "Have I mentioned the Great Furnace Catastrophe?" Roberto and I hovered at Miriam's side, our smiles fixed on our faces, waiting for the caboose of Roger's long train of thought. Miriam glanced sympathetically in our direction, but the color was draining from her face.

"I hope I'm not boring you," Roger said.

"No, I think it's this bouillabaisse," said Miriam, whose slouch Roberto was imitating until I glared to make him stop.

Then something clattered, like a trashcan tipping over. It came from Arthur's direction, by the back steps to the house. Arthur was laughing, and so was Edward, at his side and holding something circular that shone like brass.

"Excuse me, excuse me!" Arthur was shouting in his stage voice. "I have an announcement! Whoever sold me this Chinese gong owes me a refund. No wonder the Empress Dowager wanted to get rid of it!" While Edward hung the gong back on its teakwood rack, Arthur continued to speak, smiling and twisting his signet ring, his polka-dot bowtie askew, but his enjoyment of an audience undiminished.

"Of course, I gave this party to welcome you all to Province-town—and to inaugurate the season. And I'm happy to report that attendance is near one-hundred percent, except, I regret, we are missing the crew of our visiting tall ship, the *Vasa.* I refuse to believe they are confined to their hammocks with scurvy. And besides, our bartender has a plentiful supply of limes."

People laughed and glanced at the *Vasa,* floating far off-shore.

"There's a lot of excitement in town this year, in addition to the solitary Swedes. Roger Morton has redone the White Gull, making it more beautiful than ever, if that were possible."

The twins started the applause, which Roger acknowledged with a limited wave of his hand.

"And we have talent galore here today, theater talent, in the form of Mark Winslow and his friend…" Arthur had forgotten Roberto's name. "…Mark and his amusing companion, who's just too witty for words…"

To my embarrassment, my amusing companion shouted across the crowd to our host: "My name is Roberto, Roberto Schreiber—and we're looking for gigs in Provincetown this summer, doing improv comedy! Hey, we're fabulous, honest!"

"So *hire* these poor troopers!" Arthur laughed, missing a perfect opportunity to suggest Roger Morton do exactly that.

"Now for a more serious note," Arthur said, beginning his Swim for Scholars pitch. Though teeming with summer people and summer jobs, Provincetown suffered the highest winter unemployment rate in Massachusetts. Arthur was proposing a Labor Day swim across Provincetown Harbor to fund a college scholarship for local high school students. Most of the people on the terrace were listening to their host out of good manners or middle-class guilt. Except Ian Drummond. He was laughing and swilling beer with Barton Daggett. I tried to snag Roger Morton's attention, but he was fixed on Arthur, avoiding eye contact with Roberto and me.

"…It will be a worthy cause, with lots of beefcake," Arthur was saying, as someone tugged at my elbow. It was Miriam, white and distressed. "Do you have a car?" she whispered. "I feel sick. I thought local mussels might be, you know, more benign. I guess I'm allergic." Her shop was a short ride away.

"I hope I don't faint." She clasped my arm as Arthur rambled on, and we slipped through the crowd, passing Ian, who got no response by cracking, "Chin up, Miriam, the party's not that bad."

In the house, Miriam retrieved a shawl stitched with llamas from the dining room, then, shuffling in her thick leather sandals, led me toward the door to the street. She pushed open the screen door, wobbled, then screamed—a ragged cry of shock and rage. Then she fell against me and I caught the door as she began gasping and sobbing.

There, on the granite stoop, lay the corpse of a dog, its belly bloated and slashed open—the first blood of that summer of death.

Chapter Two

I had first come to Provincetown as a small boy. My mother was singing at a club on the outskirts of town, out by the ponds where it seems that everything is just sand and pines.

My mother didn't plan to become a jazz singer. She was studying classical piano at the New England Conservatory when she became pregnant by my father. He was an officer on a destroyer. They'd met one evening at a jazz club, Lulu Wright's, in the South End of Boston. He was handsome and smart, he'd been all over the world, but "the Orient," as he'd called it back then, was his favorite. That evening at Lulu Wright's, he folded my mother a piece of origami, a paper puzzle of interlocking cranes that in Japan was associated with ten thousand years of happiness.

But longevity was missing from their relationship: it lasted barely ten hours. His ship was bound the next morning for the Panama Canal. She'd loved him "oh, so passionately," they were "soul mates," they'd talked about jazz at my mother's apartment until dawn. "His name was Douglas," my mother told me. "Douglas, don't ever call me Doug." No surname was ever mentioned, nor was the identity of his ship, and the records I'd consulted—the Navy's, the Port Authority's, the newspapers on microfiche at various libraries—yielded no clues. A Liberian tanker had docked that weekend, and a cruise ship, the *Bimini Prize*, but no American vessels, so my father became lost, stolen by long-ago tides.

"Neither of us knew you were on the way," my mother said. I arrived the first day of April, under the sign of the ram.

After my mother dropped out of the Conservatory, she supported herself by singing jazz in clubs and acting in summer stock. She'd finished a run of *The King and I* at the Cape Playhouse in Dennis when she took the gig at Jubilee's. The owner of the club was quite struck by her. Grenadian by birth, almost seven feet tall, he had skin the color of toffee and a diamond set in one of his canine teeth. He'd been baptized Alphonse, but everyone called him Jubilee.

He put us up in an apartment in a series of shacks built out on a pier. It's still there today, gull-gray and hung with ropes and lanterns and blue glass Japanese fishermen's floats. It was sufficiently rickety to serve in my imagination as a pirate ship, and the smell of the sea permeated everything: our sheets, our clothing, even the corn flakes we kept in our refrigerator. I would play on the beach underneath the pier, between the wet, slick pilings, which, studded with periwinkles and barnacles, seemed part of the sea, like the wreck of a galleon full of skeletons and chests of rubies.

Sometimes, late at night, after the club had closed and Jubilee had driven us home—I always attended my mother's shows—we would sit outside on the pier in the dark, my mother drinking tea "with just a smidgen of gin" while I nursed a 7-Up and gobbled the barbecue-flavored peanuts the bartenders gave me to keep me quiet. My mother would still be in her "working clothes," the long sequined gown, glittery like a boat's wake in moonlight. She'd hum a few bars of "Satin Doll" or do some husky parody of a nursery rhyme and we'd both just stare out to sea. I'd always assumed she was thinking about my father, where he was and what he was doing, sailing off Madagascar, getting a tattoo in Yokohama…We'd stare out to sea like those whalers' wives who kept watching horizons long after they knew their husbands had drowned.

I don't remember noticing the gay men in Provincetown that summer when I was eight. Raised in a house with brassieres but no neckties, with Midol and douche but no Cruex or Old Spice, all men seemed exotic to me. Yet that first summer in Provincetown, I vividly recall seeing my first naked man, not flesh and blood, but paint and canvas—Thomas Royall's masterpiece, *The Fisher Boy*. In the Provincetown Municipal Museum.

Since then, I've seen that painting a thousand times, on jigsaw puzzles and postcards, on tote bags and key chains and magnets, even parodied in pornography and political cartoons. It's almost as ubiquitous as Michelangelo's *David,* in the gay world, anyway— this naked youth, kneeling in a dory, holding a halibut so silver and unworldly it could be an idol of some sea deity.

The light—on his chest and darker genitals, on the crests of the waves and emphasizing the scales of the fish—all this light on these naked surfaces made the scene throb with sensuality, as if the painting itself had a pulse. I wanted to plunge into that sea, swim to his dory, and have the Fisher Boy lift me from the water.

"Who is he?" I asked my mother.

"He's some model, darling."

"Is he out in the harbor?"

"I doubt it, Mark. This picture was painted in…1916, so I doubt if he's hauling nets these days. He's probably playing a harp." She drew the tube of scarlet lipstick over her lips, as careful as I was with my crayons, careful to stay within the lines…From that point on, I saw Provincetown Harbor as full of the swimming ghosts of boys.

◇◇◇

I dreamt about *The Fisher Boy* the night after Arthur's party. I saw the boy in the boat against a sky never navigated by jets. The same brigantine in the painting graced the horizon—or was it the Swedish tall ship, the *Vasa?* Then, as I looked at the Fisher Boy, I saw that he was holding something different—something brownish and swollen and wet with gore…

I woke. It was already ten-fifteen. Luckily, the apartment I'd rented in Provincetown was close to the restaurant where I'd promised to meet Ian Drummond for brunch. Why he'd called me and scheduled this meeting, he hadn't explained, but had stressed that it was "very important."

Not one to wait for anyone, Ian had already taken a table under a French poster of a chimp brandishing a bottle of cognac. Sipping a Bloody Mary, he was examining the long laminated menu with the confidence his ancestry and trusts bestowed, as though this restaurant, this town, the very world existed to please him.

Without glancing up, he greeted me with, "You're late, Winslow, by seven minutes. That will be five days of work squad, sweeping the chapel steps." Ian enjoyed referencing the authoritarian aspects of prep school.

"With all due respect, sir, you can shove it," I said, as though talking back to a master.

"No wonder you ended up at a state university, with that attitude."

What is it about a friendship forged in childhood that gives it such potency, an intimacy that can assert itself years later, almost against your will? Is it strong because you both were growing, formed when that friendship was formed? Is something embedded at your cellular level, something as fixed as your DNA? I had that with Ian.

Though he had partied through Dartmouth and barely survived law school in the south, Ian took the "gentleman" in "gentleman's C" very seriously. He sometimes teased me about the "plebeian shadows" of my background, but was careful, with one exception, not to reference the mystery of my paternity. He'd been gone from the east for two short years, but he seemed a changed man, from his musculature to his mood.

"I've given up my job," I told him, mentioning my plans for a show business career.

His face became all solemn concern. "You can't be serious."

I said I was trying to be funny.

"This isn't a punchline, Mark, it's your life." He seemed genuinely upset. Perhaps he felt an investment in my life, having once saved it.

We were eleven, or Ian was, I was ten-and-a-half. We took one of his brothers' rowboats and Ian rowed to Ten Pound Island in Gloucester Harbor. There wasn't much there: a stubby unmanned lighthouse, some weeds, gravelly beaches, but its inaccessibility lent it a certain glamour. During my turn to row, on the way back, a storm blew up. The rain was warm and soft at first, then it began lashing like bullwhips. The sky blackened and fractured with electric-white lightning while the sea all but boiled. I froze at the oars. Blinded by my tears and rain and wind, I was sure we would never see dry land again. That's when Ian took control and calmly rowed us to shore. Without comment, without scorn. He'd earned my undying gratitude.

I diverted our conversation. "Isn't it a little early for liquor? Not to mention your choice of a drink." I was recalling my dream and the gore on Arthur's steps.

"I had to fortify myself to meet the star of the morning news," Ian said.

Of course, I'd been enraged at what I'd seen as a hate crime. At the very moment Arthur was giving back to Provincetown, marshalling support for his Swim for Scholars effort, some bigot was throwing the bloody corpse of a dog onto his doorstep. A similar incident had happened in Alabama, at a women's retreat run by two lesbians; a dead dog, with a note referencing "bitches," had been draped over their rural mailbox, beginning a string of hate crimes that culminated with gunshots and one of the women dead. There was no note with the animal at Arthur's, but, tied to the dog's neck was a reddish ribbon, seemingly mocking the AIDS awareness symbol.

"You were the lead story on the Boston news."

I'd thought I'd been speaking to the local cable station.

"Know what you want, guys?" the waiter asked.

Ian wanted Belgian waffles with extra whipped cream, odd for a bodybuilder, I thought. I opted for blueberry pancakes without butter and fresh-squeezed orange juice.

"Who would do such a thing to Arthur?" I asked.

"Punks," Ian said, "just punks. I don't know why some people make everything political. There'll always be mosquitoes and people who dump trash in national parks. It's an imperfect world, but you liberals insist on redeeming it. You should learn to take the bitter with the sweet. God knows I've had to."

San Francisco had made something in him go sour. He still hadn't mentioned the purpose of our brunch, but I assumed it was yesterday's hate crime.

"Did you rent your place the last two summers?" I hadn't seen him in Provincetown either year.

"No." Ian owned a house at the beginning of Commercial Street, an ugly "futuristic" building from the mid-Sixties on a sandy hill overlooking the breakwater. All plate glass and redwood beams, it was circular, like the revolving restaurants that came into vogue when the Seattle Space Needle went up.

"I couldn't come here because of work, and I couldn't rent my house because of these damn environmental regulations. I'm having structural problems with the house because the hill it's built on is shifting."

The waiter bent his knees as he slid my plate of pancakes, flooded with butter, onto the scalloped paper placemat. Ian's Belgian waffles came innocent of whipped cream and there was no mention of my orange juice. Before we could protest, the waiter zig-zagged through the tables, back to the kitchen.

"Excuse me," said a woman with an enamel pink triangle on her shirt. "You're the man who was on TV, you were there," she told me, as though I were confused about this fact.

"I wasn't at the party," the woman began.

"We're trying to eat!" Ian said angrily, enunciating each word more precisely than its predecessor. "We were having a nice, peaceful discussion about my house caving in—"

"An attack against one of us is an attack against all of us," the woman said. "There's a meeting at town hall, tomorrow night, at seven."

She left us just as our waiter returned. "How is everything?" he asked, before speed-walking off to the cashier to change a fifty for a group at a table across the room—some Middle-American people carrying books looking like Bibles.

Chapter Three

No one knew the meaning of what had happened at Arthur's. Was it a hate crime directed at a specific individual, or against the entire gay community, using one man as a kind of totem? Like hundreds of other sweaty, sunburned people, Roberto and I crowded into the meeting about this outrage.

The room in the town hall was one of those echoing Victorian spaces that called to mind assembly at St. Harold's. The seats were hard, made of varnished slats the color of peanut brittle. They kept up a running battle with your spine. Despite this and humidity that settled on your skin like a rash, the place was packed with a populace diverse as Arthur's party: gays and straights, shop-owners and houseboys, summer residents and year-rounders, even families of tourists fanning themselves with the lavender flyers obediently accepted from gay rights activists.

A famous lesbian author nursed her baby with one dove-white breast. A prominent bar-owner, in a Santa Claus beard and leather lederhosen, had brought along his Congo parrot, which danced on his shoulder. "Why, why, I want to know why," a woman in painters' overalls was saying. The tension in the hall was as palpable as the heat, which was Bangladeshi in its intensity.

The first speaker was the Provincetown chief of police. He was a sleek man with a profile sharp as the edges of his badge. "First, let me say that everyone in Provincetown is shocked at this incident of…vandalism. And let me stress that every possible lead—"

"You told the media you don't have any leads!" one activist with flyers yelled.

"The chief has the floor!" shouted the captain of a whale watch boat.

"We have leads but no suspects," the chief of police answered. "The animal found on Mr. Hilliard's doorstep was wearing a collar but no license or any sort of identifying tag."

"It was wearing an AIDS ribbon, though! That's evidence of a hate crime!" one of the twins from Arthur's party argued.

"The animal in question was indeed wearing a ribbon tied to its collar," the chief admitted. "The ribbon was saturated with blood and may, at one time, have been red or another dark color. What this signifies—"

"It signifies hatred! It's a hate crime!" Roberto yelled. Outspoken as always, he was now all but trembling with anger.

The chief reported that the dog was "a well-nourished female, a mixed breed, German shepherd and Labrador retriever."

"Like we need its ancestry," Roberto said.

The famous lesbian author demanded, "This happens in broad daylight, yet nobody saw a thing?"

"Which seems to suggest that the people who did this had a car—to be able to dump this dog off quickly, then retreat," the chief said. "But no, there was very little street traffic at the time, and nobody saw a thing. No neighbors, for instance. They were all at Arthur's party, in the dining room, at the back of the house, or in the backyard, out on the terrace. The dining room windows open onto Arthur's driveway, so there is no direct view of the street. On the terrace, the view of the street is blocked by the foliage in the garden. The dog was bloody, but there was no blood spilt on the front path leading to the stoop, suggesting the animal was carried in some sort of container. So, please, if anyone has *any* information, contact us."

Just then, the lesbian author's baby began screeching until she pointed it back to her nipple. Some tourists' children in Notre Dame T-shirts giggled when they saw the bare breast, then their father turned their heads around like spigots on a sink.

Rumor had it Arthur had been scheduled to speak but had cancelled at the last minute. He was absent, and so were Edward and the woman from the café who'd alerted me to this meeting.

Ian was recognized and stood. "I have been a summer resident and tax-payer for more than seven years. I had had a pleasant experience here in Provincetown until government meddling interfered with my wishes regarding my private property—"

"Mr. Drummond," the moderator asked, "what relevance does this have to tonight's—"

"This is a clear-cut case of mindless vandalism," Ian said. "It isn't political and it isn't a hate crime. How many crimes are committed out of love? Just enforce the laws that are on the books and put these punks to work making license plates."

"Say no to hatred!" a gay rights activist called out. "The climate of this town must change!"

"I agree!" said a man about forty in a navy blue suit which must have felt like goose down in the heat. Upon reaching the microphone, he beamed and said, "I feel so fortunate to be a new resident of this glorious corner of creation…"

"Get to the point," somebody yelled.

Politely, too politely, he said, "I will." He fumbled with the flap to the pocket of his jacket, and, from inside, drew a slender glass jar, the sort that holds maraschino cherries or marinated mushrooms in supermarkets.

Unscrewing the lid of the jar, he poured its contents into his hand—a glittery white substance he displayed with triumph. "This," he told us, "is all that's left of Sodom and Gomorrah…A salty waste on the shores of the Dead Sea."

At this point, something jolted my memory, like your body jolts when first surrendering to sleep. I had seen this man before, televised, amid colored fountains and the statue of an angel ten stories tall. Others recognized him too, and moaned, "Oh God!"

"I'm so glad somebody finally brought Him up!"

People whispered and then shouted his name: "Hollings Fair, Hollings Fair from the Christian Soldiers!"

At this point, all decorum collapsed. The lesbian author shouted, her earrings flashing like swords. I saw Miriam for the first time, standing toward the rear and hissing.

Fair continued, "Three-hundred-eighty-five years ago, the Pilgrim fathers dropped anchor in the New World, at Provincetown. Now, we too come here, in the same spirit of hope and opportunity."

"You're not a resident!" Roger Morton shouted. "You don't belong at this meeting!"

"Opportunism is more like it," the lesbian author said. "We know what your people did out west!"

"Shame, shame!" some activists shouted.

Hollings Fair folded his hands on the podium and tried to appear serene, but he was squeezing his knuckles white with tension.

"I'd like the floor," said a blue-haired lady I knew worked at the local bakery. The chief tapped Hollings Fair, but he refused to move. Instead, he bowed his head in silence, apparently in prayer.

"Sir," said the chief of police, "please make your point in a timely manner."

"I will," said Hollings Fair. "I just wanted to tell God about it first." His voice became strident. It might have been the voice of his ten-story angel, with her sword and concrete wings: "We do have a stake in what happens in Provincetown, we *do* have a right to voice our opinion. Because we *are* property-owners as of this week!" He pulled papers from his jacket and waved them aloft. "Here's our deed, here's our deed!" He quoted an address on Commercial Street.

Many in the audience groaned or swore. "Focus, focus!" somebody called.

"We are going to change this town!" Hollings Fair announced. "We are going to take back this town in the name of the American family!"

Roberto stood and yelled, "Are you behind what happened at Arthur's party?"

"Of course not!" Fair yelled back.

"We're here to discuss the incident about the dog," the moderator pleaded. "Please yield the floor."

At last Fair obeyed, taking his deed and Dead Sea salt to a far rear corner of the room where his followers had been collecting, not anemic ladies in straw hats with veils, but crewcut men who were Parris Island-lean, some in camouflage and boots black as iron.

Then the blue-haired woman from the bakery took the microphone amid scattered but intense applause. I had often seen her, among the turnovers and Portuguese pastries. Introducing herself as Mary Almeida, she said, "I'm a lifelong, year-round resident of Provincetown," a dig at summer people like Ian and the famous author. "My son is on the police force," she said, and some people in the audience began clapping.

Mrs. Almeida made a speech about unity in the face of hatred and was the first person to praise Arthur's long list of contributions to Provincetown. Coming from someone local with a son on the police force, her words carried an added authority, especially when she ended her speech with, "And who could do such a thing to Arthur, of all people?"

There was sustained applause.

But where *was* Arthur? Frightened into seclusion in his house? If he'd been alone, I might've been less uneasy, but he was with that dubious little Edward Babineaux.

As we filed out into the humid night, Ian accosted me. "Did you believe that holy roller?" He was violating my space, as some people might say, standing inches in front of me, his breath reeking of beer, like a frat-house the morning after a kegger. "Did you see those stormtroopers he brought with him? Where did they go? I guess they cut out early." Ian's tone conveyed both indignation and delight. The delight might have been due to the Christian Soldiers' battle gear; Ian loved military history and could name divisions and commanding officers from wars most people had never heard of.

"Spare change?" a girl with a foreign-sounding accent asked on Commercial Street, then Ian laughed and edged away. The girl had crinkly golden hair and sprays of coins dangling from her pierced ears. At first, I thought she was a foreign college student, hitchhiking around the States, then I saw that she was young, fifteen at most, barefoot and dirty, in a long dress of violet batik. She and her companion, her sister, I guessed, were smoking fat, hand-rolled cigarettes that generated a great many sparks.

My pocket yielded two quarters, some pennies, and some lint. Roberto was about to give them a dollar bill when Miriam called out, "Stop! Don't do that! Don't give those girls a thing, they stole from me earlier this week!" Miriam's nerves were obviously jangling—she'd been sick on Edward's bouillabaisse, then, with me, discovered the bloated mutt on Arthur's doorstep. "I recognize you both," Miriam said, but the girls smiled as though she were telling them a riddle instead of accusing them of theft. "You," she said to the older girl, "you tried to take an amber bracelet." She pointed to the smaller girl. "And you tried to put a kaleidoscope into your handbag."

"We're from Scandinavia," the older girl said, in a singsong accent reminiscent of Abba.

"Since the *Vasa* has come here, all young shoplifters are suddenly Scandinavians who speak English when it serves their interest," Miriam told us. "But everyone knows that the crew of the *Vasa* hasn't come ashore and you didn't even know what amber was even though most of the world's amber comes from the Baltic," Miriam scolded the older girl.

Both girls, smoking their fat, sparky cigarettes, laughed. The older girl took Roberto's dollar, then they vanished.

Miriam turned her irritation on me. "Why didn't you say something at the meeting?" she said, the heiress pushing through her earth mother facade. "You're an actor, you're used to speaking in public."

"I'm not a resident. And I spoke on TV. Why didn't you speak?" I asked her.

She didn't answer, but said seeing that obnoxious Hollings Fair had nauseated her as much as Edward's bouillabaisse. And she was worried sick about Arthur. Like me, she'd called him dozens of times, only to get the "treasure" on the answering machine, repeating that they were "fine" but not up to receiving phone calls or visitors. "He's not reaching out," Miriam said. "Arthur isn't asking for support. He might need his meds again."

We walked Miriam to her shop. Her daughter, Chloe, was behind the counter, not waiting on customers, of course, but leafing through a storybook, *The Magical Radish*. The little girl had Miriam's auburn hair, but a smile that was more transforming. It lit up her being as she abandoned her book, calling, "Mum, mum, mum!"

"Thank God you're here!" the cashier said to Miriam.

"Has Chloe been acting up?"

The little girl came scampering out from behind the display case, from behind the shelves of amethysts and arrowheads, garnets and quartz and freshwater pearls, all sparkling among river stones dark like sea beans. She buried her head in Miriam's skirt.

"Chloe's been fine, but we've had shoplifters."

"Two dirty-looking girls?"

"A dirty boy. He almost made off with one of the paper-weights." The cashier, a high school girl, gestured at the shelf of blown glass paperweights, each with what looked like a sea anemone imprisoned inside. Expensive, imported from Scotland, the smallest cost fifty dollars.

The cashier said a boy "who looked like he was allergic to soap and water" slipped a paperweight into the front pocket of his jeans. When she told him to put it back, he said the bulge was "an all-natural compliment." So she called down the street, pretending to see Sergeant Almeida, and the boy tossed the paperweight onto the floor, then ran out.

"Was he 'Swedish'?" Miriam asked sarcastically.

"He was just an idiot," the cashier said.

The paperweight, full of tender-looking orange tentacles that looked like they might sting small fish, had chipped, the cashier confessed, but Miriam said not to worry about it. Then, to Roberto and me, she said, "I wonder if the Christian Soldiers steal?"

Chapter Four

Up, up, up we climbed on the following Friday. Roberto and I were climbing endless redwood steps up the sandy hillside to what Ian Drummond was calling the First Annual St. Harold's Memoriam. Ian's party list was culled from a far smaller circle than Arthur's; it was crankier, more conservative, and exclusively gay male. His guests were graduates of select New England prep schools like St. Paul's, St. Mark's, and Exeter, among which St. Harold's would be considered what Ian called "weak tea" even before it began hemorrhaging red ink.

But the fate of St. Harold's failed to tarnish Ian's social stature in gay circles. Among angry entrepreneurs who called talk radio on their cell phones, among MBAs who quoted Ayn Rand, among South End couples with hot tubs on their roof decks, Ian was recognized, and, to a large degree, respected. People might challenge his opinions or find him scrappy and smug, but few denied him the compliment of being one of Boston's "movers and shakers."

"Take everything he says with a grain of salt," I advised Roberto, as a survival strategy for this party.

Our host, obviously sloshed, greeted us with, "Welcome, Mark, what would you like to drink? I'm serving grilled swordfish, which doesn't go well with dead dog, so I want no discussion whatsoever about Arthur's little canine dilemma. Agreed?" This remark sabotaged my plan. I'd left a message on Arthur's answering machine warning that if I didn't receive some sort of reply—from him—that I'd assume he was in danger. And I'd planned on asking Ian to phone him too.

Belatedly, Ian acknowledged Roberto, or rather acknowledged his thighs and biceps with a once-over, then, to me: "And you brought your fellow thespian. How bohemian, I hope we won't bore you."

Roberto simmered, but didn't speak. Ian's house was like a flying saucer from some especially shabby planet. Built on several levels, it seemed decorated with suggestions from old *Playboy* "Advisor" columns or plagiarized from sets of an early James Bond film. It was filled with Sixties-era sculptures—a neon eye, female nudes in runny epoxy—and with kidney-shaped tables and Martian-looking lamps and acres of nubbly carpeting the beige of dirty cocker spaniels. But you had to forgive Ian for most of these lapses of taste because, strictly speaking, they were not his. He had inherited the furniture and art from his oldest brother, Fulton. Married but childless like Ian's other brother, George, Fulton had given Ian the entire contents of his Sutton Place townhouse when he'd left bachelorhood and Manhattan for marriage and Westport. When I whispered this information to Roberto, he countered, "He's still under indictment for the carpeting."

The men present, busy laughing, talking about taxes and property values, were the sort that sent us scurrying to that sanctuary of the shy, the hors d'oeuvres table. Ian's offerings were not terribly imaginative, celery and carrot sticks and broccoli florets, with onion dip conjured from some mix. And even the celery was bad, thick and spongy and riddled with those strings that wedge between your teeth for days at a time. "He can't even do vegetables," Roberto said.

"So we've got to socialize," I muttered. "We can't use having a full mouth as an excuse not to talk."

I had hoped to buttonhole a club owner or two about booking our troupe, but this wasn't a comedy club crowd. The guests might have been hired to offset the ugliness of the decor, chosen for their bone structure, which was as serene as the geometry of the Taj Mahal, and just as marble-cool. Of course the view from this hideous house was spectacular. Its site atop one of the higher hills of Provincetown, an ambitious dune, really, gave it a view of the "old" harbor and the breakwater connecting the "mainland" to the gay nude beach at Herring Cove.

Our host approached us. "Don't wolf down all my vegetables. Leave some for the masses."

Roberto swiped a spear of zucchini through the onion dip, swiftly, like someone swiping a credit card through a machine. "So you couldn't care less about what happened to Arthur," Roberto challenged Ian.

"Uh-uh-ah," Ian said. "What did I tell you? Dead dog and swordfish don't go well together. I forbid any discussion of Arthur's problem—"

"It's everyone's problem," Roberto snapped. "Even yours."

"Can you really imagine anyone hauling a dead dog up my steps? They'd have to be awfully energetic." Ian finished his Heineken and put his empty bottle next to the onion dip. "A question for you, Mark," he said. "You're a good Gloucester boy. I'm doing a little nautical survey…Define the term 'neap tide'."

It was a tide of unusually low range, influenced by the positions of the sun and moon. I said this.

"Can you imagine a marine biologist not knowing that? Wouldn't that strike you as a bit…fishy?" He didn't wait for my answer, but instead joined the discussion of the NASDAQ next to us.

Roberto nodded toward the balcony that ran all around the house, where a cook was prodding swordfish sputtering on a grill. "I need some air," he said. I said I would join him once I used the facilities.

The bathroom, like the rest of the house, was redolent of mildew and none too clean. A layer of dust the color of bone meal coated everything, from the lemon-shaped soaps in a canister on the sink to the Serenity Prayer hung eye-level back of the toilet tank. Was that a joke? I wondered, then wondered again. Ian was not widely thought of as alcoholic, but had certainly been drinking rigorously this year.

Ian's bathroom reading, in a brass bucket, was not the biographies of Douglas MacArthur and the Duke of Wellington I'd expected, but Boswell's history of Christianity and homosexuality, with the mosaic of a hare on its cover. After washing my hands, I wandered farther down the quiet corridor to peer into Ian's bedroom, to see whether he still used Fulton's circular bed and notorious black satin sheets.

Yes, the bed was still there, unmade, but the sheets were wholesome white cotton. The floor was littered with male detritus: barbells and bodybuilding magazines of men whose chests were so layered with muscle they looked segmented, like the undersides of beetles. On the walls were red abstract canvasses, smears like lab slides.

Then I realized that I was not alone. Something was moving on the balcony outside the bedroom, beyond the gauzy oatmeal-colored curtains, beyond the open sliding door—something small. My first reaction was fear, fear in the wake of Arthur's incident and the arrival of Hollings Fair's Christian Soldiers. But then embarrassment superseded this fear, as though I'd been caught foraging through someone's medicine cabinet.

Then I realized the figure on the balcony was Edward Babineaux. He was watching people trekking across the break-water, crossing the long, twisting expanse of granite, coming from the nude section of Herring Cove.

"Wishing you were at the beach?" I said to him. I felt I had to alert him that I was there, although I sensed he'd seen me all along.

"Oh, no." Edward was as devoid of humor as before. "I'm here. I live in the here and now."

Being homeless, I imagine, makes that a sensible strategy.

"I'm representing Arthur," Edward said, "at Ian's party."

"In Ian's bedroom."

"With you." His smile was sweet as a geisha's.

"I hate to be blunt, but I'm worried sick about Arthur. All of his old friends are worried sick. I'd like to hear from him *in person* to be sure he's okay."

"Don't you trust me?" Edward was obviously enjoying forcing me to be polite and hypocritical.

"Of course I trust you," I lied.

Edward reported that Arthur wasn't good. I thought he might cast himself in the role of his keeper's savior, providing gourmet cooking and comforts of the flesh, but he didn't. He said Arthur's psychiatrist had phoned the local pharmacy so Arthur had access to sedatives to dull his nerves. "He has night terrors," Edward said. "He wakes up screaming. Because of the calls."

"What calls? From the media?"

He shook his buzz-cut head. "They've called, but I took care of them. These other calls come in the early morning. They don't *say* anything. I pick up the phone and there's just…silence."

No wonder Arthur was shunning the telephone. "Have you told the police?"

Edward had come in off the balcony. He was investigating the top of Ian's bureau, which was as well-stocked as his bar, except that these bottles, of course, contained colognes, in silver flasks and sapphire-blue cubes, all with knobby stoppers you could really grip.

"We've told the police and they've tried to trace the calls. We've had *one* call since they put the tap on the line. It was made from a public telephone in Hyannis. They hung up immediately."

"I keep thinking about these fundamentalists, these Christian Soldiers."

Edward nodded.

"I keep wondering—did they do this to Arthur personally, or as a warning to the entire community? Targeting a prominent gay man."

Dreamily, like a child at play in his mother's bedroom, Edward kept unscrewing bottles of cologne, sniffing each one.

"You must really love cologne." I sat down on the circular bed.

"Not really. They're just chemicals. And I have allergies like you wouldn't believe."

"What were you doing," I said, "before you met Arthur?"

"I was at cooking school."

That explained the superb bouillabaisse. "Were you expelled for burning a soufflé?"

He didn't laugh. He advanced toward me with the dancer's grace he'd demonstrated at Arthur's party, snuffing the candles and raising the window shades and his host's spirits. He paused to stroke my earlobe, a quick erotic gesture with the tip of his finger. "Thank you for asking about us." Then he kissed my cheek and swiftly exited the room, neglecting to screw the stoppers back on Ian's colognes.

I found Roberto wandering around the living room, holding two plates of grilled swordfish. "It's getting cold," he said, referring it seemed to both the meal and his mood. "What took you so long? Don't tell me there's a back room."

"Edward was there."

"I saw him. He just left."

"Having a good time?" Ian now asked. Guilty about prowling in his bedroom, I compensated by being overly enthusiastic, saying, "I've always loved this house. Everything is just great!"

"Do you love it enough to buy it? It's costing me a fucking fortune. It's this damn erosion problem. The hill this house is built on is becoming destabilized. The whole house is threatening to break apart. It's this damn sand. I mean, I left San Francisco to avoid this situation. I didn't want to wake up with my house on top of me!"

Barton Daggett, all but bursting from his seersucker suit, could not resist joining us to bemoan his own real estate woes, so Ian was off to check on dessert. "First my woods become infested with ticks, those Lyme disease ticks, from the gee-dee deer. Deer, I call them rats with antlers. Then these people move in that make the deer seem terrific—these imbeciles who shoot things in the woods, at all hours."

"Perhaps they're shooting the deer that carry the ticks," Roberto said.

This logic seemed to irritate Barton, who changed the subject, asking Roberto, "Are you a St. Harold's graduate?"

Ian saved Roberto from responding by bellowing, "Attention, attention, gentlemen! May I have a moment of silence, please?"

The laughter and conversation subsided, then Ian vanished into the kitchen to return with our dessert on a silver tray: an ice cream cake in the shape of the St. Harold's crest. It was a warm evening and the air-conditioning was off—what with the doors flung open to the balcony—so the cake was sweating like a finalist finishing the Boston Marathon. Already, pieces of the insignia, the icing lions and some ivy, were threatening to drop away. Alone, in a boozy tenor, Ian sang the school hymn, laughing on the verse, "And eternal, like the hills, St. Harold's…lives."

Everyone cheered.

"Where on earth did you procure this cake?" Barton Daggett asked Ian.

"'Procure' is certainly the right word," Ian said. The cake had come from an adults-only bakery in Hyannis, one that specialized in edible smut, in rendering breasts and genitalia in frosting. "I'm told the baker is a failed gynecologist."

Someone had the bad taste to ask, "Who was St. Harold? He wasn't the author of any gospels."

"He's the patron saint of the bankrupt," Ian said. Then, he called out, "Let us raise our glasses…We toast the men of classes past. For at St. Harold's, there is no future."

Then we drank and Ian cut the cake with a dull-bladed sword from Barton's collection.

Chapter Five

Arthur called that evening, while I was still at Ian's St. Harold's party. Had Edward engineered that contact? Left the party early to tell Arthur to call me when Edward knew only my answering machine was home? "Mark, don't be worried," Arthur's voice said. "Edward is taking wonderful care of me, especially of my stomach. I'm gorging myself. He's feeding me riotous amounts of calories. I'm the size of a walrus. Take care."

That, at least, was sound advice. To "take care" that dangerous summer...

So it wasn't Arthur but Commercial Street that finally introduced me to Roger Morton. Both of us were peering into the office Hollings Fair and his Christian Soldiers were renting across from Spiritus Pizza. The office was empty except for an orange bead curtain from the building's former life as a Chinese restaurant. Cornering Roger, I used Arthur's name as a reference to ask for a run at Quahog. Roger had one opening next Saturday at eight, replacing a female impersonator whose mono was back.

Performers in Provincetown get saddled with generating their own audiences, so Sammy, one of our actors, a graphic designer who'd been fired by most of the high-tech firms along Route 128, had cobbled together some flyers from clip art and a photo of the troupe and shipped them to us by overnight mail. Unfortunately, he'd bungled the date of our gig, so Roberto and I had to correct each flyer by hand, using pink felt pens, then we thumb-tacked them to anything upright: bulletin boards, telephone poles, trees, the salt-eaten stalls in the men's room at Herring Cove. We distributed them from towel to towel at the beach and to people filing out from tea dance. We left piles of them in guest house halls, by the complimentary toothpicks and mints.

The five other members of the troupe carpooled down the afternoon before the show, and, over nachos and too much beer, we planned our performance: the skit types, the casts, and so on. We were giddy with confidence and terror, certain we would bomb and equally sure we'd be The Next Big Thing. "I don't have butterflies in my stomach, I have California condors," Roberto said.

We spent the hour before curtain time "barking" in front of Quahog, pestering Commercial Street's tourists to buy tickets. I've seldom depended upon the kindness of strangers, so I found barking embarrassing, a first cousin to outright panhandling. I kept pretty quiet and offered my flyers to people too timid to refuse them.

An older man in a flasher's raincoat the color of hummus thanked me for a flyer and asked, "Is your show men in dresses?" Roberto answered that we couldn't afford costumes, so he said he'd try to make it. "It's always good to broaden our audience," Roberto reasoned.

Twenty minutes before eight, a group of five men in camouflage that mimicked sycamore bark approached us—Christian Soldiers, for sure. My stomach felt like one of those balloons street vendors torture into animal shapes to sell to children.

"Does your comedy make fun of God?" one of them asked.

"Buy a ticket and find out," Roberto said.

"We're after laughs," I said, "not changing theology."

"Have you heard of Hollings Fair?" the Soldier asked.

"I heard him speak once, at town hall," I said.

Luckily, that satisfied him. "God loves you," he said, making it sound like a threat. Then they dispersed.

At ten minutes to eight, we stopped barking and went inside Quahog. There were just three people in the audience. The restaurant was decorated with the sort of kitsch statuettes, plaster sea captains, fish sporting chefs' hats, mermaids rising from painted waves, that often mean the menu is surf 'n' turf specials and baked stuffed lobster with a bad lobster-to-breadcrumb ratio.

Quahog's stage was miniscule, no bigger than the smallest traffic island, and without microphones. Our backstage space was smaller still, a tiny hallway truncated by a flight of stairs to a recently flooded basement. Was this where so many Big Names had gotten their start, amid these plywood walls and concrete steps the color of earwigs? This was Our Big Break, but everything smelled of wet carpeting and a bad night.

And all of us knew this. We avoided eye contact with each other; each person was "preparing" for the show in his own way. Justin was doing his transcendental meditation and twitching a lot. Paul was blowing bubbles from a chartreuse mass of watermelon-flavored gum; Sammy was tinkering with his newly pierced eyebrow; and Brian and Andy looked as though our nachos and beer dinner had declared war on their stomachs.

Roberto was confident, cracking his knuckles and trying out voices. "My Katharine Hepburn sounds just like my Rose Kennedy," he was complaining.

Andy told Roberto to keep it down, people in the audience might hear him. "What people?" Roberto laughed. He jerked aside the ancient curtain, so soft it seemed more dust than velvet. We counted eleven—*eleven* people huddled at the mock-colonial tables, in the red glow from hobnail glass lamps.

Andy turned on me. "You said you and Roberto have been leafletting. Then why is the house so awful?"

"Cool it, there'll be more," Roberto said, in a Bugs Bunny voice Andy didn't appreciate.

We had an unwritten rule: when the cast outnumbers the audience, the show must not go on. This wasn't the case tonight, but, unlike Roberto and me, Andy and the others had driven many miles for such a pathetic house.

Roberto peered back into the audience. "Swell, one guy is leaving."

"I hope he's just hitting the men's room," I said.

Justin was blinking out of his TM. Paul spit his bubblegum into his hand then stuck it on the wall. Everyone else was trying to act enthused. "Have an awesome night, everybody," Brian sighed. "It's eight-fifteen," Andy said. "If we're going on, we've got to go on now!"

I parted the curtain and counted ten heads, all looking uneasy, almost guilty, as though they'd done something wrong, chosen the wrong show, for instance.

Then, far back in the audience, someone shouted my name: "Mark, YES!" It was Ian, wobbling between two men from the St. Harold's party. They were emerging from the street with at least five more customers in tow.

"Hey!" I answered Ian, then ducked backstage.

At least they'd bought tickets, but performing in front of friends always spooked me; I felt the stakes were higher, meeting their expectations. Then again, was Ian really my friend? In spite of the childhood rescue, I knew that was debatable.

"Sixteen people," I reported to Andy. "A guy I know just brought five more bodies."

"It's eight-twenty-five let's go!" Roberto said. So I led the troupe into the spotlight, into the glare. Some polite applause broke out and someone, it might've been Ian, bellowed, "Break a leg!" in a beery voice. With the light in our faces, the audience was little more than a blur. My nerves were on overdrive; rivulets of sweat were coursing down my spine, but my mouth felt as dry as though it contained all of the deserts of Arizona, complete with cactus, tarantulas, and Gila monsters. "Hello!" I rasped. "Thanks for coming."

"Not in my mouth!" some imbecile yelled.

Then I began our introduction, explaining improv required audience collaboration, that skits had rules, like games of baseball, but that every skit was spontaneous as a sneeze and fuelled by their suggestions. "So, when we ask for your input before each skit, or clap to stop the action and get your advice, please be outrageous…"

"What about God?" somebody asked, and my body went on alert, sure Christian Soldiers were in our audience. I caught sight of the man in the flasher's raincoat, the man who'd asked if we were a drag show; he was stationed at a table down front covered with pamphlets with angels on their covers.

"Is God in your script? In the script of your life?"

"Well, I prayed for a bigger audience," Roberto admitted.

Two lesbians laughed.

"Anyway," I said, "your suggestions, divine or otherwise, are most welcome." Since I was "calling," directing, the first skit, I asked for a location where the action should take place.

"Mars," someone in the audience yelled.

"A gay beach," someone else said.

"A gay beach on Mars," a third person suggested.

I took the gay beach on Mars as our setting. The skit, "A Meeting," was governed by the principle that the actors involved are two gay men, strangers instinctively attracted to each other. We cast our strongest performers, Andy and Roberto, in this skit—and they came through with some good lines, about getting "an earthburn" and being "into tentacles," then ended with a parody song, "Red Scales in a Sunspot."

The applause was strong, but when we assembled backstage, Roberto kept worrying his energy was low, jealous, actually, that he wasn't being singled out as the star.

"At least the holy roller is quiet," Brian said.

"Well, he's eating," Andy said. "He's preoccupied with his giant order of onion rings."

Our mood soared as the next two skits went beautifully. Roger Morton appeared at the bar, mixing someone a cocktail requiring grenadine and a tiny paper parasol. Tristan, the bouncer, was now manning the door. It was my turn to act in a skit, "Coming Out," which involved taking an audience member's true coming out story and embellishing it with bizarre twists.

Andy, calling the skit, asked, "Who has a coming-out story he'd like to share?" The lesbian couple gave him a stare that all but sandblasted him, so he added, "Or she'd like to share."

You'd think he'd asked for a moment of silence. Sometimes it was difficult to get people to volunteer a milestone for comic fodder, but we were always gentle with our humor for this skit. "Don't be shy!" I encouraged the audience. "Tell us a friend's coming out story."

The man in the raincoat, the man with the pamphlets, was waving his hand, the only person in the audience to respond, so Andy was forced to acknowledge him. "Yes…sir, do you have a coming-out story?"

"I'm talking about the greatest story ever told," he answered, then, silently, he rose and began distributing his pamphlets, table by table, around the room. Judging by his walk, he was either drunk or sick. I hadn't seen him at town hall; he could've been a Christian Soldier or just a lone crank.

"Sir…please," Andy said.

"Where is the bouncer?" Brian whispered.

Of course Tristan and Roger Morton were now nowhere in sight.

The man sidled up to the two lesbians' table. As he held out his pamphlet, one of them enunciated, "NO THANK YOU!" Stunned, he meekly tucked his remaining literature into his pocket and shuffled out of the restaurant.

The audience cheered. The lesbian who'd spoken took a stylish bow.

"She got the biggest hand of the evening," Roberto muttered.

"Onward and upward," Andy said, struggling to re-establish momentum.

"Hey, bring back that guy with the pamphlets!" one of Ian's friends yelled. "He was the funniest thing in the show!"

"Yes, you in the rear," Andy was saying, grateful for an upraised hand. "Tell us your coming out story."

"It was back at school," the voice began. Was it Ian's posh North Shore drawl? It was so thickened by drink that I was unsure.

"It was long ago and far away…"

Everything inside me was shutting down.

"…At the late, great St. Harold's…"

It was Ian in the murk, there was no doubt.

"…It happened in chapel, a building ordinarily off-limits to animal lusts. We were both acolytes, myself and this fellow I'll call 'M.' M was reasonably attractive, but a little too sensitive and desperate…"

He was exhuming something awful, the worst part of our shared past, the thing that almost negated his saving my life.

"This sounds pretty good," Brian whispered and Sam nodded. The troupe was eager to use Ian's story, except for Roberto, who knew we'd been classmates.

"…This poor fellow had *parentage issues.* His father was a nautical person and his mother more or less followed the fleet…"

Already, my colleagues were huddling, assigning roles. "I'll be the sensitive loser," Justin said. "You be the guy who rejects him," Paul told me. All the while, Andy was talking, explaining how we could have fun with this material. That's all it was for them, just material.

"I'm sitting this one out," I said.

"It's your turn," two people told me.

I could hear Ian laughing and saw Roger Morton, in his vest of tiny mirrors, like extra eyes, at the bar.

"Let him go," said Roberto, as I ripped aside the curtain, almost splitting the fragile fabric. With Ian's laughter still bullying my ears, I felt my fury escalate at his "follow the fleet" remark, his disparaging my mother, and I saw him long ago, in the chapel crypt, among the racks of choir robes, his laughter shiny and as hard as the brass candle snuffer he'd been holding…

The "Coming Out Story" skit was concluding. "…YOU MEAN YOU'RE THE BISHOP?!" Justin was shouting, then the audience cheered and the actors came bursting backstage.

"That was professional," Andy said to me.

"Yeah, thanks for your support, Mark," Brian added.

"You're calling the next skit," Roberto reminded me.

Somehow, I walked back onstage, parted the curtains and put myself into the lurid energy of the spotlight. "Okay, for this next skit, we need some occupations, the more bizarre the better," I said.

"Mortician," someone said.

"Porn star." The perennial response.

"Astronaut—female," one of the two lesbians specified.

Most of the other suggestions were just as good.

I said, "This next skit is called 'Day Job,' and it's about someone whose fantasy career wreaks havoc with their nine-to-five responsibilities, for instance, a manicurist who secretly longs to be a tree surgeon."

"Hey!" someone shouted.

"So let's begin—"

"Hey," the heckler repeated. It was Ian, staggering through the audience in a yellow-and-black rugby shirt spotted with ketchup. His eyes and nose looked runny, like he'd been fighting flu. "How come you weren't in the last skit, Mark? I think you could've added a lot of…authenticity."

"Where is the goddamn bouncer?" Roberto was asking.

"I think you've had a few too many," I told Ian. Then, without thinking, I repeated my gesture from years before, under the Gothic arches on the chapel's crypt: I touched his shoulder.

And he repeated his response, this time in public, for my troupe and our entire audience to hear—"Take your fucking hands off me, you son of a whore!"

To my right, a straight couple was beginning a pitcher of beer. Everything felt tenuous, like the landscapes in lucid dreams; I felt that I could fly if I chose to. I said, "I don't usually use props, but tonight I'm making an exception."

Then I seized the pitcher of beer and emptied it over Ian Drummond's head.

Chapter Six

The next day, Sunday, I went to church as a kind of penance, to the Unitarian/Universalist meetinghouse in Provincetown. It's right there on Commercial Street, with its white clapboards and prim spire, amid the shops selling incense and tarot cards and tit clamps. Inside, *tromp l'oeil* paintings gave an added dimension to its ceiling and walls, pulling niches, cornices, pilasters, and rosettes from flat, oyster-colored plaster. Suspended from the ceiling hung a Victorian lamp, all prisms and glass globes, the sort Mary Lincoln might have read by. Pews which once held whalers' widows and sailors familiar with Cape Horn and islands of cannibals were now filled with drag queens and software executives masquerading as beachboys.

I felt awful, for all sorts of reasons: for disgracing myself with my improv colleagues, for fleeing Quahog as soon the bouncer pried Ian and me apart. An angry friend is more dreaded than any enemy, so meeting Roberto or Roger Morton terrified me.

And I was wary that the Christian Soldiers, or whoever was responsible for the hate crime at Arthur's, might sabotage a service at this most lavender of congregations. So when Edward settled into the pew in front of me, a little to my left so that I could observe him without his knowing, it was somehow comforting. Upon sitting, he began to pray, shutting his eyes as tightly as a child counting while playing hide-and-go-seek.

The first hymn was, ironically, "Forward Through the Ages," that is, "Onward, Christian Soldiers" with lyrics editing Jesus and war out of the picture. Christian Soldiers, I thought, would haunt this service.

And I was right. When the congregation was invited to share its "joys and sorrows," several people took the microphone to express concern for Arthur and the "spirit" or "soul" of Provincetown. A Canadian lesbian, an Olympic kayaking gold medalist, spoke sadly about "the five men—they looked like Christian Soldiers, they had the uniforms—who screamed insults at me and at my partner from a car on Bradford Street." Some in the church clapped at compliments to Arthur, while others whirled two fingers above their heads, in the Unitarian "gesture of affirmation."

Edward coughed into a tissue during the sermon, which was about hatred. The African-American minister, a lesbian graduate of Harvard Divinity School, said, "We have to look inside our hearts, to ask ourselves: Is there hatred within us too? What kind of garden are we growing within our souls? Is it full of nettles and thistles and briars? Or does it bring forth the sweet, nourishing fruit of forgiveness?"

Were Hollings Fair's followers the forgiving sort? Fair himself had left Cape Cod the day after his speech at the town meeting. He was needed, evidently, at his trademark church, with its concrete angel with an observation deck lodged in her halo. Were the Christian Soldiers praying at this very moment, to a god who existed solely to punish, who'd refined hell into a Calvinist theme park for their despised? And how big, we all wondered, was their presence in Provincetown? We saw men in battle gear all the time now, milling on the streets, driving trucks and cars, but were there others, incognito, in this very church this morning?

During the moment of silent meditation, when the associate minister played his Tibetan singing bowls, I thought Edward wiped tears from his eyes. Then a soloist from the choir sang a spiritual, "Precious Lord, Take My Hand" bringing the ache of the old South into our humid Yankee church.

After the service, there was the inevitable bottleneck at the door. Again, I worried about meeting the wrong people, but no one from Quahog materialized, thank God.

Some churchgoers were pausing outside, taking refreshments, participating in the post-service social. Edward was unlocking a bicycle from the rack in front of the church, lifting it gently, as if to avoid the violence of metal on metal, avoid the spokes of his wheels banging others. I recognized the bicycle as Arthur's, but Edward's clothes were new, a blue T-shirt advertising Quicksilver surfing gear, and black denim shorts cut to advertise his body. I remembered him kissing me in Ian's bedroom, then scurrying away.

"Hello," he said. "I heard you were at Quahog."

Had he heard about my fight, I wondered, or were he and Arthur still frightened of the telephone, of those late-night hang-up calls Edward mentioned at Ian's?

"How did you hear about our gig?"

Edward was now astride the bicycle, one muscular leg on its pedal and the other straight out, his toe *en pointe* on the ground in its fraying sneaker. "I saw you out front of Quahog before the show. Two friends of Arthur's went, Elinor and Ginny. I saw them in Adams Pharmacy this morning." He described the lesbians who'd intimidated the fundamentalist with the pamphlets.

"Did they give you a review of my performance?"

"They said…you made quite a splash." Was that his wit or the lesbians'? We both laughed.

Talking to Edward, especially about Arthur, was an oddly formal experience in which every gesture, every phrase, seemed governed by some vast, vaguely hostile code of etiquette. He was protecting Arthur from intruders, so it seemed, the way Montezuma's emissaries sought to bribe away Cortez with gifts of quetzal feathers and jade. Then, abruptly, he became accessible: "I'm sure Ian deserved it."

I mentioned Edward's early exit from Ian's party. He'd found the swordfish "tough as an old shoe" and the chutney sour. Then, blushing, he began coughing. "Excuse me," he said, choking, while I stood there helplessly, unsure whether this was an embarrassment or an emergency.

He dismounted from the bicycle, letting it clatter to the ground, and then rummaged through the leather pouch strapped around his waist. Retrieving an orange tube from the pouch, he turned away. He held the object to his mouth, his shoulders hunched like somebody with grandchildren. He had asthma, I realized. It was an inhaler, not amyl nitrate, Ian had seen him using in Arthur's kitchen.

People kept streaming from the church. "Is your friend okay?" asked a woman I recognized as the lover of the lesbian author who'd spoken at town hall.

"I'm not sure," I said. "Let me get him something to drink." I nudged my way through the crowd to the folding tables of refreshments for the social: sticky pink cake studded with pieces of peppermint, ginger snap cookies, jugs of lemonade.

When I returned with some lemonade, Edward was still coughing, being lectured by the famous author on illness as a metaphor for racism. Her child was sleeping through her speech in a sling on her back. "Perhaps you're allergic to proximity of homophobia," the famous author told Edward, then eased away.

Edward drank the lemonade, said, "Sorry about that," and stopped coughing. "Thank you, thanks for rescuing me."

I think I needed him at that moment as much as I've needed anyone: I still felt like the Outcast, the Idiot Who'd Wrecked the Show, so, impulsively, I offered to buy him lunch—and he surprised me by answering, "Great!"

I chose the Café Blasé, across Commercial Street from my apartment, where white metal tables with wide, fringed umbrellas stood beneath the twisting branches of an acanthus tree strung with fairy lights. Its porch was hung with Chinese lanterns made of loose, blistery-looking paper, and, enclosing all this was a white picket fence with flowerboxes brilliant with petunias and geraniums pink as prom gowns.

"We've both been virtuous, we've been to church," I said, "so we can indulge." I ordered a margarita, but Edward wanted nothing stronger than guava juice.

He borrowed a pen from our waiter, and then filled his placemat with sketches, with enough racing cars for an Indianapolis

500. "That Ian drinks like a fish," he said, making me self-conscious about my great big blue cocktail.

"Margaritas aren't my usual Sunday fare," I said. "...Arthur was a bit soused the day of the party."

"But since then, he hasn't had a drop. I've been very strict, keeping him clean and sober. He looks awesome." Edward paused. "That was such an awful thing—"

"To do to Arthur," I said.

He stopped sketching. The pen was broken, leaking ink onto his fingers. "And to hurt that poor dog." He put a surprising amount of emotion into his voice. "That was so cruel. I'm an animal lover. I believe living things have the right to live."

That didn't stop him from ordering a hamburger, heavy with bacon, with extra mushrooms. Considering his past, studying cooking, I thought he might choose something minimalist and broiled or full of sprouts and field greens, but I was wrong. I was midway through my grilled chicken sandwich and a second margarita before I had the courage enough to ask him the question I now realized was the reason for this luncheon. "How did you meet Arthur?"

Edward was eating his hamburger with a knife and fork, cutting it with quick, fastidious gestures that reflected his culinary background. "I'll never forget the day I met Arthur. But not because of anything to do with Arthur."

He had been hitchhiking to Provincetown. He'd gotten as far as the Orleans traffic circle without incident, receiving rides from traveling salesmen, a Seventh-Day Adventist minister, and a potter from Welfleet. "They were all very straight, very talkative, and very boring."

Then, at Orleans, all of that changed. His next ride was in an old beige van. Edward would always remember the grubby fake fur on its steering wheel and the web of wooden beads slung over the driver's seat. "For my sciatica," the driver had said. The driver himself was somewhat generic. He wore a baseball cap and those silver reflecting sunglasses that make you feel like you're talking to yourself. He had dark curly hair and a mustache graying at the edges. His skin was olive, gritty from years at a gas station or a marina; his fingernails were black.

He told Edward he could take him to Provincetown, but said little else. He played classical music, "lots of harpsichords," very loud on his tapedeck; it made Edward's ears throb. When Edward tried to make small talk, the driver shrugged and turned the music still louder.

By the time Provincetown came into view, the pond and sand on the right, Massachusetts Bay and that line of cabins on the left, Edward's uneasiness was calcifying into fear. Something told him to bolt at the next traffic light. Unfortunately, it was green and the driver shot through, miles above the speed limit. Edward prayed for a police car to intercept them, but they seemed to have the road to themselves.

When they reached the exits for the East End of Provincetown, Edward screamed for the driver to stop and let him out. He knew there was panic in his voice; he knew the driver realized he wasn't screaming just to compete with the music. For the first time, the driver smiled. Then he turned up the harpsichords, like instruments of torture.

The driver and the air-conditioning of the van both seemed to grow colder by the moment. "He just sped through the lights, red, green, it didn't make any difference."

Edward looked straight into my eyes, eager, I thought, to gauge my reaction. "He raped me." He made it sound like a boast.

He elaborated. The driver swerved down a side road where there was nothing but woods, the dry black pines, the scrub trees that barely suck life out of the sandy earth of the Province Lands. He parked the van and then overpowered Edward, pinning his arms, wrestling him still, and dragging him deep into the woods.

Edward screamed but heard nothing except the dry hum of insects in reply. He remembered the driver's hands, callused, smelling of turpentine, clamping over his mouth, and his feet, in new orange workboots, kicking and tearing through the brush on the overgrown trail. He remembered the man dragging him through poison ivy and having the ridiculous urge to warn him of its presence, hoping this small act of kindness might somehow temper his brutality.

The driver was squeezing him so hard he thought he'd fractured some ribs. Exhausted, too frightened to fight further, Edward went limp and the driver gathered him almost tenderly in his arms, slinging him over his shoulder. Edward said nothing; the woods were deserted, and he'd screamed his throat raw.

"He had a knife. I was lucky to get out alive."

So, bleeding and all but broke, Edward had staggered into Provincetown. He bought a meal of fried dough and salt water taffy, then spent the night on the beach, where Arthur found him the following morning in back of his house.

Chapter Seven

Was he telling the truth? Or was this a fantasy cooked up like his bouillabaisse, his payment for my treating him to lunch? I had no idea, but I wanted to believe him, for Arthur's sake and my own.

It had been three weeks since it had last rained and lawns were yellowing, farmers worrying and experts predicting a drought. But there was ample sunshine to be enjoyed, so I suggested Edward ask Arthur to come to the beach. I would drive and pick them up tomorrow at ten.

The next day, June fifteenth, broke sunny and hot. When I stopped at Arthur's house in my rusting Volvo, Edward, alone, answered the door. "Arthur isn't up to Herring Cove," he informed me.

Bear in mind that I'd known Arthur for a good ten years, and here was this boy he'd found like a sand dollar four short weeks ago, suggesting my company was some sort of ordeal. A boy Arthur himself admitted needed a bottle of Kwell and a dozen showers before being allowed near good linen.

"What is there to be 'up to' about the beach?" Was the whole town going to shun me because of one night, one mistake? "Is Arthur okay?" I asked, loudly, so that my voice would travel well beyond the front hall, beyond the China trade umbrella stand and the Rowlandson prints of gambling rakes.

Edward used the full howitzers of his charm. "He's napping now. He's having a new security system installed. They're coming this afternoon from Plymouth. But I'd love to go."

Without waiting for my response, he gathered some beach things, Arthur's things, from a closet, then grabbed a hardback book from the sofa. Arthur had bought Edward the clothes he was wearing, the ice-blue gym shorts and a polo shirt in a color catalogues that year called "mango." "I think we'll both feel better once the alarm system gets installed."

My taking him to the beach alone had ulterior motives, of course: I could ask him about his background. Would he answer?

The upholstery in the car seared my thighs, even though it was only mid-morning. Edward was all coy silence, the silence of a withholder, as we drove slowly through this prettiest section of Provincetown. White picket fences separated lawns and gardens from the street. Many of the houses, barn-red, white, or cedar worn to a twig-like November-brown, were older than the country, older than the United States of America. They were overwhelmed by the greenery surrounding them, tunnels of sycamores and silver maples, of wisteria, rhododendrons, and masses of bridal wreath in their last vigor before drought finally sapped them.

Edward was ignoring the scenery, examining my car, grinning at the odometer and gas gauge as if they were tricks. He even had the audacity to open my glove compartment, to thumb through the Volvo owner's manual.

"I don't believe you've mentioned where you're from."

"Oh, we moved a lot. I don't think about the past. I'm really sort of concentrating on my future."

"Are you here just for the summer?"

"I'm not really sure." He crammed the owner's manual back in its place, then shut the glove compartment a bit too forcefully, as if to shut off my line of personal questions. His silences had an edge; he had a way of making *you* feel responsible for his share of conversation. "…Have you ever owned a Jaguar?" he said at last. "It's been my lifelong ambition. Owning a Jaguar."

He pronounced it "Jag-you-are" like British actors do in their commercials, but he was some sort of New Englander because he dropped his R's and revved up his A's.

"That's beyond my budget, a Jaguar."

"I thought all you preppies had big bucks." He was grinning.

We'd come to the beginning of Commercial Street, where it meets the shore road. On the left stood the big hotel, the one that really belong in Hyannis; on the right were some houses, bleached wood, all Danish Modern angles. In front of us were the tidal flats and the granite breakwater snaking through them, and, in the distance, the dunes of the National Seashore, buff-colored humps like a lost piece of Arabia.

I took a right onto the shore road so that the lushness and history of the West End became just nature. We drove past salt marshes, ponds green with winking coverings of scum, and miniature pines draped with southern-seeming silvery-gray moss.

Edward was talking, but about Formula One racing. "Well, you follow the Grand Prix, don't you? You've heard of Monte Carlo, haven't you?" He began quoting statistics, about drivers and races and circuits, about Ferrari and McLaren and Maserati, all while running his hands over the luminous, icy fabric of his running shorts. He was doing everything he could to make his small talk as small as possible.

"This is our lucky day," I said. I was gliding into a just-vacated space in the parking lot at Herring Cove Beach. In retrospect, that was stupidest remark I've made in my life. If I'd been the least bit psychic, I'd never have said that, never gone to Cape Cod that summer. We parked near the beige-wood-and-cinder-block snack bar so that we could smell hot dogs and relish cutting through the fragrance of salt and roses. Wild roses thrived along the parking lot fence, their loose pink petals trembling in what little breeze braved the heat.

"I hope you don't mind a walk," I said to Edward. "I thought we'd try the nude section."

I thought that might get some sort of reaction. Since everyone assumed he was hustling Arthur's money and that his brain was locked on all things carnal, I thought he'd play the prude and insist we stay here. Instead, he clasped my arm with the authority of someone older, taller, and stronger. He said, "Arthur says you're an okay guy, so that's enough for me." As though he were the one who'd shared a prep school with Arthur, who'd toasted New Year's Eve in front of his fireplace on Beacon Street.

There are just two buildings at Herring Cove Beach, the snack bar and the bath house, then sand and water. The beach is just a succession of sand and dunes that empties of people the farther you walk, except for the men's nude section. The water that day was almost tropical blue, bursting into breakers that were the exaggerated white of shaving cream.

It was a hot, half-hour walk to the nude beach. The sand, gravelly and coarse at the water's edge, sucked at our heels. It was littered with all sorts of gifts from the tides, the things that I'd collected as a child; tangles of kelp, like the combings of some sea god's hair; clamshells with purple streaks the Indians had cut to trade as wampum; wet pebbles veined with greenstone that could almost pass as jade.

Continuing to do his best to avoid real conversation, Edward strode along just ahead of me, keeping enough distance so that we couldn't be perceived as being together. I should say right now that I don't break any mirrors. That summer I was twenty-nine, "considered good-looking" as the personals ads would say, 5'10", slender, with reddish-brown hair cut as fashionably as Newbury Street could manage. Nothing for Edward to be ashamed of.

We passed the women's section, then the clothed men's section, then a Foreign Legion's worth of empty sand, scorching and seemingly endless. Edward apparently knew his way because he accelerated his pace until at last we reached our goal. It was actually marked, this oasis, but not by date palms or some bubbling spring. Instead, two huge branches of driftwood had been screwed into the sand to form a fork, like the whalebone arches sea captains built for their gardens throughout nineteenth-century Cape Cod. Draped from one of these branches was a fading rainbow flag, along with countless strands of Mardi

Gras beads—silver, lavender, gold—glittering in the still, blazing air.

Seeing no one I knew, I felt relieved in spite of myself. "Make yourself at home," I called to Edward, who'd already begun settling in. He unfurled a towel Arthur had swiped from a hotel at Cap d'Antibes, then propped up a gauzy collapsible tent. Finally, with all eyes upon him—there were thirty or more men in the vicinity—he began disrobing, without the slightest hint of stage fright, until he stood stripped, desired, and unobtainable. You could see the effect in other men's reactions: the lovers nudging each other to look, a middle-aged man putting down his Foucault just to stare. They saw what compensated for rent at Arthur's—a chest with a delicate play of muscles, and a penis, that, liberated from his underwear, was large and seemingly moist, almost erect, bobbing as Edward rubbed his body with tanning oil.

"Need some help with your back?" a handsome black man was reckless enough to ask. A smile flashed then died on Edward's lips when he answered, "Thanks just the same, but I'm fine."

His body language was all about exclusion. I didn't have the confidence to sit close to him, and he didn't invite me, so I claimed a spot about fifteen feet away. He spent much of his time in the tent he'd borrowed, something Arthur had bought for his sister when she'd developed skin cancer. My lunch, fake crabmeat and a package of oatmeal cookies, decidedly downscale compared to some of my neighbors' fare, was half eaten when I saw *him* and lost my appetite. Ian, of course. Ian Drummond. The cause of my disgrace, the reason I was alone.

He was with his crowd, gay Republicans with summer houses in the vicinity, including Barton Daggett. Ian was using his hoarse, bearish laugh, often unleashed at someone else's expense. I turned away, wishing I could hide in Edward's tent. Then Ian and his friends filed up into the dunes flanking the back of the beach.

It was gorgeous weather, hot, with a sky hard and blue as tile. The sun was burning; you could feel your shoulders cooking like sirloin. Don't think of Ian, I told myself, don't think of anything

but this day. I swam every hour or so. The water was clear close
to the shore, then aquamarine farther out, with a gem-like cold-
ness that seemed to stop your heart when you dove in. It gave
you a blade-like awareness of your body the first few minutes,
then, once you swam in the slow, clear swells, it was marvelous,
especially naked, with everything floating and free.

But most of the men stayed on shore, marking crossword
puzzles, getting peeved at the grit in their sandwiches, and cruising Edward. There was little interaction between the groups on
the beach; they sat on their towels, in close proximity but with
vague distrust, like Italian city-states during the Middle Ages.
Several times, as soon as I emerged from the water, Edward went
strolling languidly toward it, always naked, always smiling as he
passed me. To follow him back into the Atlantic would be an
open act of shameless desperation, so I didn't dare.

As the day wound down and the sun completed its arc across
the sky, people began leaving the beach—Barton Daggett and
his friends, the black man Edward had refused. But not Ian.
Couples shook sand from their blankets and folded them as
crisply as soldiers folding the flag at a military funeral. Guys
wiggled back into sneakers, pressed fingers into reddening flesh
to confirm they'd "picked up a little color." They stuffed favorite beach stones into pockets to join guest house keys on long
plastic lozenges, and began the trek back across the breakwater
to town, or to the Herring Cove parking lot, full of all sorts of
cars from all sorts of states with the same Celebrate Diversity
stickers on their bumpers.

By late afternoon, only three people remained in sight:
myself, Edward, and an Asian boy. The Asian appeared to be in
his late teens, with spiky hair and studs in his ears that looked
like droplets of mercury. He wore a black Lycra thong, and his
dusky skin suggested he could be Cambodian.

Somehow his presence here felt validating, as though the
bumper stickers about diversity were at last becoming true, and
that war, emigration, and his parents' prayers to a thousand joss
sticks couldn't prevent him coming here and being himself, on

this beach at the edge of America. Finally, he too made gestures to leave, swigging the last of his Evian water, standing, brushing the sand from his tawny thighs, all the while glancing invitingly in Edward's direction but getting no reaction whatsoever. Edward had emerged from his tent, but was absorbed with reading the bulky hardback book he'd snatched from the sofa at Arthur's.

Then the Asian boy peeled off his thong, wrung the seawater from it, and walked across the sand, the DMZ separating him from Edward. I could hear snatches of their conversation, like the words, ragged with static, of broadcasts from Winnipeg and Calgary fading in and out on my late-night car radio.

Whatever the Asian's line, it failed. He stepped indignantly into his briefs and jeans, then came marching in my direction. He was breaking through the erotic wall of silence that separates naked men at this beach, so I felt a little self-conscious.

"What's with him, anyway?" The Asian had a chili-thick Texas drawl. "Talk about mixed messages, the way he parades around! You should've seen him carrying on while you were in the water!" Then he was off, late for tea dance.

I was shaking out my deck shoes when Edward approached, saying, "You've been awfully quiet this afternoon."

Don't psychiatrists call that "projection"? "It comes with the territory," I said.

He was holding the book he'd gotten from Arthur's sofa. "Arthur says you're interested in this guy." The book's title was spelled out in gilt Gothic lettering: *A Prince Among Painters: The Art of Thomas Royall*. It was mostly plates, and contained little information. The one Royall biography was something rare published in the Fifties.

"He painted *The Fisher Boy*," Edward said. "It's in the museum back in town."

He was kneeling now, exuding the scent of warm skin and tanning butter, flipping through Arthur's book with his beach-greasy, damaging fingers. "They're having a retrospective on Thomas Royall at the museum. Here in Provincetown."

He actually seemed eager to talk, but, having been slighted the entire day, I felt less than flattered being the center of attention now that the beach was empty except for gulls, sandpipers, and some tiny figures in the distance by the bath house.

"Would you like to borrow it?"

He doesn't want to carry it back, I thought. He wants me to lug this heavy book back to the parking lot, then drive him to Arthur's.

"I'll take a rain check." A joke that year, what with the drought.

"Are you leaving now?"

"Actually, I'm not." I'd been ready to go for more than an hour.

"I've got to get back to Arthur's." Suddenly Edward was all responsibility. "I mean, those security people will be leaving pretty soon, and he won't want to be all alone."

He knew there was a shuttle between the bath house and town, costing all of one dollar.

"Hey," he said, giving me his widest smile, "thanks for the ride to the beach." Then he quickly dressed and packed up his things, Arthur's things, and walked away.

I was picking the icing from an oatmeal cookie, worrying that my shins had gotten sun-burnt, when I heard someone call my name. It couldn't be Edward, he was already miniature, far down the beach toward the parking lot.

"The other way!" the voice shouted.

Looking back toward Long Point, I saw Ian Drummond in the dunes.

"C'mere!" he called as dread flooded my system.

He was kneeling, his body hidden by the dunes and clumps of beach grass, that coarse grass that cuts your legs and stays green like conifers all winter. I hesitated, knowing I should yank on my pants, but if I did that, I'd just leave, head for the parking lot and ignore him. Exactly what most people would have done in my circumstances. After what had happened, after what he'd done.

"Come as you are," Ian shouted, as if reading my mind.

He'd been drinking but didn't sound completely polluted, the way he had the night of our show. He exerted a pull, not entirely due to his saving me in Gloucester. We were equals here on this naked sand and had unfinished business with each other that only we, alone, could conclude. This time there was no one to referee us, and Ian owed me contrition, an apology, for insulting my mother in public. As I walked across the sand that separated us—one of the longest walks of my life, even though it was two hundred feet or less—I actually wondered if this were some sort of ambush. Ian, after all, was the ambushing type.

"Mark, my man, welcome to my world." He was as naked as I was, sitting on a towel in one of those hollows in the dunes that look like sand traps on golf courses. Hidden from the National Park rangers who sometimes patrolled the flat parts of the beach.

We hadn't been naked together since prep school, in our pungent old gymnasium. For all his athleticism, for all his money and the ease it gave him, Ian had always been modest about his body, but it seemed that had changed now that he'd pumped himself up.

His chest was muscular in an exaggerated way, like some idealized ditch digger or dock worker in a WPA mural. He'd crossed his legs so that I couldn't see whether he was aroused, but I confirmed my suspicion that he'd been drinking. A bottle of Russian vodka with St. Basil's Cathedral on its label was propped against a wicker picnic hamper. Ian's latest reading was an oversized paperback, *Chorus Against Fascism: The Greek Resistance During World War Two,* by Stavros Zarefes.

"Still reading about war?" I asked breezily, then regretted it. War was a poor opener, given our recent fight.

"It isn't very good. He makes the Germans all but sub-human. The author obviously has an axe to grind. His uncle died being interrogated by German troops."

Leave it to Ian to worry about demonizing Nazis.

"Have a seat. Don't stand there on view for the Decency Patrol."

I didn't want to, not really, not my rational side. I kept remembering what he'd said that awful night of the performance at Quahog. His lip was still split, daubed with mercurochrome. Did that make us "even"? Could I ever be even with one of the Drummonds?

He pulled a peach, cold as a snowball, from his hamper. "Care for a fruit?"

"Thanks." Saying that made it easier to sit on his towel.

I refused a Swiss Army knife to peel the peach.

"You're buffed," I said. Ian was tanning a caramel color, and shaving his chest; he was much less hairy than I'd remembered. He was handsome in a blond, heavy-jawed way, much more adult than, say, Edward. You can't help but notice beauty, even in your enemies.

He inspected my groin. The wind sent granules of sand stinging against my body. Because I was conscious of him evaluating me, I was determined not to reciprocate. He uncrossed his legs, showcasing himself. He said, "It's always good to get a rise out of people."

He was going to play games. Very much in character.

"I saw you chatting up Arthur's little protégé, his bit of beach-combing." Then Ian crossed his legs, again censoring himself, again confusing me. His features tightened. "I haven't been very nice to you, Mark." He sighed while thrusting the vodka bottle in my direction. "I haven't been nice to you since way back when. At St. Harold's and in Gloucester, when we were kids."

Feeling vindicated but slightly embarrassed, I took a slug of vodka.

"I'm sorry, man." He never usually used "man" or other dated hipster slang, so perhaps this apology was equally bogus. He clapped his hands onto my shoulders so that he forced me to look directly into his face. He looked fatigued, gray around the eyes.

He squeezed my shoulders in a quick, confiding way, then drew me toward him so that our chests were touching. He licked at my ear and I could feel his hot breath as he nibbled my earlobe.

This is betrayal, I thought, of my mother whom he'd insulted, betrayal of all of my family, going back generations. But I took another swig of vodka, raw like paint thinner, down my throat. I remembered all he'd done, all he'd apologized for, then tried to stand but lost my balance.

My heart was pounding the way it does when my blood pressure gets taken, when the sleeve begins tightening, crushing my arm.

"Hey, man, relax." A sexy leer transformed Ian's face. I had another hit of vodka then another, my eighty-proof excuse for what was happening.

"It's not like we're total strangers," he said. Conservative in his politics and clothing, he was liberal in ways of the flesh. His chest was like stone. He was far from the beefy stripling of St. Harold's. I'd done my time with free weights and jogged hundreds of weedy-smelling miles by the Charles, but I felt thin and naive at that moment compared to Ian.

I was enjoying the sex, but felt a little detached as though I were hovering above us in the hot, salty air, like a soul afloat above its newly-dead body. I was confused about the work my mouth and hands were doing—to someone I half-despised.

After it was over, he became brusque. He stared out to sea. The coast, the crook of Cape Cod stretching toward Plymouth, was grayish-blue in the distance. He lit a cigarette and smoked with a kind of hunger.

"You never used to smoke," I said, and he snapped, "Don't get on my case, okay? I don't need an extra physician. I've got enough people on my case already, so I sure as hell don't need you!"

He slipped the Swiss Army knife back into his wicker hamper, then brushed me and the sand from his towel.

"You're not staying to watch the sunset?"

"You sound like a greeting card." Ian sounded more weary than hostile. He pulled on his clothes roughly, as if they'd misbehaved. "If you want to watch something, I suggest you watch little Edward."

"Why? Are you after him too?"

Hugging the hamper and his beach things, he headed toward the breakwater and his house. *"Vaya con Díos,"* he said, over his shoulder.

I felt very alone, and a bit drunk from the vodka Ian had insisted I share. He'd left me the bottle, now my only companion on this empty beach.

Why didn't I leave right then? Why didn't I pack up and return to the Herring Cove parking lot? I stayed, I suppose, because there was something magical about the beach at that hour, the cooling sand, the ocean like quicksilver, so dense and metallic, and the full moon white as a shaman's bone amulet in the pale sky.

I swam, and the water was frigid. Colder currents must have come roiling in from somewhere out toward George's Bank. When I ran to my towel, I was shivering, so, to warm my gut, I finished the last of Ian's vodka. I meant to watch the sunset but my insomnia had kicked in since that awful night at the club, since my disgrace. Sleep overwhelmed me.

When I awoke, it was dark, nine-forty by my watch. I was alone in a black windy landscape. I didn't want to chance taking the beach route back what with the threats from those Christian Soldiers. Provincetown was in such a mess. I wanted the lights of the shore road in my sight as a beacon, a kind of comfort. So I decided to cross the granite breakwater—the long string of stones across the inlet separating Herring Cove Beach from the mainland.

The breakwater seemed to stretch forever in the moonlight. The tide was in: you could hear it gurgling and sloshing between the stones. There's no mortar in the breakwater; it's just heaped together, like the stone walls marking the pastures of long-dead farmers in rural New England. It's tricky walking. The stones, quarry scrap, are the size of car hoods, tilted every which way and sometimes loose, so you have to watch every step, plan every move. Even in daylight, you could slip and twist an ankle or break your leg.

The breakwater is long, a good half-hour walk. Soon, I began tiring, but with hundreds of yards behind me, I'd already gone too far to turn back. I was also realizing the foolishness of my choice; at least the beach route was relatively flat. But here you could see the lights of Provincetown, glittering along the harbor shore in an uneven tide, as if each building had been gently, haphazardly, deposited by a different tide.

I was relieved, happy, to see a man in the distance. Not a basher, I hoped, not some hostile visitor from the west. He was on the right side of the breakwater, facing the harbor, leaning against an upright slab of rock. At night, at high tide, you see people fishing here, but I couldn't make out his line or reel.

Days, people nodded as they crossed paths here, those coming to the beach and those leaving it. Mostly men took this route, a lengthy but direct hike to the gay nude section of Herring Cove. Here the sense of "community" actually rang true: the handsomest men gave you a cheery hello, forced to confront you face to face on this narrow, slightly hazardous structure.

This man was just the other side of a part in the breakwater where the sea had knocked some stones askew, so that, at high tide, you were compelled to wade through about five or six inches of water where the breakwater is intact but not as high as intended.

Removing my shoes, I sloshed across this gap, not longer than a yard or so. I was just about to joke about this gesture, but wasn't sure this was the right thing to do. I'd have ignored a couple who were here at night, figuring they wanted privacy in the moonlight and salt air. And if this man was fishing, I didn't want to startle him, to make him inadvertently jerk his line, then lose his catch.

So, I paused, momentarily, to study him. No, there was no fishing line, so it was safe to speak. "Beautiful night," I started to say, but got only as far as the first syllable. I stopped when I saw his forearm—it was soaked in something thick, not the cold guts of bait...

He had a startled look, his eyes were open. So was his mouth. His throat was leaking streams of blood from a deep, ragged gash.

For an instant, I actually wondered whether he was still alive. That was before I realized who he was. His shirt was matted with blood, all but obliterating the Izod insignia. Instinctively, I reached out to touch his shoulder, but there was no place to touch, no part of his clothing or flesh not wet with thick arterial blood.

So, instead of touching him, I said his name out loud...

Chapter Eight

"…Ian." I said his name in a whisper, as if frightened to confirm it.

Because, without a doubt, it was. I'd recognized the Rolex watch and the bodybuilder's shoulders swelling the Izod shirt. I'd recognized those things before I'd admitted I recognized his face. I'd been postponing the decision it was him.

I couldn't see his beach things, his hamper and towel and book on wartime Greece, but his killer could have taken these. The man who had saved my life had now lost his, and not to something impersonal like the sea or a car crash or a retrovirus. Someone had killed him. Someone had done this. Someone had stopped his existence.

I'd never seen so much blood. It was everywhere, gleaming in the light of the full moon. Blood had run down his bare legs, then dripped onto the granite slabs to collect in the grooves the stonecutters had drilled in the quarry. It looked as though someone had taken a saw to Ian's throat and cut it through to the bone. There were wounds to his chest too; the fabric of his polo shirt was torn.

Nausea seized me like a tackle in football. I knew I was going to vomit, the way Miriam had at Arthur's. But then I knew I couldn't, that I'd be contaminating a crime scene. I'd also be leaving a clue that I'd been here. Because I knew, without a doubt, that I would not report this horror to the police. Everyone knew about my fight with Ian, my public brawl in the audience at Quahog. I would be Suspect Number One, or at least high on the list of people to question.

I pressed my arm against my mouth as bile rose then caught in my gut. To distract myself, I looked at the moon. Somehow, the spasms in my stomach eased. Then I covered my face with my fingers and began to cry, deep, ragged sobs until I bit my knuckle to make myself stop.

Someone had killed Ian, someone had cut his throat. I had to get out of here as soon as possible, but first I had to be sure that I didn't touch anything, that I hadn't touched anything.

Had I touched the stones? Had I braced myself against them in my shock, leaving fingerprints behind? I couldn't remember. I stared at my hands. Thank God they were clean, thank God there wasn't any blood on my hands.

Then I noticed my beach bag. I'd dropped it and scattered some of its contents: one towel, my sunglasses, the swim trunks I'd brought in case the National Seashore rangers came patrolling…A wind had risen, and the towel was whipping along the breakwater, as if to evade me. I stamped it down, then snapped it up. Then I grabbed my sunglasses and swim trunks.

Had I picked up everything? Yes, this was it. Had I touched anything else? Not as far as I could recall; I'd been careful. I bent to check a crevasse between the stones. Was that my comb in there? I reached…Then as I did, I felt something dislodge from inside the beach bag I'd wedged under my arm, something bright that caught the moonlight as it fell, hitting the stone then exploding into hundreds of incriminating fragments.

I swore, then wept. It was the vodka, the bottle Ian had given me. It had broken and fallen into the space between two chunks of granite. I picked up the neck of the bottle, still with its cap…For God's sake, don't cut yourself, I thought, don't leave your DNA in addition to your fingerprints.

There was no comb, it was a twig of driftwood. I kept picking up glass. The more I picked up, the more seemed to appear, sparkling amid the straw, dried seaweed, and crumbly remnants of a styrofoam fishing float. My fingerprints were all over the bottle, I kept thinking; if I left even one shard of glass it could connect me to this murder. It could say, *he* was here, the man who fought Ian. I was stuffing the glass fragments into my beach bag. The label of the bottle, with its embossed design of St. Basil's Cathedral, remained intact, clinging to the largest pieces of glass I could find.

There was no one in sight, but how soon would that change? I had to leave, I had to run. Clutching the beach bag, twisting it shut to prevent anything else spilling out, I leapt from slab to slab of rock and was soon out of breath. It was both dangerous and useless to hurry. It also looked suspicious, but then, anyone crossing the breakwater this night would look, in retrospect, suspicious. And if I *did* meet people—anyone—on the breakwater, what would I do? Ignore them? Speak, but turn away? They might continue along the breakwater far enough to find Ian, then remember my photograph, from our comedy troupe flyers, the ones I'd posted with Roberto all over town. In my mind, each flyer became a "Wanted for Murder" poster.

I met no one on the remainder of the breakwater, thank God, and my walk to my car in the Herring Cove lot was uneventful. I took the right side of the shore road, with the traffic to my back. When traffic approached me from the opposite direction, I hung my head, hiding my face, stared at my deck shoes.

Every step I took brought me farther away from murder, away from everything except the horror of the memory.

Chapter Nine

I had some chloral hydrate at my apartment. I took two, washed down with some bad Chablis. Showering, I cried into the spray, then fell into bed.

When the sun rose and stung my eyes awake, I realized immediately that it had set on Ian forever

Until last night on the breakwater, I hadn't realized the potency of my feelings for Ian—almost fraternal, we'd shared so much. Vignettes from our past kept playing in my head, of swimming, games of baseball, building forts in the sumac and cat briar of Eastern Point, and, of course, of his saving me in the storm in Gloucester Harbor. And our sex in the dunes kept screening in my consciousness, like a snuff film on endless loop.

My milk had soured, so I dribbled some tap water over my muesli before deciding this was unsatisfactory. So I drove partway up Bradford Street, but it was seven-thirty, so the supermarket of course was closed. Instinctively, I headed toward Arthur's. I had to speak with Arthur, whether he was "up to it" or not.

His BMW, the gray of an old fedora, was parked in his driveway. The buttercup-yellow house looked serene, the peonies bending under the weight of their open, globe-like flowers. I heard someone singing—singing!—on this horrible morning. It was Arthur's voice, damaging something from *The Pirates of Penzance*.

"Hello?" I called, stepping toward the garden.

Instantly, the air filled with noise, like the sirens from every fire engine on Cape Cod.

Arthur came running in a terrycloth robe. "Don't move!" he yelled to me, then vanished inside the house. After an interval that seemed endless, the racket ceased.

"Your new alarm," I said, when he returned.

"It's a bit hypersensitive, like its owner."

A neighbor's shar pei was barking from the yard across the street.

"They're adjusting the alarm later today," Arthur said, "before my neighbors evict me." He began pouring birdseed into a Plexiglas cylinder wired to his silver maple. "You're up early." He was his buoyant old self, the Arthur of summers past.

I was casual. "The early bird gets the worm."

"And then some." Arthur closed the top of the feeder and then the bag of birdseed. "Well, you might as well be the first to know. My bird has left his gilded cage—along with two very valuable ormolu candlesticks. Can you beat that?" He plopped the bag of birdseed onto the flagstones on the terrace, then brought a plate of raisin bagels and two cups of coffee from the kitchen. "You look like you could use a hit of caffeine."

He went on about the candlesticks. His great-aunt Harriet had given them to him when he was twenty-three, when he had published his first poem in the *Yale Review.* "They were French, Empire. Harriet claimed they came from the *salon* of Madame Récamier." He was lathering cream cheese onto his bagel. "The little hustler," he muttered, obviously not referring to Madame Récamier.

Only now it registered. "Edward is missing?!"

"Gone with the wind."

He was savoring the theatricality of the moment. Certainly he was upset about both losses, but his new security system, his electronic safety net, apparently gave him confidence, restored some humor, and from his pocket he drew a plastic bottle of pills. "My new prescription," he laughed, shaking the dull turquoise capsules. "My bluebirds of happiness. Mother's little helpers. Did I ever tell you I had a mad crush on the Rolling Stones during the Sixties? Don't tell a soul!"

Everywhere—in my coffee cup, in the waves winking from Provincetown Harbor—I saw the murder. As the sole witness to that scene, I carried all of its brutality alone. Arthur, obviously, had yet to hear the news. Ian's body might still be on the breakwater, with no company but the gulls and terns. But I had to keep silent and use my acting skills, to pretend to be absorbed by some missing antiques, stolen by a kept boy who'd suddenly hit the road. Because everyone knew how I'd fought with Ian. Lots of people knew we'd both been at the beach. So I'd be a logical suspect.

"You know," Arthur was saying, "that Edward was something of a prude. He didn't even like to be touched."

He was "that Edward" now. I thought of Edward's story, of the man assaulting him in the woods. Who wouldn't have qualms about intimacy after that? Supposing, of course, his story was true.

"We slept in separate rooms last night," Arthur said. "The pollen was bothering him, or a summer cold. Or me."

So Edward hadn't mentioned his asthma. He'd kept his inhaler secret, like so much else.

"He knew the value of those candlesticks. He knew the David painting of Madame Récamier. 'Oh, we had that in art history,' he told me."

"He slipped away without triggering your new alarm?"

"I'd switched it off before we went to bed. As you saw, it's got opening-night jitters."

Then the phone in the kitchen began ringing. To my tired ears, it sounded almost as loud as the alarm.

"Everyone is so early today!" laughed Arthur.

I stared into my cup of coffee; I felt as quavery as my reflection. Cupping the cellular phone to his ear, Arthur came striding back onto the terrace. Surely this was the call; surely this was the news about Ian. Bad news is an early riser, and it was all of eight-fifteen.

Arthur's face assumed the frozen look of a mime's. "Good God, I can't believe it!" he was saying.

I starting cutting a bagel, then I put the knife down, reluctant about using it while Arthur was hearing about Ian.

"…Well, thank you," Arthur said, in a strangled whisper. "I'll break the news to Mark."

He walked toward me. "That was Roger Morton. The manager of the motel near the breakwater just phoned him. A photographer found a body on the breakwater this morning, some photographer doing a calendar of sunrise shots. The body has been identified. It's Ian. Oh God, it's so horrible!"

◇◇◇

Ian's funeral was held in Gloucester, in a Gothic sandstone church the brown of cough drops, with some of the same Anglican touches as our chapel at St. Harold's: the brass memorial plaques and Tiffany stained-glass windows glowing like sectioned mineral samples. These windows didn't open, of course, so inside it was stifling, smelling of carpeting, old hymnals, and the lemon oil that emanated from the pews.

The church was mobbed, owing, frankly, as much to the Drummonds' prominence as to their youngest son's popularity. For years, Ian's father Duncan and all his children—Fulton, George, Ian, and Sallie—had ridden to the hounds at the Essex Hunt Club. Ian's mother Janet, a tennis star during her youth, had aborted her first child, rumor had it, to play in the semifinals at Wimbledon.

Of course, Mrs. Drummond had been off the courts for years. She and her husband were elderly now, both Ian and Sallie having been "change of life" children. Today Mrs. Drummond was gaunt as one of the Fates, a black veil covering her features like an old-fashioned oxygen tent. Mr. Drummond seemed unsure exactly where he was, folding and refolding the funeral program as if making a piece of origami. Ian's brothers—each years his senior—their eyes bright with grief, carried the mahogany casket while staring straight ahead, as if fixing their attention on anything but the gilt cross on the altar would endanger their brother's soul.

The organ music surged through the church like electricity, like an earth tremor, through the floor, through the pews, through our bones. It pulled me back to prep school, to evensong after soccer practice, when Ian would arrive just as the opening hymn was beginning, all arrogant ease, his blond hair still wet from the shower, the collar of his blazer upturned against the autumn chill. For once, today, he was on time for a service.

Arthur, Miriam, and I rose with the congregation to sing "A Mighty Fortress Is Our God." I joined in, hoarse, with conflicting emotions. I was thinking of the Ian I knew, from childhood to prep school to Provincetown. I saw Ian in the Gloucester woods, forcing a crying Jonathan Robson to eat green blueberries; I saw him at St. Harold's, steering Suki Weatherbee around the floor at Spring Dance; I saw him naked in the dunes, then muttering, *"Vaya con Díos,"* his last words addressed to me in this world. Then the hymn was over and the mourners shut their hymnals with a series of soft, papery thuds that generated the only breeze inside the church.

"Ian Drummond was confirmed in this church," said the robust old Episcopal priest officiating. "So, today, Ian has come home." Then the priest spoke extensively about a person I barely recognized, describing "a seeker, a seeker of truth, a man impatient with the orthodox answers, someone who sought to forge his own spiritual path."

I kept wondering about other seekers, the police. Had they lifted my fingerprints from the crime scene, from the pieces of glass, parts of the vodka bottle I'd missed? Should I go to the police on my own, I wondered, as the priest quoted the Book of Wisdom. No, that was foolish, I decided, as Ian's oldest brother, Fulton, ascended to the pulpit and spoke about the family's famous tradition of athletics, citing Ian's soccer successes on the North Shore, at St. Harold's, and at Dartmouth. Fulton broke down reading "Envoi," the Robert Louis Stevenson poem, on the line, "Home is the sailor, home from sea…"

At that point, a female voice joined Fulton's sobbing. Tracing the sound to a pew just across the aisle, I saw that it came from Suki Weatherbee, elegant and almost matronly in a peach silk blouse, pearls, and frosted blond hair. A black man was handing her a handkerchief in an intimate gesture. Arthur, Miriam, and a good many mourners stole glances at Suki with sympathy that eventually curdled into annoyance as her crying intensified, then mercifully stopped.

The Drummond family plot was in a surprisingly old cemetery in Gloucester full of slate gravestones from the seventeenth century, carved with skulls and skeletons lugging oversized hourglasses full of time. "I didn't think they buried anyone in places like this," Miriam said. "I thought these cemeteries were all filled up…with people like Paul Revere."

Ian came from an old New England family, I reminded Miriam, and privately considered it somehow appropriate for a person with Ian's politics to share ground with neighbors familiar with snuff and the ducking stool.

"Good heavens!" Arthur whispered when confronted with the Drummond family plot, guarded by the cemetery's most modern monument, a Victorian sphinx of indeterminate sex with a male face and bare female breasts protruding from a necklace of scarabs and ankhs. Though I'd never seen this monument before, I remembered the explanation for its existence: one of Ian's ancestors, a prominent Egyptologist, had helped the Museum of Fine Arts acquire its Middle Kingdom sculptures before dying of typhus in Cairo at thirty-one. Two years Ian's senior.

The crowd assembled around the open grave. Just beyond the cemetery, past a boatyard and a bed and breakfast, was the big fish processing plant, so the odor of cod was carried on the wind, mixing with the fragrance of earth from the new grave. The grass in the cemetery was long and wet, and some of the mourners began worriedly checking their shoes.

"Let us pray," said the priest, and we bowed our heads. He read a prayer of interment and a lone piper—we couldn't see him—played "Amazing Grace." The Drummonds were certainly emphasizing their Scottish heritage. I felt that Ian, who'd spent a miserable college semester "studying abroad" in Edinburgh, would've found these touches over the top.

In fact, the whole service, at the church and the cemetery, had little to do with the breezy, cynical man I knew. There wasn't a word about Ian being gay, no mention, actually, of his having been murdered, for God's sake. Were both topics dismissed as equally unsavory?

Miriam must've been clairvoyant. "This isn't about Ian," she muttered to Arthur. "Listening to these people, he could've been a married man who died of a coronary!"

This impression was further strengthened at Cold Cove, the Drummonds' baronial mansion on a pinkish outcropping of granite above Gloucester Harbor. The place was teeming with Yankee Boston: Marblehead yachtsmen, State Street bankers, girls from the Junior League.

A small contingent of old St. Harold's boys was present, but no one from Ian's Provincetown parties. Kittredge Rawlings, our senior prefect, pinned me in a corner of the garden between a Roman sarcophagus and the Drummonds' fishpond, where the carp, bright as chain mail, shot through the peat-colored water. Then he delivered one of those long, boastful monologues people usually save for alumni magazines.

"…So, after Harvard, what do I do but apply to both law school and medical school, then end up choosing neither…After I left the bank, I married Catherine and we moved to Geneva… We call Kittredge the Second *our little Swiss surprise.* They say chocolate is an aphrodisiac, have you read that?"

At last Kittredge mentioned Ian, his face distorted with puzzlement and irritation. "But what was he doing in Provincetown?" Kittredge was watching the carp rather than me. "We've only been there once. We were in Chatham at Catherine's mother's place and it was raining cats and dogs, so we got desperate and went to Provincetown to hit the shops. But it was just T-shirts and ice cream and Third-World junk. Of all the places to be mugged, to be done in. Poor Ian!"

Was he staring at the carp because he was ashamed to meet my eyes? Had he heard Ian's story about my gesture in our chapel? Did he want me to out us both then and there? This screen of decorum was infuriating. Now, I had the chance to puncture that screen, but I balked. "Ian was on vacation," I said.

Kittredge acted as though the great tragedy wasn't Ian being butchered but being caught dead—literally—in a tawdry summer destination. Kittredge had no more idea Ian was gay than did Suki Weatherbee, now approaching us with her black companion. Before they reached us, Kittredge excused himself to visit the bathroom.

"Mark," said Suki, who smelled of face powder and some woodsy fragrance as we kissed the air next to each other's cheeks. "This is Gaston," she said. He was her husband and African, not African-American. "Darling," she asked him, "could you get us another crabmeat sandwich?" When we were alone, she confided that their marriage had taken even her by surprise. "Not to mention my family and half of Charleston!"

She'd met Gaston in Senegal. She was working there after earning her MBA at Wharton. Suki began giggling. "So Gaston never met Ian. Remember Ian back at St. Harold's? How full of the devil he was? But sweet. Remember Spring Dance when we all got so stoned that we broke into the chapel late at night and ate *all* the communion wafers?"

Not being part of Ian's clique, I didn't remember, but I nodded as if savoring the story.

"Are we almost done?" Gaston asked, seeming to grow peevish and less deferential once he returned with the sandwich. "We've paid our respects. Let's get an early shuttle home."

"Gaston *swore* he couldn't function away from Mother Africa, but now that we're living in New York, he just loves it," Suki told me.

Gaston was not about to let this sweeping statement pass without modifying it in some way. There was a certain vitality to Manhattan, he admitted, but it was "imbued with the innate violence of American society."

"Eventually we'll go back to Senegal," Suki explained. "The skyscrapers make Gaston claustrophobic."

Gaston bombarded the carp with pieces of crabmeat roll. The fish were colliding with each other in their quest for the bread, slashing back and forth through the water as Gaston kept tossing them crumbs. "Americans are fundamentally unsure who they are. Unsure whether they even belong on this continent," he said.

"We've had one sermon already today, darling," Suki reminded him.

"Look," Gaston said, tossing the last bit of bread at a giant carp that was silvery white like the dough rolls Chinese serve for dim sum. "No, not at the fish. Look at that man!"

Gaston indicated a tall, black male among the mourners across the garden. His sleek dark suit fit his body like skin, but his hair was worlds away from either Gloucester or St. Harold's—a mane of dreadlocks, tumbling over his shoulders, bleached peroxide-blond.

"He's utterly ridiculous," Gaston snapped. "He's not sure whether he's Haile Selassie or Madonna…It's this confusion you have, your mongrel culture."

The man with the dreadlocks, in his early thirties, I guessed, was nursing a drink and wandering absentmindedly through the crowd.

"This Provincetown," Gaston said. "I understand it's…a very promiscuous environment. Many nightclubs, lots of, how do you say it, *low* life?"

"Yes," Suki said, "it's Fag Heaven. Now why did I think Ian summered in Katama?"

Everything gay about Ian was being obliterated. I felt like I was being obliterated too. A scalding force was threatening to erupt, like the night I'd poured beer onto Ian at Quahog. I said, "You know Ian had changed a lot since Spring Dance at St. Harold's. He really wasn't the Katama sort at all. He enjoyed Provincetown more, for the same reason I do…"

Gaston was acting bored and Suki was faking a smile.

I said, "The dick tastes better than on the Vineyard."

Gaston began laughing, but Suki's face was transformed into the mask of some Tibetan demon. "You liar!" Suki spat. "Ian always loathed you. He felt sorry for you, that's why he tolerated your company…you twisted, pathetic little freak."

"Great to see you," I told her.

I navigated my way through the crowd until I located Arthur, browsing the long, linen-covered table laden with silver platters of food: mounds of shrimp, salmon mousse, fussy triangular sandwiches.

"I'm afraid I just disgraced myself," I laughed. "I outed Ian to Suki Weatherbee, the St. Harold's mattress. She spent every weekend in one of our dormitories. With either Ian or Kittredge Rawlings. She went to Braemere, you know, our sister school."

"Our incestuous sister," Arthur said.

Miriam joined us. She seemed a bit light-hearted for the day of a funeral, eating a jungle of a salad. "An adequate salad bar," she whispered. "Will wonders never cease?"

We found a quiet corner of the garden where we could relax, speculate about the murder, and hear Arthur's plan to dedicate his Swim for Scholars to Ian's memory. While we were talking, Ian's sister Sallie strolled by, arm-in-arm with a tall, dazzling stranger.

"Her fiancé," Arthur whispered. "Or so I heard over the cucumber sandwiches. He's a marine biologist. The ultimate small fish in a big pond."

Chapter Ten

Arthur and Miriam returned to Cape Cod while I called on my mother in Gloucester. She lived a short distance from the Drummonds in a strange stone gatehouse, a mossy tower Rapunzel might have inhabited, so darkened by overhanging spruce trees that it seemed as though sun never penetrated its dampness. My mother had bought the house years ago from the Snows, distant relatives of Ian's father.

At the time, the Snows were moving to England, something to do with North Sea oil, and the grounds of their estate, Bellevue, were going to be subdivided into a development called Bayberry Heights. Then Mr. Snow dropped dead of an embolism in the first-class cabin of their jet to London. His widow and children began a litigious dispute about Bellevue, and, eventually, the house was pulled down—some museum in New York bought the Grinling Gibbons carving from the library—and the family donated the land to the Nature Conservancy, for tax purposes. But before Mr. Snow booked his fatal flight, when it looked like Bayberry Heights would make the transition from the drawing board to the cement mixer and saw, my mother bought the gatehouse "for a song," as she would say. And now that it abutted conservation land instead of an outbreak of plywood townhouses, its value had skyrocketed.

My mother was in back of the house when I arrived, painting at her easel, a canvas of Halibut Point, Rockport. She had hair like mine, the tarnished copper of hoarded pennies, my sharp features and the mouth someone once called "licentious." She'd liked a drink since her nightclub days, while I was wary of liquor. She was wearing something she'd salvaged from a yard sale, a housecoat appliquéd with fat red strawberries. On her feet were ballet slippers, and, as always, she rattled when she moved; she wore a dozen silver bracelets and a necklace of pottery beads. Why she bothered with jewelry when she was content with such clothes, her "painting rags," was a mystery.

"Hello, darling," she said, although her back was toward me and my feet were muffled by the browning spruce boughs littering the lawn like rushes on the floor of a medieval palace. She had the hearing of a guard dog; I guess that came with her musical training.

"How can you paint such a sunny landscape in this gloom?" I asked. "A bomb shelter couldn't be any darker."

"I have the sun in my head." She dipped a brush in turpentine and wiped it clean. "It's in my memory. Besides, I was just touching up."

"You weren't at the funeral."

"That's right, I was painting."

We hadn't spoken since Ian was killed. My mother stepped back to appraise the canvas. She'd taken up painting late in life but was quite good. You could see the waves swelling; almost experience the odor of salt and kelp.

"What do you think? It's already been sold to a homesick Bostonian in Minneapolis." My mother's art sold well. Between painting and giving piano lessons, she made a comfortable living.

"It's the usual masterpiece. He'll love it."

Wiping her fingers on a rag she'd wet with turpentine, she said, "Mark, I'm not being callous, but mourning doesn't undo what's already been done. I believe in being nice to people when they're alive. Not that Ian always did. Good Lord, I still remember him torturing poor Jonathan Robson. Of course, coming from that family, from that privilege, that arrogance."

She recounted a story often told in Gloucester, of how Ian's mother, Janet, had run over a mailman while returning from a tennis match she'd lost in Brookline. "Going sixty in a thirty-mile zone. That poor mailman was in a body cast for months. That family was *always* reckless."

I smiled because "reckless" was an adjective sometimes flung in her direction.

"I suppose I'm saying that because it's comforting, I know. It makes it seem less random if Ian put himself in the line of fire. If he came from a family that used poor judgment." She was putting the brushes to soak in an old peanut butter jar. "I was hoping you'd drop by. I've marinated some chicken. I'm done painting today. I'm ready for a stiff vodka gimlet. How about you?"

I nodded. We sat in the back yard, beneath the blue-black spruces. My mother loved the sea, and turned out seascapes for corporate boardrooms, and tourists and transplanted New Englanders, yet she had one of the few pieces of property in this part of Gloucester lacking a view of the ocean. "Why don't you trim these stupid trees?" I asked her, after the vodka made me a bit bolder. "If you trimmed these trees, you could see the water."

"I'm an earth sign, darling," my mother said.

That excuse was ridiculous because my mother thought astrology belonged in its place on the comics pages of newspapers. "Are you avoiding seeing the sea because it makes you think of my father?"

"Of course not, darling." She was still in the ratty housecoat with a Jackson Pollack's worth of paint dribbled down the front. "Would you like another gimlet?"

"My head is swimming. I'd better not."

"Well, you drank that first one like it was lemonade. Just go easy. You're not driving back to the Cape tonight surely?"

"No." I surrendered my empty glass for a refill, to be sure I kept my word and slept over.

After dinner, after I'd consumed generous amounts of marinated chicken, potato salad, and corn on the cob, my mother mentioned one of the Snows. "I saw Geoffrey Snow at West Beach. Last week. He was visiting from Phoenix."

I hardly knew Geoffrey. The Snows kept to themselves and kept their distance even from the Drummonds.

"Geoffrey has done well. He designs golf courses, imagine, and the Snows were all so uncoordinated, such poor athletes. Not like Duncan and his gang." My mother served us home-made rhubarb pie: tart, slimy, and delicious. She said, "Geoffrey says Duncan Drummond isn't well at all, he's becoming confused."

I remembered Ian's father at the funeral, his bewildered expression during the service, his folding the program over and over. "He looked lost at the funeral," I said, "but who wouldn't?"

"Mark, I worry about you so. I mean, I'm sure you're careful, but do you have to go back to Provincetown this summer? Couldn't you commute like the rest of your troupe? I've seen that horrible Hollings Fair speaking on television, so smarmy and vitriolic. And those Christian Soldiers are everywhere, like gypsy moths."

I said, "I can't quit everything." We both knew what that meant. I'd bailed from the ad world to concentrate on acting. Now, thanks to the fight, I'd blown that as well, but didn't mention this.

Drinking the last of my gimlet, I remembered the vodka I'd shared with Ian and the bottle broken on the breakwater.

"Provincetown is dangerous this summer," my mother said. "It's not like when I sang there way back when."

Feeling drunk and self-confident, I surprised even myself: "Maybe Ian was killed by someone he knew. Not by a basher." I thought of myself: "Ian pissed off his friends more than anyone."

"But these incidents," my mother said, "the dog on your friend's doorstep, the whole climate of the town—"

"So you saw me on TV?"

"Geoffrey Snow saw you. He mentioned it. I called you, I left three messages on your machine."

It was true, I remembered the messages, but I'd postponed calling back because of dreading this conversation: the Dangers of Provincetown Conversation. Of course the issue was more than my summer on Cape Cod. Like many "bohemians," my mother wanted conventional, placid children. She provided enough originality for the family.

"It wasn't bashers, I'm sure of it. People would like to think so, because, as you say, it's comforting."

"Yet for some strange reason, wasn't Ian popular? In with the in crowd, that sort of thing?" My mother gathered up the remains of the chicken, which, stripped of their meat, with their bones and structure revealed, looked more like carcasses than ever. "I called you about the exhibit too," she said.

"Exhibit?"

"Centered around the first love of your life, remember? *The Fisher Boy?*"

Of course. I'd meant to write it on my calendar before I left Boston. I'd figured I couldn't help but remember it—such a big event right in Provincetown. Provincetown Municipal Museum was a planning a massive retrospective of his work, with paintings on loan from collections throughout the world.

That night, awake in my childhood bed, I kept thinking of Ian, newly in his grave, spending his first night in the Drummond plot, guarded by that atrocious, bare-breasted sphinx. Someone, somewhere, was very much alive—the person or persons who put Ian into that grave.

It must have been about midnight when I heard the sobbing, faint and stifled, like a child's ghost. I followed the sound through the darkened gatehouse, down the cool stone stairs and into the kitchen. My mother was sitting at the kitchen table, still in her painting clothes, with the Gloucester newspaper spread out in front of her, and the vodka bottle, just the bottle but no glass in her hand. Her face was streaked with tears.

I asked the stupid question we all ask when the answer is all too obvious: "Are you all right?" I thought she'd jump, be startled, or nonchalantly shoo me away, but she set the bottle on the table then began smoothing the newspaper, smoothing the obituary page with its bad news in fine print, its advertisements for funeral homes and tombstones.

"It's an awful thing, just awful." She smoothed the newspaper as though it were her sketchpad, ready to receive her impressions of an esteemed local view. She'd consumed a good deal of vodka; I remembered the level of the liquor in the bottle during our dinner.

Something priggish and self-protective made me speak. "If you were this upset, you should've come to the funeral."

She laughed, running her fingers over the newsprint. "Good Lord, darling, they paid me. They paid me to stay away, they were rather generous."

"What do you mean?" Everything suddenly seemed light, as if gravity had been abolished. As if everything in the room seemed made of helium.

"When I was at the Conservatory, I think I told you I sang in a little club called Lulu Wright's, in the South End."

I sat down in one of the hard oak chairs. I had the urge to confiscate the bottle of liquor, but I knew there were more, legions of them, there always had been, hidden creatively throughout the house, like Easter eggs.

"There were some pretty big names passing through there back then, and, hard as it is to believe, some people from the North Shore showed up. On occasion. We didn't do anything special to encourage them, I mean, there was no Stuffed Shirt Night." She laughed her drinker's laugh—raucous and sad and embarrassing.

"One man…from the North Shore brought along some colleagues from his bank. I'd always thought of him as the consummate Philistine. A man with a tin ear, an intimidating member of the local gentry. I thought he was slumming.

"And then, Good Lord, he came back on his own, for five nights in a row. I was floored. Well, we talked after the show, and, lo and behold, he was a jazz buff, an aficionado, really. He'd waited for five hours in the rain outside a studio in Chicago just to get Ella Fitzgerald's autograph. He knew songs by Charlie Parker that people at the Conservatory had never heard of."

She'd heard tales of his wild youth, expelled from Harvard, totaling enough Jaguars to empty a dealership. Her mother had warned her that the whole family was reckless. She'd quoted that famous line about Lord Byron—the family was "mad, bad, and dangerous to know."

"I was young," my mother said, "and a bit reckless myself… He was handsome, and almost courtly. It sounds so silly, but he made me believe in myself, in my singing. My mother was opposed to my pursuing the arts, she was practical to a T."

He wrote poems to her, in lower-case letters like ee cummings. They met secretly in places his family would never frequent, over plates of tripe in the North End, in the Monet room of the Museum of Fine Arts. His grandmother's portrait was hanging in that museum. Sargent had painted her, all firelight and pearls; he'd made that mercenary old woman who re-used mousetraps in her house on Beacon Hill seem as enticing as a mirage.

"He came back to my apartment one Friday in June. I was renting a studio so small you didn't have room to change your mind. I said how much I hated it, but he said he lived in a much smaller space. In his marriage. His marriage felt like the character in that Edgar Allan Poe story, "The Premature Burial." He was buried alive in his marriage. His wife was obsessed by her tennis game—imagine! His two young sons had each other. And his job at the bank was an utter bore; money was to be enjoyed, not managed."

As I listened to her speak, a fantasy died as my father became something palpable, someone real—a man I'd known all my life, a man whose presence had consistently diminished my confidence. I could see him, years ago, with the faintest of smiles on his face and a gin and tonic in his hand, asking what I'd been "up to" and then listening to my answer with a detached amusement, as though I were the punchline to some joke he'd already heard.

I remembered his party tricks—with origami, of course—and his collection of birds' eggs, some rare, mounted and labeled, under glass in his library in Gloucester. He sang "Summertime" once, at his daughter's coming-out party. He had a beautiful voice, rich and low. My mother had trespassed into that reckless family, following her seduced young heart.

"Do his children know?" My voice and calm were faltering. "His other children, I mean."

"No," my mother said. "His wife was several months pregnant at the time." She was holding Ian's obituary in her hands, which trembled faintly like dying birds. "He provided for you, Mark. He established a trust for your education, for prep school and college. He bought me this gatehouse from the Snows. He made me sign an agreement I wouldn't reveal his identity until after he was dead. But now, in his condition…"

He was as removed, of course, as if death had taken him. The dementia that was smothering his being was the neurological equivalent of Poe's nightmare.

"You knew," I said, meaning everything about my father. "You knew, yet you let me wonder for twenty-nine years. You let me comb through records at the Port Authority. Looking for some mythical destroyer."

She took the bottle of liquor into her lap. She held it like it was a baby. "Be kind," she said, in a strangled voice.

Why had she confided in me, for her benefit or mine? Her secret had become a burden she could not longer hold, a burden she needed to put down, if only for a moment, for a conversation. Or the death of another of Duncan Drummond's sons—and the vodka—had loosened her tongue. She was always horrified by violence. In the house, she couldn't crush a moth or step on a beetle without a ripple of regret, so I supposed the violence of Ian's death, the deliberateness, had unhinged her.

But thanks to her, I'd had sex with my brother, the brother I'd found dead and been denied the privilege of knowing, of really knowing. And my father—Duncan Drummond—was he anything more redeemable than a rake? Could I ever find out? His dementia was a fortress more formidable than any trust or the walls of an Eastern Point estate.

"Be kind," my mother repeated.

So I went south, to Cape Cod, back to the place where my brother Ian was so brutally slaughtered.

Chapter Eleven

The week of Ian's murder, the Christian Soldiers opened a small office opposite Spiritus Pizza. Dotted Swiss curtains brightened its plate glass windows. No grisly crucifixions were on display, or sinners blistering in hell, just two cardboard posters depicting scenes of the Holy Land, Manger Square and the Sea of Galilee. From the street, it might have been a travel agency. You expected El Al airfares to be posted daily.

Their people were in the street too, not Parris Island toughs in combat fatigues, but handsome men, young like Mormon elders, in brown ties and starched white shirts. They carried clipboards but no pens or petitions, and approached groups of straight tourists, saying, "Have you heard the good news?" At first, the tourists paused, expecting discount coupons for lobster or two margaritas for the price of one. The tourists kept smiling but edged away once the Biblical content of the good news became evident. "God bless you," the young men said, making it sound like a rebuke.

And there was a second group in town that blistering summer that could not have been more different from the Christian Solders in manner or hygiene. Commercial Street was also clotted with girls and boys, teenagers with vacant or piercing stares, with bare feet and a kind of nineteenth-century sense of fashion, a liking for gingham skirts and overalls that might have been found at grange meetings a hundred years ago. In fact, the rings on their toes and puncturing the cartilage of their ears were the only indications the new millennium was imminent. Some of the runaways banded together to play instruments made of strange things: hollowed-out African gourds and logs. They congregated under the chestnut tree outside the Provincetown Public Library, on the town hall steps, and on MacMillan Wharf when the ferry from Boston was docking. "We're Scandinavians," they said, as if this explained their presence. The *Vasa,* the Swedish tall ship, was long gone from Provincetown Harbor, probably sailing into Chesapeake Bay, nearing her final American port of call, Annapolis.

Occasionally, the street kids sold things, including flowers. I bought a glorious bouquet of lilies for Roberto, tall and spindly and pink as flamingoes, like something from the hot soil of the Congo. These were a peace offering. And I bought a Hallmark card, just this side of clever, with a cartoon mouse and a message about forgiveness. "Can you come for dinner at my apartment at 4:30?" I asked in my accompanying note.

Arthur had claimed Roberto was now a houseboy at the White Gull. Climbing the guest house steps, I expected to confront an enraged Roger Morton, berating me for fighting Ian that night at Quahog. But neither Roger nor Roberto was on the premises. Gary, the houseboy manning the desk, said that Roger was in Boston on some sort of business and Roberto was on break, swimming at Herring Cove. Gary promised to give Roberto my flowers and card.

Roberto appeared at my apartment at four-thirty sharp. Wearing lime-green Speedo trunks and a sprinkling of sand like salt on his pretzel-brown legs, he'd come straight from Herring Cove via the front desk of the White Gull. I had never seen him shirtless and could have given him the compliment he made about my view of Provincetown Harbor: "Very nice."

"Thanks for the fabulous lilies," he said.

"If they wilt, put a penny in the water. The copper is supposed to revive them."

"My room at the White Gull is sweltering," said Roberto. "It's in the attic. Got an extra roll of pennies to revive *me?*"

"No," I said, but I had some new Chablis.

"Does everybody hate me?" I asked Roberto as we lazed on my back deck. He wore a gold star of David on a chain as fine as powder. By "everybody," of course, I meant the guys from the troupe, for setting my most memorable scene in the audience.

"The troupe voted to take a little breather. To think about reconvening in the fall." Roberto was diplomatic, considering every word like a contestant vying for the jackpot on a quiz show. He said Andy had a new job in human resources at John Hancock; Sammy had quit the troupe to take a course in HTML. "But the general consensus was that Ian deserved his free beer. And Roger Morton agrees…"

He was my brother, I almost said, I just learned it from my mother. Half of my life isn't missing anymore, I know who my father is, but it's upended my world. Since I couldn't share this—or the horror on the breakwater—I described Ian's funeral and the sphinx at his grave and my fight with Suki Weatherbee about Provincetown.

"Of all the people in the community to become a martyr," Roberto said. "Ian Drummond!"

A vigil had been held last night, while I was in Gloucester, Roberto explained. More than three-hundred people had marched from the Unitarian/Universalist meetinghouse up Commercial Street to the breakwater, many carrying candles or signs like "Ian Drummond: Killed By Hate" and "Disarm the Christian Soldiers."

"Do you think it was a random hate crime?" I asked Roberto.

"Isn't it obvious?" he asked. "The thing at Arthur's, then Ian being murdered. Both after these lunatics show up? You do the math."

Then, through the buzz from the Chablis, I heard someone calling at the foot of my back stairs, the wooden stairs descending from my deck to the ground.

"Hello? Mark Winslow? Sergeant David Almeida, Province-town police."

Roberto actually stood, like a St. Harold's boy greeting the headmaster's wife.

"I'm Mark Winslow." I remained seated while extending my hand, which Almeida clasped to steady me and assess me with eyes that were dark yet cold.

"I have a few questions I'd like to ask you about Ian Drummond," he said.

Then I noticed he wasn't alone. A second man squeezed past him up the stairs so that the two of them were overpopulating my deck, already crammed with K-mart summer furniture, with aluminum chairs and a table.

"This is Detective DeRenzi," Almeida said of his colleague who could be typecast as a pathologist: pinched and ascetic, I could picture him around tweezers and refrigerated samples of dead flesh.

"Do you mind if we tape you?" Almeida asked.

What could I say but, "Oh, no, go right ahead."

Almeida spoke to the tape recorder, reciting the date, time, and place of our conversation, and noting the names of those present, including Roberto. He knew Roberto's name without asking, and that bothered me. As he and DeRenzi each took a chair, he said, "What was your relationship with Ian Drummond?"

"We were friends…" I felt foolish not offering them wine, with the bottle right there, but they were obviously on duty, and offering it even as a courtesy might seem like bribery. "…And Ian and I were at school together." I shouldn't say more, I should get an attorney, I thought. But mentioning that might seem to amplify my guilt, my guilt at never reporting finding Ian's body.

"St. Harold's?"

"Yes." I could see the tape gleaming through the pane of darkish plastic as it turned on its slow, steady spool, like ropes turning on the wheels of a medieval rack.

"St. Harold's was located in Stark, Massachusetts?"

"Yes," I said. They had seen Ian's body, these policemen. It wasn't theory for them, they didn't have to imagine it, the stones soaked with blood, the opened throat. Yet the accounts in the media didn't mention his throat wounds, only the wounds to Ian's chest. Remembering the horror on the breakwater, I remembered the broken vodka bottle and shivered.

"When did you last see Ian Drummond, Mr. Winslow?"

My very name, Winslow, now felt like a lie. "I saw him June fifteenth, at Herring Cove." That was the truth, but of course blood was throbbing through my temples, burning my ears scarlet.

"You saw Ian Drummond June fifteenth at the beach at Herring Cove?"

"Correct," I said. It was the wrong word to use; it sounded hostile at worst, pompous at best.

Then I remembered it, my beach towel on the breakwater by Ian; the wind had blown it along the stones, flipped it into a pool of Ian's blood. And a corner of the towel, just a tiny corner, had stained. I'd thought it was blood, but it could've been tar, tar from the beach. I'd meant to throw it out, but it was "evidence," so I didn't. That towel was inside my apartment. Would they search it?

"What time did you see Ian at the beach?"

All of them were staring—Almeida, DeRenzi, and Roberto. The gleaming tape kept winding behind the darkish pane of plastic. It was all being recorded, not just my words but my tone, my hesitations. The hesitations would seem incriminating, I thought.

I would have to lie now, lie again. I couldn't link myself to Ian by admitting we'd talked late that day. That might make me the last person to see Ian alive. But if I did tell the truth—that we'd talked later, shared vodka, had sex—at least that would demonstrate we weren't enemies at the end, that the rancor from the Quahog fight had faded.

"What time did you see Ian at the beach?"

"Mid-afternoon. He was with some friends. I knew one, Barton Daggett." Again, I massaged the facts: "I'd gone to the beach alone." Surely mentioning Edward would be asking for trouble—and he had walked away from me, walking down the beach; he'd walked as though we were separate, I'd have witnesses to that.

"Did you speak with Mr. Drummond?" Almeida was doing all the talking. Was this police detective new—or the ambushing type, like Ian?

"I saw Ian from a distance. He was walking near the water. I was further away, up toward the dunes."

"So you didn't exchange words with Ian Drummond June fifteenth?"

"No." A complete lie.

"Do you have any idea who killed Ian Drummond?"

At last I could be honest again. "I have no idea." And the relief that came from saying something honest almost made me break down, then and there. Roberto was regarding me with protective concern, for which I felt an immense gratitude.

"You're an actor, aren't you, Mr. Winslow?"

Was he implying my answers were a performance? "I'm in an acting troupe, an improv troupe."

"He's very good," Roberto said. He was trying to be helpful, giving a compliment. "I'm in the troupe too. We did a show at Quahog."

"Yes," said Sergeant Almeida, "I know."

The "I know" made me realize Roberto's compliment was disastrous.

"Your performance at Quahog, the night of June thirteenth, I wanted to bring that up. Ian Drummond attended that performance, did he not?"

The "did he not" was hostile. I wanted to take a sip of my Chablis because my mouth was dry, just like onstage during that awful gig, but I thought needing liquor would seem incriminating.

"Yes. Ian was there."

"Was it a successful night?" Sergeant Almeida asked.

"Ian was a bit tipsy. He was drunk, actually. He was harassing us, shouting out comments—"

"Isn't that the whole point of improv, the audience participating?"

"There's a distinction between participation and disruption," Roberto said.

"We're speaking with Mr. Winslow," DeRenzi stated.

Would they read my Miranda rights now? Would they brandish their warrant then search my apartment? Would they find my towel with Ian's blood, stuffed under the bureau in my bedroom? They were twenty feet away from evidence placing me squarely at the scene of the crime.

"Ian arrived with some friends, they were pretty bombed."

"Go on," Almeida told me.

"Ian was disrupting the show. He brought up an old incident from prep school." As I spoke, Almeida's face was beginning to look familiar. I had seen it reproduced in both *Advocates,* the Provincetown newspaper and the national gay magazine. Of course, he was a Provincetown native, the police officer who'd come out last October. His left earlobe was pierced; I could see the faint puncture, although an earring was absent. "Ian mocked me about an incident at prep school, about touching his shoulder. He wasn't out then, not even to himself." It sounded petty saying it, in light of Ian's murder. But I continued: "He made fun of me."

"At Quahog or St. Harold's?"

"At both…We became friends after college. We'd lost touch during college. He went to Dartmouth, I was at UMass Amherst. We'd grown up together, in Gloucester."

I reached for the wine and popped it open, so that the cork shot up and out of my fingers, dropping down the stairs and hitting each step like the bouncing ball hits each word of a song you're supposed to sing. I filled my glass with Chablis and drank deeply.

"Ian was a bit of a bully," I said. "That was always an element of his personality. You had to accept that to get along with him. That the bully part might activate at any moment. He got way out of control at Quahog." I let my eyes meet Almeida's. "I emptied a pitcher of beer over his head."

"Did you kill Ian Drummond, Mr. Winslow?" Almeida asked, casually, with no more emotion than he'd displayed on any previous question.

"No," I stated. "I didn't."

Almeida said, "Just a few more questions about another incident. Did you know an Edward Babineaux?"

Was he questioning my story about the beach, about going there alone, and not with Edward? "I knew him socially. He… was staying with Arthur Hilliard for a while."

"Mr. Hilliard is accusing him of stealing some valuable antique candlesticks."

I nodded.

"Do you know where Edward Babineaux might be staying now? He disappeared the morning after Ian Drummond's murder."

With relief, I was able to answer truthfully, "I have no idea."

"Did this Edward Babineaux know Ian Drummond?" asked DeRenzi.

Here I could cooperate, more or less. I described seeing Edward and Ian at the two parties, Arthur's inauguration of the Provincetown season and Ian's St. Harold's "memoriam." I didn't mention meeting Edward in Ian's bedroom—or our brunch after church at the Café Blasé, where he'd spilled his assault-in-the-woods tale. Edward was probably not a suspect in Ian's death because he'd been with Arthur when Ian was killed.

"Thank you, Mr. Winslow," said Sergeant Almeida. "By the way, you're an excellent actor. I've had the pleasure of seeing you with your troupe."

To be polite, I asked, "When?"

"On the night of June thirteenth, this year, at Quahog."

Chapter Twelve

After that, my apartment seemed contaminated by my encounter with Sergeant Almeida and his detective, and by that towel hidden beneath my bureau.

Or was it love that made me move? I guess it was love. A love that began when I saw Roberto, fresh from the sea, like the youth in *The Fisher Boy.* Love and a gentle desperation. That was there too—a hollowness expanding inside of me when I thought of my mother's deceptions and of Ian's bleeding wounds on the breakwater. Wounds that had yet to be avenged.

So I moved into his attic at the White Gull, and we decided to stay in Provincetown for the summer, to try our luck together doing improv or standup in the clubs.

In May, Roberto had left work as a courier, left pedaling his bicycle through Boston traffic, a sort of Mercury in Spandex, always carrying a package that was the corporate equivalent of the president's nuclear black box. He'd left in good weather, when the ice ruts, road salt, and sleet were long gone, so, he reasoned, he'd better have a good excuse for quitting Provincetown without giving show business his best shot.

My new quarters were as hot as my old apartment, hot as Timbuktu, in the attic of the White Gull, under splintery eaves studded with vacant wasps' nests. Roberto shared this space with another houseboy, Tim, who was at Cape Cod Hospital with an especially bad case of poison ivy, the result of safe sex in dangerous foliage. While he recuperated, I was welcome to use Tim's bed, a futon thin as a paperback book.

Roberto's day began each morning at five, when he was charged with baking dozens of cranberry muffins for the guests' breakfast at nine. There was always wash to do, sheets, blankets, pillowcases, and towels, which Roberto handled using translucent disposable gloves. The White Gull parking lot was even smaller than its lawn, so all day Roberto moved cars like Rubik's cube pieces as guests came and went. Through all this, he never tired. He was thrilled to be "in the middle of so much material."

He studied the guests and staff: their walks, how they carried their luggage, their method of applying tanning butter or sunscreen. He developed a theory of personality based on the strength of sunscreen guests applied and whether they were "random smearers," "thorough strokers," or "total body-immersion people." He'd say, "That couple, Tom and Pete? They're going to break up by Labor Day because Tom is a random smearer who uses SP15, but Pete is a total body-immersion person who is substance-abusing SP29, if not 35."

In his precious spare moments, Roberto rented videos of comedy programs to watch in the guest house lounge. He loved the television of our parents' youth: Sid Caesar and Jackie Gleason and Lucy and Ethel committing industrial sabotage, screwing up the candy factory. Roberto didn't just watch these tapes, he was an active participant in every show, talking to the actors, miming their gestures, praising or upbraiding their timing. He could pick out familiar voices from laugh tracks on *I Love Lucy*. Sometimes, transfixed by mimicking Bill Dana or Topo Gigio from old Ed Sullivan tapes, he'd forget his work and let the muffins burn or the sheets in the dryer all but scorch, but, most of the time during our early days at the guest house, he was focused, energetic, and up. No one was better company.

Nights, we seldom went out. Roberto was exhausted and I was afraid. In the dark, in the heat, we'd lie on our mattresses like brothers in their bedroom. The windows in the attic were small, with wooden louvers that censored the wind, so that the heat from the roof persisted late into the morning. On nights we couldn't sleep, we traded lives, told our stories. You can tell almost anything in the dark.

Roberto spoke of growing up in Puerto Rico, of the stucco house in old San Juan the color of pistachio ice cream, of his street with iron cobblestones that gleamed like minerals in black light, gleamed sapphire like the carapace of some jungle insect, a beetle from the rain forest, El Yunge. He spoke of his first sex, on the beach in Ocean Park, outside a gay guest house, late one Saturday in the shelter of some sea grape bushes. His partner was a soldier from a base on the island. Roberto wasn't good at differentiating uniforms, but he remembered the soldier's broad chest and shiny shoes. He was fifteen at the time, and the sex felt wondrous, as though the soldier had restored some part of himself he wasn't aware was missing.

Two months later, Roberto met a boy his own age, at El Morro, the old Spanish fortress. They met in the field, watching boys playing Frisbee. They'd flirted, following one another along the eroding, yellowish walls, ending up in one of the circular pillboxes vagrants occasionally used as toilets. The pillbox reeked, so all they did was quickly grope, rumple each other's clothing, and kiss. The boy's kiss, Roberto remembered, tasted of cinnamon, from gum he'd been chewing.

Many Jews on the island had emigrated from Cuba, but Roberto's parents had both come as small children from South Africa. Growing up gay and Jewish in Puerto Rico was being "the Other within the Other." It was estranging being Jewish on that Catholic island, with its convents, their huge doors and locks requiring keys a foot long; its cathedrals with altars busy with golden ornaments and saints with stiff skirts Roberto longed to touch. The bones of Ponce de Leon, the crosses you saw everywhere—on churches, on rosaries dangling from rearview mirrors in cabs, gleaming with whitewash in cemeteries—all these fed his sense of "otherness" so that it grew tangled and strong, like lianas around his soul.

Daily, Roberto struggled with this, but his parents were not especially religious. His mother kept Shabbat once in a blue moon and sporadically attended the conservative temple in San Juan, one of only two on the island. But his father, then associated with the big observatory at Arecibo, thought of the universe as being a great cold space filled with asteroids and stars made from luminous gasses, all governed by the beauty, by the perfection, of the laws of physics. The prophets of ancient Israel were myth, he believed, no more real than the lost gods of the Taino, the indigenous tribes of Puerto Rico. "There is no valid archaeological evidence *whatsoever* for the existence of Moses," Dr. Schreiber would state proudly.

It was a kind of spiritual defiance that made Roberto wear a *kipah* in college—for two short weeks, until it blew from his head into a puddle, "a divine sign." He'd eaten kosher for a full month before defiling himself with a plate of Cajun crawfish. There were many kinds of Jews in college, orthodox, conservative, reformed, so that this embarrassment of riches overwhelmed him, exacerbated his otherness of being gay. "I think getting religion is like getting inoculations. It's best to get it early so it can take," Roberto believed.

"But at least you have a name," I said.

"What do you mean?" he asked in the dark.

So I told him my tale, my mother's, really—about my unknown father, about growing up in Gloucester, first in our apartment above the garage at my grandmother's, then in the gatehouse, with the spruce trees brushing against our windows, and, winters toasting marshmallows with my mother in our fieldstone fireplace, with the owl andirons.

"In Europe, Jews' surnames were often randomly assigned. During the Middle Ages, way back," Roberto said. "Names weren't important, being alive was." He gestured at the wasps' nests, the gray of the withered cardboard of egg cartons. "I'll bet those wasps thought they'd live forever. So did Ian, probably."

I felt weak at that moment, weak with fear and loneliness. Provincetown heightens the potency of loneliness, like liquor heightens the potency of barbiturates. Naked, I felt all skin. No bones, no arteries, just skin, with a hollowness inside.

"Don't you sometimes feel like 'the other' here?" I asked. "In Provincetown? If you're single, I mean?"

I thought about something I'd read in a magazine, about our human need for loving skin contact. I'd read babies could die, "failure-to-thrive babies." You could feed them and change them and keep them quiet and warm, but without skin-to-skin contact with someone who loved them, they'd shut down, stop growing, and die. "People need skin contact," I said, as we lay in the dark, naked, the heat pressing down upon us.

I almost told him, then, that night. I almost told him about Ian, how I'd yearned for his body, for the companionship of his skin, so I'd had sex with him in the dunes the day he'd died. I was the last person to see him alive, I almost said—except that wasn't true: I wasn't the person who'd killed him.

Roberto asked was my futon comfortable and I admitted it was thin. "That's surprising? For a mattress from a country where they make rice paper walls?"

We both laughed.

He could laugh at anything. I envied that, I said.

"I'd like to write a new show," Roberto said, "a two-man standup show." Then he asked, "Are you interested?" He said it again, but it wasn't about the show, or a gig, or the summer. "Are you interested?" he repeated, in a whisper.

"Sure." Meaning everything he was suggesting. I turned on my side so that I could see him—brown and muscular in the moonlight.

"Come here," Roberto said. "I don't want to shout." He squirmed to one side of the generous mattress, which was set on the floor on its box springs. "There's room."

I lay beside him, our shoulders almost flush. I could feel the heat from his body. He was on his back; I was on mine.

He edged closer, so that the hairs of our legs touched the other's flesh. "I think we just need a new strategy, we just need to adapt our Provincetown material and write a bit more and we'll be fine."

The heat pressed down onto our flesh.

Roberto continued speaking, about his plans for the new show, about writing material appealing to women because more lesbians were vacationing in Provincetown, about making our comedy "less Bostonian" for people from outside New England.

He turned his head, his eyes large and deep with what I hoped was yearning. "Are you game?"

I nodded.

He rose to hug me closer, then, with delicate gestures, tickled the nape of my neck with his fingers. "You're so tense," he said, holding both my hands.

He kissed my face, from my forehead to my mouth—the lids of my shut eyes, my cheekbones, the tip of my nose. "Don't be afraid," he kept saying, "don't be afraid."

Later, we lay together in the dark, on the chaotic sheets, until we fell asleep, skin-to-skin, healed, one.

Chapter Thirteen

The last day of June, I took everything that was mine from that shabby apartment above the leather shop: I brought my books, my radio, my clothes, even my favorite beach stones to our stifling garret at the White Gull. Of course this move was temporary, I knew. Tim, the absent houseboy, had been discharged from Cape Cod Hospital, his poison ivy abating but he'd flown to Virginia for a couple of weeks. So, while retaining the lease on the apartment, I started working as a houseboy at the White Gull, in lieu of rent. Roberto siphoned off a few chores to me, like some of the laundry and waking up nights to water the small lawn, to violate the ban just imposed due to our now-serious drought.

Roberto was writing in his precious spare time, even while watching his favorite Ernie Kovacs videos. He wrote in his khaki shorts and those fashionable sandals with the Velcro straps and hieroglyphics. "The show is coming along fabulously," he'd say, scribbling onto one of his wire-coil notebooks. Sometimes he'd stay awake entire nights, writing and reading dialogue softly to himself, testing the voices of characters he was creating.

We made love mornings, once the muffins were cooling and before we shaved and showered. Roberto enjoyed shaving me, scorning my electric razor, saying, "Those are for girls," and applying clouds of slightly burning lather to my face, then obliterating my whiskers with his dangerous straight razor.

He filled our attic with all sorts of kitsch: a lava lamp and rubber chickens, glow-in-the-dark yo-yos and those false teeth you wind up to walk, a backscratcher shaped like Frankenstein's hand with long, emerald-green fingernails. "I hate good taste!" he'd sometimes say. "It's the first sign of encroaching middle age."

He'd get irritated by the menus in Provincetown, by the pretensions about garlic mashed potatoes and cod baked in blue corn tortilla chips: "I want some real American food! American food for Americans. I want food cooked by somebody who can't spell 'aioli.'"

We found a hamburger stand dispensing plastic mermaids in conjunction with an animated film. "This has Chloe's name written all over it!" he said, waving the toy. We were joining Chloe and Miriam to help Arthur weed his garden, which had gotten out of hand while he'd been secluded with his treasure.

"This is for you!" Roberto said to the thrilled little girl.

She clutched the mermaid, moving its fragile arms, then began circling us and giggling while tickling our bare legs.

"Most men don't give her a second look," said Miriam.

It wasn't a reprimand, but it felt like one. Especially to me. A tingle of shame rode lightly along my nerves as I realized that she was right, that Chloe had been left fatherless—the price, I'd always assumed, of Miriam's using a sperm bank. As her way of thanking Roberto, Chloe clasped his legs, rubbing her face against them, like a kitten marking its territory. "Thank you, that tickles," Roberto laughed, his experience gained from having sisters serving him well.

Then we dispersed throughout Arthur's garden to help him weed. He'd neglected this duty since that awful party, so all sorts of unwelcome growth was literally having a field day. It was hot, sparrows were quarrelling in the bird feeders, scattering the seed, and the sky was blue and hard and dazzling, the kind that should shine on the great sandstone buttes of Arizona. Working close to the earth, I thought of Ian buried beneath it. "I can't stop thinking of Ian," I told them.

They all nodded or sighed. Arthur mentioned speaking with friends from the gay business guild. The Christian Soldiers were picketing some guest houses, harassing others with phone calls, tying up the lines, making bogus reservations. Luckily, we'd had none of this at the White Gull. "It's one of them," Arthur said, bitterly. "One of them butchered poor Ian." There was no escaping the fear; it flourished beneath the surface of life, like crabgrass germinating throughout a lawn.

"But we have to live our lives," Miriam said. "Are you getting out at all, Arthur? You're not becoming housebound, I hope."

He was tearing out a vine as long and tough as an extension cord. "These things take time," he said. "By the way, I gave Sergeant Almeida a complete description of Edward. Bad Man Babineaux, as I call him. He left drugs in my bathroom, you know. A bag of white powder I'm sure was cocaine."

"Really?" I said. This surprised me. An asthma sufferer using a drug you'd inhale?

Edward had stashed it in the bathroom, along with a paperback about gay love signs. And I'd imagined him appearing with just the clothes on his back.

"Well, since he's gone, I guess it's okay to mention this…" So I told them Edward's hitchhiking saga, about the man who'd picked him up at the Orleans traffic circle then taken him deep into the Province Lands. "…He dragged him into the woods, at knifepoint," I was saying. Unfortunately, all four of them were listening, including Chloe, who'd stopped dipping her mermaid into Arthur's fishpond and was eagerly awaiting the conclusion of my story, as though it were a cartoon.

"Darling," said Miriam, "look at the nice bug." She indicated a damp spot in the soil where a wood louse was trundling through the debris. "Look at the bug, Chloe!" Miriam suggested, but the little girl's attention was focused solely on me. "Then what happened?" she asked.

"Yes, then what happened?" Arthur demanded.

Chloe began dancing her doll in circles around the wood louse.

"Edward was…" I spelled it: "R-A-P-E-D."

Sitting the mermaid squarely atop the bug, Chloe asked her mother, "What does that mean, what he said?"

"It means Edward became a little sick," Miriam answered.

"Did he get better?" Chloe's voice was soft with worry.

"Better enough to run far away," Arthur said.

Chloe removed the mermaid, distressed because the wood louse was now still. "I wish you'd told me this earlier!" Arthur snapped at me. "That thug in the van could've traced Edward to this house. He could've harmed me, he could be responsible for that dead dog!"

I'd never thought of that—that the dead dog could have been meant for Edward. "You were in seclusion," I said. "Edward was screening all your calls. I wasn't even sure the story was true. He almost seemed proud when he told it."

"That must explain his abhorrence at being touched. Perhaps it wasn't me *per se* he was rejecting," Arthur sighed. What he said next put my heart on hold: "Almeida said Ian's killer left something behind. He wouldn't say what it was." Then Arthur began talking eagerly. His meds must have kicked in. The police had searched the area around the breakwater. They'd found nothing that could qualify as the murder weapon, just a fishing knife so corroded it had obviously been submerged for years.

"Almeida visited me too," I said.

"I was there," Roberto said. "At Mark's. When Almeida came."

"He was very tight-lipped, as far as theories, as far as suspects." Or was he just tight-lipped around me?

Chloe was manipulating the mermaid, inching the doll up the trunk of the silver maple, as though imitating the movements woodpeckers use shopping for food.

"I don't believe it was a random hate crime. Most people are killed by someone they know. And Ian made enemies easily, even among his 'friends.' Besides, the breakwater is a bizarre place to be mugged."

"Actually, it's ideal," Roberto countered. "There's nowhere to run, nowhere you can run. It's a ready-made obstacle course. An obstacle course at sea, at high tide."

"You haven't mentioned those late-night calls. Those hang-up calls," Miriam said to Arthur.

"They've stopped," Arthur said. "They stopped while Edward was still here. He told them off. So he wasn't exactly good for nothing, he was good for something—a little something."

Just then, Chloe began crying. She'd snapped an arm from her mermaid doll.

Chapter Fourteen

She didn't even say who she was, but I knew her voice. It was unmistakable—husky and aloof, with a kind of perpetual patrician laryngitis—Sallie Drummond. She was telephoning from Ian's Provincetown house and had left three messages on my apartment's answering machine. She was sorting through some of Ian's things and wondered whether I wanted "some St. Harold's memorabilia."

Fulton and George, her older brothers, were Exeter alumni, not interested in articles from the second-string prep school Ian had enrolled in only after being booted out of Exeter. Ian was "the keeper of the St. Harold's flame," as Sallie put it, and, since I was "his oldest friend from St. Harold's," I got first crack at this stuff. I was relieved she said nothing about the fracas at Quahog or my fight with Suki Weatherbee at the funeral, so when I got her messages, I called and told her I'd be right over.

I couldn't confront them at their house in Gloucester. That fortress, that Romanesque pile, always put the fear into me, not the fear of God, but the fear of property. But now I had to ask Sallie whether my mother's story was true. Was she really my half-sister? Had my half-brother seduced me, knowing our blood tie?

It was my imagination, I'm sure, but it seemed, climbing the sandy hill, that Ian's house had shifted still further toward the precipice, as if made suicidal by its owner's death. And it seemed that the cliff of sand was somehow animate, disintegrating before my eyes, trickling down like the sand in an hourglass, like the sand in the Biblical aphorism about building your house upon a rock.

"When you say 'right over,' you're not kidding." Sallie came to the door wearing a bikini bottom and a diamond tennis bracelet— and nothing else. This shocked me into silence—Sallie and being in this hideous spaceship of a house, given the circumstances.

She was a muscular girl with the take-charge manner of a sister raised in a household of brothers. Many women in Provincetown could have taken her for a lesbian, which she was not. She'd briefly dated Jonathan Robson, of all people, before he'd moved to Denver to marry a cattle heiress. Then she'd been serious with one of the Saltonstalls, but they'd broken up over differences in politics. Sallie was even more conservative than Ian, so her nudity was even more startling.

"I've been living in Seattle, so sun, *any sun*, is most welcome," she was saying, leading me through the nubbly beige carpeting of the living room and onto the redwood deck, now littered with boxes containing the unwanted innards of my prep school. "Oh, don't look so shocked, Mark. It's not like I need to worry around *you*. I mean Ian told me the whole bit."

"The whole bit?" I'd assumed Ian had been killed before meeting anyone but his assailant, killed on the way back across the breakwater from the beach, so that his story of our sex, of our *incest* in the dunes, had died with him. No, "the whole bit" meant she knew my sexuality, so her being naked was somehow acceptable since I was no more male than the pine trees below the deck, than the ivy dying in terra cotta pots by the gas grill. She wouldn't suspect our blood ties. There was nothing Drummond in my face or physique: my mother's Winslow genes had vanquished theirs.

Sallie ripped open a carton marked "St. Harold's #6" in Ian's always legible script. Inside were tablets engraved with winning soccer scores and an ancient football swollen like some delicate kind of fungus. "When that silly school closed, Ian drove out there to cart off all this junk." Without a trace of irony, she blew the dust from a lacrosse trophy, a silver jug, all dents and tarnish. "I wondered if you'd like it."

Was this the way they'd bought off my mother? With a check that did minimum damage to their assets and a breezy kiss-off?

Letting the trophy bang to the deck, Sallie yanked open a carton of yearbooks with embossed covers. "What's next?"

I was wondering that myself. "Are you selling this house?"

"Why? Interested?"

A sarcastic comment. She knew I couldn't afford it.

Being male I felt an obligation to stare. Sallie's breasts were full, with wide areolas. She'd probably been working all morning, hauling cartons, taking inventory, because her dark apricot skin was glittering with droplets of sweat. She must have spent hours with sun lamps to nurture a tan this serious in Washington.

She flicked her tawny mane of hair. "If you're interested in this house, I'd like to sell you a bridge in Brooklyn."

Suddenly I agreed with Suki Weatherbee's African husband. "New York gives me claustrophobia."

She put the yearbooks back into their carton. "Well, speaking of geography, Provincetown isn't exactly my idea of a good time, Mark." She shrugged and the sun caught on the diamonds of her tennis bracelet. She had broad hips for such a delicate bikini.

"Ian enjoyed himself here," I said.

"Not in the end." Sallie took a swig of some poison-green sports drink, the kind spiked with vitamins and caffeine.

"Have a look," she said, all bonhomie, changing her tone like an actor in improv taking a strong suggestion from his audience. She shoved the cartons toward me with a brisk movement of her large-size foot. The variety of things in them was amazing: an iron Victorian microscope, a bolt of damask, hymnals drier than the Dead Sea Scrolls, a sign with an arrow to a fallout shelter, a terrarium containing a turtle shell and a china shipwreck, needlepoint pillows of the Lamb of God done by a headmaster's wife…Ian must've needed an eighteen-wheeler to cart all this stuff away.

Of course Ian specialized in real estate law. He'd helped St. Harold's liquidate some of its assets.

"They may pull this house down," Sallie said. "It's structurally unsound, so we're told." Below were pines in the cliffs of trickling sand.

Frowning at a black onyx pen set, Sallie asked, "Who do you think did it?" She was abrupt, almost accusatory.

"That's what we're all asking."

"But you were here, you must have theories." Sallie tucked the onyx pen set into a throw rug of Middle Eastern cotton.

"I have no idea who did it." It wasn't me, I'm your brother, I could have said. Except that I didn't feel that; I tried to, but even now I felt no bond whatsoever with this woman.

"Ian saw your show." Sallie was finishing her bottle of the energy beverage. I braced myself for a crack about our fight. She wiped her mouth with the back of her hand. "He said you were very good. You were always very theatrical."

She made "theatrical" sound like it carried a lot of baggage—like the view of the breakwater we were so busy ignoring.

One carton contained newer books, some Buddhist meditations and a biography of Thomas Merton. These were clean and had been carefully read, scored in places, whole pages, with yellow highlighter. "I never knew Ian was so…metaphysical," I said. "I knew he read a lot of military history, I knew he was big on battles."

"Big on battles" certainly described Ian. And he'd been reading a book on war, on occupied Greece, that day in the dunes before he'd died.

"Ian was conducting a study on early Christianity," Sallie said.

He'd had the Boswell book in the bathroom, I remembered.

In an old Lowenbrau carton, I found an alabaster statue of St. Harold, missing his staff and part of his beard. I ran my thumb over these sugary, flaking parts of the stone and was about to mention that this statue occupied a place of honor in the Common Room when Sallie said, "Is that Santa Claus? Oh, no, I suppose it's St. Harold. He's all yours, if you want him."

At last she opted to don a T-shirt, a very big one with Seattle Mariners in extroverted lettering. "Do you know Ian left a generous bequest to the Episcopal church in Gloucester? They'll get the new slate roof they've been harping about. That's why Reverend Tyler was so obsequious at the funeral. He was sickening." Sallie frowned. "Do you want these New Age books or not?"

I didn't really consider Thomas Merton or the Buddha in the same category as crystals and aromatherapy, but, to be polite, I took three of these paperbacks. After all, these were Ian's things and not just memorabilia from our defunct school.

"There's some gay policeman on the case," Sallie said. She realized her tone had been insensitive, a small miracle, because she mitigated her sarcasm in the next sentence. "I suppose that's good. He must know your community down here."

Then I had to tell her, not about us, not about my mother's story, but about something I'd felt from the very beginning. "I want you to know, Sallie, I'm, um, asking around…" She stopped what she was doing. "…I think Ian was killed by someone he knew."

She seemed startled. "Why, thank you for your concern." Then she leaned across the carton of leather-bound books to quickly kiss my cheek, and I'm afraid I cringed, which was doubly embarrassing because a tall, handsome stranger was just sliding the screen door aside to emerge from the darkness of the living room. "Honey, he's agitated," the stranger said. It was her fiancé.

"Mark," Sallie said, "this is my significant other, Alexander Nash. Alexander, Mark Winslow. Mark was at St. Harold's with Ian."

He was dark, with the added attraction of very blue eyes, so blue you'd mistake them for contacts. He had the shy but virile manner of a handsome male unaware of his beauty.

"Alexander is working at Woods Hole," Sallie said. "He's in marine biology, studying the scallop population of Buzzards Bay. It's mysteriously crashed."

I was about to ask him about who was agitated when Alexander cut me off, saying, "This must be pretty precious material for you, Mark," indicating some sepia photographs dark as tea in a pile of artifacts that seemed to have grown rather than diminished, despite Sallie's efforts.

"Alexander thinks all this is history," Sallie said.

"Coming from the west, where something from the Seventies gets a plaque stuck on it," said Alexander.

"Alexander loves New England," Sallie said, chucking a volume of one headmaster's memoirs. "He's tracing his family tree. He's into genealogy. It's a Mormon thing."

There was something clean-cut and western about him, like a champion skier from an up-close-and-personal profile on the Olympics.

"My folks were Mormon," Alexander said, "but I consider myself a staunch Episcopalian."

"Oh, no!" Sallie suddenly moaned, waving at a figure at the screen door.

"I told you he was agitated," Alexander said.

The old man picking at the screen was thin as a shoelace. His hands were desperate as moths, trying to beat their way through the restrictive mesh.

I felt sick, like the time I'd found the dog on Arthur's stoop, but I leapt up. Bumping against a carton of St. Harold's relics, I stumbled across the deck and drew the screen door aside. He looked years older than at Ian's funeral, and he smelled old, like thick toenails and Ace bandages. I couldn't call him "Father" or "Mr. Drummond" or anything else. I took his veined hands, his old wrinkled hands, in both of mine. Then made a fool of myself—and wept.

"Mark and Ian were very close," I heard Sallie explaining to Alexander.

"It's me," I kept saying to the frightened eyes, which were vacant and intense at the same time, as comprehension came and went, flickered on then off, like current in a faulty socket. "It's Mark," I kept repeating, just this side of angry, as if he should know his son, even through that wall of dementia.

Sallie wiped her hands on a strip of grimy cheesecloth. Duncan Drummond's shirt looked no cleaner. "Where is his carrot?" Sallie said, and then Alexander produced a stuffed cloth carrot that he gave to the old man to knead.

"It's Mark," I told him, but he was staring out to sea.

"We're not sure he realizes," Alexander said. "About the tragedy. It could be a blessing."

"Isn't it time for his medication?" Sallie asked Alexander. To me, she remarked, "Having him here gives Mother a little break."

"Sir?" said Alexander, brushing the old man's back, brushing the shirt where you could count the vertebrae, guiding him out of the sunlight, into the op art and darkness of his dead son's living room.

"Is it…Alzheimer's?" I asked, remembering my mother's comments.

"He's confused," Sallie said, for once using a euphemism. "He's been this way for three years. Don't feel bad, Mark. Most days he doesn't know *us*."

I'm an "us," I wanted to say.

Gently, persistently, Alexander was telling Mr. Drummond to "swallow the applesauce." Sallie dropped my three paperbacks into a plastic bag, my hint to leave.

I had to speak: "Sallie, I've…known your family a long time, we go way back…"

She regarded me warily. The sun caught the diamonds of her tennis bracelet.

"My mother was…friendly with your dad."

"They both liked jazz, they were Ella Fitzgerald fans." Sallie laughed, but her square face was humorless.

She could know that from parties—the jazz link, I thought.

"I think they had a little…" I began. "…You're my half, my half…" She looked terrified. "…My half-sister," I said. Her face went blank. Then I became aware of a presence behind the screen—Alexander, holding a spoon and a jar of applesauce, and sighing. "I crushed the pill," he said, "but he keeps spitting it out."

"Daddy's a little agitated," Sallie said. "You'll excuse us, Mark. Take St. Harold if you want to." Then she did something that startled me again: she hugged me against her muscular body.

She hadn't believed me. Or had she? She'd admitted they'd shared an intimacy, our father and my mother. "Our father"—it sounded like the beginning of a prayer. I'd always fantasized about my father, heroic in his Navy whites and bringing me strange shells from dangerous oceans. But now that I'd found him—elderly and sick, his mind wrecked—my fantasy withered. This father could never answer any of my questions or provide the "why" of his perspective. I'd never speak to him as my parent or let him know me as a son. He'd remain the aging rogue I'd met at North Shore parties, the man who'd playfully tugged my tie to confirm it wasn't silk.

Of course there was the chance my mother was lying. But hadn't I always shown a Drummond recklessness? On my job, for instance, smoking weed then resigning, giving two days' notice? Dousing Ian with that pitcher of beer? But why should she lie now about this? She had nothing to gain. She risked my speaking to the Drummonds, violating their contract. And what a mess it would be if she somehow lost her house and ended up, desperate, on my doorstep.

So I resolved to keep silent about my Drummond blood—if it existed.

Chapter Fifteen

July Fourth weekend, the Thomas Royall exhibit opened at the Provincetown Municipal Museum. Miriam coaxed Arthur into attending the opening reception, but Roberto and I were very busy at the White Gull. We'd finally been targeted by the Christian Soldiers, in the form of picketers with professionally printed signs like" A Double Room in Sodom, Harbor View?" and "Worried about Global Warming? Hell Is a Lot Hotter." Only one of the picketers wore battle fatigues, a female, oddly enough.

They picketed two days, until eight o'clock at night, then, abruptly, they left. So Roberto and I missed the opening, which included the crab-stuffed mushroom caps prepared by the Hungry Gull, Roger Morton's catering business, and a few words by an old man who'd once delivered kerosene to Royall's Provincetown residence and remembered him as "a great strapping fellow who smelled of violet toilet water."

So Roberto and I went to the exhibit the first day the picketers failed to arrive. Roberto was letting his hair grow, looking wonderful, like a Samson who'd stopped dating Delilah. Instead of the jawbone of an ass, he held something equally unwelcome to the museum attendant selling tickets, a bag of that crumbly, all-natural licorice they sell in art-house movie theaters.

"I'm sorry, sir, but there's no food allowed inside," the attendant said.

"Fascists," snapped someone beyond the entrance.

I could smell him before he emerged from inside the museum; smell the rank odor of his unwashed flesh. He was thin, about thirty, shirtless and in overalls. He had blondish hair of Jesus' length, and his bare shoulders were dense with freckles. "Gestapo, Gestapo," he called the woman selling tickets. "You should let him have his food," he said. "People have the right to eat, don't they?"

"Not in the presence of art," the woman answered.

"It's no big deal," Roberto told the foul-smelling stranger, surrendering the candy.

Stiff as her hairdo, the attendant deposited it on a shelf next to some leaflets about an exhibit, "Whaling in Oils," which had long since closed.

Then the foul-smelling stranger retreated back inside the museum.

"We're interested in the Royall exhibit," Roberto said, and she gave us directions without bothering to look up from the yellow legal pad she was filling with writing no larger than dust mites.

"This place is getting more homophobic by the moment," Roberto complained, but I reminded him that, even people as benevolent as us had our cranky days; on the desk at the White Gull, with demanding guests, for instance.

◇◇◇

The Royall exhibit was in the new climate-controlled wing. It included more than forty paintings from museums and private collections, ranging from oils with almost life-sized figures to watercolors so small they could trick you into thinking you could afford them. Almost all were inspired by the sea: fishermen gutting cod, waves challenging piers, brigantines in opalescent fogs. One wall was full of nudes—youths diving from wharfs, wrestling on sand, tossing a ball near cliffs the color of nougat.

"They're either dead or in nursing homes now," Roberto observed.

"Not so loud," I said, mindful of other visitors, elderly liberals migrating from painting to painting in the sequence the exhibit literature suggested.

"So where is the painting that changed your life?" Roberto asked, tickling my back.

"You'll see it, eventually."

At the beginning of the exhibit were cardboard panels with photographs of Royall and the so-called artists' communities he'd established throughout New England. Some of the story on the panels was familiar. Royall had been born in 1880, in Dorchester, Massachusetts, the son of a hardware merchant, Ezekiel Royall, and Emma Root, the famous clairvoyant. His formal schooling ended at age eleven when he almost died of diphtheria. While recovering, in bed, he made a series of pencil sketches—of a pear, his canary, and of his own feet, with their distinct hammertoes—the toes which convinced his mother that he was a uniquely gifted artist, the reincarnation, to be precise, of Angelo Bonelli, the sixteenth-century Florentine master.

Royall senior resisted the reincarnation idea, principly out of anti-Italian prejudice, but agreed that his son was ill-suited to spend his days selling shovels and wrenches. So, Thomas was allowed to become apprenticed to Wendell Sleeper, the Boston painter who paid for the boy's journey to England, where he met Edward Carpenter, posed for Henry Scott Tuke, and drank absinthe with Aubrey Beardsley. Carpenter's writings on Uranian love would eventually fire Royall to imagine founding his male Utopias.

When he returned to Massachusetts, Royall began painting. He produced grittier canvases than Boston contemporaries like Benson or Tarbell: his subjects included Gypsy encampments; maids at soapstone sinks; newsboys picking lice from each other's scalps. Slowly, his work began selling, but his very subject matter, Boston, with its slums and soot and buildings plastered with advertisements selling spats and tooth powders, began to depress him. He left the city, never to return. Eventually, he settled on Cape Cod.

"He came here to escape," I told Roberto.

"Escape what?"

"People in Black Dog T-shirts," I said, spotting yet another tourist with the canine logo of the Vineyard restaurant.

Royall moved to Provincetown in 1907, settling in a house in the East End later obliterated to make way for a gas station. But he was also busy founding communes: Brook Farms for artists, Jacob's Pillows for craftsmen. Ascetic, all-male, almost monastic societies where one could paint, sculpt, weave, and throw pots while espousing the vague Nordic paganism Royall was formulating in dreams, with help from his late mother's shade.

A video monitor had been built into one of the exhibit's cardboard panels. I punched a button and a narrator, whose deep, reassuring voice I recognized from PBS nature documentaries, informed us we were seeing the sole footage in existence in the Cape Cod community. The film was grainy, flecked with age, as if photographed through sleet, although it depicted a summer meadow and a circle of men costumed like druids dancing around a flat glacial stone picked with petroglyphs.

"Interesting," Roberto said.

The thirty or more men ranged from college boys to men Merlin's age.

"Is that Royall?" Roberto pointed to an old man.

"No, that's him there." Royall was the only man bare-chested, in some kilt ancient highlanders might've worn, with a tusk or crescent of bone suspended from a chain around his neck.

"He's quite the dish," Roberto said, approving of Royall's eyes, dark with anger, as though something about the ritual had gone wrong—the dance or the offerings heaped on the stone, the grapes, melons, and ears of corn.

An elderly couple now hovered behind us, consulting their pamphlets about details of Royall's life. The woman said to us, "My husband likes the paintings of ships."

"He does ships well," the husband said. "I was in the Navy. At Midway, during the war."

"This Royall gets the sails and rigging right," the husband continued. "And I should know, I was born on an island. Off Nova Scotia. I'm a naturalized American citizen."

The wife said, "He's not much on nudes."

"They look silly," the husband stated. Then, guessing we were a couple, he added, "But they're fine for you fellows. It's not like we're Christian Cuckoos." He squinted at the video. "Now these people in robes look like they're worshipping an idol, an elephant. That would be Ganesh, the Hindu god of luck. We took a tour of India in eighty-eight."

"It isn't Ganesh," his wife corrected him. "It's just a long flat stone. He won't wear his glasses, he's too *vain.*" Using the exhibit brochure, she jabbed her husband in the ribs. "Uh-oh," she muttered. "Here comes trouble."

She was not speaking about the group of Japanese tourists who had followed their leader's upraised red umbrella into the room.

"Over by the window," the wife whispered to Roberto.

It was the reeking man in overalls, with the Biblical hair. He had rolled his exhibit program into a tight cylinder, which he used to beat the palm of his hand as he paced back and forth by some of the nudes, including *The Fisher Boy.*

"He's been here for hours," the woman said. "The woman at the desk told us all about him. He gave her a terrible time. He was waiting outside when the museum opened and he only left to get his lunch. In fact, he tried to bring his lunch in here, a big plate of fried clams, when it was perfectly obvious it's against the rules. There's a sign that says so, for all to see, unless you're my husband and you leave your glasses in the car."

The wife leaned closer to Roberto and me. "Well, he threw the clams all over the lawn, then just glared at the woman like it was a perfectly normal thing to do. Of course, the seagulls were delirious, happy as clams…"

"He's a little off," the husband confided. "Swearing, talking to himself about 'the last days.' I heard him. He has pamphlets from the Christian Cuckoos in his pockets."

"I mean, if he doesn't like the paintings, why did he come?" the wife asked.

"I don't see why he wouldn't like the ships," the husband said.

His wife realized it was "almost time for the whale watch." Her husband drew a coconut candy bar from his shirt pocket and ate half of it in one bite. "I smuggled it past security," he told us, as his wife laughed and led him away.

We stayed away from the wall of nudes because the man in the overalls was pacing in front of them, humming. He seemed as likely to desert his post as a guard at the Tomb of the Unknown Soldier.

Copy on the cardboard panels informed us that Royall's communes outside Cape Cod all "failed" within two to five years, but "the Pamet experiment" lasted a full seven years, from 1911 to 1918. At Pamet, Royall and his followers raised all their own food and made their own clothing, weaving the cloth and dyeing it with extracts from roots and leaves. Royall was fascinated by Norse sagas and the speculation that Vikings had reached New England. "Royall was obsessed by runes," Roberto read, "although the runes on this stone are now known to be a colonial-era hoax."

A still photograph, sepia like tobacco spit, showed some of the same men from the footage of the ritual seated at a long wooden table, doling gruel out of an iron cauldron. They were in a sort of hall, with sheaves of grain tied to its rafters.

The next photograph was much more startling. In it, Royall—naked, clutching a dagger—was lying on a large flat stone, possibly the one the elderly man had mistaken for the elephant god. Any petroglyphs on the sides of the stone were concealed by a cloth draped over it, a bolt of what might be velvet embroidered with interlocking swastikas.

I winced, massaging Roberto's shoulder, but he didn't act upset. "It was taken in 1912," he said, noting the caption. "Long before the Nazis. Swastikas are an ancient talisman."

It was impossible not to notice Royall's body, taut from the regimen of exercise he imposed on the commune's inhabitants: calisthenics three times each day, a workout with barbells each noon, morning and evening swims in ponds or the sea, from May Day through October. Royall was holding the dagger so that it pointed directly toward his genitals, toward his heavy, uncircumcised penis. Seeing genitals in old photographs always startled me; you see them so seldom that it almost seems they're a modern invention.

"Why is he lying there like that?" Roberto said. "Like he's some sort of sacrifice."

The Japanese tourists were collecting in murmuring knots behind us. I expected the women to giggle and the men to gawk at these pictures from a lost private world, but, instead, they consulted their guide with expressions no doubt as baffled as ours.

The guide was a small man with a great many moles. In English, he said to us, "A group of strange bohemians."

"Do you mean us?" Roberto asked.

"Sun worshipper," the guide said, of Royall lying naked on the stone. Then, in rapid Japanese, he commented on the exhibit, thrust his umbrella into the air, and ushered his flock out of the room.

The man in overalls remained, pacing in front of *The Fisher Boy.* He was still swatting his hand with the rolled-up pamphlet. His gesture, repetitive and obsessive, called to mind Duncan Drummond kneading that stuffed cloth carrot at Ian's house.

I kept hoping he'd move away from *The Fisher Boy* and investigate the watercolors of ships. "Let's look at the ships," I whispered to Roberto. "Until he moves."

We had looked at the ships twice, but he was still in front of *The Fisher Boy.* I said, "I think he'll be there all day, let's just ignore him." He edged away from us, mumbling something I couldn't understand. He reeked of a combination of cigarettes and body odor—acrid, punishing your nostrils, odd among these paintings of water and clean, naked skin.

The Fisher Boy was large, six feet by four feet, I'd say—and still youthful, of course. I'd grown older, but he'd stayed the same, nineteen or so, smiling as he held the giant halibut. "I had no idea this was here. I mean, I've seen this before," Roberto said, "but I thought it must be someplace like the Louvre."

The boy in this painting, Thomas Royall's model, would be well over one-hundred today, knotted by arthritis and closed tight like a fist, in worse shape than my pitiful possible father.

"Is this your favorite?"

I almost jumped. The man with the long Jesus hair was addressing me. He'd asked a perfectly sensible question, but my guard went up, the way it does when a panhandler approaches.

"Is this your favorite?" His smile revealed teeth that were yellow as kernels of corn. "I like this painting a lot," he said. He kept smiling, as though he'd just told a joke, and drew closer.

Roberto put his arm around my shoulder. I was suddenly alarmed at his gesture, seeing the pamphlets in this man's overalls. His dyed hair was dull with grease, and black roots were growing from his scalp.

"This is a good painting," he said, and he laughed, showing his broken teeth. "I like this painting very much."

I don't know why, but I was afraid he was going to do something. What that might be, I wasn't sure. Maybe it was no more threatening than just to touch me, to touch us, but he smelled so rancid and acted so strange that this seemed threat enough.

Then Roberto took control of the situation. "Nice meeting you," he said, setting his hands on my shoulders and steering me briskly toward the exit.

The militaristic woman at the entrance was filling a rack with brochures about other attractions, everything from Plimouth Plantation to Aqua-World, the big water park in Hyannis. She handed Roberto the bag of licorice she'd confiscated earlier.

"There's a man back there who's acting very bizarre," Roberto said. "And he smells."

"We're not responsible for our visitors' hygiene," the woman said crisply, stacking some brochures about dune buggy tours.

"He keeps pacing back and forth in front of *The Fisher Boy*," I said.

"Thank you for your concern," she said. "I'll inform the guard."

Afterward, we acted like tourists, strolling up and down Commercial Street. A hot wind was blowing through the town, like something you'd expect in Tangier, like something off the Sahara. It hadn't rained for weeks, and the Christian Soldiers were claiming the drought was punishment from God.

We ate vegetarian sandwiches at a place with an open second-story deck. We could look down onto Commercial Street, where we recognized some of the same tourists we'd seen all day, traipsing up and down, over and over, looking more depleted with each trip.

The East End begins about there, the gift shops and restaurants gradually surrendering to art galleries of two distinct types: those selling Cape Cod landscapes paying homage to Edward Hopper, and, what might, at one time, have been called avant-garde art, Rothko knock-offs and sculptures of brutalized metal. Most of the tourists turned back at this point: day trippers seldom buy art.

Our sandwiches were delicious, bursting with a pasture's worth of field greens, messy with soy sauce. I was pushing some stray dandelion leaves into my mouth, when, beneath us on Commercial Street, I saw a familiar—and unmistakable—head.

I nudged Roberto to bring the man with the golden dreadlocks to his attention. "Have you seen him before?"

"I can't see his face."

"How many blond Rastafarians have you encountered?"

His hair was platinum. He was formally dressed for Commercial Street, in an Oxford-cloth shirt with peppermint stripes, linen trousers, and tasseled loafers. "He was at Ian's funeral!" I said.

"I can't picture Ian having black friends."

The man with the dreadlocks ducked into Scents of Being, a shop that specialized in home-made jellies and other Cape Cod products: bayberry soap, stoneware from potters in Welfleet, and potpourri originating in local herb beds.

We were still watching the shop, waiting for the man with the dreadlocks to emerge, when the sound of sirens ripped through the afternoon, startling the crowds on Commercial Street. People stopped in their tracks and began talking, pointing back toward the West End.

The boy busing plates at our restaurant, a townie about sixteen with a nose ring, leaned over the railing and yelled "What's happening?" to a friend in the street below.

"Someone got stabbed," the friend yelled, "at the museum!"

Roberto and I scrambled down the stairs, as if evacuating the place. We hit the pavement so hard the soles of my feet were stinging as we ran.

A crowd was collecting outside the museum. An ambulance and two police cars were parked on Commercial Street, in front of the building, and a fire engine was wailing up Center Street. Police and firemen were speaking into walkie-talkies. I noticed a paper plate lodged in the shrubbery growing flush with the foundation of the museum.

The woman at the ticket booth emerged from the entrance to the museum, her hands smeared with blood. She seemed to be in a state of shock: she kept touching the clasp of her white straw pocketbook, as if making sure that it was locked, as if this small gesture, this indication of normality, might somehow mitigate the horror around her.

"She wasn't the one who was stabbed," someone was saying, as the crowd in the street became more anxious.

"It was the guard, Mr. Peever," another person said.

"The Christian Soldiers are behind this," said a separate voice, and a number of voices answered in agreement, saying "Absolutely!" and "No kidding!" and "Something like this was bound to happen."

Two ambulance attendants with a stretcher went running up the steps of the museum. Another siren, from Bradford Street, drilled through the air. The woman from the ticket booth, Roberto's old adversary, was being helped toward an ambulance. She was soaked with gore; I thought I could smell it. It was the breakwater experience all over again.

Miriam came pushing through the crowd, asking, "What's happened, what's happened now?" Someone answered before I could speak and she began crying. "Oh, poor Mr. Peever, he's on the board of our church, and his wife just died. Oh, this is awful!"

Then the ambulance attendants came out, carrying an old man whose face was obscured by an oxygen mask.

"Is he dead?" a voice asked, sounding eager or excited or both.

"Oh, shut up!" Miriam snapped. "Have a little respect!"

"He's alive—barely," said one of the policemen, speaking to Sergeant Almeida.

Miriam was still crying, pressing a Kleenex to her eyes, when two other policemen led the squirming, screaming suspect down the museum steps. Everyone gasped.

It was him, of course—the strange man we'd encountered at the Royall exhibit. His Jesus hair was flying, his features contorted with rage. His denim overalls were splattered with blood.

"Good God!" Roberto groaned.

He lunged at his captors, as if trying to bite them with his broken yellow teeth. The police, wearing disposable gloves, were simultaneously restraining him and recoiling from him.

"Ashes, ashes!" he was yelling. "And the sun shall be covered in ashes!" he was shouting, as the police wrestled him into the cruiser and the crowds parted so that his captors could drive him away.

Chapter Sixteen

The Provincetown police station is small, a white clapboard building that would fit in a Fifties subdivision. All it's missing is a black metal eagle above the door, or pottery cat climbing a chimney. The police had scheduled a press conference at six o'clock sharp, so vans from several Boston and Providence television stations were in the street, as well as many spectators, residents and tourists. Some gay activists were distributing hastily prepared flyers linking the museum stabbing and Ian's murder to the Christian Soldiers.

"He was quoting the *Book of Revelation*," one woman said.

"Don't they all?" another asked.

Rumors were multiplying like tadpoles in a warm pond: that the assailant was Hollings Fair's nephew; that the knife used to assault Clarence Peever matched "the fatal wound to Ian's Drummond's throat"; and that, during the struggle in the museum, Thomas Royall's masterpiece called *The Fisher King* was slashed beyond repair.

"They must mean *The Fisher Boy*," I told Roberto.

Miriam was accompanying us, with Chloe. Miriam spoke of how violent rhetoric spawns violent actions. "But I hope the police work him over," she added, referencing the suspect.

A reporter and cameraman from a Boston UHF channel were sampling crowd opinion before the press conference. "People here seem to believe that a troubling murder mystery that has darkened this resort town this season may soon be laid to rest," the reporter was telling the camera. "Is this incident related to the brutal murder of Boston socialite Ian Drummond? This town is wondering that tonight, and tensions are high. Police are guarding the local headquarters of a fundamentalist religious group, Hollings Fair's Christian Soldiers, that has recently leased office space on Commercial Street…"

"Guarding murderers!" a voice yelled from the crowd.

"This will force them out of town," said the voice that came from, yes—Arthur! With a faded tan but a vivid grin. He'd cut his gray hair short in a style at least a generation too young.

The UHF station reporter was weaving through the crowd, heading toward Miriam, who was still holding forth about a right-wing conspiracy. To save herself from being interviewed, Miriam tattled, *"They saw him*, earlier in the day—Mark and Roberto saw the suspect at the museum."

"Sir?" Suddenly I found a microphone ready to broadcast my words, and the intense, powdered face of reporter Erin Leary asking for my "impressions" of the suspect.

But I was saved from responding, because, just at that moment, the Provincetown chief of police stepped up to the bouquet of microphones, his manner austere as a maximum-security cell. "At three-fifteen p.m., we were summoned," he began. He described the stabbing of Clarence Peever in the most dispassionate manner possible: "knife wounds…lacerations…critical but stable condition…"

Already, the media people were impatient and began peppering him with questions.

"Chief, chief, what about the suspect?"

"Who is he?"

"Is he linked to the Drummond murder?"

"Is he affiliated with the Christian Soldiers?"

The chief stiffened and looked above the heads of the crowd. "The suspect was carrying no identification, no driver's license. He has declined to answer any questions and refuses to speak."

"He was carrying pamphlets from the Christian Soldiers!" a man shouted.

"The suspect was carrying a variety of literature—flyers and coupons—that are given away to everyone on the street here in town."

"Born-again killers!" Miriam shouted.

"The suspect persists in quoting the Bible," the chief said. "As far as we know, he was not an acquaintance of either Clarence Peever or Eileen Sturmer, the other museum employee he allegedly assaulted."

"Don't you love the 'allegedly'?" Miriam said. "My God, there were eyewitnesses!" Ignoring the adult world, Chloe was picking at a Creamsicle somebody had dropped. Now, Sergeant Almeida was joining the chief.

"So, you have no idea who this man is?" Erin Leary asked.

"He is not known to this department," the chief replied.

"When are you going to do something about what's happening in this town?" Roberto had the audacity to demand.

"We have a suspect under arrest and the investigation is proceeding. The knife allegedly used in the assault is undergoing tests." The chief leaned forward toward the microphones. "Thank you," he said with finality.

A flurry of dismay and resentment ruffled through the crowd as the chief and his colleagues slipped back into the station. "Can you believe it?" people kept saying. I wanted to leave, to avoid being buttonholed by Erin Leary. Roberto hooked his warm, muscular arm into mine.

Arthur alone seemed satisfied, only hinting at his nervousness by playing with his oversized signet ring. "We can all rest easier," he said. "The nightmare, the atrocity, is over." He suggested we adjourn for an early dinner; he was dying for a good Portuguese fish stew. But Miriam had bought some sea bass and insisted she cook for us at her place.

But was it really over? Had I just met the man who'd slaughtered Ian? When I asked myself these questions, instinctively I answered no. Arthur was chattering away about the benefits of his new medication. He said, "I have a dry mouth but a light heart. Life is about tradeoffs. Smell that salt air! I'll take it over Obsession any day!" We walked through the soft summer light, through the gossiping, agitated crowds.

Miriam's studio was in the East End of town, an ex-fishing shack once plain as a mud hen but now a bright bird-of-paradise thanks to skylights, a deck, and coats of tangerine paint. Lots of buildings in Provincetown were like that: wallflowers made up to be supermodels. Miriam bought works from local artists, and, in the grass of her front yard, bleached yellow like corn silk, stood a sculpture of porpoise-gray stone called *Mother and Child* and a copper piece symbolizing nuclear war.

The house was filled with jars of beads, malachite and faience and jade, from Africa and Crete and Sri Lanka, and spools of wire and silver and gold—the stuff of her jewelry-making business. It was sweltering inside, even in the coolest rooms facing the water, so we opted to eat on the deck built over the sand flanking Provincetown Harbor. Miriam changed Chloe into a sun dress decorated with seahorses, and the little girl began thumbing through a storybook, the old classic *The Dragonfly's Suggestion*.

"I'd much rather have her read that," Miriam said, "than some corporate commodity like *The Loneliest Starfish*." She said this in Roberto's presence, perhaps forgetting he'd given her the toy mermaid from that film. Noting his frown, she added, "She's still upset that she broke her mermaid's arm."

Roberto volunteered to try mending the doll. I began reading Chloe the book aloud, the story of the little boy in the magic nightshirt who climbs onto the dragonfly's back for the journey to the Snail King's palace under the pond. My mother had read this to me when I was Chloe's age, the same book, with lacy Victorian woodcuts. As I read and the fragrance of fish and asparagus cooking in wine came trespassing from Miriam's stove—she was the sort of cook who dirtied innumerable dishes—the little girl edged closer on the settee as the hold of the story and her trust in me grew. Her skin radiated warmth.

Roberto used Krazy Glue to fix the arm, but told Chloe not to disturb the mermaid until she was discharged from the hospital. He made the doll a bed out of cotton batten and some ripped old crochet, and, speaking in a voice that was Robin Williams-does-Viennese psychiatrist, he told Chloe to let the patient get plenty of rest "until ze glue iz not zo crazy, understand?"

Miriam phoned Clarence Peever's family and spoke with his niece. His vital signs were stable and he was holding his own; the doctors were "optimistic." She seemed soothed by this, her movements in the kitchen became less frenetic. She stopped slamming pots and pans.

She served the sea bass on blue bubbleware plates she'd bought at an antique shop in Barnstable. Unusually for her, especially in the wake of her rhetoric, she requested we bow our heads before eating to pray. She prayed for Clarence Peever, "for his recovery, and for the recovery of our town, from violence and divisiveness."

"May the same hold true for our country," Arthur added. Then we devoured Miriam's marvelous meal, and the peace of the moment soothed me. Provincetown Harbor filled with a light fog which seemed to glow like something holy and divine.

Finishing his meal, Arthur clasped his hands like a child in Sunday school. "I have egg on my face."

"There's no dairy in this recipe." Miriam was as literal about food as the scorned Edward.

"Rhetorically speaking. Your plates, from the antique shop, prompt my confession. The candlesticks have come home."

"*Your* candlesticks?" Miriam said.

"The ones you said Edward took?" I said. "Has Edward brought them back?"

"No," Arthur said, "he's still gone with the wind. But I blackened his name a bit too thoroughly."

A man from Remembrance of Things Past, the antique store in Brewster, finally returned with the candlesticks. Edward had sent them out to be repaired, at Arthur's request, as Arthur himself belatedly recalled. That was why he had associated Edward with the candlesticks—Edward had sent them away when Arthur was at a medical appointment in Boston. "I'm afraid I began drinking when Edward was with me. It was the thrill of having something so beautiful under my roof. So Edward wasn't a thief after all. Vulgar, tongue-tied, and narcissistic, yes. But not a thief. He stole only my heart. But that has returned too."

As Miriam cleared the blue bubbleware plates, the fog thickened like a sweater that's too heavy. Then Miriam herself broke the taboo she'd imposed before dinner. While serving us chocolate cake drizzled with raspberry sauce, she asked, "Do you really think this is it? The arrest of that creature at the museum? I don't feel closure, I don't feel safe. The Christian Soldiers are still here, with police protection. The police are functioning as enablers."

Arthur was sectioning away the frosting from the cake so that he could devour a cornice of it first. He said the Christian Soldiers would be on their very best behavior, for the short time they'd dare remain in Provincetown. They'd barged in here to attract media attention. They knew they couldn't close the gay businesses here; we were far too essential to the economy. Their efforts in Provincetown were simply a trial balloon for their real ambitions out west—defeating gay rights initiatives in Oregon and Colorado. "Their presence here has been *a disaster*—Ian's death and now this assault on an elderly, straight, year-round resident…"

"But why?" I asked, as the foghorn sounded over the harbor. "Why did this violence happen?"

"Because they're evil," Miriam said.

"Homophobia," Roberto added.

"So that explains Ian's death and the dog on Arthur's doorstep, but why would they attack Mr. Peever and Eileen Sturmer?"

Their expressions went slack with bafflement, then Roberto resumed his line of thought with irritation. "Well, he slashed *The Fisher Boy*, isn't that homophobic enough? He slashed your fantasy."

That was rumor, I reminded them. Confirmed by no one.

"But why Ian? Why at night on the breakwater?" I turned to Arthur: "And why you? Why your party?"

With patience and pride, Arthur said, "I'm a prominent person in this community. So was Ian."

"There are much bigger targets," I said. *"Nationally* known gay people who summer here." Like the lesbian author, the kung fu movie star, a closeted conservative columnist.

"Perhaps he wanted to start small and go big, with his targets," Miriam said.

Arthur removed a raspberry from his chocolate cake. "Raspberries don't agree with me," he said. Neither, apparently, did being called a "small" target.

Miriam cut into her cake with confident strokes. She pointed out that knives had been used in Ian's death and in the museum stabbings. All of this had happened since Hollings Fair's people had come to town. "It can't all be a coincidence. That creature was quoting Scripture! You saw him! You saw how strange he was! You're acting as noncommittal as the damn police!"

"You said a bad word," Chloe told her mother.

"He was different from those right-wing people," I said. "He was different from those people with the petitions, the people who picketed the White Gull. Look at his hair, it was long, like something from the Bible…"

"Exactly!" said both Miriam and Roberto.

"Ian knew his killer," I said.

Miriam turned toward me. She used the low, cold tone of a prosecutor. "Well, then, you'd be a very logical suspect in Ian's murder, now, wouldn't you? You'd known each other since St. Harold's and before. He'd made your life like something from *Lord of the Flies.*"

She was savoring this mini-attack, the self-righteous part of her, the leftist crusader.

Ian and I were like brothers, I almost said. "What precipitated the attack at the museum? I mean, that man had been there all day."

"He took a swipe at *The Fisher Boy,* so I understand," Arthur said. "Clarence Peever tried to stop him, so he stabbed him. He slashed Eileen Sturmer when she came running to help Clarence, when she heard Clarence screaming in the exhibit."

"But if that was his plan, attacking *The Fisher Boy,* why didn't he do it right away? Why did he linger all those hours? Why didn't he do it after Eileen Sturmer told him he couldn't bring his lunch inside the museum? That's when he was maddest."

"Mad—exactly," Arthur said. "You expect logic from someone who uses the *Book of Revelation* to plan his actions?"

"What was he like, Roberto?" Miriam asked.

"Like a street person who puts you on your guard. The kind you cross the street to avoid."

"Was he muttering anything anti-gay?" I said. "No. Was he quoting Leviticus about Sodom? No. If he was so anti-gay, why didn't he attack *us*—or some other gay couple instead of two straight staff from the museum?"

◇◇◇

That night, we were too tense to make love. We lay awake in each other's arms until sleep abducted us. The next morning, while we were readying the muffins, Roger Morton reported the news he'd heard on his scanner—the man being held for the museum stabbings was dead. He had killed himself in his cell at the police station.

Chapter Seventeen

There were no bars to serve as a desperate man's gallows; his cell was sealed behind a panel of Plexiglass. He'd worn no belt, and the laces of his rotted sneakers had been confiscated by the police. So he'd choked himself to death, swallowing a plastic bag he'd secreted on his person.

He died after being in custody less than twelve hours, after extensive police questioning had produced no information about who he was, why he'd attacked the people at the museum and slashed the frame of one of the paintings—not *The Fisher Boy.* No evidence yet linked him to Ian's murder or to any earlier events.

Yet, in the court of public opinion, in the restaurants, bars, and guest houses of Provincetown, he'd been tried and convicted, executed by his own hand. We could all get back to "normal."

"He got what he deserved, the bloody bugger," said one of two Australian lesbians at breakfast on the back porch of the White Gull the next morning.

"He'd have been more useful alive," I said.

I was helping Roger and Roberto water the pots of fuchsia, which sported trailing vines with pink flowers tiered like pagodas. I kept soaking the plants so that they quickly became incontinent, splattering the premises with muddy droplets of water. "Sorry," I'd mutter, half to myself, half to Roger and Roberto.

"You're dangerous around liquids," Roger commented, alluding no doubt to the incident at Quahog.

We were all ignoring the Australians' diatribe about the violence of American society, "the Wild West cast to the culture."

"The autopsy will tell us a lot more." Roger was scanning an article in the *Cape Cod Times* written just after the body was found. It was frustratingly vague.

"Do you believe the fundamentalists are behind this?" I asked Roger.

"Mark doesn't," Roberto said.

Roger read aloud: "The suspect refused to answer questions posed by police. Instead, he quoted the New Testament concerning the Apocalypse. At a press conference in San Diego, Hollings Fair of the Christian Soldiers adamantly denied the suspect had any affiliation with his organization." Roger said, "Hey, suicide bombers seldom carry IDs."

The suspect's photograph was on the front page of the newspaper.

I said, "Why hasn't anyone claimed the body?"

"The Christian Soldiers are preventing his family from claiming him," Roger theorized. "One of their own took their rhetoric too literally and right now they're dreadfully embarrassed. They'll wait until the furor dies down, then they'll claim him. Please don't drown my plants, by the way."

"Forget that vagrant! Polish your sketches," Roberto told me. He began filling the birdbath using the same watering can he'd used for the fuchsia. I advised him to empty the birdbath and start again, since the liquid plant food the fuchsia enjoyed might well prove fatal.

◇◇◇

I tried to squirrel myself away with my coil notepad and flesh out a sketch for our planned two-man show. It would be scripted, about a tourist who's allergic to all the scented tsochtkes in his guesthouse, the sachets and soap roses and so on. The White Gull of course was nothing like this because Roger Morton loathed sachets and the baskets, Victorian dolls, peacock feathers, and jars of shells, the sort of Haight-Ashbury-meets-Pollyanna clutter that often passes for period decor on Cape Cod.

But my thinking of sachets made me think of the Elizabethans, who carried sachets to mask their aversion to bathing. And thinking of unwashed flesh made me remember the man at the museum again, his acrid smell, sharp as spoilt cheese. I remembered his yellow teeth with their tartar deposits, untouched by a dentist's instruments for years. His slovenliness, his sheer dirtiness, distinguished him from any of the fundamentalists I'd seen here. He was just too filthy to be one of them.

I wanted to tell this to Roberto, but he was busy at the desk, booking an elderly straight couple into their room. So, I decided to hit Adams Pharmacy to buy a Boston paper's account of the suicide. It was arctic in the drugstore as usual, and the papers were up front, by the window, held in the same wire dispenser caging the tabloids, an inadvertent comment on the state of American media.

Sallie Drummond pushed open the door, bringing in the heat of the street.

"Never a dull moment," she said, in her petulant, deadpan way. She retrieved a *Globe*. "So do you think this wraps everything up?"

She'd usurped my question. "Do you?"

She was skimming the paper. "'No positive identification,'" she read. "'The suspect was a white male, twenty-eight to thirty-five years old, blond, clean-shaven, with a tattoo of *a cross* on his upper right arm.'"

I hadn't seen the cross. I said, "Lots of people have crosses. Hell's Angels. Street gangs."

"Did you know this…man?"

"Of course I didn't know him."

"So you hadn't seen him…preaching in the street or at some bar."

"No."

She was staring at the *Globe* again, as if dismissing me, as if I were the servant who'd brought the morning coffee and should now be gone. "I've hired a home-health aide for my father," she said, glancing at the sports page. "She's with him now." There was a catch in her voice. A bruise was healing beneath one of her eyes. "My father is getting out of hand, physically. He's so paranoid." She'd realized I'd noticed the bruise.

We paid for our newspapers and went outside. "I wish I could say this felt like a bad dream, but it hasn't felt like a dream at all. It's been hideously real from day one," she said.

This brief sharing of thoughts made me trust her momentarily, enough to risk confiding in her a bit. "I saw him at the museum," I said and related my encounter with him, that strange, reeking man.

She stood in the sunlight on Commercial Street, in a Talbot's dress with spinnakers on it, more suitable for Edgartown or Chatham. Hugging the newspaper against her chest, she looked intense, controlled again, like an athlete competing, like a tennis star concentrating at Wimbledon. "He was nothing like these fundamentalists. He was more like a street person."

"You think they're all squeaky clean?" she said. "I guess there's one way to find out—if he was one of them, I mean."

"What's that?"

"Go ask."

She was actually serious. She'd read their denials, heard Fair on the news, but she was "a believer in showing up in person." She strode along at a pace suited to power-walking, getting an admiring glance from the Australian lesbians, which she ignored.

Sallie knew the location of the fundamentalists' office, opposite Spiritus Pizza. Some queer activists, people who could've passed as skinheads given their shaved skulls and studded armbands, were staring threateningly at the little storefront, at its dotted Swiss curtains and posters of the Holy Land.

By poetic justice, Sergeant Almeida was doing guard duty at the office.

"Hello, Ms. Drummond," he said. So he knew her.

"Miss Drummond," she corrected him.

"May I go inside?"

"For any particular reason?"

"Just looking," she said, sternly. "I'm not carrying any weapons. Want to frisk me?"

"Go ahead."

Most shops in Provincetown were cold compared to the street. Sweaty tourists like chilly shops, but this was ridiculous. It was like stepping into a meat locker: bloody sides of beef should have lined the walls. Instead, they were bare, eggshell-white.

The room was sparsely furnished, containing two metal desks and two folding tables crowded with telephones and Cape Cod directories. A Lucite stand held crosses "fashioned from olive wood from the Garden of Gethsemane" for sale.

A young woman, thin, wan, and smiling, rose from her desk, shy but eager. Properly patriarchal, she said, "Good morning," to me first.

Sallie answered. "It's a rather troubling morning, actually."

"Pardon?" The woman frowned.

"The violence in this town," Sallie said.

The woman's expression became sympathetically clouded. "Oh, I know," she said. She was alone in the outer office, wearing pink barrettes and a mustard seed suspended in a clear globe of glass on a chain around her neck.

"My brother was attacked—" Sallie began.

"Is your brother Mr. Peever?"

"My brother never worked in that museum!" Sallie snapped. "And he obviously wasn't eighty years old!"

"I didn't know the ages—"

"Was that creature a member of your organization?" Sallie demanded in a loud, husky voice. "That creature who killed himself in jail?"

"No, ma'am, he certainly was not," said the tall man in camouflage gear who nudged past the bead curtain left over from the Chinese take-out place.

"There are lots of rumors," Sallie said, her voice still hard with anger. "My brother was Ian Drummond. He was murdered."

The man in camouflage resembled all the other Soldiers I'd seen earlier and had the clipped, all-business manner of most zealots. "We have never believed in violence to achieve our ends," he stated.

There were other people behind the bead curtain. I could see figures moving behind the plastic jewels. Their backs were to us: a man changing the cartridge of a copying machine and a girl stacking cardboard boxes.

"Miss Drummond's brother was stabbed to death," I said. As I spoke, I kept an eye on the figures behind the bead curtain. I kept thinking we were in danger, that somehow this was a set-up, but of course that was nonsense, we had come here of our own free will. I said, "There's speculation in the media—"

"The media!" the Soldier scoffed.

"There's speculation that the man who attacked the people in the museum also killed Ian, Miss Drummond's brother." I was playing, I felt, to my most hostile audience ever.

Then the man changing the cartridge of the copying machine turned, and, head bent, examining the spent cartridge, pushed through the bead curtain and tugged at the Soldier's arm. "What should I do with this?" he asked.

It was Edward.

Chapter Eighteen

His hair was darker, a tawny brown, and he had lost weight, so that he looked somber, delicate, and, somehow, desperate. He kept his gaze fixed on the Soldier, as if the Soldier owned him.

"There's a carton out back, by the thermostat," said the Soldier. "Put it there."

Before Edward retreated to the back room, he glanced at Sallie, then at me. His face registered no change of emotion. Did he recognize me? He acted drugged. Perhaps the bag of white powder he'd stashed in Arthur's bathroom really was narcotics. He might be innocent of stealing Madame Récamier's candlesticks, but was he guilty of other crimes besides hypocrisy?

What, in God's name, was he doing working here? In God's name, exactly. Had he been one of them all along? Did this somehow explain the dog's corpse on Arthur's doorstep? Did this somehow explain Ian's murder?

"I'm a Christian," I heard Sallie say to the Soldier. She used the word in the exclusionary way that weighted it with aggression, with politics.

The Soldier nodded sympathetically, and I felt the tension in the office subside. The woman at the desk began moistening stamps with a little yellow sponge and sticking them precisely onto envelopes with a logo that said ONWARD in red lettering.

"This town, and what it stands for, is, frankly, alien to me," Sallie told the Soldier.

Then the bead curtain rattled and Edward was in the outer office once again. He deposited another pile of envelopes on the woman's desk and she said "Thank you" with such enthusiasm that his gesture might have come as a complete surprise. He might've been a stranger who'd dropped by to donate these office supplies as some spontaneous act of largesse.

I was by the Lucite stand holding the olive wood crosses. I thought of the cross tattooed on the man from the museum, the man lying chilled in the morgue. "These crosses are beautiful," I said to Edward, forcing him to acknowledge me. "You must have a hard time keeping them in stock."

He paused and looked at the crosses and me with the same vacant expression. "They're from the Holy Land. They're cut from trees from the Garden of Gethsemane."

He recognized me, I was sure, but acted stupefied. I felt like shaking him. I was relieved to see him alive and angry to find him here. I wondered all sorts of things I couldn't ask aloud: Had he heard about Ian's murder? Where was he living? Had he been a Christian Soldier all along?

"Do you have chains to go with these beautiful crosses?" I asked.

The woman at the desk stopped stamping the envelopes. "Oh, Paul is fairly new here," she told me. Then, to Edward, she said, "Paul, the chains are out back, on the shelf with the booklets about Armageddon." She said this as cheerily as she'd thanked him for bringing the envelopes.

Paul, she called him. Was that his real name?

While Edward was getting the chains, the woman at the desk confided, "They're not solid gold, they're just electroplated with gold. But nothing on this earth lasteth forever."

I wanted to make conversation. "How large is your staff?"

This question caused her to become as businesslike as the Soldier, who was now discussing theology with Sallie Drummond. "We don't divulge that sort of information," she said. "It's just policy."

"Policy," I said, "not theology."

Her smile was contracting.

The man I'd known as Edward returned, holding plastic envelopes containing chains. Without looking at my face, he explained, "We have three styles to choose from: light, medium, and heavy mesh."

"I think the heavy chains are more masculine," said the woman at the desk.

Of course, masculinity was highly valued in this culture, Christianity at its most muscular. Sallie and the Soldier were now discussing the Book of Isaiah.

"This is all very interesting," I said to Edward. At last he looked me in the eye but gave no sign of emotion; he might've been under anesthesia. "I'll take a cross and your heaviest chain," I said.

"The chain is ten dollars," Edward said. "The cross is twelve ninety-five."

"Don't forget the sales tax, Paul," the woman at the desk said cheerily.

I thought of asking to use a credit card, so that I could write Edward a note asking why he was here, but, at second thought, I shuddered at these people having access to my name or address. They might not be killers, but they held their own sorts of danger.

Edward was at the other desk, scribbling a record of the sale onto a pad of paper. When no one but Edward was looking, I seized his pen and wrote on a fresh page: "Why are you here? Where have you been? Do you know anything about—"

Then he snatched back the pen and scribbled onto the pad beneath my questions: "Be careful. You're in danger from the Golden One." All dullness had left his expression, replaced by the tautness of fear.

Now Sallie was at my side. "Let's go," she said.

"I bought a cross," I said, covering our writing with my hand.

She studied the crude cross, made of light wood the color of cocoa, and wrinkled her nose with disapproval.

I gave Edward thirty dollars and he gave me my purchases and my change. "We don't have bags," he apologized.

"But we will," said the woman at the desk. "We're expanding."

Chapter Nineteen

I had heard the phrase before, the "Golden One," and I brought Miriam and Chloe with me when I revisited the museum to confirm my theory. The Royall exhibition was mobbed. The attraction wasn't the oils, watercolors, and sketches, but the fact that this was a crime scene, a nationally publicized battleground in the "culture wars."

New guards and docents were fielding questions about the attack. Visiting the exhibit had become politically correct, showing posthumous support for Thomas Royall, who was under siege from the religious right. Queer activists circulated through the crowd, self-appointed like Guardian Angels, making sure no other paintings were jeopardized.

"There," I said, pointing to a small watercolor next to *The Fisher Boy*. It portrayed a naked youth on a boulder by the sea, sitting with the confidence of a prince on his throne, as the sun emphasized the mica in the granite and the bright, sharp something he was clasping, a razor or a razor clam.

Miriam read the title out loud. "*The Golden One*. So what?" She shrugged, fingering her necklace of Zuni fetishes.

Needing to tell someone, I said, "I visited Edward yesterday."

"Edward?" Miriam said. "I thought Edward was missing."

When I told her he was working for the fundamentalists, she called him a traitor, but listened about my scribbling my questions, and about him claiming I was in danger from some "Golden One."

Miriam held Chloe flush against her dress. "You think you're in danger from this painting? I think you need a rest, Mark, you're disassociating from reality."

Tourists were gawking at the gouges in the gilt on the frame of the painting to the left of *The Golden One*, an oil called *Youth in the Dunes*.

Miriam told me I was a fool to believe anything Edward said. Obviously he was trying to frighten me away; I was an embarrassment from his sinful past. Now that he'd joined these militant bigots, he'd picked up the zeal of the convert. They were always the worst.

"He looked scared to death writing that note."

"Scared you'd expose him, sure."

It was more than that, a more virulent fear. As we wandered back to Miriam's house, I told her I was sure that the painting's title being identical to Edward's warning was no coincidence. And the vagrant going berserk near that painting was no coincidence either.

"But he didn't strike *The Golden One*, he struck at *Youth in the Dunes*. You saw the scratches," Miriam said.

"He missed."

Besides, *The Golden One* was in the permanent collection of the museum, so Edward's reference to it could pre-date the opening of the big Royall exhibit in July.

Miriam muttered something about fearing no art. We adjourned to her house, where she began stringing a necklace of aventurine beads the light celery color of certain Chinese porcelains. She'd brought her work out onto her deck, along with a pitcher of sun-brewed iced tea. The afternoon was still and hot, the turquoise sky hard as a gem set in Navajo silver.

"There's a mystery around Thomas Royall, you know. Royall didn't die—he disappeared."

"What?!" She stopped stringing the beads, while I related the story.

On July 21, 1918, a German submarine was sighted offshore, near the naval air station at Chatham. The submarine fired on the *Perth Amboy*, a tugboat out of Gloucester, and throngs of people from the lower Cape crowded the shore to watch the action, the Great War right here in New England waters. The incident inspired a wave of local anti-German hysteria, which was common enough throughout the country: dachshunds were being stoned in the streets; families with German surnames were petitioning courts to change them, from Schultz to Smith.

"Royall, of course, was an ardent admirer of Nordic culture: runes, Wagner's operas, Viking sagas. So his community became a convenient target, a scapegoat for people on Cape Cod."

"Of course, the bluenoses had been sniffing at Royall all along. His nudes were going out of fashion. War makes the home front break out the fig leaves, the whole culture becomes puritanical... Anyway, Royall vanished. His clothes were discovered at Scusset Beach in Truro, but his body was never retrieved. The police assumed he drowned himself, figuring his career was finished.

"But I'm going to grill Edward," I told Miriam, "because he's some sort of link between this Golden One and, well, anyway, he's key."

Miriam exaggerated her sigh. "The key to your heart? You couldn't take your eyes off him the day of Arthur's party. Of course he's pretty enough in a surfer-boy way."

"He was half-naked when I arrived."

"Chloe," said Miriam, "go play with your mermaid. You left her in the kitchen."

The little girl went bounding away.

"Forget Edward. He's been trouble from the word go."

"Edward didn't put the dog on Arthur's doorstep," I said.

"And Edward didn't make the late-night calls Arthur kept getting. And he didn't kill Ian, that maniac did. But all of this trouble began once he showed up. And he's with those fascists now, helping them disseminate hate." She used the worst cliché possible: "Let sleeping dogs lie, Mark."

Then Chloe came running from the kitchen, holding her mermaid's broken arm. Even the Krazy Glue hadn't held.

Chapter Twenty

The next day, the Christian Soldiers' office was closed. The dotted Swiss curtains and posters of the Holy Land were gone. The building was full of Soldiers in Army fatigues, hammering, sawing plywood, measuring bolts of fabric. Indeed they were expanding, just as Alicia, the receptionist, promised. "My boss is a Jewish carpenter," the new sticker on the front door proclaimed.

The guard from the Provincetown police was across the street, buying a slice of pizza at Spiritus. The police, apparently, thought the threat to the fundamentalists was diminishing, thought the violence this year, Ian's murder, the museum stabbings, were the work of a man on the fringe of the movement, a loner scorned by mainstream Christian Soldiers. The Christian Soldiers would linger to save face, then close up shop and skulk away. But if that were true, then why were they expanding?

Inside the shop, I said, to no one in particular, "I bought this chain but it broke right away..."

"We'll take the broken chain, then send you a new chain in the mail," someone said. I turned to confront the Soldier I'd seen in the storage room with Edward. He was frowning, lugging a piece of Formica. "We have your name and address, don't we?"

"Of course," I lied. "I gave it to...Paul."

"Paul is a little scatterbrained," the Soldier said. "He mixed up the order on those chains, he chose the wrong manufacturer."

Did he suspect Edward knew me? For the first time, I worried that my presence could endanger Edward.

"You have to make allowances. Paul came to us from difficult circumstances. Very difficult circumstances."

Was that a dig at Arthur, at me, at Edward's gay past? Or was he referencing something earlier? I wanted to ask so many questions. Since Edward was absent, I wanted to interrogate the Soldier about who—or what—was this Golden One.

"We'll be opening again next week." A boyish enthusiasm crept into the Soldier's manner as he began boasting about their new technology. "We've bought brand new computers and all the latest software. We'll do all our ordering online and buy from American manufacturers." He added, "Paul is being transferred," while gauging my reaction. A wide smile animated his features and vanished as quickly as it had begun.

◇◇◇

The Soldier wasn't the only one whose mood was changeable. Roberto abruptly entered a blue funk. He'd been manically planning our show, sharpening his mime skills. But now his mood was low as the tide. We were strolling through the muck flanking Provincetown Harbor. That's when he mentioned the reason for his mood, a telephone call from Dr. Schreiber.

We'd walked from the White Gull to beyond MacMillan Wharf. There, on the beach, an actual shipwreck was resting on the sand, a rusting fishing boat smelling of tar and fuel. It was not the least bit like the sunken pirate vessels of my fantasies, thick with sea fans and coral, doubloons and ingots and pirates' bones spilling from their broken bulwarks. No, this was hazardous waste. Some lawsuit was stopping the town from removing it.

Roberto kicked a coil of rope from the boat. "For an atheist, my father is very religious. He was dead set against me having a Bris, being circumcised, and my mother forced him, almost at gunpoint, to have me Bar Mitzvahed. Science is his theology, but he's the most homophobic person I've ever encountered. He keeps talking about laws, not God's laws, but the laws of science. How can he take my 'lifesyle' seriously when I belittle it onstage in my comedy? How rational is that?"

He climbed barefoot onto the deck of the little boat, all sharp, rusting edges, a case of tetanus waiting to happen. A Keep Off sign was posted on the bow. Fuel from the ruptured tank was staining the sand opalescent, blackening some nearby scallop shells.

"Be careful."

"He promised to come to our opening night, then reneged. He says he'd forgotten about some conference at MIT, but that's bullshit. I checked my calendar—it doesn't conflict with our show. And I double-checked with MIT, just to be sure."

He jumped from the boat, splattering my shins with sludge. "Quick whiz," he said suddenly, and, stepping closer to the wreck, unzipped his shorts, stroked his penis as if to reassure it, then guided an insistent stream splattering against the hull. The sight of his peeing, this masculine yet vulnerable gesture, released a vast tenderness within me, so, when he was done, I encircled his waist with my arms and hugged him, and he smelled of the Drakka Noir he wore when he was testy.

We were heading back, passing the carcass of a skate, its vertebrae pushing up through its flesh like the frame through the skin of a ruined kite, when he gave me more news. "Tim is coming back. I, umm, didn't want to tell you until it was definite."

The other houseboy, whose futon I'd used, until Roberto invited me into his bed. Did he regret that invitation? Was he finding living and working together claustrophobic?

He said, "Sorry," and I wasn't sure he meant it.

The sand was winking with the burrows of submerged clams. Roberto picked up a pebble and sent it skimming along the ground in a happy, boyish gesture. Having told me this news, he seemed better already.

Tim returned, but only to collect his things, before resigning to take a job in Rehoboth Beach. That same day, we learned that the museum assailant was buried in the anonymous earth of a potter's field. And I felt something else being buried too: the affection and trust I'd been building with Roberto, the bond that would allow me to confide in him about Ian, about our sex in the dunes and my finding Ian's body. And that Ian was my long lost brother—if he was.

Chapter Twenty-one

But I still had the stage, that little shelf of plywood at the club. There was magic there; it was thrilling, the risk of trying each new line, casting it off like a fisherman's lure to see if an audience would bite; then the burst of laughter like a marlin breaking up out of a once-calm sea. You knew that that moment was yours, yours alone. Yours in its utter and temporary perfection.

And hadn't I always been *acting*, hadn't I literally rehearsed for this career long before I'd joined that troupe? I was realizing now I'd never believed my mother's tall tale about the Navy man and his phantom destroyer. Her imagination worked best with paint and song; the spoken word just wasn't her medium. She was a charming but ludicrous liar, no better at being truthful than staying sober. Those years of trying to verify her fictions were just my part of her script. But that was over.

People packed Quahog the night of our new show. The lead act, a lesbian comic built like a bowling pin and rumored to be a major diva, was graciousness itself to us. She was a shy Smith graduate whose passions were raw cookie dough and her paperback of poems by Emily Dickinson. "Did you know that Emily Dickinson was what we'd call a 'big, beautiful woman'?" she asked us. "In her later years, I mean. There's a dress they keep under wraps at her house in Amherst, and, let me tell you, Emily did some *serious* eating."

We were opening for her, and although the audience was ninety percent female, their response to us was fantastic. Standing on a stage, you can feel a room change as you win the crowd over, subtly at first, like barometric pressure, then the energy swells to a thunderclap.

We saw a few familiar faces in the murk, some Boston actors and Roberto's college stage combat instructor, but not his father, not Dr. Schreiber. Roberto waited until the end of our act to complain backstage. "It's his loss. He's missing a fabulous night. He'd travel ten thousand fucking miles if I were a lunar eclipse."

Roger Morton seemed elated. "You're on your way, you're on your way," he kept repeating during our brief intermission.

As our headliner was packing the next morning, she asked, "Do you guys have an agent?"

"We wish," I said.

"Well, mine isn't taking new clients." She licked cookie dough from her fingers. "But there was one there last night, asking a lot of questions, a tall guy with a ponytail. He said he'd give Roger his card." She pointed a sticky finger toward me. "He wanted to know all about you. He kept his eye on you all night, so he said."

We'd neglected to network after the show; we'd been too busy greeting friends from the audience. Roger Morton had slipped out of Quahog after the last curtain call, and was sleeping late this morning. When he came yawning onto the porch in a Hawaiian shirt, all catamarans and volcanoes, he was beaming. "How are the stars?"

But the headliner's story baffled him, he claimed. No "agent" had been circulating, asking about us. Sometimes our famous colleague overindulged in diet pills, although she'd seemed reasonably coherent last night. Anyway, no one "professional" had approached him about our act, except one writer from a bar rag in Boston, and *she* didn't have a ponytail, just a padlock in one ear, and no one had given him a business card, certainly no agent wanting clients.

By the time we'd spoken with Roger, our headliner was flying to a show in Montreal, so we were unable to question her further. She could have fabricated her agent story to boost our morale, or Roger could have been fending off agents to keep booking us at his stingy rate.

"He kept his eye on you." She hadn't said this "agent" thought I was funny, and there was a suggestion of surveillance in the compliment. And, to be truthful, even when I was at my best, it was odd for anyone to single me out for praise when Roberto was so obviously The Star.

My uneasiness increased when I stopped by my apartment to pick up my mail. Eleven calls were blinking from my answering machine, all hang-ups. Were these calls from the "agent" who'd kept his eye on me, or from Edward, to elaborate about his warning? Could they be from Ian's killer, who'd seen me find his body? Could he—or she or they—have hidden from view? No, that was unlikely; there was no place to hide on the breakwater, and the moon had been generous with its light.

Trying to stay calm was like willing my pulse to go down. I kept on down this road. The killer could have been waiting on the shore road: there were trees and cars and buildings to hide behind, shadows to absorb a silhouette. Whoever was responsible for Ian's death could've seen me walk from the breakwater to the parking lot, then followed my car to this apartment.

It was time to dispose of that awful towel, the physical evidence that linked me to the crime. I would burn it in the woods, then scatter the ashes. Of course burning was illegal during this record-setting drought, but destroying evidence was against the law too.

I found some wooden kitchen matches that came with the apartment, then went to get the towel. I'd moved it a couple of times. I'd last stashed it under the bureau in the bedroom, among some dust, paperclips, and a roach motel. I'd left this litter from a previous tenant because it made the towel's presence look innocent, haphazard. All of this was hidden by the bureau's decorative panel, a cheap maple filigree hanging almost flush with the floor.

I reached under the bureau, but felt nothing. I stretched out my arm, but felt no dust, no paperclips, no towel...Desperate, I crawled closer to the bureau, patting the floorboards beneath it and praying, then swearing.

Standing up, I shoved the bureau aside so roughly it almost toppled. The space beneath it, once so filthy, was bare. My towel and the previous tenant's refuse were gone. "Damnit!" I screamed.

I tried to convince myself that the landlord had cleaned…But he never did that, he had no right, no business throwing anything of mine away. Then I thought of the police, of Almeida and his ghoulish detective on my apartment porch, questioning me, watching me sweat. But the police would need a warrant, they'd have called and left a message—wouldn't they?

Glancing around the apartment, I was sure, now, that things had been moved, just slightly, an inch here, an inch there: the brass floor lamp, the iron bed, the sofa with ratty upholstery. Everything had been handled and examined.

I ran downstairs to the leather shop owned by my landlord. The fragrance of fresh hide overcame the chemical cold of the air-conditioning. I asked the clerk, verifying a credit card, whether Michael, my landlord, had been in my apartment. "No way, man. Michael's in Palm Springs, visiting his mom. Like it isn't hot enough around here."

"Someone's been in my room!" I all but yelled. I was losing it. Amid the rawhide and tourists, I was losing it.

"Did they rip you off? Is anything missing?"

A woman was modeling a fringe jacket for her husband. "You look just like Annie Oakley," he told her.

I elbowed them aside.

"Hey, call the police, man!" the clerk yelled in my wake. "You ought to call the police!"

Chapter Twenty-two

Someone was investigating my life. "Your silence will not protect you," the AIDS activists' bumper stickers say. Waiting for the authorities to act wouldn't either. I knew Thomas Royall was somehow associated with this summer's horror through the title of his painting, *The Golden One.* So I went to the Provincetown Public Library to do some research.

The Provincetown Public Library reminded me of an old-fashioned house. Despite the fluorescent lighting and linoleum floors, it still seems domestic with its narrow wooden stairs and gingerbread flourishes. There's something homey and small-town about the staff there too: eager to help, grateful for your interest, glad you haven't stopped by just to use the rest rooms.

The one Royall biography had been published during the Fifties, when there'd been a brief flurry of interest surrounding the fortieth anniversary of his disappearance. The book's plastic cover crackled as I opened it. Some pieces of angel food cake, pressed flat like flowers in a Victorian's Bible, fell from one chapter, the contribution of the book's last, messy reader.

Some of the book's photographs duplicated what I'd seen in the museum: six year-old Royall in velvet breeches and curls; as a youth, arm-in-arm with Edward Carpenter; in robes, with gilded horns in his hair...There were some photographs of Gilbert Dyer, the model, the text claimed, for *The Fisher Boy* and *The Golden One.* In one photograph, Dyer was posed in the branches of a tree, all but naked amid the apple blossoms. The caption read, "Gilbert Dyer: Unwholesome Adonis."

"Is this the only book on Royall you have?" I asked the librarian.

"Where did you find that? You know, I've been looking for that all morning."

"It was on the shelf, in the art section. I was browsing."

"Misfiled." She was wearing a small ceramic pin, a cartoon stereotype of the spinster librarian: hair in bun, Ben Franklin glasses. "There are some people in Truro who've asked us to hold this book for them. There's been so much interest in Royall since that horrible stabbing at the museum."

"Oh, I always appreciated his work." I must have spoken too loud because a man who was all belly, like a clam, put down his *USA Today* and hissed, "Sssssh!"

"You may read this book here," the librarian said, "but I'm sorry, I can't let you borrow it."

I couldn't even skim its entire 375 pages, so I chose the last chapters, about the collapse of the Cape Cod colony and the events preceding Royall's disappearance.

"Chapter 22: The Pamet Colony—Prelude to Disaster

"*Thomas Edgar Royall had been attracted to the lower Cape by the light and ambiance of Provincetown. How he loved the little hamlet, its fishing shacks and dunes, its churches and shops selling nautical gear. He loved the old salts and their wives and families. He loved the actors and playwrights and poets and labor activists: those refugees from the Greenwich Village heat who gave the town a bohemian flair.*

"*He loved to paint his adoptive home: ships, steeples, masses of lilacs in May rain. The sensuousness of Provincetown enthralled him: the Portuguese boys, dusky as Samoans, diving for pennies tossed by passengers from the ferries; the muscles of young fisherman; the fish, bright as swords, being shoveled from boats onto the piers. Royall painted it all, in his unique style that seemed somehow to trap sunlight onto canvas.*

"But Royall dreamt of something more, more than a way of painting: a way of life. He longed for a community, a community of artists, with all of its possibilities of peace yet cross-fertilization. And this new colony would benefit from the mistakes, from the bickering and bitterness of his previous efforts elsewhere.

"He had always been intrigued by the sagas of the Vikings, by the possibility that those strong blond pagans had reached his beloved New England centuries prior to the Genoese captain dropping anchor at San Salvador. He was enthralled by the old tower in Newport that some said was Norse and others, a colonial mill. When he heard of the rune stone by the pond near the Pamet, his pulse quickened and he hired a car to see it for himself.

"Royall was bewitched. The gray granite boulder with its mysterious markings, zigzags that might have been dug by Leif Ericson, spoke to his very soul. Its surroundings—the woods of birch and pitch pine and oak, the salt marsh, the kettle pond, the Bay side beach with its shell middens left by ancient Indians—called him to his New Home.

"Here, he was convinced, he could build his community of men, his home for artists, in this place that was somehow sacred. How wrong, how tragically wrong, he was."

I glanced up. The librarian was circulating around the room, neatening the shelves of books, pushing some that patrons had disturbed back flush with their neighbors. I skipped ahead in the biography.

"...By the spring of 1911, the little colony was ready. Both the Cox farmhouse and the old Robbins mansion had been refurbished, and Royall had completed many buildings of his own—Quincy granite "sleeping halls" with rows of beds (a bit like dormitories in orphanages!), saunas, barns, and an eating hall with a dais for Royall. Royall was adamantly against men of his colony owning personal property, except, of course, their art. While their studios, situated throughout *the woodland and marsh, were private—with ateliers, kilns, looms, and so forth—their lives were to be shared.*

"They would sleep, eat, and bathe together. In this way, solitude was reserved for creativity, yet the isolation of the artist, suffering in his garret, alone at his table at the cafe, penniless, misunderstood, all this was banished. The electricity of intercourse, the healthy outdoor communal life Royall so admired in the German Wandervogel movement (those troops of sunny Bavarians with their walking sticks and lederhosen, trekking through the Alps and Black Forest, singing songs, swimming in cold streams, living on honey and peasant breads) could be brought to Truro..."

I stopped. Of course. The Pamet was a river that flowed through *Truro*. There was a sign referring to it on Route 6: "Pamet Roads." I'd always sped past it, eagerly gunning for P-town. Royall's colony had been right next door, one town away, not in Brewster or Barnstable, as I'd imagined. I resumed reading.

"...The men slept nude, like people during the Middle Ages, and bathed in the pond first thing in the morning, from May through October. Before breakfast, year-round, the men did calisthenics, naked, outside in the sun. They worked with barbells and weights to strengthen the bodies that Royall considered Temples of the Soul..."

"Sir?"

I looked up. The librarian was acting chagrined. "I'm sorry, but the girl who put that book on reserve just phoned and she's coming right over."

"I was just getting to the good part."

"Yes, and everything on Royall has been checked out, for weeks at a time. And with these budget cuts, we can't buy—"

"Has it been checked out since before the museum stabbings?" I asked.

She leafed through the book, discovered more fossilized pieces of angel cake, and picked them out. "Now that you mention it, yes, I believe it has. Of course, the exhibit, the retrospective, was bound to generate interest."

The big-bellied man had abandoned the *USA Today*, so I read the headlines from around the country. The heat wave persisted. There was a water crisis in New York, what with children opening hydrants to cool off in their spray. Four people had died of heatstroke in their sweltering Newark tenement. A forest fire was scorching the Adirondacks, the sort you associate with Idaho or California; towns were being evacuated and three firefighters had been killed when a sort of flaming tornado had torn through a valley north of Rhinebeck. Ants and hornets were swarming, doing courting dances out of season. Even sea creatures were being affected. Several dolphins had beached themselves in Hyannis. "They're mad with the heat," one biologist believed.

Then I heard her at the counter. "Do you have the Royall book we put on reserve?"

She was a girl, a teenager, skinny in a long calico dress. Her frizzy blond hair fell below her shoulders. She wore rings on every finger, on both thumbs, even on her toes. She was barefoot and her feet were filthy.

"I'll bet it's hot out there," the librarian said.

The girl nodded.

"Have you seen the Royall exhibit? Or have your parents?"

The girl giggled as the librarian checked out the book.

As I passed her, I could smell her, a smell of patchouli fighting the odor of unwashed flesh. Without a thank-you, she seized the book from the librarian with the quick, practiced gesture of a purse snatcher.

Chapter Twenty-three

Truro Center was a lie. The road sign on Route 6 fooled you into expecting something like Welfleet: chaste white houses, a church with a white spire and gilt cod weathervane. But Truro Center that summer consisted of a strip mall with a gift shop, a grocery store, and an office where you could buy stickers for beach parking. There was a town hall and a post office, each the size of a prefabricated woodshed. There was little else. It was not a place to linger or converse.

"The old Royall community? Where the painter lived?" I asked. People shook their heads, then ducked back into their station wagons. From the library book, I'd memorized a few landmarks in the vicinity of Royall's colony, now, seemingly lost as old Roanoke and Virginia Dare.

Everything abutted the Pamet River, so that was of little help, but the author cited Old Barn Road and Deep Pond. Consulting my battered book of maps of Massachusetts towns, I could not locate Old Barn Road, but saw Deep Pond toward the Massachusetts Bay side of Truro, which agreed with Royall's biography alluding to ancient shell middens on his land. I was determined to find Royall's lost community because I felt it was no coincidence that Edward's warning and Royall's painting both alluded to a Golden One. It was no coincidence that the museum assailant went berserk in the Royall exhibit, near that painting. I believed that Edward's warning and Royall's colony and Ian's murder—all the perverse events plaguing the summer—were somehow related, tangled together like cat briar.

Truro, unlike Provincetown, is very wooded and spread out. Forests of oak and pine and birch suddenly break open to reveal a marsh fanning out toward the horizon, the greenest grass imaginable cut by a shallow meandering river. But in all this expanse, the buildings are few, and there's nothing as urban as Commercial Street. A good number of the buildings in Truro are old, many farmhouses built before the Revolution, with broad chimneys and small-paned windows, glass being precious back then. There is less Victorian whimsy than in Provincetown, and that's appropriate because Truro has always been more conservative than Provincetown, very straight, full of journalists from New York and Harvard professors and an occasional famous novelist or photographer. It's the sort of place where you can drive for a mile and not see a house, just rolling hills and trees, then you'll notice a small stand selling fresh fruit or vegetables, a place where they weigh your produce on a creaky old scale and pack it in brown paper bags.

I stopped at just such a stand to ask directions. I should've bought a little something, but the drought had diminished the supply of native produce, and what was available had a stunted, dulled look. "I'm looking for Old Barn Road," I began.

An old man whose skin was leathery and cured-looking from many profound sunburns, wearing a flannel shirt in all this heat, went back to reading the local paper. "There's no Old Barn Road, not that's public."

"Well, do you know where Deep Pond is?"

"That's private too." He shooed away a bee cruising a carton of berries. "Can't help you. Better move along."

Using my mime skills, I pretended to be interested in some peppers that were sunken like the hollows of the old man's face.

"Better move along," he said, sharper. "Just move along."

The staff at the Christian Soldiers' office had been friendlier, and I had a Massachusetts license plate: I wasn't some Yankees fan from Westchester.

I kept driving, down the winding roads with generous soft shoulders that sent clouds of dust and grit to coat the foliage at their sides. Some of the road signs were missing, leaving just metal poles, and all of the landscape looked alike, the trees, the undergrowth vivid with poison ivy. There was virtually no traffic, no one else to ask for directions, but, eventually, if I kept driving. I figured I'd reach Massachusetts Bay, stumble upon a beach and there would be people there, families swimming or at least parking lot attendants.

Eventually, the asphalt gave way to dirt. The car buckled as it hit potholes and gullies washed by rain. As the road narrowed, bushes groped the sides of the car like brushes in a car wash.

Suddenly, a stout woman was in front of my car. "This is private property," she said.

"I'm lost."

"Back out until you hit the tar, then turn around by the white post."

"I'm looking for Deep Pond—"

"Back up."

"I'm interested in the old Royall place—"

"This is private property." The woman was local, not summering gentry. You could tell by her accent and her apron, stitched with Dutch windmills, and by her blunt hands, toughened by hoeing and weeding.

"I'm visiting from Boston."

"Are you looking for relatives?"

"I'm just curious—"

"Then go back to Boston."

Obeying, I backed the car out as she watched me like my driving instructor. I had nothing to offend the locals on my car, no rainbow decals or "Hatred Is Not A Family Value" bumper stickers. So why were the people of Truro so hostile? Did Royall still have a bad reputation, eighty years after his death?

Some locals get sick of the summer people, but not this early in the season. In Provincetown they call this attitude Augustitis, and it usually hits year-rounders three weeks or so before Labor

Day, when the crowds, the jostling, the bumper-to-bumper traffic inching along Commercial Street slower than lichens growing on old tombstones makes residents overtly territorial. But this was late-July and that man selling vegetables owed his living to summer people, or part of it.

Back on the asphalt, I found myself at a fork in the road. I had three choices, according to a white post with signs every which way, like a weathervane: Corn Hollow Road, Standish Street, and Deep Road.

I opted for the last. It didn't say Deep Pond, but, a few hundred yards further, I found a sign reading Pond Road.

Again, the landscape was a Xerox of other bits of Truro: woods, dry in this blazing heat, full of briars and the rustling of chipmunks and squirrels in the incendiary detritus. Again, the tar gave way to dirt and my car swooped down into bowls and ruts then slowly climbed out, scraping its bottom and making me anxious about my muffler.

Then it rose from the greenery, blocking the road—a chain-link fence bright as the edge of a new knife. It was of very fine mesh, like medieval chain mail, difficult to climb because you couldn't get a foothold, and crowned with spirals of razor-like wire like so much vicious tumbleweed. The gate in the fence was locked, and burdened with enough chains to defeat Houdini.

I jumped when something pounded my car. Where had the sound come from? Not from under my car, from behind it! I stamped on the brake and turned my head around to look.

A young girl—skinny and blond, in a long dress like a hippie or a pioneer matron—glared at me. She rapped on my trunk with her hand.

"Excuse me?" I yelled, in a combination of anger and bewilderment, then I realized she couldn't hear me, with the windows shut tight and the air-conditioning blasting.

She rapped on the trunk with her knuckles. As I reached to switch off the air-conditioning, I leaned forward and accidentally let go of my foot on the brake, just a bit, so the car lunged ahead, and the girl, who must have been leaning on my bumper, lost her balance.

I cut the engine and tried to open the car door, but some bushes encroaching on the road kept me pinned in my seat. I couldn't get the door fully ajar, but I could hear the girl, swearing, cursing me, using every expletive in the English language permits.

"I'm sorry!"

"Bastard! You tried to run me over!"

"The car was moving forward, I'm sorry if I startled you!"

"Why are you here?"

"You shouldn't be leaning—"

"Why are you here?"

I wasn't trying to be witty, or ironic. There wasn't any motive behind what I said next. It just came out of my mouth, spontaneously: "I'm on a quest."

The anger left her expression. I realized then that I'd seen her before. She was the girl from the Provincetown Public Library, the one who'd borrowed the book about Thomas Royall. Or was she? It could be her, it could be her sister—or any of the young girls panhandling through Provincetown this year.

"Do you work with Jason?" she asked.

I almost said yes out of daring. I said, "I'm looking for Deep Pond," without answering her.

She acted as if she expected me to say some kind of password. I was tempted to try saying "the Golden One" because that's what struck me about her, there in the sunlight filtering through the forest—her flaxen hair, long as Rapunzel's. She was like a princess in a fairy tale, this girl from the woods.

She tugged at her hair. "Who are you?"

Something made me hold back. "I think I saw you at the library in Provincetown."

She moved toward my side of the car, by the bumper. Craning my neck, I could see that she was barefoot, like the girl in the library. She'd come out of those woods barefoot, through the poison ivy, through the briars. Her feet had to be tough with calluses. And there was something tough about her manner, in spite of her Little Match Girl thinness. I remembered the girl at the library, snatching the Royall biography, pickpocket-quick, from the librarian.

"I'm interested in a man called Thomas Royall."

"Go away!" The anger had returned to her voice.

"He was an artist in the early nineteen-hundreds. He built a community in this part of Truro."

"Are you a reporter?"

"I'm an actor." Although she was small, the intensity of her fury was threatening.

"Sigrid?" The man's voice came from the woods. "Sigrid? Who's there?"

"An actor," the girl answered. "From Provincetown." She'd noticed the beach parking sticker on my window.

From the woods, a man stepped into the road next to Sigrid. He was tall enough to qualify for the Boston Celtics, with a body any gym rat would envy. He'd shaved his head, but had a beard the color of burrs and antiquated clothing—pants and a shirt—that Royall's followers might have woven.

"Who are you?" This Giant's voice was soft.

The girl became angry again. "I tried to stop him, he tried to run me over."

"Be quiet," the Giant said, which seemed to devastate her. She put her hands over her mouth and her expression crumpled. It took me a few seconds to realize she was crying.

"I'm…in the arts…I'm interested in an artist named Thomas Royall. I'm looking for the site of his community, for the ruins."

"Runes?" the Giant asked.

"Thomas Royall's community."

"There's nothing to see."

I wanted to prolong the conversation, but the questions I longed to ask would be perceived as intrusive, and we were alone in these woods, and I was lost. "You're in danger," I remembered Edward warning me.

"There's nothing left," the Giant said. "This is private property."

Indeed. All of Truro was private property, at least today.

"Sorry to bother you. I'll be off."

When I turned my head back to face the steering wheel, three more girls—young, underweight, with light hair—had materialized in front of the car. Gaunt and as otherworldly as figures in a daguerreotype, they might have been sisters from a sod house in frontier Nebraska.

"I'm leaving." I shifted into reverse, and, in an instant, the girls and the Giant, like phantoms, like swamp gas, were gone.

Chapter Twenty-four

I'd noticed them before, they were everywhere in Provincetown: groups of thin, straggly-haired young people, like time-travelers from the Summer of Love, asking for spare change and playing dulcimers and tambourines under the chestnut tree by the public library, and on MacMillan Wharf as the ferry from Boston was docking.

I'd noticed them, but paid little attention. I was too concerned about the fundamentalists, the Christian Soldiers' holy war. "Have you seen all the street kids? There's so many this year," people would remark rhetorically, not expecting an answer, then go on to complain about the Bible-thumpers and the heat. "Lots of Scandinavians in town," I'd heard someone observe, noting that many of them were fair and some were beyond their back-packing years. "We're from Scandinavia," the street kids would say, with no accent to their English, and, if you questioned them further, they'd just laugh or ask for more money. Once, I'd thought they were connected with the *Vasa,* the Swedish tall ship—everyone had. But not any more.

Miriam mentioned more trouble at her shop. She'd caught two of them, boys this time, stealing amethyst beads. They'd just laughed when she'd forced them to empty their pockets, full of hashish, and, of all things, gum drops. They'd wrapped the beads in cellophane bags with the candy. "Can I keep them? They're my birthstone," one boy whined to Miriam when she'd confiscated the amethysts.

"Were they Scandinavians?" I'd asked. "Dumb ones." Miriam said they hadn't even known about Dala horses. Miriam sold them, carved wooden horses painted orange, with folk art flowers, imported from Sweden. One "Scandinavian" called them "carousel ponies," Miriam remembered. "That's like a Dutchman not knowing Rembrandt." Still, I kept my Truro trip secret, as secret as my alleged Drummond blood, secret from Miriam and everyone else.

I saw some blond teenagers on the beach back of the Boatslip, sitting in a circle, eating Milky Ways and cotton candy and sharing a bottle of tequila. Simultaneously, as unified as a school of fish, they turned to stare with dull suspicious eyes as I approached.

"How's it going?" I said.

They didn't so much as bother to shrug.

"This is the hottest July on record," I said.

I didn't recognize any of them. One boy drew a circle in the sand with a fish bone. A girl picked at her toenails. "Do you speak English?" I asked.

"We're from Scandinavia," said the boy sketching with the bone. His hair, like the girls' in the woods, was fair as flax. Suddenly he seized the bottle of tequila, offering me a sip and laughing "Skoal!"

I had thoughts of hepatitis, even, irrationally, of poison, so I laughed too. "I'm on the wagon." I edged away.

Within a minute, they were passing the liquor around again and divvying out pieces of pink cotton candy with eager, dirty fingers.

That night, while Roberto manned the desk and Roger Morton met with Arthur about the Swim for Scholars benefit, I slipped into the White Gull office to surf the Internet.

"Golden One," I typed and the computer screen flashed and regurgitated listings for jewelry stores, metallurgists' conventions, and Chinese restaurants. Not very promising. So I typed "cults" and the computer retrieved URLs of deprogramming groups and cult-monitoring organizations, plus stores selling relics of dead-at-a-young-age movie stars, no "Golden One" or anything to do with Truro or Thomas Royall. And typing "Royall" and "Truro" and "Cape Cod artists" yielded nothing of consequence. Just some websites of small galleries, none local, selling bad reproductions, mostly of *The Fisher Boy.*

◇◇◇

Then came the fundamentalists' Public Relations Spectacle, the next Sunday noon, appropriately. It began with fleets of busses and cars clogging the town's parking lots. They had southern license plates with peaches or palmettos, and from them streamed people of all ages, retirees in sunshades, young families, handsome men. They were casually dressed, but more formal than your typical tourists, in clothes so neat they might still be dangling in the dry cleaners' bags.

We were bound for brunch: Arthur, Miriam, Chloe, Roberto, and I. We had just celebrated "a service of community healing" at the Unitarian/Universalist meetinghouse.

"They can't all be heading to Spiritus," Arthur said. "I know they've done miracles with loaves and fishes, but I don't think pizza goes forth and multiplies."

"I'll bet they're heading for the Christian Soldiers' office," I said, remembering its location opposite the landmark pizzeria.

Some of the visitors were carrying Bibles, others, small vials of liquid. We joined them surging up Commercial Street until we reached our destination. "GRAND OPENING," read the sign in the office window. Pinned beneath the sign was an American flag on which fifty white crosses usurped the places of the states' stars.

Sunday mornings were usually quiet on Commercial Street, and there were no police here, or none that I noticed. I recognized an exuberant man in a suit the gray of duct tape, escorted by what had to be bodyguards. This was not Hollings Fair but one of his less frenzied colleagues, a positive-thinking sort of evangelist.

The crowd applauded as the evangelist accepted a microphone from one of the Christian Soldiers. "On this glorious day, in the footsteps of the Pilgrim fathers, we too come here to bring new life. We too come here to heal…"

"Didn't we just do this?" Miriam wondered.

Then Arthur gasped, but not at the preacher. "It's him, that shameless little parasite!"

Indeed, Edward was at the evangelist's side, wearing an electric-blue suit and a knitted fawn tie. His hair looked stiff, as if laden with old-fashioned brilliantine, so that he resembled a grammar school boy dressed up for his class photograph during the Depression.

"Oh, this is nauseating," Arthur whispered. "This is positively vile!"

A beaming Roberto was enjoying the damage to Edward's reputation. Edward himself didn't seem too comfortable. His electric-blue suit looked heavy, wool possibly, and, being small and unimportant, he was overshadowed by the evangelist, his bodyguards, and the Christian Soldiers. When I stared in his direction, his eyes found mine and he hung his head.

"Let us pray," the evangelist said, and hundreds of heads bowed, people shutting their eyes tightly.

Excusing myself from my companions, I threaded through the people praying aloud. I almost collided with one of the few African-American families from the busses and apologized.

A couple of buildings away from the Christian Soldiers' office, I slipped down an alley, a sandy space where some acanthus trees were growing, until I came onto the beach by Provincetown Harbor.

Trying to appear casual, the toughest acting assignment you can have, I walked back toward the rear entrance of the Christian Soldiers' office. Somehow, by luck or coincidence, I thought that eventually I might rendezvous with Edward there. I knew he knew something about Ian's murder; he'd run away the morning his body was found. Seeking Edward was risky, but I'd seen him at the office in the past.

The rear of the cedar-shingled building was flanked by a Dumpster and some bushes of beach roses, their milky pink petals scenting the air. I pulled at the screen door just as a walkie-talkie crackled behind me.

It was one of the bodyguards, huge and menacing, even with no emotion on his face. "The service is out front, sir."

"I know." I wished I had my alibi, my olive wood cross.

"This door is locked. I have to ask you to leave."

"What's happening next?"

"There's the prayer service, here on the beach."

"Oh, right." I said, "Thank you, sir," like a motorist thanking a cop for issuing a warning instead of a ticket.

I re-joined my companions just as Miriam whispered to Arthur, "Can you believe he said that?"

"Said what?" I asked.

"'Judge not lest ye be judged,'" Miriam said. She was almost disappointed, seeing an evangelist this equivocal, this mild. Certainty was their one enviable trait.

"We will now proceed in an orderly and respectful manner to the harbor," the evangelist announced. Like graduates rehearsed for commencement, the flock knew precisely where to go. Sergeant Almeida came muttering along. "They don't have a permit to do this." He spoke half to us and half to himself.

On the beach near MacMillan Wharf, the evangelist led his followers in prayer, then suggested that those who had brought "water from the River Jordan" sprinkle it over Provincetown Harbor in a gesture of closure and reconciliation. "God bless you all," the evangelist emphasized. "And may this blessed place be healed once again."

This apparently concluded the service because the crowd became secular instantaneously. Their quiet conformity broke open and people remarked what a scorcher it was and began snapping photographs of the fishing boats and Pilgrim monument. "Is Plymouth Rock far?" one of them was wondering. None of them stared at our little group. With Miriam and Chloe, we passed for some sort of nuclear family.

Since the stands flanking MacMillan Wharf were handy, they raided them for lobster and soft-serve ice cream. "I want some clams," a man with a string tie announced. "But I hope they take those bellies off them."

They were all around us, overwhelming us, the way we over-whelm the year-round residents every summer. I told my group I wanted to check my apartment, since it was so close by.

"You're not going to watch them send their clam bellies back?" Arthur asked. My companions would wait for me by the public telephones by MacMillan Wharf.

I felt a little afraid, unlocking my apartment. I was after my olive wood cross; I could use that as my excuse to again tour the Christian Soldiers' headquarters. Of course, all of the faithful from the busses wore laminated IDs with their photographs.

The heat made me a little stupid. I kept trying keys from the White Gull in my apartment door. Finally, I fitted the right key and the lock was pleased enough to let me enter.

The contents of the apartment, the things in the kitchen, the bedroom furniture, had not, as far as I could tell, been touched since my last visit.

I'd propped the olive wood cross on my pillow on my bed. I was picking it up when I heard him in the kitchen.

"I'm sorry about that," he said, in the doorway to my bed-room, in that awful electric-blue suit.

I should have been glad to see him, I'd been looking for him back of the Christian Soldiers' office, but something—him surprising me instead of the reverse, I guess—made me furious. "So, is it Edward or Paul you're going by this morning? What's your alias of the day?"

"They're...both real. My middle name is Paul," he said. "I never liked it," he added, almost eagerly. "There are lots of things about myself I don't like."

Since he knew the location of my apartment he could have been the one riffling through my things. But he couldn't have known about the towel, unless...

"Have you been here before? Did you break into this place, by any chance?"

"Of course not! I followed you here. You'd been staring me down. Obviously you wanted to talk. Mark, please. I can explain everything. Almost everything." Unknotting his tie, he sat wearily in one of the metal tube chairs at my kitchen table. "May I have something to drink? Not alcohol. Just juice or some Coke."

I remembered Arthur finding the white powder in his bathroom. "I don't have any cocaine. I don't do drugs."

"My God," he said, "you sound like one of those nutcase evangelists."

So he was ready to betray them too, so soon. Squirming out of his suit jacket, he caught his elbow in the lining and began snickering. He seemed to be snickering at me, and at everyone foolish enough to trust him. It was all a joke, a summer hustle: him startling me, Ian's murder, him pulling a fast one and ditching Arthur.

Then it happened—I hit him. To make him care, if caring was possible. I just walked across the room, across the kitchen, and hit him. I hit him harder than I'd intended, punched his shoulder so that the silvery lining of his suit jacket tore open.

Shielding his face with his hand, he began whimpering. "Please, oh, please!" he whispered as the whispers turned to sobs, first quiet then louder, and his face became the red of an awful sunburn. "Don't hurt me, Mark, please, I've been hurt enough!"

I yanked open the refrigerator. I had nothing to drink but a carton of cranberry juice, so old its spout was soft and dog-eared. I poured him a glass and slid it onto the table. He nodded a thank you and began gulping it down.

I was feeling ashamed. "I'm sorry, I got carried away."

He'd stopped crying.

"Who is the Golden One?" I asked, quietly.

"I can't tell you."

I pounded the table so that the salt and pepper shakers, ceramic pigs, leapt up. "Damnit! I want some answers! There's been a murder, there's been a stabbing, and some idiot has killed himself in jail! And you've got something to do with it all, haven't you?"

"NO!" he screamed in the ragged cry of a toddler. "I just spent some time with your stupid friend Arthur! Is that a crime? To make a lonesome old man a little happy?"

He began coughing, coughing into the glass of cranberry juice as he drank. Then he set the glass on the table and pulled something from his pocket and held it to his mouth. His inhaler, for his asthma—what Ian had mistaken for amyl nitrate at Arthur's party. On that we'd judged him too harshly.

I poured him more juice and his coughing subsided. Helping him out of his jacket, I realized I needed to be persistent but less abrasive in my questioning. Like Sergeant Almeida had been with me. "Why did you leave when you did? Why did you leave Arthur's the morning after Ian was murdered?

"Because the old goat kept copping a feel."

"Why can't you tell me about this Golden One? You warned me I was in danger, and I appreciate that. You warned me in your note at their office." I found that I was speaking almost tenderly to him, like a lover after sex in a shared bed.

He unbuttoned his shirt, so that I could see the sweat trickling down between his nipples, down his breastbone. He was wearing an olive wood cross on a chain, like the one he'd sold me earlier in their office.

"Do you know who killed Ian?" I asked gently.

"I dunno."

"Have you any idea why Ian was killed?"

"Got me."

"Ian had his moments of being a major-league asshole, but he meant a lot to me. We'd grown up together." Then I risked saying it, just to test it out: "We were like brothers."

He began gliding a salt shaker in circles around the table, pretending it was a racing car probably. He was a child-man, stunted somehow.

"There are people in the street, runaways, vagrants."

He kept gliding the salt shaker in circles around the Formica.

"They say they're from Scandinavia, but I think they're from some cult, some cult that's headquartered over in Truro."

He sighed.

"Do you know who killed Ian?" I asked a second time.

"Why would I?"

"Because you're hiding so fucking much!" I bellowed.

"That has nothing to do with Ian!" Edward yelled. Such a strong voice from such a small body. He put the inhaler back into his mouth, pumped it, then took it away. "Ian was a dangerous man."

"Why? Why do you say that?"

"Just look how he provoked a nice guy like you."

I ignored his sarcasm. "Why am I in danger? You said I was in danger."

"I shouldn't have said that. I feel faint. May I take a cold shower? A quick shower?"

"Of course." Granting him this small favor might cause him to cooperate, alter the tone of this encounter. After all, I had him alone, away from his keepers, and letting him shower might make up for my hitting him, for my bullying him and acting like...Ian.

He stripped off his shirt with the same practiced grace he'd used at Herring Cove. In a moment, he stood naked, carefully draping his shirt, pants, socks, and jacket over my kitchen chairs. Shedding his clothing seemed to bolster his confidence, just as it had at the beach.

Backing away from me into my bathroom, he smiled. "I'll only be a minute, I promise," he said, like a youth from Royall's turn-of-the-century libido.

I followed him into the bathroom. He was showering like a child, pirouetting slowly in the spray, then pausing to drink from the nozzle. He was like a Victorian slum child who'd never used plumbing. He was reacting with delight to the sensuous play of water streaming and glittering over his body.

My light cotton clothes were saturated with sweat. The spray from the shower—the curtain was bunched to one side—teased my own bare legs and arms. Edward finally saw me watching him, or let me know he'd seen me, and, lathering the bar of soap against his pubic hair, which was brownish not blond, I now noticed, he said, "Come on in, the water's fine."

I couldn't let him seduce me, but I'd have to play along to get him to talk. "Who hurt you?" I asked, recalling what he'd said in the kitchen. When he shifted, revealing his back, I half-expected the drama of welts or scars, but there was nothing but the perfection of his muscles, from his nape to his waist. I remembered his hitchhiking story, about the man raping him in the Province Lands.

He was getting an erection, this choirboy with the equipment of a satyr. My own loins were activating: he knew I was fighting the urge.

"I don't have much time." He stepped naked onto the fluffy little bath mat with the *Mayflower* worked in synthetic fibers. "On Wednesday nights, I'll be at their office. Soliciting contributions." He helped himself to my towels, patting himself dry. Since I'd rebuffed his advances, he was losing his erection; it had become an inconvenience.

"Have you seen that man who raped you?"

He didn't answer, just kept drying the soles of his feet.

"Your hair was blond before. You used to dye it. Now you're letting it grow brown again."

"Mark, you have to understand. I was raised…in a very rigid system. It's all I've ever known."

"So that's the attraction of these…Soldiers?"

"I went with them for my safety!" He sidled past me, cupping his genitals in my towel. In the kitchen, pulling up his pants (he wore no briefs), he repeated, "Ian was a dangerous man."

"So you're happy he's dead. It's only logical. You and this Golden One you spoke of."

He kept silent.

I switched tactics, became the good cop: "You're afraid. I can tell you're afraid, we all are. Look, perhaps I can help, but only if I know more."

Just then the rickety stairs outside my back door began to vibrate and Arthur called, "Mark? Mark? Are you okay?"

Arthur scowled at the sight of his former treasure. "Good God in heaven. I hope this little rendezvous wasn't planned."

"It wasn't," Edward said. "I saw Mark and followed him, after the rally. He let me use his shower. I'd had an asthma attack, I almost passed out." He kept bungling the knot of his tie. "Nothing happened between us, Arthur, honest."

"Let me guess—you swear it on a stack of Bibles," Arthur said.

"I've caused you a lot of trouble, and I apologize," Edward said. He'd put everything on again, even his suit jacket, ripped silver lining and all.

Arthur clamped his big hand around Edward's wrist. "You're a very troubled young man," he said.

"I know that," Edward whispered.

Arthur held his wrist for an instant, then released it. Edward retrieved his inhaler from the kitchen table, then made the swift, offended exit of the boy kept late after class.

Chapter Twenty-five

The flip side of Arthur's benevolence, his "shadow," as Miriam would say, was his love of gossip. He spread gossip the way day care centers spread colds: relentlessly, efficiently, and without conscious malice. So he waited all of twelve hours to tell Roberto about finding me with Edward.

I knew something was wrong. Roberto was redolent with Drakka Noir, simmering the entire afternoon, full of the menace of anger or creativity, as if ruminating about a skit in rehearsal. The Big Fight happened Tuesday, July 29th, at 11:19 in our room in the attic of the White Gull. Undressing, Roberto was silent, handsome and unapproachable, folding his briefs instead of slinging them over a chair. He kicked one of his joke shop toys, the walking dentures, across the floor.

Then a hornet began buzzing along the ceiling, buzzing as loud as hedge clippers, knocking against the rafters as it sought escape. The attic felt steaming. I was about to turn on our big electric fan.

"Kill the wasp first," Roberto commanded.

It was an intriguing slip of the tongue. "It's a hornet." I had seen its yellow markings.

He detonated: "I don't need a fucking Audubon lecture, just kill the godamn bug so I can sleep!"

"I" not "we."

I tugged the case from my pillow and began throwing it, always hitting the wood just beside the seemingly psychic insect.

"Your timing is as bad as onstage," Roberto snapped, snatching my pillow and pressing it against the hornet until the bug fell to the floor, sputtering like a downed power line. A smack of Roberto's Teva sandal killed it.

"Arthur told me everything. About finding you and Little Mr. Wonderful in his birthday suit. Is that why you kept the apartment? So you could plow little Edward on the side? Arthur says he's hung like a horse."

I told him the truth, how Edward had followed me there after noticing me listening to the evangelist. I told him about Edward's seductive shower, how I'd challenged him, hit him, demanded he tell me what he knew about Ian and all the catastrophes of the summer.

"This isn't working," Roberto said.

I felt nauseous, felt that heaviness at the back of my tongue.

"This living and working together, it isn't working." He lay down on the futon I'd used before we'd become lovers.

Why was I surprised? He'd been so calm the other week by Provincetown Harbor, telling me I'd have to leave because the other houseboy was returning. He'd been distancing himself emotionally more and more, spending his free time watching videotapes of *The Honeymooners* instead of swimming at Race Point with me. I thought of telling him all my secrets, about Ian being my brother, about the trauma of finding his body after our sex in the dunes, about my visit to Truro and meeting that giant and those spooky girls materializing from the woods.

But I didn't, I held back. Still, I needed the best acting of my career to say one word: "Fine."

Roberto telephoned his father, then got Roger Morton's permission to spend some time with his family at the house they were renting in Owl Island, Maine. It was true that his sister Elana was "recovering from surgery," but it was minor, orthodontic, not the emergency Roberto described. Now he was literally distancing himself, so I decided to do the same, to take on all Roberto's duties at the White Gull but to abandon our attic quarters, with its mattress full of memories. I'd sleep at my grungy apartment, haunted though it was by the theft of the bloody towel and the subtle shuffling of the furniture.

I was unable to visit Edward at the Christian Soldiers' office that Wednesday, unable even to phone him. On duty at the White Gull, I had no privacy, I was frantic without Roberto's help, quoting rates, taking reservations, moving guests' cars in the parking lot. I discovered that Roberto had let a number of ongoing chores slide, like cleaning the oven and fertilizing the plants and buying staples for the kitchen. I ran out of muffin mix and detergent for the wash. Roberto was spoiled, I decided, immature even for his younger age. And his immaturity wasn't confined to the guest house, it leached over onto the stage. He was always jealous of other actors' applause, critical of everyone, of my mime skills and rapport with the audience, even critical of my using an electric razor.

For an instant, I remembered his straight razor, and I pictured him on the breakwater, seizing Ian and opening his throat, so that Ian's reactionary voice was forever stilled. Silence Equals Death indeed. But that was spite, not logic.

My mother claims I have "People Issues." She'd cite the Lisa Incident, from work, as an example. "Just talk things out," she'd always say. "Don't write people off right off the bat." But when you've lived with rumors all your life, about your parentage and everything. I enjoyed advertising for five years, then a kind of rot set in. So, sometimes, during breaks, I'd sneak up onto the roof of our building and sit there on the gravel with just the pigeons and the skyline, and smoke a joint. There was a kid from the mailroom who'd do the same thing, and he became my dealer, more or less. We'd smoke afternoons, mostly Fridays when the weather was decent. Everything was fine until Lisa found out.

Socially she was my saboteur. Technically, she was my administrative assistant. "And not your personal slave," she'd be sure to add. She had a pug face and silver fingernails and a battalion of yarn animals thumb-tacked along the rim of her cubicle. She'd go on about her diet, trips to Aruba, and tickets to the Barry Manilow concert. She was the niece of a city counselor, a night student at law school, and a self-appointed guardian of virtue.

She was put out in the extreme if you asked her to do anything after three-thirty. "If you concentrated afternoons, you wouldn't give me all this last-minute work," she'd say, with a slight collapse of her shoulders. And this was long before I'd begun hitting the roof.

I know what turned her against me. It was about Reza, the Iranian intern. It was something that had happened on Halloween, when our whole office went to Sligo, the pub at Quincy Market. Lisa kept drinking her "yard-long" glass of Guinness and giving me the evil eye because, by coincidence, I was seated next to Reza, and he was actually enjoying himself, which was due more to his intake of Long Island iced tea than to anything related to me. And, by coincidence, we left Sligo simultaneously. Then something in the Middle East—a coup or a wedding—resulted in Reza leaving the office and America the following week, leaving Lisa convinced I had seduced or defiled Reza, transforming me into The Reason Her Man Got Away.

Then she found the "evidence" on the roof, some roaches or a few bits of grass; the mailroom kid was getting careless. Suddenly, the door to the roof was locked.

I heard Lisa had mentioned the dope to my manager, who became distant, circumspect, dropping hints about our excellent Employee Assistance Plan, the counseling they offered for stress…and substance abuse. Then came my scrap with our big software client—and I quit to do improv in P-town.

"People are fallible, darling," my mother had always said. "Colleagues, lovers, everybody. They're fallible. It's human nature."

Roberto was fallible. I kept playing and re-playing our quarrel in my mind. During my scant free time, I roamed Commercial Street, seeing the same jaded residents and trolleys of sun-weary tourists. Miriam was helping Arthur plan his Swim for Scholars benefit, so I sometimes took Chloe on my excursions.

She seemed shy at first, then became delighted to see me. She would express this delight by circling me in a brief dance of joy, then she'd tickle the crook of my elbow and giggle. She seemed terribly small in the summer throngs, a world of knees for her. Fearful of losing her, I clutched her hand with a protective ferocity that once made her howl. I had to adjust my speed, too. She took tiny steps and often stopped, fascinated by things on the ground: pennies, Popsicle sticks, glitter in the gutter, a Yorkshire terrier like a walking toupée.

We built a sandcastle on the beach near MacMillan Wharf. Some psychologists claim that boys build pointed things, subconsciously honoring the phallus, while young girls dig burrows, expressing the wombs swimming through their psyches. If so, Chloe defied these stereotypes by patting together a castle that bristled with battlements and towers. She decorated it with shells and pebbles and gull feathers, a skate egg sack serving as a flag. She was beaming, but desperate to show her handiwork to her mother, so I suggested we buy a disposable camera.

Luck was with us, the castle was safe upon our return. No bully had kicked it apart and the tide was just easing in. So Chloe posed next to her castle, joy radiating from her features.

To celebrate, we went for ice cream at the stand at MacMillan Wharf. "What flavor do you want?" I asked and she looked terribly somber, wide-eyed, with one wrinkle, a zigzag of concern, marking her forehead. "Would you like chocolate or vanilla or black raspberry?" Again, the wide eyes and worried forehead.

She stood there, in her purple sun dress and sandals of clear purple plastic, like grape candy. "They have bubblegum and pistachio and maple walnut and ginger." Gently, I removed her from the path of some French-Canadian tourists concentrating on their guidebook instead of watching where they were going. "I'd like piña colada," she finally decided, and the man serving us laughed.

"That was my ex-boyfriend's favorite flavor…I'll take a medium piña colada and a medium black raspberry cone."

We had just licked our ice cream to a manageable size when Chloe asked, "Can we go back?"

"Back where? Back home?"

"To make sure the sandcastle is safe."

So we returned to the beach and finished our cones there.

◇◇◇

I must have missed Roberto or missed the idea of having a boyfriend, the emotional convenience, because I became lonely enough to telephone my mother. She'd obviously been drinking, as she was only semi-coherent, talking about painting a mural across the back of the gatehouse, telling me to "forget everything" she'd said about Duncan Drummond while never denying that it was true.

Just for the hell of it, I asked her about *The Golden One.* Had she heard of such a painting or heard the phrase in any context? She focused enough to say no, then went back to describing the mural: "It'll be a jazz funeral, see, in New Orleans…"

◇◇◇

Then I saw him again, when returning from Miriam's after dropping off Chloe. I saw the African American who'd been at Ian's funeral—and on Commercial Street, the day of the museum stabbing. Dressed in a shirt with lime pinstripes, khaki pants with creases so sharp they could cut you, and woven-leather Mexican sandals, he was carrying a cardboard tray of clinking jars.

Of course. When I'd noticed him from the deck of the vegetarian restaurant, he'd ducked into a shop specializing in local products: I knew its name, but my mind had misfiled it. Pretending to tie my shoe, I paused to observe where he was going.

He had a jaunty, confident walk, almost a bounce, and his noble head was like a bronze cast from some lost culture from the Bight of Benin. He was used to being stared at, what with his dreadlocks and his beauty, so he probably hadn't noticed my fascination, here or at Ian's funeral.

He went into a shop on the right-hand side of the street, almost opposite the vegetarian restaurant. Scents of Being, yes, just like before.

I trailed him. I figured he might know something, and he'd seemed so out of place at Ian's funeral. Scents of Being wasn't air-conditioned. It was stocked with potpourri kept in the heavy glass jars I associated with Victorian stores selling horehound drops and molasses candy. The odors of the potpourri were at war with each other: lavender, then lilac, then something like mown hay. There were other fragrances too, of bath salts and oatmeal soap and wreathes woven from dried herbs.

Unfortunately, the shop was all but empty, so I couldn't casually spy on my quarry in the anonymity of a crowd. He was counting out jars of strawberry preserves for the small, dark woman at the cash register.

"That's all?" the woman said. "I thought you promised us *three* dozen. Jason, don't do this to me, please!"

Jason. I had heard that name before—in the woods in Truro, from that little girl. She'd asked me, "Do you work with Jason?"

He was extraordinarily handsome, his only flaw being a gap separating his two front teeth. On his wrist, he wore a gold watch with an onyx face.

When he'd finished his transaction, I approached him in the street outside the shop. "Excuse me," I said. His manner was Wall Street-whiz-meets-power-at-the-ashram. "What can I do you for?" he asked, rolling a perfect cigarette using paper and tobacco from a pouch from the pocket of his baggy trousers. He lit the cigarette with a gold lighter, and, when exhaling, let the smoke leak from the corner of his mouth as he talked.

I told him the most bold-faced series of lies imaginable, that I'd loved his preserves, like everyone else, and was considering starting a small business of my own, an artists' cooperative. There was so much mass-market junk here in Provincetown, it was discouraging; so little was really New England. I was making this up, sentence by sentence as I spoke, sure he was aware this was a ruse. To temper the lies, I spiced them with bits of the truth. "I've been in improv a while, I'm getting restless."

I convinced him, surprisingly easily, to have a drink at the Café Blasé. It was my idea to come here, but I was nervous about my choice because my apartment was just across the street. I didn't want him visiting me by surprise.

"So what brought you to Provincetown?" He added something none of my friends would think necessary: "Be honest now."

"I was at loose ends." Our improv group was having growing pains, we were moderately successful, earning $900 per gig, but that was divided by seven, and we were having trouble with varying levels of commitment; actors were missing rehearsals, skipping shows, being diverted by day jobs and backstage scraps.

"The usual *maya*."

"Excuse me?"

"Yearning for more, but getting less. Seeking the truth while living a lie."

We were sitting under an umbrella, drinking guava juice the pink of tropical sunsets. He dragged on his cigarette with such intensity that the tobacco emitted a few sparks, and then expelled it from one side of his mouth so that he grimaced. He smoked the same loose, fat cigarettes as the skinny girls I'd seen outside town hall after the meeting. "You seem like a lost soul." He smiled as though he'd just paid me a compliment.

I decided to wait, to let the silence force him to explain that comment, but he just rolled his cigarette between his long fingers with their blunt manicured nails. There was a solid torso beneath his shirt, the kind familiar with martial arts, and familiar with using them. Finally, he spoke. "When I come into town, I get checked out a lot, by men, women, and some in the category 'none of the above.' But that's about them, that's not about me." He asked, "Is your comedy troupe gay?"

You ought to know, I thought. You were at my last show, asking questions and pretending to be an agent. And you were at Ian's funeral, or the gathering at the house, Suki Weatherbee's husband was criticizing your blond hair.

"Yes, our troupe is gay."

The sun ricocheted off his gold watch. Was this the Golden One himself, the man Edward was warning me about? But what was a black man doing in a cult based on Norse folklore? If that's what these Truro people were. And if Jason was the link between Ian and the "Scandinavians," why did he—or they—want Ian dead?

I had last seen Jason the day of the museum stabbing. He had been walking to Scents of Being from the direction of the museum. Was it possible that Jason had met the filthy museum assailant and somehow instigated that attack? I couldn't ask him any of these questions, of course, but the arrogance of his manner called for some sort of challenge.

"Are you gay?"

"All of that has fallen away. The dichotomy of sexuality, the chase, that's all done."

It was typical of cults to speak in parables or jargon, in language difficult to challenge because it's so opaque.

I would play into his hands to gain his confidence. "You're right." I kept sipping the pink juice. "You're right about my searching. It's this quest…"

"You came to the end of the rainbow."

Another cut, I thought, the *Wizard of Oz* analogy. "I was desperate." I remembered staring out to sea as a child, with my mother, wishing my father would sail up in his destroyer. Not knowing the destroyer was Duncan Drummond.

"You're a talented comedian," he said, finishing his juice.

"So you have seen me perform."

"I can tell by this conversation."

Would he admit he'd been the man who'd been spying on me before? Who'd been posing as an agent at our show at Quahog? Had he been rummaging through my apartment too? Had he taken the towel with the stain that I'd worried was Ian's blood? I couldn't mention that, of course. That would place me at the crime scene, reveal the reason I was questioning him.

"Did you see our two-man show? Our standup show at Quahog?"

He shook his head.

"There was a man there in a ponytail, with blond hair. He said he was an agent, he asked the headliner about us." She hadn't described him as black, but she could have left that out so as not to seem racist; he wasn't "a black man," just a man. I mentioned our headliner's name.

"Never seen her. Never cared for her material, to be perfectly frank."

You're lying, I felt like saying. You were at the Drummonds' house and at our last show at Quahog.

He tried shaming me now. "Of course, we all look alike. Peas in a pod." He glanced at his watch, an onyx face with no numbers, just a diamond where the 12 belonged, an odd watch for a businessman with appointments, since, in a way, it was "timeless."

He consulted his watch again, not to learn the time but to convey that our meeting was over. I'd brought him here on the pretence of being interested in starting a small business, which he knew was a sham, yet, earlier he'd been the one interested in me, posing as an agent, questioning people at Quahog. And what was he doing at Ian's funeral?

"Attitude is everything, Mark, my man. Good luck with your business, whatever that might be." Taking my hand, he felt it before shaking it, exploring the bones in a gesture that was intimate yet not quite sexual.

I said, "I'd like to learn more." Which was perfectly true. "What you say interests me."

I slapped down the money to pay for both drinks.

"I'm celibate."

"That's fine with me." He thought this was a come-on. That was good.

"I have to come back in town tonight. Meet me at the store at seven-thirty."

Chapter Twenty-six

That night, at Scents of Being, I was frightened: could I carry out this offstage scene with Jason, pretending to be interested in his business? I browsed through the soaps because these were farthest from the cashier; I didn't want her to ask if she could help me. Some soaps were clear like blocks of honey, some cool as newly thrown clay pots, others cloudy and flecked with bits of herbs. I remembered a grisly association: the Nazis processing human flesh for use in soaps. I thought of Nazis with runes on their uniforms, and the runes on that stone that lured Royall to Truro.

I assumed the cashier, small, dark, jumpy as a sparrow, had a tenuous connection with Jason, a vendor/supplier relationship. She was busy counting small pins made from a South American nut with a white, hard texture which mimicked ivory. She told me, "We've had problems with shoplifters."

Could they possibly be the street people that had bothered Miriam, like that boy who had tried to steal from her shop? It didn't seem likely, if one of their own sold their products to Scents of Being. It was a brilliant choice for this cult to sell preserves, something associated with grandmothers lovingly sweating over stoves, associated with the wholesomeness of fruit and vines and earth.

"Believe it or not, I caught a couple of born-again Christians making off with a dolphin pin. Well, one of their kids, actually, about seven or eight. He'd slipped it under his belt. His father was furious." She began counting the pins out loud. "Thirty-one, thirty-two, thirty-three…We're missing two pins. I can't keep my eye on every customer."

The way Jason had kept his eye on me, during our show. "I'm waiting to see Jason." I figured it was safe to talk, since we were the only two people in the shop.

"Jason's such a character, so happy-go-lucky. I've got a wicked crush on him. Are…you guys dating?"

Happy-go-lucky hardly applied to the brusque man I'd met earlier. Despite his stance with me, Jason struck this woman as gay. "We're having a business meeting."

"Well, if you're hoping to find the secret to their great preserves, their recipes, forget it. He won't tell, I've asked him a million times." She held up one of the small carved animals, a dolphin. "Imagine stealing one of these. They're very reasonably priced. But that born-again father wouldn't buy one for his kid because he said it was pagan, a totem."

Making sure Jason wasn't in the vicinity, I asked, "Who makes these preserves? They're delicious." The preserves had cornucopias decorating their labels and were marketed under the name Olde Nature's Finest.

"Jason's people make them." The cashier knocked open a roll of quarters. "His people over in Truro."

Jason, lugging a large carton of preserves, then entered the shop and deposited the carton on the counter. "I've got two more cartons, then that's it for a while. We have to make more." Unsmiling, he acknowledged me with a flat, "You're here already?" He was late, it was seven forty-five.

"I told him it was useless to try coaxing any recipes out of you," the cashier said. Then, thank God, she validated my story. "He's a huge fan of your preserves."

"Can you give me a hand?" Jason asked me. "I threw my back out." So I trailed him outside to a battered maroon Mercedes, the insignia ripped from its hood.

"If you take the heavy one in the front seat, I'd be much obliged."

Fine, I wanted him to be much obliged, to gain his confidence. When I pulled the carton off the seat, I felt my vertebrae rebel. Most air-conditioners weighed less.

"Keep yourself in shape, do you?"

"I'm flattered that you noticed." I struggled not to gasp.

"It's my business to notice everything."

The preserves business, I thought sarcastically.

"Being an entrepreneur and all," Jason added.

The cashier at Scents of Being wrote a check, then tore it up. "Sorry, I forgot you prefer cash."

Outside, on Commercial Street, he said, "Let's go to my place."

"My car is down by the Café Blasé. I'll just follow you."

When he smiled, the gap between his teeth seemed to have widened. "Why two cars? It's a waste of energy. I'll be glad to give you a ride back."

Taking my car gave me a means of escape. But I couldn't appear panicky or suspicious. "Let me get my briefcase." I scurried to my car, in the precious parking space behind my apartment. In my blue canvas briefcase, I'd hidden a can of Mace I'd bought to spray at bashers and a more aggressive weapon, a thick, serrated steak knife from the White Gull's kitchen.

"My, my, my, aren't we the workaholic?" Jason nodded at the briefcase. He was nothing like Edward, so tongue-tied and mysterious. He talked while he drove, all spiritual generalities, about ego and "the light" and "the light's source." Every once in a while, he'd turn toward me and snap, "You've got to be cleansed, my good man, cleansed."

He was successful in business because his soul had been cleansed, he stressed. "Before you begin a business, you put your life in order. Before you begin a meal, you wash your hands. First things first."

Dusk was giving everything gray, soft edges, and the narrow woodsy roads of Truro offered few landmarks. Small street signs flashed by like spasms from a migraine headache. I quickly became lost.

A dry wind was blowing through the trees, upturning their foliage so that masses of leaves appeared silver. The air-conditioning in the ancient car was long gone, and it was sweltering because several of the electric windows were jammed shut. Keeping one hand on the wheel, Jason unbuttoned his shirt to let it unfurl. His stomach was ribbed, hard like sand at low tide. Was that beautiful body the last thing Ian had seen?

He turned left down a rutted, unmarked road. Was it the same road where I'd encountered the Giant and the blond girl, the girl who'd asked whether I worked with Jason? What on earth would I say if I encountered either of them tonight? They'd know my meeting Jason at Scents of Being was planned because they'd caught me prowling earlier on their property.

In the headlights, I could see that the oaks were old, their rough bark invaded by lichens and moss. We were descending a hill, slowly winding through a forest with the weedy odor of swamp water permeating everything, in spite of the drought. Were we approaching Royall's pond?

Then came the fence with that strange fine mesh, blocking the road but not Jason. He shifted the car into park, and then leapt from his seat to punch a code into a panel on one its posts. Then, from his pocket, he drew keys to appease the tangle of padlocks and chains. He punched another button and the gates slowly opened.

We drove a short distance, then a white house swam up out of the night, a white house busy with gingerbread, like heat lightning fracturing the dark. Jason cut the engine, and I found to my embarrassment that I was clutching my briefcase like a flotation cushion after an air crash at sea. He must have sensed my apprehension because he played a joke on me right then, using the happy-go-lucky side the cashier appreciated.

"Got to load the preserves back into the house," he said. So wanting to please, I said, "Sure," and he burst into laughter. "There are no more preserves in the car," he said, laughing. He pressed the long-defunct horn. "Honk, honk." He was laughing at me. Then, he snapped, "Let's go," like an order.

Would I dare to use the steak knife or even the Mace? Of course, if it saved me from ending up like Ian. "Is this where you live?" I followed him onto the porch of the white house. I thought, this must be the Robbins mansion mentioned in the Royall biography.

"No one lives here." He beckoned me inside.

The cold, the air-conditioning, bit my bare arms and legs, drying the sweat from them in seconds. We passed through an empty hallway with floorboards gleaming with polyurethane into what had once probably been considered the parlor. It too was virtually empty except for a couch of scratchy custard-colored wool and some cushions scattered over the floor. It seemed exactly like the archetypical ashram, the couch for the guru and the cushions for his adoring followers. What was odd, unexpected, was the fireplace—it was blazing. Flames were devouring birch logs like the ones crammed into the iron bucket by the hearth.

"A fire in all this heat?" Instantly I felt foolish because, here, inside, it was colder than in the Christian Soldiers' office. I might have been Robert Falcon Scott, freezing to death in the white immensity of the Antarctic.

"The fire is legal," Jason said, in reference to the ban. "It's not outdoor burning." He kept his shirt unbuttoned, while I was wishing I'd brought a sweater. "Are you going to let go of that briefcase?"

I was staring at the wall. Fixed to it above the mantle were two swords, crossed. They were thick, ponderous. I thought of Ian's wounds, and of the knife among the scripts in my briefcase.

"They're not as old as they look."

Their handles were stylized to resemble bearded warriors in helmets. Their dark iron blades were corrupted with rust.

"They were made in the general vicinity," Jason said.

By Royall's people, I was sure.

He sat on the couch and tossed me a cushion, meant for the floor. "What's in the briefcase? I take it you've brought something to show me. A business plan for this shop of yours?"

"There's nothing in it but jokes."

"Jokes?"

"Scripts, sketches. For our show."

"But not the script for your life. Not the script for your future." He was sitting on the couch, calm as the Buddha. He sat square in the center of the couch, so that it was plain that he wasn't expecting me to sit next to him, at his level. I settled on a cushion on the floor, at his feet like a dog or disciple. He nodded toward the briefcase. "Let me see."

I unzipped the briefcase and opened it wide to purposely reveal the can of Mace as I rummaged through the manila folders of material. If I showed him the Mace, he might think this was the only weapon I'd brought.

"You came armed." He had noticed the Mace.

"So did you." I indicated the swords above the mantel.

"Those aren't mine." Then he stretched out his hand and softly snapped his fingers. "Say something funny, make me laugh."

So much in comedy depends on delivery, tone, gestures. I'd written a sketch about manning the front desk at the White Gull. It was still rough, but enlivened with a few strong lines, so I passed this script to Jason. Solemnly, he scanned it, as if trying to see beyond its content, trying to psychoanalyze its author. Handing back the script, he laughed, like the low ricochet of a machine gun heard from a distance—hahahahaHA—nothing like the belly laugh he'd had teasing me about unloading more preserves. "Very amusing, very amusing. Now let's get down to business. You didn't come here to talk comedy." His tone was cold as the room. He was wringing his hands. Had he wrung a neck in his time?

I'd thought he'd give me another barrage of doctrine, like cult recruiters I'd encountered on Boston Common, with open faces but the rapid speech of telemarketers. I had only one card left to play, so I risked everything.

"I'm also interested in Thomas Royall." I said. I told him about seeing one of Royall's paintings as a child—careful not to mention any of their titles—and told him how this art had helped define my sexuality, forge a kind of personal connection to Royall. "I've been studying his life…"

"A worthy life to study."

He could be an admirer of Royall, I thought, so I put more enthusiasm into my voice. "Some critics found Royall kitschy, even embarrassing, but I admired his sense of the erotic, the way he could replicate sunlight on canvas."

"He got it wrong."

"The sun?"

"Everything."

I was intrigued by the concept of artists working together, I said, not like our comedy troupe with all our bickering, but like the Bloomsbury Group or dancers at Jacob's Pillow.

"He got it *wrong*." Jason shifted on the couch and grimaced, like he'd ripped a tendon on the soccer field. "He started out right, then got it wrong. He got it totally wrong, totally wrong!" He glanced at the damaged swords above the mantle, then at me, as if Royall's errors, whatever they were in his mind, were somehow partially my fault. Did it all boil down to homophobia?

Now he delivered the doctrine, vague ideas delivered in a clear voice: about *maya,* "reality posits," and "paradigm shifts." I couldn't visibly betray my discomfort, so I hid my hands behind my back and scratched at the cushion I sat on with my fingernails, taking all my uneasiness out on the fabric.

My knife is right here, I told myself, right under the scripts in my briefcase. Of course, he might know karate, might kick the knife out of my hand. And he could summon colleagues who would help him; all of the lights were on throughout the house when we first drove onto the grounds.

"Does anyone know who they are?" He was laughing now, really laughing. "Does anyone? Do you?"

Just to react, I laughed. Lots of actors can't laugh on cue, but I can.

"You're anesthetized, anesthetized!" He was shouting like a madman, then he stopped and his face relaxed into an easygoing smile.

So I did what I do when being recruited for cults on Boston Common. I smiled and nodded, the noncommittal nod of the psychiatrist hearing the visions of a schizophrenic, of the police officer hearing the confession of a killer. Just let me listen, tell me more. I tried to choreograph these thoughts into my body language. I brought my hands out from behind me to rest serenely on my knees.

He went on, with no mention of any Golden One. I couldn't keep focused on his abstract ravings, so I glanced around the room, observing a little more with each glance: books interspersed with the cushions on the floor, the same book actually, a paperback with a yellow cover and "Light" in its title. And, scattered among the cushions and paperbacks, cassette tapes and a Walkman or two.

Jason stopped his tirade and stared in my direction. "I'd appreciate it if you paid attention." What he said next indeed caught my interest. "This property has a sinister history."

I felt like asking: Because of you? Because of what you did this year?

He rose, crossed the room, then took one of the swords down from its pegs above the mantle. He ran his fingers along the rust dulling its blade. "Did you know there was a murder on this property?"

"When?" Adrenaline sluiced through my system.

"When Royall and his false Utopia were in full bloom." He held the sword between the tips of his fingers, as though it were a delicate thing, capable of being damaged by the oil from his palms.

"Who was killed?"

"I can't say."

"Royall disappeared. I thought the inquest concluded that he'd drowned himself. I know his body was never recovered." I was emboldened by his evasiveness. "A friend of mine was killed this summer…" I would say it, it was only two words, and I wasn't accusing Jason or his colleagues, not overtly. "…Ian Drummond."

"Dwell on the positive, Mark," Jason said. "Leave those matters to the authorities."

Aren't you all authorities here? I could have said. But it was time for me to compliment him about something. "Your preserves are so delicious. Do you grow the fruit here?"

"We grow a great deal here, fruit and corn and beans and herbs, using the most advanced technology available. We've also invested in aquaculture, raising flounder and oysters and clams. We've brought this place out of darkness. Once, it was unclean."

"Why was this place unclean?"

"Because Royall defiled it. He defiled a sacred place." Then worry confused his features as his beeper went off, and, cursing, he went scurrying from the room, without apology or explanation.

For a few moments, I sat still as though I were posing for my portrait, aware of the possibility of hidden cameras. This might have been planned, some sort of trick to get me to commit some infraction of their rules. But a paperback copy of the cult's book—*Purity of the Light*—was tempting me. It was on the floor, almost within arm's reach, half-hidden by a cushion, so perhaps Jason hadn't seen it. On its cover, a disembodied eye loomed above a pyramid, like the design on the back of one-dollar bills. Surely this was their Bible, the teachings of their leader, but no author was listed on the cover.

I dared to pick it up; after all, reverence and curiosity are compatible. No author was listed on its title page or spine. I thumbed through the chapters, "Renunciation of the Self," "The Shining Word," "Germination," and "Message from the Runes." Runes—yes! —the Giant in the woods had first thought I was interested in runes. Royall had been attracted to this land by the granite boulder in the photographs at the exhibit. Flat like an altar, it was inscribed with designs that some argued were Norse and others, pre-Columbian Native American or a hoax. Obviously, it held significance for both Royall *and* these people. I skimmed the next few pages, but it was abstract to the point of meaninglessness, leavened with apocalyptic threats about something called "the Fall."

Leafing through the book, I felt as self-conscious as actors in an improv skit going nowhere. So I mimed some distracting gestures with my papers, with my scripts, then I covered their book with a manila folder and tucked them both back into my briefcase. If caught stealing the book, I'd say I'd slipped it away by accident, or say I'd taken it on purpose because I wanted to learn more, that's why I'd come…

I could hear nothing of any activity happening elsewhere in the building because of the white noise, the hum the air-conditioners in the windows were generating. But I wondered why Jason and this building were so clean, scrubbed, and the children in the woods and in Provincetown were so dirty, and why had Jason volunteered information about a murder, even a murder committed so long in the past? Why bring up the subject of murder, if these people were responsible for killing Ian?

Fifteen, twenty minutes passed. I wanted to leave this refrigerated building. If I'd brought my own car, I'd have driven away. Through the window, I could see Jason's junky Mercedes parked in the long grass of the yard. If he'd left the keys in the ignition, I'd have stolen his car to escape. Of course, I hadn't seen whether the gate had shut behind us…This room felt suffocating, even though it was bright and large. I was standing by the mantel, hugging myself against the cold, examining the swords on the wall, deciding they were too fragile, too rusty, to have caused Ian's wounds…Then Jason barged in.

"We can go now." He made no further comment. Since I was thrilled to go, I just said, "Okay."

He hardly spoke the whole way back, but drove faster and faster, tailgating, passing on the right, using the breakdown lanes or soft shoulders of roads. All the while, I wondered whether I'd done anything to inspire his foul mood, been caught lifting the book by surveillance devices.

"I'm sorry you're having such a bad day," I finally muttered as he steered the car onto Bradford Street. "What?" he seemed surprised. "I'm fine, man."

Getting out at the MacMillan Wharf parking lot, I said, "Thanks for your advice."

He didn't answer. He cut the engine and fished through some road maps in the rear of the car. "Yes!" he exclaimed, yanking his discovery out from the maps—one of those seat covers composed of fat wooden beads that always remind me of an abacus.

He draped this cover over the driver's seat. "My fucking back, I've gotta get it X-rayed." Then, he drove carefully through the traffic, away, ignoring my feeble wave.

Then the backrest made me remember, remember Edward and his hitchhiking story, of the man in the van who'd blared classical music, who'd taken him to the Province Lands to rape him. That rapist had used one of those beaded seat covers. Was this a coincidence? Was Edward telling the truth?

In my apartment, I pressed the play button and a tinny rendition of Miriam's voice came quavering out of the speaker: "Mark, where are you? Please call me as soon as possible!" and "Mark, come quick, it's an emergency! The police are here!" then "Oh, God, please call me! Please come! Somebody's taken Chloe!"

Chapter Twenty-seven

Miriam was clutching a toy, a beige plastic horse. She wasn't sobbing, but her face was flushed and swollen with grief. Police crowded the living room, incongruous amid the art books and bowls of beads.

She hugged me with a hunger, desperation. She told me Arthur was in Easthampton, visiting an old friend from Yale. Concentrating on me, the one face that wasn't official, she related the horror of her day. She had been designing a special commission for a debutante from Houston. It was a kind of crown, a net, twisted wires of gold set with the girl's favorite stones, Australian fire opals. These Texans, not oil or cattle people, their money derived from laundromats, had bought a place on the Vineyard and the father loved Miriam's designs and commissioned this crown for his daughter's coming-out party, a huge bash featuring jungles of orchids and holograms by engineers from theme parks in Orlando. Miriam had been driving to Hyannis to pick up the opals from the father; they were expensive, so he was reluctant to ship them.

Gemma, a girl from the high school, was minding both Chloe and Miriam's shop while she went on this errand. Chloe was behind the counter with her favorite books and the mermaid doll Roberto had gotten at the fast-food place. Miriam began crying. "Chloe felt sorry for the mermaid because she'd broken her arm."

A customer at Miriam's shop who had been in the day before wanted a certain kaleidoscope with watery colors that reminded him of his favorite stained-glass windows at the Sainte-Chapelle in Paris. So he and Gemma had had to look through all the kaleidoscopes, while Chloe sat contented behind the counter. This could have been a major sale; these wood and brass kaleidoscopes were hand-made, some costing hundreds of dollars. So Gemma's attention was focused on the bright, fracturing scenery inside them.

"Someone ducked behind the counter and just took her," Miriam said.

"Or she could have wandered outside then been abducted in the street," one policeman added.

Gemma remembered no one asking for Miriam, no one checking to be sure she wasn't there at the shop.

Sergeant Almeida said to Miriam, "We really have to insist, Ms. Hilliard, *who* is the little girl's father?"

"Her name is Chloe." Like a child, Miriam ignored the question and wound the key in the plastic palomino's stomach. It played a version of "Happy Trails to You." "This pony was mine, when I was Chloe's age. You can still see my tooth marks in the plastic. Chloe bites her toys the same way." Deep, dry sobs interrupted Miriam's speech. "She is afraid of the dark. Chloe is afraid of the dark…"

"Mr. Winslow, can you please tell Ms. Hilliard how important it is that she cooperate fully with this investigation?" Almeida asked.

I felt like a hypocrite. "You've got to tell them everything, Miriam."

Almeida's tone was tart: "In most instances when children disappear, the root cause is trouble between their parents. How can you be sure Chloe isn't with her father? Who is Chloe's father?"

"I was desperate, I'd tried everything." Miriam put the plastic horse down on the coffee table, by a book about Cezanne and a dish of carob candy.

She'd been engaged long ago, just after graduating from Bryn Mawr. Her fiancé was a Philadelphia boy from an old Main Line family. They'd met during a teach-in at Penn, then joined the Peace Corps together. They were posted in different parts of Peru, she near Lima, he in a village in the Andes. "Brad Arkwright was his name." The warmth of memory softened Miriam's voice. "I called him Brad. My friends called him Mr. Right, and I guess he was."

Miriam became pregnant in Peru, on one of Brad's visits to Lima. "His uncle was in the state department. He smoothed my exit from the Peace Corps. I felt guilty about leaving those poor people I'd been helping, living in houses made from packing crates and cardboard—Lima's in the desert, it hardly ever rains—but Brad and his family insisted I take an apartment in Miraflores, somewhere clean, with no fleas, for the baby's sake. I moved when I was three months pregnant."

"We were going to be married when Brad came to Miraflores." There'd been trouble in his village, a land dispute, so they'd been forced to postpone their wedding, which was to be quick and intimate, just themselves and an Episcopal priest from the American colony.

Then, one winter night, Brad called from the Lima airport. He'd flown in from Cuzco, spur of the moment, giddy and eager, having notified the priest to perform the wedding the next morning. When Miriam drove to meet Brad at the airport, it was foggy; a grit-colored mist hung in the air. It was hazardous to pause, dangerous to stop, at red lights in certain districts of Lima: carjackers and thieves frequented some intersections. Miriam was driving fast.

"Brad was so happy. He was wearing this little clay charm a village elder had given him..." Her voice trailed away. "...To bless our wedding."

"It was...a police car, of all things. At this intersection that was usually empty. It hit us broadside, on the passenger side of my car. Brad was killed instantly. I lost the baby. Almost every bone in Brad's body was broken, but that little clay amulet was whole, on the cord around his neck." She was crying softly, in a kind of moan. "I sometimes wondered if that charm...was some kind of curse."

Miriam quickly composed herself. She'd had other relationships, but nothing special, nothing lasting. At forty, she'd begun placing ads for a known sperm donor in the alternative press. She attended meetings of Single Mothers by Choice.

When she was transitioning out of social work, taking a course at the Boston Center for Adult Education, jewelry-making, beginning to solder and set semi-precious stones, the start of the business that brought her to Provincetown, she met a man named Martin, just Martin. He was a claims adjuster at an insurance company in Copley Square.

Miriam said, "I was taking a terrible chance."

After one class, they went to a Spanish restaurant for tapas—"rabbit, quail, and baby eels, I can still remember"—and a pitcher of sangria. The restaurant's grille work and rough stucco walls reminded Miriam of Peru, and she kept remembering Brad and the accident. It had been her idea, choosing the place, but it had backfired.

"By dessert, I was a wreck, crying into my flan. Martin insisted on taking me home. What happened next was one-hundred percent my fault." She arranged the things on the coffee table, so that the book, the dish of candy, and the plastic horse didn't touch one another. "That was the last time I ever saw Martin. He dropped out of the class. Shortly afterward, I found out that I was pregnant."

Almeida said, "He never tried to contact you, this Martin?"

Miriam shook her head no.

Almeida said: "So he knew where you lived, he'd been to your apartment. Did you keep the same Boston address? Or did you move?"

"The same Cambridge address."

"So he could have contacted you, but he didn't."

"He just vanished. I checked with the people at the Center, but no Martin had ever officially registered for the course. He was just auditing it, apparently…illegally."

"He never knew that you'd had his child?"

"No," Miriam said, pleading for us to leave her alone.

◇◇◇

Police and volunteers searched for Chloe. The news broadcast footage of men, women, and children scouring the underbrush, of dogs with trained noses sniffing at moss and at the roots of the stunted pines. Without success. A pond was drained in Welfleet. Just that thought drained Miriam's strength, as if she were losing blood as the pond lost water. "But we can't think that way," she told me, husky with grief. "Chloe will be fine."

State parks and forests were thoroughly combed. Missing-person posters were distributed throughout the Northeast, so that Chloe smiled from telephone poles and supermarket bulletin boards, on screens on the Internet.

A devastated Arthur hurried back from Long Island. We both kept close to Miriam's side; Roger hired temporary extra help to manage things at the White Gull. Roberto, incredibly, stayed in Maine, without so much as a word of concern. I remembered his repairing Chloe's broken mermaid, his improvising a doll's hospital bed from scraps of old crochet. He had two sisters of his own, he ought to have had some compassion, some decency, even some curiosity, but kidnapping, I guessed, made poor comic material, so he wasn't too interested in Chloe's trauma. It wouldn't pull laughs onstage.

Miriam became, alternately, hysterical then serene, sure Chloe was injured or dead, then certain some form of contact—a request, a ransom note, an explanation—would come. Miriam's was a living hell where sleep and food were irrelevant. Overnight, exhaustion sharpened her features. She pulled out some old family albums, photographs from the Seventies, of Brad with his freckles and wooly sideburns: with the village mayor in the Andes, in a pen of llamas, swimming in Miriam's pool at Miraflores. The color of the pictures was already fading, making them prematurely antique. Miriam was in the photographs too, resembling a younger, more adventurous sister. "I wonder if Brad would give me a second look today," she said. "Why, I'm old enough now to be his mother." Then the word "mother" made her weep.

My own photographs were ready, of Chloe and her sand-castle by Provincetown Harbor. I kept remembering her small, hot hand, holding it as we walked to the beach. A panic kept washing over me, a sensation that the goodness, kindness, the stability of the world, had come undone, that chaos at best, evil at worst governed all things.

Her helplessness was what tortured me most. Her utter dependence on the kindness of her captors—who would be people without kindness, of course.

Any harm to Chloe overwhelmed the hideousness of Ian's death. I couldn't imagine this little girl—the indulged only child of a middle-aged mother—in captivity.

Miriam had no enemies that I knew of, had had no fights with employees at her shop, or within her circle of friends. Arthur was her closest relative, except for elderly aunts in Scottsdale and Grosse Pointe, whom she seldom saw.

Lying at night on Miriam's couch, I kept wondering where Chloe was at that very moment, in what frightening circumstances. Any fear I'd had this summer was dwarfed by hers. I thought too of Ian, in his grave with the granite sphinx, with the fumes from the fish plant wafting past the tombstones, and of the madman buried in a potter's field.

Why had any of this happened? What chain of sordid links bound all these events together? Now, more than ever, I was determined to find answers. Not just for myself but for Chloe, for Miriam.

Chapter Twenty-eight

I had to be more open with the police, about what I'd discovered. So, the day after the kidnapping, without mentioning it to Miriam, I stopped by the station to tell Sergeant Almeida that if Miriam didn't remember any possible enemies, I now did—the street children she'd caught stealing in her shop who lived on land once owned by Thomas Royall. That madman had gone berserk at the Royall exhibition…There had to be some connection to all of this.

Listening to me, Sergeant Almeida was as calm as though I were reporting a lost cat. "The commune is in Truro."

Was he introducing the idea of police jurisdiction? I couldn't believe it! "They're panhandling in Provincetown, smoking dope on our beach—"

"We're quite confident that Chloe Hilliard's disappearance is unrelated to the Truro community."

I remembered something from my visit with Jason that could prove him wrong: Jason's beeper sounding the very evening of Chloe's disappearance, while we were in that chill room with the fireplace and Royall's swords. Something had shaken Jason that night; someone had phoned him with news that transformed his manner from ashram hipster to very worried man. I almost told Almeida this, but stopped with an account of my first visit to Truro, my meeting with the Giant and the girls in the Truro woods. I didn't mention Jason at all, I couldn't divulge how far my investigation was going without revealing my motive for doing all this—my finding Ian's body and the suggestion that he was my brother.

Almeida scraped back his chair, signaling our discussion was done. "Mark, you're not a policeman. Even if you play one on the stage." He smiled at his joke, then, when I was halfway out of the room, he called, "Be careful. Don't get in over your head. Leave this investigation to professionals."

◇◇◇

No one was suggesting the fundamentalists were behind Chloe's disappearance. The third day Chloe was gone, they collected outside Miriam's house. Like carolers lost in the wrong season, they were singing hymns and holding candles protected by punched-out Dixie cups.

"They think they have a monopoly on issues about children," Miriam snapped. "They're not going to co-opt my little girl."

The singing seemed to grow louder. Arthur felt compelled to acknowledge them. "Perhaps that will drive them away," he hoped.

But when he returned from the porch, he was more agitated than before, and the singers had failed to disperse. "*He's* with them. That punk."

Edward, of course.

"See for yourself," Arthur told me.

Miriam stepped into her buffalo-hide sandals.

"Stay here, spare yourself," I told her.

I recognized a few of them: Alicia, the receptionist from their office, and the Soldier who'd ordered Edward around, angry he'd bought chains from a "foreign" manufacturer. Edward himself was singing at the back of the crowd, in the shadow of a dogwood, outside Miriam's fence. His candle, I noticed, had blown out.

On Miriam's porch, I became the de facto center of attention. I waited while their hymn spawned verse after verse. When they finally finished, I spoke words as hackneyed as any I'd ever heard, ending with, "Thank you for keeping Chloe in your hearts."

Then Arthur joined me. While he thanked the Christian Soldiers for their prayers and concern and subtly suggested they grant Miriam some peace, I slipped out the back of the house to circle around and accost Edward.

"You're bothering Miriam," I whispered.

"It wasn't my decision—"

"It never is, is it? Where have you been? You haven't been at their office."

"They've been reorganizing," Edward answered.

Defying Arthur's wishes, the fundamentalists began a new hymn. Alicia was singing in a clear contralto voice only a few feet away, so I motioned for Edward to move into the driveway, so that a sculpture on the lawn, a sheet of tormented copper, blocked her view of us talking.

"Do you know anything about Chloe Hilliard's disappearance?"

"Of course not."

"This Golden One isn't behind it?"

"How would I know?! Don't use that tone on me."

"Miriam's daughter is missing. If anything happens to that little girl because of you—"

He stepped back toward the fundamentalists, who were singing "Abide with Me."

I switched tactics. *"Please.* Meet me, I want to talk."

He agreed, to get rid of me, to prevent my embarrassing him further.

"Nine o'clock tomorrow night, on the beach just in back of our office."

Our office.

Chapter Twenty-nine

He actually showed up, on time, alone in the night fog. His wardrobe was suffering. Gone were the clothes he'd "borrowed" from Arthur, the flashy new things of his kept period, replaced by items culled from second-hand stores; tonight, a yellow shirt of something like cheesecloth and pants the drab green used for painting military vehicles.

The beach was empty, the fog thickening, so that it was like being in the center of a cloud, like heaven in old Sunday school pictures. Edward took my hand and squeezed it between his palms. I wondered, could he *act* this well? "Thank you for coming," he said. "Thank you for coming to see me."

This after I'd ordered him here. And I was coming for information about Chloe, about Ian, not a social visit with this man-boy of fragile loyalties. But there was no seduction in Edward's manner, just the sexlessness of desperation.

He seemed eager to confide. "I knew the man in the museum."

At first, I thought he meant Clarence Peever, the elderly guard who'd been stabbed, now recovering at his son's house in Cotuit.

Edward clarified his remark. "I mean the man who was disturbed, the man who went crazy, the man who passed away in jail."

We were sitting on the damp sand, dark as ash in the fog. We huddled against a seawall, partially hidden by a couple of dories, belly-up like dead fish.

"I knew the man who attacked those people…He was my brother."

"What?" He said it again. I had thought they might have some sort of connection, but not this close. It took a second to register, then I assessed his features, comparing them with the madman with broken teeth and Biblical hair.

I'd had a brother who'd died too, I thought. Instinctively, I reached out to touch him, to comfort him as he began crying, but he flinched and drew away toward the rust-streaked concrete of the seawall. "We don't look very much alike, I know. He—Clark—was schizophrenic. He was okay, manageable, when he took his medication. But they took it away, they wouldn't let him have it. So he kept just the bag, the plastic bag for his pills. That's what he swallowed to commit suicide."

"Who are 'they'?" I said. I knew, but wanted him to answer.

"The Circle of the Harmonic Peace."

That wasn't the answer I'd expected. "Who?" I knew it was wrong, but I said, "From your church?" To see if he'd dodge assigning the blame.

"Of course not. They're tight-assed bullies, but they're not murderers." Then Edward pumped some asthma medication into his lungs and wiped his face with his sandy fingers. With vehemence he said, "I didn't grow up with a silver spoon, like you and your buddy Ian." He sneezed. "Bless you," I said, and my blessing seemed to appease him.

He said, "I grew up in Vermont. In a shithole you tourists avoid." Then he told his story—or the most I'd heard to date.

He grew up with Clark and his parents in a rickety wooden house with a metal roof, with a barn full of rats and rusting tractor parts, on a farm whose long-fallow fields were reverting to forest. His father drove milk trucks, those gleaming silver tanks you see on the road. It was strange, Edward said; they seldom drank milk. City people think rural families eat healthy, surrounded by rich earth to generate produce, by animals to yield eggs and meat, but Edward's family "lived on Kool-aid and Spam."

Their hardscrabble existence darkened as Clark became worse, as he heard voices, saw angels in cornfields and demons riding the backs of cows. "My mother was very religious," Edward said. She joined a religious book club and began reading about the Essenes, about the Gnostic Gospels, about the Kabbalah. He described an exhausted woman, letting the macaroni burn on the stove while scanning the sacred texts of the world to see if any of them offered a reason, even an excuse, why her son was mad, in the barn, thinking the rats were whispering prophecies. Edward was an A-student, but Clark left school at fifteen, wandering the roads, nights, in all seasons, in the rain and sleet and snow, praying and seeing visions, almost getting killed by an oil truck near Cornish.

Then Edward's father was laid off from work. He held a series of odd jobs, in a factory making boxes, in a quarry cutting granite for gravestones, then these too ended and he became restless and distraught. Like his eldest son, he took to the road, driving aimlessly in his rotting Oldsmobile, sometimes disappearing for longer periods than Clark.

Once, on a highway in western New Hampshire, he met a man who changed his life. He was a hitchhiker with a backpack of pamphlets about a group called the Circle of the Harmonic Peace. "It was ironic, after my brother's visions and my mother's reading, that it was my father who became the real religious fanatic," Edward said. He'd been a lukewarm Methodist who'd come close to atheism when Clark was first diagnosed as schizophrenic, but, quickly, this group, this Circle, took over his life.

"What about the Golden One?"

"That came later." Soon after his father began studying with the Circle of the Harmonic Peace, he found a new job. "Or the job found him, as he liked to put it. He believed everything was destiny. My mother wanted him to junk all the mysticism bullshit and become his old practical self again. She burnt her religious books in the incinerator, the day my father started spouting his God-speak. She said, 'You can't let this cult interfere with your new work.'" Edward didn't specify what his father's new job was, but from what I could gather, it was something manual, like construction.

But Edward's father grew more and more enthralled with the Circle. He believed Clark's illness was "punishment for harm done in past lives."

Again, I asked, "Who is the Golden One?"

A beagle emerged from the fog, followed by a taut chain, then a woman, a brunette.

"They bleach their hair—"

"Some of them."

"They pass themselves off as Scandinavians."

"In Provincetown, at times."

Eventually, his father left his new job, shuttling his family to communities in Maine and Massachusetts.

"In Truro."

"No," Edward stated. "My father never made it to Truro. He died of pancreatic cancer, with shame as an underlying cause. He died six months before the move to Truro."

"Shame?"

"For breeding at all once he'd fathered a child like Clark. 'A child with a blight,' they called it, defective."

Despite his humble wardrobe, he still retained a boyish beauty. "But there was nothing wrong with you."

He laughed.

Then I realized these people would of course consider his sexuality a blight.

Stoic, determined, his mother adapted to life in the group, becoming their chief bookkeeper. She had little choice; the medication for Clark was becoming more and more expensive, and her husband had sold their house and most of their possessions and given the money to the community.

"They trained me as a chef," Edward said, "cooking expensive, foreign recipes for visiting dignitaries, people they wanted to impress, potential donors." Edward added, "They called them 'seeds.' Then they got some bad publicity, in New York and out west, and the donors, the seeds, took a hike. So I became less useful."

"Not much call for a good bouillabaisse."

"I ran away. I hitchhiked to Provincetown. To the beach where Arthur found me."

"Where does Ian fit in?"

"He was the Anti-Midas."

"The Anti-Midas?"

"Everything Ian touched turned to shit."

"What do you mean?"

"He was obnoxious. Like I need to tell you? You're the guy who gave him the Budweiser shower." He was cocky and coquettish again. "Hey, you could've killed him. You were the last guy in the nude section the day he got offed."

Except for the Asian. "Did Ian know those people in Truro? Did Ian know those bogus Scandinavians? Or this Circle of the Whatever-You-Call-It?"

"I think so."

"How did he know them? Why did he know them?"

"I really have to go," Edward said.

"Did Ian know those lunatics in Truro? I want an answer!"

"Yes!" Edward bellowed into the fog so that even I became self-conscious that the Christian Soldiers might hear us.

"How did he know them?" I asked quietly, to calm him.

"Through some legal bullshit. I don't know the details, so don't ask me."

"Did those people in Truro kill Ian?"

"It's possible," Edward said, using his Mona Lisa smile. "Unless you got him first."

"You disappeared the morning his body was found—"

"That was just a coincidence, I told you that before. Arthur kept copping a feel."

"Why didn't you go to the police? About those people in Truro abusing your brother? Withholding his medication, that's abuse. Then forcing him onto the street…"

"My mother is still there!"

The woman exercising her beagle was now returning.

"I have to go. They'll miss me at the office." He added, "To you, these Christian Soldiers are bogus intruders, annoying wackos. To me, they're protection. They've saved my life. I mean it."

How much of the rest of it did he mean? "Was Ian connected to the Christian Soldiers?"

"Not that I know of."

"Do the Christian Soldiers know you lived in the Truro community?"

"Sort of."

Getting a straight answer was like trying to bottle the fog. I took both his shoulders in my hands and he squirmed. "If those people in Truro had kidnapped Chloe, would you know about it?"

"No way, I'm out of the loop." He brushed the sand from his donated pants, then scurried through the fog toward the rigid embrace of the fundamentalists.

Chapter Thirty

Although the theology books of Ian's I'd gotten from Sallie Drummond contained nothing useful—Ian hadn't scribbled any notes about his life or beliefs, just highlighted practically every paragraph in yellow—I had a 310-page clue I had yet to use: *The Purity of Light,* the tome I'd stolen from the Truro people. Though the book's contents baffled me as thoroughly as any calculus text and no author, no Golden One, took credit for the dense prose, a publisher was listed on the title page: The Igneous Press in Rockport, Massachusetts. This was the town adjoining Gloucester, where I'd grown up.

The Igneous Press was located in a shabby part of Rockport, by an abandoned quarry full of water, junked cars, and, according to local legend, the tuxedo-clad ghost of Franklin Pearsall, the football star who'd drowned while swimming there, drunk, after his senior prom.

"No," said the man at the plywood counter, catching sight of the book with the eye above the pyramid on its cover in my hand. "We're not printing more until you pay for the last run."

I put the book on the counter, next to a dish garden with snake-plants and china lambs. "I'm not one—"

"Take your business elsewhere. And take that book off my counter."

"I'm NOT one of them!" I finally shouted.

"Are you from the police?" His voice was quiet.

"A friend has become involved—"

"Go to the police," the man suggested. In a back room, machinery was rattling. "What makes me ashamed is the whole thing started here."

"What thing?"

"The baloney in that book, their leader's ideas. Lucas Mikkonen's damned ideas." He must have enjoyed the surprise in my expression, because he continued talking. "Their guru— Lucas Mikkonen—grew up right here in Rockport. His mother, Patricia, runs a shop on Bearskin Neck. She sells dolls."

Bearskin Neck is a small peninsula dense with gift shops, crowded as closely together as barnacles on the jaws of an old whale. The shops are in shacks where fishermen once mended their nets and sorted their catches of mackerel and cod. Now, the buildings have been sanded, painted gray or russet or periwinkle-blue, and given gardens of begonias and petunias with beach-stone borders. They have carved wooden signs of old salts and pirates and lobsters and sell the same sorts of trinkets offered in Provincetown, but there's less art here, fewer serious galleries. My mother remembers the Rockport of the Fifties, when first-rate antique stores flourished on the Neck, full of China-trade Buddhas with subtle bronze smiles and junks and minute armies carved out of elephants' tusks. Now, there are cheaper foreign crafts around: abalone shell earrings, ebony elephants mass-produced somewhere in Kenya.

But Rockport lives up to its name. It has the granite headlands Cape Cod lacks, granite impregnated with mica, like the stone comprising the Provincetown breakwater.

You can look into Rockport Harbor from the Neck. It's a small bowl of greenish water ringed at low tide by stone wharfs dark with limp wreaths of bladder wrack. The harbor is full of stubby fishing boats, presided over by the most famous fishing shack in New England. "Motif Number One," the shack was nicknamed by the artists forced to paint and sketch it for generations. Barn-red, seemingly primeval, this building actually dates from the late Nineteen-Seventies, when its century-old predecessor washed apart in a winter storm. With its beaky roof and single window, it looks a little like an oversized outhouse, but it's been reproduced literally thousands of times, the East Coast version of the famous lone cypress above the Pacific near Monterey.

Mrs. Mikkonen's store had a view of this landmark, but it was down an alley on Bearskin Neck, back of a "lobster in the rough" restaurant, by a gravel townies-only parking lot. Not a prime location. The shop sold reproductions of antique dolls. Inside, there were dolls everywhere, still, glassy-eyed, making it look like a Victorian orphanage or an infirmary filled with children newly dead from some antique disease like diphtheria.

Mrs. Mikkonen was a sturdy woman, short, with blond hair surrendering to gray. Her cotton dress was decorated with teddy bears, and she wore terrycloth slippers, as if she should still be in her kitchen, frying the morning bacon. Unsure what sort of reaction her son's book might inspire, I carried it in my pocket.

She looked me up and down, without letting a smile or any reaction alter her squinting pink face. I pretended to examine two dolls, as if undecided which to pick, a girl with braids or a boy in a velvet Little Lord Fauntleroy suit, like the young Thomas Royall's.

"Every detail is authentic." Her voice was deep as Garbo's. "All done by hand," she said, of the female doll's lacy bloomers. "By hand, not by machine." I found this hard to believe, since I had seen similar dolls advertised in women's magazines I'd thumbed through in doctors' offices.

"Who is the doll for?" Her voice was so stilted, so gruff, it was hard to tell whether she had an accent or not, whether she'd been born in this country or abroad. I balked at lying and saying it was for my wife, even though my whole visit was a lie; I wasn't interested in her dolls, but in her son and his community. Was she one of his followers? I saw no Nordic clues that led me to believe this.

"It's for a friend," I said, not specifying the sex.

"How old?"

I was thinking the same question about her. Her face was as smooth as the heart of a cut potato, a wide peasant's face, someone out of Brueghel. She could have been sixty-five, seventy, or older.

Then, in this shop of still children, I thought of Miriam and Chloe and her broken mermaid doll. "My friend is in her forties."

She scuffed along in her terrycloth slippers. Her ankles were chafed and she exuded a smell of dough, of fresh bread or pastry. Standing on a stool, she reached to take down a strange doll from the top shelf. It was a child-soldier, a drummer boy. He had the stare, I realized, of those street kids in Provincetown, the same bright deadness in the eyes.

"How much do you want to spend?" She handed me the miniature drummer boy, and I realized I'd been sucked into this discussion too fast. Even if I bought this doll now, there was no guarantee she would discuss the community or her son, even supposing she knew anything useful. Cult members, even cult leaders, so often alienated their families.

"I'm not sure this is right. My friend is…very religious, anti-war."

Frowning, she pulled the doll from my hands. She climbed back onto the stool, and, straining, placed the doll back on the top shelf. The doll teetered momentarily in its licorice-black boots, and I worried it might topple and smash, but she steadied it. Then she shuffled back toward the cash register, and, with a sweeping gesture of her blunt fingers, said, "Look around, take your time," as if she wished I'd be on my way as soon as possible.

She thought I was another tourist, always dissatisfied with what was on sale. So, as I again began browsing through the dolls, I decided to establish that I was local, from Gloucester, the next town; this might give me credibility of sorts.

I picked up a doll dressed as a princess, in shimmery fabric and a tiara. "Has it been a good summer?"

"Hot." She was writing something in a ledger.

"I've spent most of the summer on Cape Cod," I said, volunteering more information than I'd planned, but desperate to resuscitate conversation.

She made no reply, just kept writing. A cat materialized, a Siamese with eyes as unreal as the dolls', unnatural as star sapphires. The cat leapt from the counter near the cash register onto a shelf with a squadron of babies in wicker prams. Mrs. Mikkonen took no notice. Obviously, the cat was experienced, trained not to knock over the merchandise. The cat leapt back onto the counter, rubbing its face against Mrs. Mikkonen's hip, against the shabby dress with all the teddy bears.

"It was hot even on Cape Cod."

She licked one of her blunt fingers and turned a page of the ledger.

"I'm actually from here."

"I know," she said.

I felt as if life had suddenly entered all the dolls' eyes, as if all of them suddenly were staring at me. But only the Siamese cat was actually paying me any attention. It hopped to the floor, weightless as down, silently landing at my feet, then rubbing its face against my legs, marking its territory. Mrs. Mikkonen was still enthralled with her ledger, or pretending to be.

"I've seen you before." She closed the ledger.

I took a doll in my hands, like a hostage. "Where?"

"At the funeral," she answered.

"Whose?"

"Are there that many funerals in your life? I feel sorry for you." She looked me straight in the eye, but there was no more sorrow in her expression than in her cat's. "At Ian Drummond's funeral. Are you allergic to cats? She's just marking her territory. Come here, Helga, over here."

A Siamese cat named Helga. I almost took out the cult's book, but I didn't, and didn't answer her question about my allergies, didn't respond to her subtle intimidation. Instead, I stroked the cat's back and gently tugged its tail. "Were you a friend of Ian's?" It seemed like a ridiculous question.

"The Drummonds are a prominent family. Everyone knows them. I knew Duncan, the old man. He came into my shop. The son was killed on Cape Cod."

"Yes, in Provincetown."

"A horrible thing." She sounded like a peasant speaking of the death of a reckless young noble. She was philosophical, remote, as though the death somehow was apt, God dispensing justice with democratic severity.

"I'm flattered that you remembered me."

"You were a few rows in front of me in the church. Then I saw you at the house, afterward. I remembered you because you spoke to that woman who'd been crying. The woman who came with the black man."

Suki Weatherbee and her African husband.

"Poor Mr. Drummond. Such a nice old gentleman."

My father, I could have said. "Nice" was hardly his reputation during his prime: drinking away his liver, seducing other men's wives. And my mother. "Was he a regular customer?"

"He stole things. He picked up things and forgot to pay. His mind was going."

"The Alzheimer's."

"Whatever they call it."

It was evident by this time that she had no accent. Just a stilted way of speaking, clipped, militaristic. Yes, there was something militaristic about her. Perhaps that's why she'd shown me the drummer boy first. Did she keep this shop of artificial children because her flesh-and-blood-son had been such a disappointment?

"The family always paid. He'd come down with the chauffeur. In a big car the size of a boat. He was looking for dolls for his daughter. He'd forgotten she was all grown up."

So there was a link, tenuous but ongoing, between the Mikkonen and Drummond families. Ian himself could have come here, to this room of staring glass eyes. And Edward could be right—Ian could have done some "legal bullshit" for the people in Truro.

"I was at school with Ian Drummond." I pretended to examine a pale resin baby in a christening gown with enough lace to please a bride.

Mrs. Mikkonen was writing something with a pencil capped with the head of a miniature Cabbage Patch Doll instead of an eraser.

"I went to a place called St. Harold's."

Mrs. Mikkonen continued writing, muttering something about "fancy schools for fancy people."

I was holding the resin baby, which I felt compelled to support with both arms, as though it were real. Dolls had become so much more lifelike since I was a child. The doll in the christening gown looked like a baby, but not, I realized like a *live* child; it looked like a dead baby "prepared" by an undertaker. The resin had the hardness of dead rouged flesh.

"My son went to public school, right here in Rockport. It was good enough for Lucas." Then her expression became hard as the resin dolls in her shop. "That school—St. Harold's—closed down," she said, with triumph.

The remark stung, small but sharp like a shaving cut. She stunned me when she added, "My son bought that school."

"What?!"

She put down the pencil with the Cabbage Patch Doll like a head impaled on a spike. She must've known she'd said something significant, something she shouldn't have revealed. "Are you interested in Baby Victoria? Because, if you're not, I'm closing for lunch."

Chapter Thirty-one

Was Ian connected to Lucas Mikkonen through St. Harold's? Was the "legal bullshit" Edward had spoken of helping the school sell its assets to these fraudulent Nordics? Since I was already here on the North Shore, there was someone in the area I could ask.

I hadn't gotten the chance to express my condolences in person to Mrs. Drummond the day of Ian's funeral. She was mobbed by mourners and busy attending to her bewildered husband. So I brought her a bouquet, a half-dozen roses with baby's breath in a cone of the florist's green cellophane. I also brought my questions, many questions.

The Drummonds' estate seemed to grow out of the granite of Eastern Point, squatting among the yews and rhododendrons. *You're entitled to some of this*, a grasping little voice inside of me insisted. You're more of a Drummond than she is; she's a Drummond by marriage. You share genetic material, you share DNA, don't be awed by their house or their things.

A plump maid with a moustache greeted me. Mrs. Drummond was in the library, a dark paneled room full of books whose gilt bindings had never been cracked. Janet Drummond had been "a great beauty" in her youth, so people said. You could still see that beauty in her high cheekbones and thick wavy hair, now silver but still brushing her shoulders. She was sitting on a low leather couch, the kind I associate with analysts' offices, sorting through a pile of notes and cards, sympathy mail concerning her youngest son's death. From somewhere in the room came the soft thwack of a ball then ripples of applause. Of course, she was watching a tennis match. I saw the portable TV on a spindly chrome stand, the sole cheap piece of furniture in a room of rich surfaces.

"Hello," I said, and she glanced up just in time to say, "Ssssh! Sazonov is serving!" On the screen was the dripping face of Yuri Sazonov, the Russian tennis star rumored to be Mafia property. He slammed the ball toward his stunned American opponent, Matt Milner. Milner swung but missed, and Mrs. Drummond resumed writing on her heavy, cream-colored stationery.

"I'm terribly sorry about Ian."

"You can't know how a mother feels," she said, which was certainly true, and a remark which needed no reply. "You needn't feel guilty," she added.

"Guilty?" With a tingle of dread, I was thinking that somehow, with a mother's intuition, she knew I'd found her son without reporting his murder.

"About that silly scrap at the nightclub."

"Nightclub" was such a Fifties word. It called to mind El Morocco and Porfirio Rubirosa. But that had been Mrs. Drummond's world, café society. She was a Midwesterner, from Gates Mills or Lake Forest, a tennis star who'd met Ian's father out carousing in New York. Someone claimed the Duchess of Windsor introduced them.

I said, "We'd known each other so long, we were bound to have our moments…" I was still holding the flowers.

"Ian valued your friendship."

Mrs. Drummond hadn't invited me to sit, but I did, in a wing chair by a jade plant in a Chinese pot all courtesans and plum blossoms. The windows of the library were thrown open, so that I could see Gloucester Harbor beyond the granite ledges, see Ten Pound Island in the distance.

"Ian saved my life once." I thought mentioning that might somehow make up for our fight.

"Really?" She put down her Mont Blanc pen. "How?"

I explained about our rowing to Ten Pound Island, then the storm blowing up, the sky boiling with black clouds, then the rain like bullwhips—and my freezing at the oars, unable to row home. "He took over and saved both our lives."

Her face became streaked with tears. "You were at St. Harold's together." She wore a small pin, a gold tennis racket, fastened to her black and white blouse. Ian had once mentioned the story of that pin: how she'd bought it in London while competing at Wimbledon and wore it at tennis-connected events. She wore it even today, while answering this wrenching correspondence. That athlete's spirit helped her survive times like this.

"You know I accepted Ian for whatever he was. Just as I accept you, Mark. I mean, any number of the girls I competed against…" She was talking about tennis, of course. "Any number were veritable Amazons…What's the zip code for Prides Crossing?" I told her. "God," she sighed, "I hope I never get like my husband."

My father. I couldn't say it. "I saw him in Provincetown."

"Did he recognize you?"

"I certainly hope so. His…friendship means a lot to me." My tone and the break in my voice had a desperation that should have surprised her.

"Of course it really doesn't matter, does it? We should be thankful he gets pleasure from our company. I wish I had more patience, but he's so frustrating to deal with, so recalcitrant. It's awfully hard on Sallie. She was his little princess, his blue-ribbon equestrienne. Sallie was the best athlete in the family. The best amateur…Fulton and George have such busy lives, I've asked Sallie and Alexander to settle Ian's affairs."

This was an opening of sorts. "What was Ian doing out west?"

"Real estate. A development north of San Francisco. In Marin County, a gated community. The whole thing fell through, the financing went bad. It was just as well, I wouldn't have wanted him settling out west. I think family is awfully important, don't you?" She glanced at me with a trace of pity; the sadness in her face was not just for herself.

"Awfully important—"

"I had a lovely note from your mother," she said.

Who'd avoided Ian's funeral to paint in her back yard. Did she know about my mother and her husband? It was hardly a state secret that he was the Casanova of the country club circuit. It occurred to me then, for the first time, that he could've fathered other children outside his marriage. Either way, both she and my mother were wronged, used by a faithless charmer. He'd collected women the way he'd collected the eggs of rare birds, damaging the environment in each case.

"It was too bad your mother was away the day of the services. Duncan would have enjoyed seeing her. All of us would have." She was pressing a stamp onto an envelope. Her tears had dried, and her voice was as crisp as her Shreve, Crump & Low stationary. "I always liked your mother. She always 'did her own thing' as they used to say."

Was she was being sarcastic? I couldn't tell. Her face remained mask-like and genteel. My mother seldom spoke about Janet Drummond, and I couldn't recall Mrs. Drummond mentioning my mother at all.

"She persisted with her first love," Mrs. Drummond said. Did she mean Duncan? I wondered for an instant, but she said, "She persisted with her art."

"She began as a musician." I was about to mention Lulu Wright's and my mother's phony story, which had survived all these years like an intricate but unexpectedly sturdy piece of origami.

"Your mother didn't cave in to the bluenoses." By having me, I assumed she meant, in addition to heeding her muse. She deleted a name from her list of people to thank. Was it ruthlessness that made her so mechanical today, made her write while watching a tennis tournament? No, that was unfair. She could be sedated, or numb.

I wanted to say, I'm not interested in your money, but I'd like the chance to get to know my father. But then she changed the subject, as if anticipating some unpleasantness. "Ian wasn't out west very long."

"I thought he was gone two years."

"Well, he maintained an apartment in San Francisco, on Telegraph Hill. But the Marin County project fell through quite quickly."

"How quickly?"

"I think he was through with things in six months," said Mrs. Drummond. "So we discovered once he was…gone. Ian wasn't the most open fellow around. We disagreed about an awful lot. We fought like cats and dogs about politics. I'm a Democrat to the end, you know."

I didn't. She was full of surprises.

"Ian had changed these last two years. He'd matured, become a seeker. He was reading Emerson and Thomas Merton, all those tortured, questioning souls."

The books I'd seen Sallie jettisoning back in Provincetown, stuffing into a green plastic trash bag. Had Ian's financial losses made him more spiritual? And caused him to apologize for his past bullying that day in the dunes? Something big had been preying on his mind.

"Did Ian know a Lucas Mikkonen?"

"Not that I recall."

I would broach something mildly controversial before daring to bring up my parentage: "There wasn't any mention of Ian being gay…at the funeral."

Any youth in her being seemed to recede so that her tired expression matched her silver hair. "Is everything an occasion for some political statement? Are we always obliged to educate bigots, or cater to activists? Aren't we ever allowed just to be sad?"

Before I could answer, someone said "Mother?"

In the library doorway stood Alexander Nash. He wore sea-blue Bermuda shorts, revealing his strong, tanned calves. He was extraordinarily handsome.

"Alexander is helping me hold down the fort while Sallie minds my husband on Cape Cod," said Mrs. Drummond.

"When I saw your husband—"

"He'll find a vase for those beautiful flowers."

I was a fool, an idiot, a coward! I'd squandered my chance to discuss my mother's claim. Why had I wanted to do this? To be sure she was telling the truth, I suppose, to discover if the family had been informed, if they knew, to learn Duncan Drummond's version of the events, some fragments of the story the Alzheimer's hadn't yet stolen.

Shepherding me from the library, Alexander kept repeating that the North Shore was gorgeous, how lucky I was to have grown up here. Did folks around here really appreciate it? Everything was so historical. He rattled off a list of sights he'd visited: Beauport just down the road, Fort Sewall in Marblehead, the House of Seven Gables in Salem, the Saugus Iron Works...He'd bought postcards and a pot of candy, some Boston Baked Beans.

Infuriated at not tackling my own story with Mrs. Drummond, I asked him, "Where are you from?" just to be polite, to distract myself.

He'd grown up "mostly" in a small town east of Santa Barbara, a place that was half oil fields, half lemon groves, where the oldest piece of architecture was a plaster-domed Greco-Roman gas station dating from the Depression.

In the kitchen, he found a tankard-like vase, something pewter, for my sympathy bouquet. I realized now that baby's breath was not the most sensitive flower to give the mother of a murdered son.

"So you've known the family all your life, Mark." Alexander poked the flowers into the vase until they were positioned just so. His finding a vase for my flowers and escorting me to the door implied a vaguely servant-like status. As a future son-in-law he was on his best behavior, in the family yet not quite of it, a situation not unlike my own.

"That's very nice. Did you take flower arranging classes?" I asked as a joke.

"Actually, I did. Ever the self-improver." Alexander was one of those people who hold a stare until it makes you self-conscious. His eyes were the deep blue of the northern Pacific, where he tagged walruses and measured the spiky legs of gigantic crabs. For a moment, I thought he was cruising me, drinking me in with his stare. Instead he lobbed an unexpected question: "Did Ian have any significant others?"

"He wasn't that domestic. He dated now and then, mostly Log Cabin Republicans, but there was no real lover that I can remember."

"What about women?" He was staring with those Pacific-blue eyes. Not bedroom eyes. Was he studying me? At Mrs. Drummond's request? He'd called her "Mother," so they had to be close, or else he was putting on a show. Perhaps she admired his princely athletic ease, the way he occupied the physical world. And he wanted the status of a son as soon as possible.

"Ian was involved with Suki Weatherbee at St. Harold's. But so was our whole class, so was anything male in the Berkshires."

"It's kind of sad. Ian dying without ever being loved. Romantically, I mean. Hate crimes are so senseless."

"Ian didn't believe in them."

"Beg pardon?"

"Ian didn't believe in hate crimes. He said, 'How many crimes are committed out of love?'"

He acted a little baffled. The heat could have affected his alertness. The kitchen with its big restaurant-sized stove was stifling. Rather than explain my reference to the incident at Arthur's, which had happened before he and Sallie had come east for Ian's funeral, I paid him a compliment instead. "You seem to fit into the family pretty well."

"It isn't always easy. I mean, Sallie was already devastated, what with her father's condition. Then Ian dying…But Mrs. Drummond is a trouper. An amazing lady. She can beat the beejesus out of me at tennis. Even with the copper bracelet I wear to improve my serve."

Alexander—at least at that moment—didn't strike me as particularly bright, Woods Hole association or not. But at least he admitted his discomfort, slight though it was. That inspired me to risk my next question. "Sallie didn't mind my not taking the things Ian had brought from St. Harold's, did she? I mean, I took some books that belonged to Ian, spiritual books."

"Oh, Sallie really appreciated your stopping by. She considers you like family."

That was perfect. Now I could speak. Being Sallie's fiancé, he'd be able to tell me her frank opinions. He didn't seem to have the guile or eloquence to disguise them. "Some people say…" I was unable to meet his stare, unable to meet his eyes, so I looked instead at some tall bottles of vinegar with herbs like rotting water weeds inside them. "Some people say Duncan Drummond and my mother had a fling…and that I'm the result."

Alexander paused then said, "Holy Toledo. That's got to be tough for you, Mark. That's got to be awkward as hell."

Then I just kept speaking: "I just found out the day of Ian's funeral. My mother's been alcoholic for years. They met at this jazz club. In Boston, in the South End. They were intimate, as you say, just once. Or so she says. The Drummonds' lawyer worked out some sort of settlement. Now…Mr. Drummond has dementia, as you know. So I'll never know the truth. Know him or his side of the story…" I began to choke up, I couldn't help it. I felt like a fool. "…Has Sallie ever mentioned any of this?" I managed to ask.

"No way."

"Have any of them? Fulton? George? Janet?"

"Not a word. I knew Sallie's dad had sown his oats."

"Well, sometime I'd like to talk with him."

"With your dad. Who wouldn't? Gosh, Mark, my heart goes out to you."

"Could you arrange it? On the QT?"

"His memory is just like a sieve, Mark, I've got to be honest. I'm not sure you'll get much information."

"Don't mention it to Sallie or the rest of them. Not until I ask you. Okay?" I'd made a mistake, I thought, telling him. But at least he'd listened, he hadn't dismissed my story, hadn't laughed or cut me off. "I'm not after money. That's the last thing I'm looking for."

"You just want to be recognized. You want validation. Of who you are. Hey, family is everything, Mark."

We'd been gone a while, and I was worrying that Mrs. Drummond might come wandering in. I didn't have the energy or nerve to repeat my story to her.

I tried to be jaunty but failed. "Stay cool," I told Alexander in the front hall. Knowing that was impossible in this heat.

Chapter Thirty-two

The Berkshires are different from the rest of Massachusetts; there's a luxuriance to the growth there. The soil must be richer than near Boston or on Cape Cod, and sometimes it seems as though the Berkshires are a fragment of something further south that pushed itself north into New England: tobacco can be grown on the banks of the Connecticut River. There's real forest here, too, great stretches of it darkening whole hillsides, whole valleys, and rivers that run wild, unencumbered by cisterns or culverts or dams. Some are deep and silver-gray, others flow shallow, rippling over stones beneath the occasional covered bridge.

St. Harold's was on the outskirts of a mill town, Stark, which once manufactured corsets and Dr. Elias Bennett's Miracle Elixir, a patent medicine alleged to cure everything from impotence to whooping cough. Both factories had closed by the time I was a student, of course, their smokestacks innocent of any crimes against the ozone layer, their cobblestone courtyards invaded by weeds.

Now, Stark seemed bleaker than its name or any of my memories. The heat there had a staleness, as though the valley had somehow trapped it. Potholes, veritable canyons with their own geology, punctured the main street. The drugstore, Butler's, with the marble counter veined blue like Roquefort cheese, was closed. Inside, where they had mixed the best lime rickies in all of New England, was full of dust and broken furniture. The metal thermometer nailed by the entrance suggested I should "Drink Moxie" and reported it was 97 degrees.

My stop in Stark made me even more uneasy about visiting St. Harold's. Schools, like constellations and the Lincoln Memorial, are supposed to outlast you. You're not prepared for the demise of your school. It's too total, like the collapse of an entire culture: Aztec Mexico, Imperial Russia.

So, braking at the entrance, I braced myself. The school's wrought-iron gate, with its pretentious vines and berries, had been sanded and painted; not a lesion of rust was in sight, a good sign. The gate resembled that of a Newport mansion. Indeed, St. Harold's occupied the grounds of Fayrlawne, an Italianate monstrosity thrown up by Stoddard T. Stark, the Corset King—whose factory dominated the local economy at a time when nearby Lenox was called "the inland Newport" and the Berkshires germinated mock palazzos and faux chateaux. Stark sold Fayrlawne after his wife died in an archery accident. After its founding in 1893, St. Harold's had grown, engendering an abundance of classrooms and dormitories and the magnificent chapel, a scaled-down copy of Ely Cathedral here above the banks of Lake Chiccataubett.

The carved inscription on the gate remained intact: the school's name, seal, and date of its founding in Latin. No guards or roadblocks deflected visitors.

In defiance of any ban, a built-in sprinkler system was drenching the green lawns with arcs of water. Indeed, water was puddling on the soccer field, creating miniature Okeefenokees, swamps that might yield egrets or alligators. In fact, animals, like people, were seeking refuge in cool nests, away from the heart-stopping heat.

The Stark mansion had served as the school's administration building. I'd expected memories of my past to come crowding into my consciousness on its steps. But to me St. Harold's was people, the rowdiness of the dormitory or the wonder and drudgery of the classroom. These deserted buildings were devoid of all that, sad as an empty funhouse.

I pulled at the brass knob on the door to the mansion, brilliant as a planet in the sunlight. The door was locked. Through a window, I could see a familiar Tudor table with bulbous legs, like an old man with swollen ankles. I banged on the door and rang the bell, getting no response.

I wandered through the various parking lots. Not a car was in sight, although the asphalt was new, freshly marked with white lines delineating the spaces. No handicapped parking was offered. Physically, the buildings had been improved: brick sandblasted clean, a tower's clock revived, some urns and pediments and other ornamentation restored, but something essential, something deeper, was missing. The school's soul had been hijacked.

My last destination was the chapel, built of Indiana limestone, with flying buttresses delicate as the bones of an extinct bird. Its exterior all but glowed; the moss had been dug from the gargoyles' eyes, the oxidation scoured from the drainpipes.

Merely as a formality, I nudged the heavy door. To my surprise, it creaked aside on its Gothic hinges. Inside, I followed a cool, mosaic-floored corridor that led to the main chapel. The sound of my shoes echoed off the stone, and, for a moment, I stopped, swearing I detected something else—a bubbling, like a motor churning water. When I turned into the nave, the bubbling grew louder, and a sour smell, like something rotting, dominated the air.

In the center of the aisle, between the rows of carved pews facing each other as in college chapels at Oxford, gleaming in the light from the donated stained glass, stood three huge green tanks. A sound like an outboard motor churning water while docked rumbled inside them.

I couldn't believe these things were here, in this space where we'd taken communion. The tanks were made of dark, firm plastic, six by ten feet, five feet deep. Their smell—a stench now, a rotting that assaulted your nostrils—became so strong I held my breath.

I climbed into the pews to peer over into the first tank. The water was roiling with a silvery mass, crowded with hundreds of fish. They seemed to cover the entire surface, like herring on a run, choking a stream with movement. Then, I noticed that most of the fish were not moving the water. Some submerged pump or motor was moving them. Most of the fish were dead—stiff, bloated, stinking.

Cupping my hand over my nose, I drew in a deep breath, again inhaling the stink of decay. Quickly, I peered into the two other tanks. Pumps or motors were running in them too.

"Who are you and why are you here?"

The voice made my skeleton jump inside my skin. Someone had followed me up the aisle, a woman about forty, with skin dark as cloves but with the long blond hair of a Lorelei on her rock in the Rhine. "Who are you and why are you here?" Her voice was clear, with the directness of a therapist. The lilt of her accent suggested she was from India, but that hair fought with the rest of her appearance; she seemed bizarre as the blue-skinned Hindu goddess Kali.

Something made me blurt the truth: "I'm Mark, from Cape Cod."

A smile transformed her face. "Ah yes, of course. You haven't earned your name yet. How are things in Truro?"

I hadn't earned my name. Earned my Nordic name, I assumed. When I'd said I was from Cape Cod, meaning Provincetown, she'd thought I'd meant Truro, thought I was one of them.

I found something to say: "The Cape is having a terrible drought, like everywhere else." Then I remembered the sprinklers on the lawns here, squandering water, dispersing it so freely it formed pools.

"Of course, there's no drought here, here at the compound, thanks to the Master." She gave a quick laugh, light as music. "M-I-T, Ph.D. The Master created an ingenious sprinkler system which taps Lake Chiccataubett. So we're free from the watering ban."

We were standing closest to the tank by the altar. From their niches on the chapel walls, narrow stone apostles glowered at the scene. The stench from the fish was overwhelming, yet she said nothing about it, nor did she bother to introduce herself. She might be some sort of leader in their world and assumed I knew who she was.

"Is the engineering proceeding on schedule?" she asked.

Was she testing me, or making conversation? She seemed accepting, even warm, but with a certain sense of formality. She was treating me with care, the way a non-native speaker treats the English language. I had no idea what "engineering" she'd referred to. Then her incongruous hair made me remember Jason and his crates of strawberry preserves for Scents of Being.

"The preserves are selling like mad." I hesitated to link myself directly to him because he knew I wasn't one of these people, and knew I was after something more than jam recipes.

"Jason was here the other day." She giggled. "He's adorable." Then she bent low beside the tank and scooped something from a canister which she sprinkled across the surface of the tank, meal for the fish. "We use the dead fish for fertilizer," she said, not seeming disturbed by the stench.

I was wondering if somehow I could learn if Ian had been here, if she knew Ian at all. Since he was an alumnus of the school, I tried to broach the subject of St. Harold's. "This is a beautiful chapel."

"It isn't a chapel anymore. Remember, it was deconsecrated."

"Wasn't it a school at one time?" Sallie Drummond had told me Ian was involved with liquidating many of the school's assets. Of course, Ian was a lawyer with an interest in real estate. Were his interests "out west" actually in western Massachusetts?

I marshaled all my acting skills, struggling to make the remark sound casual: "It still says St. Harold's on the gate."

She cast scoops of meal into the other stinking tanks.

"Do many nostalgic alumni drop by?"

She set down the scoop in a canister of meal, and then rubbed her hands together, brushing them clean. "There were some nasty people connected with that school, that St. Harold's," she said.

Was this insult to the chapel, to the school's spiritual heart, a way of vanquishing the old purposes of this land? Or the twisted whim of an all-powerful leader.

She turned to leave.

Chapter Thirty-three

Back in Provincetown, I went straight to the police, finally ready to tell them everything. It was way beyond my scope as a private individual to solve this case, to bring anyone to justice.

"It's all connected," I told Sergeant Almeida.

He was sitting at a gray metal desk, eating a meatball submarine sandwich that was doing its best to drip over his hands onto the stack of paperwork in front of him. "Come again?"

"Those people in Truro, that pseudo-Scandinavian Manson Family, Ian's murder, and maybe Chloe's kidnapping. Who knows?"

"*We* know, more than you. That's our business."

"If you know so damn much, why haven't you made any arrests or found Chloe?"

"Sit down."

The chair was molded plastic, a little too low to the ground. "You don't mind?" He produced his tape recorder and recited the date and time and names of the people present. Once again, the tape began turning.

Chloe's picture was thumb-tacked on the wall, along with missing children from throughout America; some of them missing for years. I checked for a man matching Edward's description of his assailant, his rapist, but found none.

"Where were you on the night of June fifteenth?" Almeida asked. "The night Ian Drummond was killed."

"I have new information."

"Just answer the question."

"I told you, I'd been to Herring Cove that day. I spent most of the day at Herring Cove."

"That day. Until what time?"

"Until a little after dark."

"And you got there how?"

"Using my car." They had obviously seen my car, late, in the Herring Cove parking lot. He was placing me at the scene of the crime, at the time Ian had died.

He smiled, not at me, but at a sheet of paper adjacent to the sandwich on his desk. "You have a dark green Volvo 240 sedan?" He reeled off the number of my license plate.

"Yes."

"And that car was parked at the Herring Cove lot until at least ten on the night of June fifteenth? Correct?"

I nodded.

"One of my colleagues, Officer John Hammond, noted your car in the Herring Cove parking lot at ten-oh-eight on the night of June fifteenth. The car was empty, so, presumably you were still on the beach. You were on the beach, in fact, when Ian Drummond was killed."

The air-conditioning in the station was inadequate, and the humidity seemed thicker than chowder. Sweat was darkening my polo shirt, turning the blue an incriminating indigo.

"The coroner estimated the time of Ian Drummond's death as nine-fifteen on the night of June fifteenth, a time you—and your Volvo—were in the general vicinity."

"I didn't kill Ian!" I snapped.

His smile was one of suppressed satisfaction.

I was going to fill in some blanks. I didn't kill Ian, the people from Truro did, I was thinking—not Clark, Edward's schizophrenic brother; he was too fragile, they'd sent someone tougher, someone reliable. Of course Almeida's questions suggested he had his doubts about blaming their John Doe for Ian's death, for blaming him for anything beyond the slashings at the museum.

I forced myself to say it, I said it quickly, blurted it out, to make sure I couldn't hesitate, couldn't stop—"I saw Ian that day, I saw him twice. Once when he was alive, and once when he was dead."

Almeida almost choked on his mouthful of sandwich and Sprite.

Some part of me felt back in command.

"You were enemies. You had a bust-up at Quahog, I saw you."

"We kissed and made up. Literally."

"Don't get wise with me. Go on." Almeida checked the tape to make sure it was behaving.

So I told him what had happened that day at Herring Cove, my lingering at the beach until no one else was there, then Ian calling me to his hollow in the dunes. I told him about getting drunk on Ian's bottle of vodka, about Ian apologizing for his bullying in the past, about our quick sex and his leaving, telling me, *"Vaya con Díos."*

"Then what?"

"I swam for a while. Then I fell asleep on the beach. When I woke up, it was dark. I took the breakwater back to the shore road. I wanted to see the lights from town, for re-assurance. I was worried about bashers, about Christian Soldiers. I was scared to walk back along the beach in the dark."

"What time did you leave the beach?"

"I'm not sure. But when I first saw Ian, saw his body…I thought it was someone fishing."

"Fishing?"

"From a distance. People fish off the breakwater at night. Of course once I was close and saw his throat cut open." The throat wound was a detail the media hadn't reported.

Almeida stood. "You actually were there. You were smack-dab at the crime scene yet withheld this information! You withheld this information when we questioned you at your apartment! What kind of game are you playing, Mr. Comedian? If you think because I'm new here—"

"I'm not playing anyone! I came here voluntarily!"

He sat down then picked up the telephone. "C'mere, it's important," he said into the receiver. Seconds later DeRenzi rushed in, the skinny, sallow, detective who'd been with Almeida at my apartment. "Tell him," said Almeida, "tell him what you just told me."

My shirt was saturated with sweat. My bare arms felt glued to the Popisicle-orange chair. "I found Ian's body on the break-water. We'd had sex in the dunes, then I'd fallen asleep. I found him when I walked back to my car."

"He came here on his own," Almeida threw in.

"Did you plan to meet Ian?" DeRenzi asked. "Was this tryst prearranged?"

"Uh-uh," I said.

"Answer Yes or No," DeRenzi said.

"No, our meeting was impromptu."

"Were you lovers?" DeRenzi asked.

Only for ten minutes. But this was no time to be sarcastic. "No."

"Did you touch anything?" Almeida asked. "Or take anything from the crime scene?"

"No. I dropped the vodka bottle Ian gave me on the beach. It broke, and I picked up the shards of glass. I touched Ian's shoulder, just to make sure."

"You needed to 'make sure' in the shape he was in?" To DeRenzi, he said, "Ask him about the body, what he saw."

I volunteered, "There was blood all over. His throat was slashed open, you could see the bone. He was sitting, propped up against a rock. There was a wound to his chest too. The moon was full, I could see pretty well. It was awful, I'd give anything not to have seen it."

Almeida asked again: "Did you kill Ian Drummond, Mr. Winslow?"

"No. He was dead when I found him."

"Was there any weapon, a knife or any sort of projectile, at the scene?"

"None that I saw."

"Why did you cover this up?" Almeida asked.

"Because everyone saw me fight with Ian at Quahog. I assumed I'd be Suspect Number One."

At that point, I wanted Almeida to say, No. But he didn't, he just wiped the pickles and hot peppers from his hands.

"Ian once saved my life. He saved me from drowning. When we were kids. I couldn't kill him."

"Did you want more than Ian Drummond would give you?" Detective DeRenzi asked. "Perhaps you murdered him in a jealous rage or because he rejected you."

"No!"

That's when I decided I wouldn't tell them everything—out of what—vanity, pique, stubbornness? And I wouldn't mention Edward or Clark, let them do their own work. Besides, it could jeopardize Edward's mother, still living at the commune.

But I had to mention Truro somehow, that's why I'd come: "I came here to talk about those people in Truro, I've visited them—"

Almeida crumpled his empty Sprite can with one strong squeeze.

"Chloe Hilliard has been kidnapped," I said, "and those people in Truro are somehow behind it!"

Almeida said, "You're the only person who's admitted he saw Ian on the breakwater."

"When were you in Truro?" DeRenzi said.

"I was there twice, actually. I'd been interested in Thomas Royall. They live on the old Royall property, his old colony. Once I just drove up to one of their gates. They have this humongous fence surrounding the whole place to keep them in and us out." I tried to smile but didn't succeed.

The tape was spooking me, that and their grim expressions.

"There was a kind of…giant guarding the gate. Then these little girls just appeared out of the woods. Kids like you see panhandling here in town. Anyway, the Giant told me to get lost. The second time I went there…"

Almeida and DeRenzi exchanged looks that suggested both wonder and exasperation.

"The second time I went I'd met this black guy, Jason. A tall guy with blond dreadlocks. He sells strawberry preserves to this shop, Scents of Being, on Commercial Street."

DeRenzi was studying me like I was a specimen in his lab. Almeida let go of the crushed Sprite can. He said, "Mark, you've seen what happened to Ian, have some common sense. Do you want to end up on the coroner's table?"

"Let me tell you why I think Chloe might be with these people." I described seeing Jason after Ian's funeral, at the Drummonds' house back in Gloucester. I told how I'd seen Jason at Scents of Being, how he'd taken me to Truro because I was curious about their business, their business making preserves. I described the white Victorian house, the freezing room, Royall's swords above the mantle, Jason's "cult-speak."

"Here's what's important," I said. "Something interrupted Jason that night. His beeper went off. He lost his cool, he got very upset. My visit was over like that. He drove back here like a bat out of hell. And guess when that was? The very day Chloe was kidnapped—that can't be coincidence."

"Why?" asked Almeida.

"Something big got on Jason's nerves—"

"But you suggest that this Jason was surprised. About something which you assume was Chloe's kidnapping. But if these people in Truro were actually her kidnappers, they'd hardly be surprised it was happening, would they? And there's been no request for ransom money. And they have more than enough children in their ranks."

"There's more," I said. "These people in Truro bought Ian's old school. My old school, St. Harold's, in the Berkshires. Ian helped liquidate their assets. When they went bankrupt. So there's a direct connection between Ian and these nuts. This guy Lucas Mikkonen is their leader. He's from Rockport."

Almeida began to speak, but DeRenzi cut him short: "Mr. Winslow, we are quite, quite sure that these nuts in Truro, as you call them, have no connection to the disappearance of Chloe Hilliard. And the Drummond case is yielding new information—"

"So you admit the guy from the museum didn't do it—"

"Do what?"

"Kill Ian."

"Mr. Winslow, you can help us most by remaining available for further questioning, by remaining in Provincetown," DeRenzi said. "Ian Drummond's murder is an open case. Your meddling in these matters could alert his killers or the kidnappers. You've contaminated the murder scene, that's trouble enough. May I suggest you confine your playing detective to the stage?"

As I rose, my polo shirt stuck to the plastic of the chair, so that I had to peel it free with my fingers. Wiping the sweat from my forehead, I thanked them, for what I had no idea. At least they hadn't arrested me for withholding evidence about Ian.

When I returned to Miriam's, there was the very last person in the world I wanted to see: Roberto Schreiber.

Chapter Thirty-four

"I didn't know!" Roberto kept repeating. "I didn't know Chloe was missing, Mark, I swear!"

"It's true," Miriam said.

Seeing Roberto—in that silly T-shirt with the kissing lavender dinosaurs, with his gorgeous but slightly bowed legs—made my anger change to a subtle but growing, yes, happiness. He was here, and it made a difference. I was surprised and relieved.

Roberto was with his father. Professor Schreiber was a husky chain-smoker in a parrot-green silk shirt, so youthful he could've passed as Roberto's rakish older brother. "It's my fault," Professor Schreiber admitted. He explained that he prized isolation while vacationing. The Owl Island house had no televisions, radios, or Internet access. "Peace and quiet are a fetish with me." Just like his tobacco habit and clear fingernail polish, his way, Roberto had once informed me, of "deconstructing the MIT stereotype, you know, *Star Trek* fan—fashion victim."

"Why didn't you call me?" Roberto asked. "I'd left my number with Roger."

"I was waiting for you to call us," I said. "Chloe was on the news from coast to coast."

Chloe had been gone eight days. And we were worried about Miriam too; her morale was deteriorating. She had unearthed her family Bible, a huge old book all but falling apart. She prayed for hours on her deck, with this Bible and a cell phone and a bottle of wine in her lap.

Alicia, the receptionist from the Christian Soldiers' office, had insinuated herself into Miriam's life, bringing an olive wood cross and a coconut cream pie one scorching morning six days after Chloe's vanishing. Too tired to be anything but polite, Miriam had invited her inside, so, since then, Alicia had shown up every morning assuring Miriam Chloe was in God's hands, holding Miriam's own hand, and reading her passages from Hollings Fair's condensed *New Testament*.

Arthur and I accepted Alicia's presence. She was doing some good, since, previously, Miriam had been refusing most food, subsisting on Graham crackers, tranquilizers, and chamomile tea. Alicia was able to stuff her with high-calorie desserts: the mousse, sheet cake, and brownies she cooked at home. "Home," we learned, was an RV out by the beach, by Herring Cove. They were all staying together, the people from her office: she, Paul, and others. They had been living there for several weeks; it was "way nicer than some motel with TVs wired to all the pornography channels."

Paul was "fine," studying the *Book of Luke* and automobile racing magazines. "He comes from a horrific background," Alicia said, but she was ignorant about specifics.

Nine days after the kidnapping, along with some trifle for Miriam, Alicia brought me a new chain for my olive wood cross. The chain was blessed, she said, by Hollings Fair himself, at an outdoor service in Bakersfield.

"Why don't they contact me? Why don't they ask for a ransom?" Miriam would moan. Even with Arthur's generous reward offer, no real leads had developed that we knew of. Gemma, the girl minding Chloe when she'd disappeared, had been questioned again and again, but could recall nothing unusual happening that day, no suspicious person or persons loitering at the shop, just one man looking for a special kaleidoscope who tried and refused every model in stock.

Soon this man came forward, a day tripper, Howard LeClair of Woonsocket, Rhode Island. He wasn't planning on buying a kaleidoscope, he'd only told Gemma that story to impress his girlfriend, a Kieran McKenna of Providence who was a stained glass artist. The police checked the backgrounds of both LeClair and McKenna, finding nothing but the occasional speeding ticket. So the couple wasn't connected to Chloe's kidnappers, they weren't distracting Gemma so that someone else could quickly spirit Chloe from the premises. They were interested in Miriam's kaleidoscopes, more or less. The police even investigated Carlyle Brackett, the Texan who'd commissioned the fire opal crown for his daughter, but he too was clean, except for some "misunderstandings" with the IRS.

On the day after he returned, I told Roberto what I'd discovered, I told him in Miriam's driveway, by the copper sculpture where I'd cornered Edward. I told him more than the "everything" I'd told the police: about finding Ian and Edward's history, about Clark and Jason and both my Truro visits, about Rockport and St. Harold's and my speaking to Almeida and DeRenzi. Roberto stood there, his mouth a perfect "O" except when he'd mutter "Holy shit!" "And remember my mother telling me my father was in the Navy? Well, that was a bunch of crap. He was Duncan Drummond, can you believe it?"

"Do you?" asked Roberto, whose tan, in Maine, had become lacquer-rich. "You and Ian don't look anything alike. You don't *act* anything alike. Thank God."

We could find out more, Roberto thought. Provincetown was full of youngsters from the Truro community, and they didn't get here using bicycles or cars, they hitched. We could get information by giving them rides, rides *back* to Truro, after confirming their destination during the requisite small-talk. They were often drunk or stoned, so, with the two of us urging them on, they might talk.

So we became the Provincetown-Truro shuttle, traversing the shore road, past the cabins and beach roses and the bay. We ignored hitchhikers over thirty, and, sheepishly, those with pink triangle or rainbow flag patches on their backpacks. We picked up the scruffy ones, those with haircuts months old, with odd clothing or musical instruments. We picked them up, off the soft shoulders, among the sand and roadkill and rubber from blown tires, smiling, squinting in the sun. Casually, we asked, "Where you headed?"—and our hearts dropped when they didn't reply, "Truro."

Over a period of two days, we picked up: a genuine Swedish college student, studying international relations at Georgetown; an acupuncturist from Iowa; a houseboy who'd once worked at the White Gull; and a six-foot tall drag queen, Vanda Orchid. None had ties to the Truro community, and the Swede had never heard of the tall ship, *Vasa*—or of Dala horses, the folk art cliché Miriam swore all Swedes should know like their shoe size.

Discouraged, we detoured to Welfleet, buying ice cream at a store that also sold candy. Not just salt water taffy and barley pops shaped like stained-glass lobsters. Here, glass shelves tempted you with slabs of fudge, veritable sidewalks of white and dark chocolate, and with liquid cherries and half-dips and nonpareils. The selection was so complete it included dietetic candy and "gourmet treats for the canine connoisseur." The atmosphere was decidedly upscale, with pastel figurines of milkmaids and shepherds and peasants with teams of ceramic oxen, so it was all the more surprising when a clerk in pearls and pink seersucker bellowed, "I saw you take that, and I've told you before not to come here!"

The accused shoplifter was in her thirties, at least, a fairskinned person scorched almost mocha. She was smiling, pleased with herself, as though she'd just told some memorable joke and the entire shop was her adoring audience.

"I live in Truro, I know about you people," the clerk continued, even louder.

The accused was standing on her toes, like a ballerina. She was barefoot, her legs so heavily tattooed they looked paisley. Her clothes—a dress the dark brown of mead, sandals with complex leather straps up to her knees—completed the illusion of someone fast-forwarded from the Dark Ages. Then she shattered all that by retrieving a cigarette from her fraying nylon satchel and lighting it with a Bic lighter. "Paranoid old fart," she muttered, so that everyone could hear.

A young man in a sleek suit came striding out from an office and gently took the woman's arm. "Let's just say the candy is our little gift. A going-away present. But I've got to ask you to smoke outside, and request that you *not* visit us again."

"I've seen the children from your community!" the clerk called to the woman.

The man in the sleek suit guided the woman to the door. Roberto and I followed, so fast our ice cream almost toppled from our cones.

"They sure are rude in that place," I said to the accused, as she hungrily smoked her cigarette.

She smiled, she was missing several teeth. "Could you give us a ride?"

"Us." Surely she was one of them, so the "us" made me expect street children or a giant might appear from nowhere.

"I don't need to go far. Just to the next town."

The next town was Truro. "Could we talk a bit?" I said.

The woman's teeth had rotted, like styrofoam left out in the elements. "I don't know why I bother patronizing that place. Especially when the food we grow is so superior. It's almost like alchemy, what we do. Like the philosophers' stone. Ever hear of that?"

"Wasn't that supposed to turn iron into gold?" I asked.

"Damn fucking right." She climbed into the back seat of my car. Discreetly, we tossed our ice cream cones into a trash barrel. I had Roberto drive so as to deflect attention from me; people usually focus on the driver of a car.

She rummaged through her satchel, which was full of, among other things, chocolate, peanut clusters, and caramels she'd stolen from the candy store, plus loose cigarettes, some flasks of expensive perfume—and a Buck knife. I flinched when I saw the knife. Smiling, she zipped the satchel shut. Like Edward's brother, Clark, she exuded the rancid odor that can only be earned by weeks of abstaining from all hygiene. Luckily, the car windows were still rolled down.

"Hot," I said, to jump-start the conversation. She crammed a caramel into her mouth, then, to my alarm, unzipped the satchel and took out the Buck knife. "Take this road until I tell you to turn," she said.

She was holding the knife in her right hand, her cigarette in her left. She smoked the last of the cigarette, a half-smoked stub when she'd lit it, then pitched it, still glowing, into the road, ignoring any fire hazard, any drought. She began running her left index finger along the blade of the knife, stroking it. Was she going to rob us or slit our throats, like Ian's? She delved back into her satchel and produced a dirty hunk of unwrapped cheese. Cutting a slice, she said, "The days are numbered," very matter-of-fact.

Not "Your days are numbered…"

"Left or right?" Roberto asked when the road forked. "Left," she answered. Roberto had seen her knife in the rear-view mirror and was visibly frightened. I wanted to touch him, comfort him somehow, but could not, could not alert her to his distress. She was armed, we were not.

"Would either of you like some cheese? It's home-made." The cheese was as grubby as her fingers, coated with lint and hair.

We both said No, we'd just eaten, so she put the cheese, again unwrapped, back into her satchel. The people in the community were under strict control, I thought. She smoked with the same hunger as Jason—and, like him, like the youngsters in Provincetown, she engaged in this behavior—using tobacco, sneaking candy—while away from Truro, away from the power of their leader. Yet didn't these guilty pleasures also show cracks in the monolith, the fact that these people dared do these things at all?

"Stop!" the woman suddenly commanded, and Roberto hit the brakes so that we all lunged forward. Giggling, she pointed backward with the knife. "I should've told you. Turn left back there." Roberto snapped on the signal that we were turning left and gave me a look that was equal parts fright and exasperation. Though the initial scheme was his.

Our passenger rested the Buck knife on her knees while running her fingers through her hair, which was reddish with outbreaks of blond and disorderly as Medusa's. Wanting to revive the subject of her background, I asked a deliberately foolish question: "Do you summer in Truro?"

She threw back her head and laughed. "I summer, winter, spring, and fall." She turned the Buck knife in her hands, taking tactile comfort from its presence, like a grandmother with a rosary. Then, with a crazy half-smile, she told me, "The Fall is coming very soon."

"What do you mean?" I asked, then she went silent as we drove through the woods with the sunlight gilding the leaves. I said, "This drought is affecting everything," wondering if she'd take the bait.

"It isn't affecting *us*. It isn't affecting us one goddamned bit." She was pulling at her dress, as if a mention of the heat brought her back to reality so that it bothered her. "We have our own irrigation system." She added, "I live with an engineer."

She was impressed by the system set up by the Master.

She slipped the knife back into her satchel. "Right at the white post. We're almost there."

This was not the road I'd discovered on my own, where the girl and the Giant had confronted me. And it was not, from what I could tell, the road Jason took the night I'd accompanied him deeper into their property, to the strange white house with the fireplace blazing and the numbing air-conditioning. This road was unpaved, but was wider than the others; it might lead to their main entrance. A wilting forest of deciduous trees interspersed with pines flanked its sides, but the foliage didn't sweep at the car as we passed. Here and there, someone had built cairns of stones, and, once, we encountered a large rock with the beginnings of human features, vague, like those forming on a fetus, carved into its surface.

With the knife away, our passenger became, paradoxically, more hostile. "Go faster," she said, but the road was riddled with ruts and holes, and was nowhere near wide enough for two cars, should we meet another. "I'm going as fast as I can without breaking an axle," said Roberto.

"Nothing breaks here," the woman said. "Things get mended, parts become whole."

We rounded a bend near an ancient oak with lichens and moss sheathing its trunk and its glossy foliage muted by dust from the road. "Who's there?" a gruff voice demanded; the tree itself seemed to be speaking, the spirit of the wood, the Green Man with his face of leaves from old pagan Europe. We stopped the car. Our passenger replied, "It's me, the wife Helga." This was the name of Mrs. Mikkonen's cat! She clutched her satchel, like a schoolgirl protecting her lunchbox.

From the woods in back of the oak came the Giant who'd ordered me away. Roberto, in the driver's seat, and the woman, behind him, were closest to the Giant, who stood at the car's left. Of course, the Giant might recognize my car, or notice me.

"Helga, is that really you?" Crunching through the under-brush, the Giant came closer. He bent low and peered into the car. His bloodshot eyes, small in proportion to his face, ignored us and sought our passenger.

Then, suddenly, he reached into the car and seized the woman by her hair; he pulled her hair like someone shucking the husk from an ear of corn, so that her head collided with the rim above the car window and she emitted a piercing yelp. "Don't ever try that again!" the Giant shouted, then, without further comment, he motioned to Roberto to proceed down the road.

Was being seen with us, outsiders, her offense, bringing us this deep into their land? Surely it was nothing to do with shoplift-ing in Welfleet. Had she neglected to perform some duty, some ritual? She kept touching her forehead near her scalp, where a large cut was now leaking blood. Roberto, shaken, asked, "Are you sure you're all right?"—speaking to both of us.

I offered her a packet of tissues from my glove compartment, which she refused. She instead toyed with the zipper on her satchel, while blood dripped from her cut.

Coming here, I now realized, was utterly insane. Roberto steered the car around a long curve in the road, then the woods parted, like a cliff breaking open.

Chapter Thirty-five

The metal fence, with its open gate, seemed like the only contemporary thing around. High and crowned with glinting razor wire, it was as out of place as a UFO. Because the scene before us might have come from some old woodcut of Grimm's fairy tales—a village, the kind of enchanted community that shimmers in Irish folklore at the bottom of a lake, or glows in German legend inside the stone heart of a mountain. Here were dozens of homes made of wood dark as the knots in pine, with steep roofs and window boxes hemorrhaging red geraniums. Here was a stone hall, the biggest building in the clearing, bearing a thin pole crowned with a beaten metal likeness of the sun, a sun spiky as a virus under a microscope.

All eyes in this village locked on us. All of these people were handsome or beautiful. Many of the adults were young, in their twenties and thirties. Few had reached middle age.

Some wore denim or hippie/peasant dresses busy with embroidery, but many wore clothing knights from the Crusades would have found familiar: tunics, robes, kilts, baggy pants, fastened by gilded pins and clasps, clothing made from rough fabric, the product of spinning wheels and hand-powered looms. Some small children were naked, and some, like most adults, were tattooed with sun designs and wore circular sun amulets on cords around their necks.

Roberto was struck speechless, as was I. Then I realized why this scene seemed familiar. It wasn't from my memory of fairy tales

or folklore, but came from Thomas Royall's Teutonic commu-
nity—the woven robes, the gilt sun capping a pole on a stone hall.
All these had been present in old photographs at the museum in
Provincetown. Of course here were added women and children.

Our passenger ducked out of the car, slammed the door, and
disappeared. "What the fuck do we do now?" Roberto whispered,
as the motor idled. "Leave." I struggled to keep my expression
calm. Then something banged on the back of the car.

Through the car's rear window, we saw three children, all
blond, all seemingly naked, balancing on our rear bumper,
banging on the trunk of the car, squealing and laughing. I was
about to ask the children to get down when the engine of the
car went dead.

A man whose hair seemed to emanate light had just pulled the
keys from the ignition. Now he was smiling broadly, his perfect
teeth so different from our dirty, beaten passenger's.

He stood beside the car in his kilt and began laughing. I
expected this to be some sort of cue, for the other people to laugh
as well, laugh at us, of course. The people of the community
had drawn close to us, like the parts of a piece of rope drawing
together to form a knot.

The Giant and the woman he abused, our passenger, were
gone, and Jason was nowhere in sight. The man beside the
car was one of the handsomest men I had seen in my life, like
someone posed naked in a mountain pond in a soft-porn coffee
table book. But he exuded menace.

He gestured to us to get out of the car. For an instant, I speculated he was deaf: he made no effort to speak and didn't seem
bothered by our silence. He beckoned us with his hand, and, as
we nervously followed, the other people who had been staring and
smiling retreated to their gardens and houses and the woods.

A narrow road bisected the village. This was paved, not with
asphalt or cobblestones, but with crushed oyster shells, like early
settlers used. The houses were small, like buildings designed
three-quarter scale for movie sets. Some reminded me of the
miniature Swiss cottages with figures that swing out, predicting

the weather, a maid for fair days, a man for foul, while others were crude like the yeomens' huts reproduced for tourists at Plimouth Plantation. I kept trying to get a glimpse inside them, but their windows were shuttered, their doors, apparently, bolted.

Between two houses, I saw a stack of plywood and rolls of silver-and-pink fiberglass insulation. This is really no different than some faux-colonial subdivision thrown up on a filled marsh or cranberry bog, I thought. Knowing full well this was faux comfort.

I nudged Roberto to notice the gardens substituting for grass in their front yards. Indeed the drought was no factor here: vegetables grew to freakish proportions, cucumbers longer than rattlesnakes, and tomatoes, taut as blood blisters, bigger than skulls. Suns with calm, archaic features, hewn from stone, baked in pottery, were set in the midst of these gardens. Even the air smelled different here, enlivened by spices or herbs.

The man we were following said nothing. The same sun face so predominant on antique maps, along with cherubs blowing wind and sea monsters all green scales and fins, was rendered in dazzling tattoo inks on his back, between his shoulder blades. Roberto, uncharacteristically, had gone silent, but I thought being quiet was surrendering our power, so I ventured to speak. "Everything here is so lush, and so beautiful." And bizarre, I might have added. The village had the smug independence of a gated community, the cleanliness of a lucrative theme park. That cleanliness contrasted with Clark, Edward's brother, and with Helga, our grimy hitchhiker.

I longed to see more evidence of the outside world, a McDonald's wrapper, the comforting trash of our consumer culture, something to pull us back into the mundane, the rational, anything but this lost Norse colony. The young man kept quiet. He kept walking down the path of bone-white shell. I remembered another walk, along the breakwater in Provincetown, eerie in the indigo and moonlight. Thinking of the children scrambling over my Volvo, I thought of little Chloe, of her helplessness and fear. If we were frightened here, imagine her, so small and young. If she was here at all, if she was even alive…

Roberto tugged my shoulder, broke my stride, made me stand still. The silent man sensed this change and wheeled around. Roberto said, "I'd just like to know where we're going. Or aren't you capable of conversation?"

The silent man didn't get mad. His smile, in fact, became broader than ever. Did he have a knife strapped somewhere in his tunic? His silence, size, and confidence carried a certain degree of authority. He was a kind of weapon all by himself.

Then, with an abrupt bow, he strode away. We were at the entrance to the great stone hall, the building that seemed to be the center of the community.

He went back of the hall, leaving us alone. We could see no one—in the woods, by the houses, along the path…"Let's go, while we can!" Roberto said, and then we remembered, they had the keys to my car. We were behind that towering fence topped with razor wire, something you'd see at a maximum-security prison. These people were capable of violence, even with their own, we'd just witnessed that. And we'd be in further trouble if we encountered anyone I'd met on my earlier excursions—they'd know we weren't casual visitors. Then what would they do? Anything they wanted. We'd told no one we were coming here today; this was a spur-of-the-moment action on our part. Was it on theirs? Had we blundered into a trap? Was that hitchhiker the bait? We were literally a captive audience.

"Sorry to keep you waiting," a male voice said.

This man behind us was about forty, in khaki pants and a hot-pink button-down shirt he'd rolled up beyond his elbows. He could've come from teaching history at St. Harold's, so the tattoos covering his bare arms, of suns and labyrinths and tribal bands serrated like sharks' teeth, seemed all the more incongruous. Like Jason, he had nothing mystical in his manner.

As if dismissing Roberto, he concentrated his energy on me. "This is the third time you've honored us with your presence."

So they knew who I was. Their whole hierarchy knew I'd been here on my own, had visited with Jason. Did they know it was me asking questions at St. Harold's? Did they know about my visit to Rockport, to Mrs. Mikkonen?

Roberto's face hardened with frustration. I was going to have to compensate for his silence, but our host was quite talkative enough. He could have been the vice-president for marketing at some Silicon Valley start-up: "What we have here is a world-class agricultural miracle, thanks to genetic engineering. And genius."

He went on, trying to impress us. Here, our host said, they were isolating the strongest genes "from many forms of life," preserving them for the benefit of the planet. Take fruit, for example. They were finding obscure types of apples, in defunct orchards in West Virginia, in upstate New York, apples abandoned by growers since the Cleveland administration in favor of popular varieties like the Delicious and the MacIntosh. They were grafting branches from these varieties onto other trees, thus preserving these once-plentiful kinds of fruit. And they were cultivating corn found frozen with Inca mummies, maize forgotten since the conquest by Pizarro.

"The more society cultivates the same few crops, the more vulnerable our food supply becomes." He glanced toward the two of us. "What if a previously unknown blight, a kind of AIDS of the grain world, were to decimate the wheat of North America, wipe out our wheat the way *phytophthora infestans* wiped out the potato in Ireland during the eighteen-forties? It's possible, we're taking that risk. And this is all the more foolish with our exploding population and global warming."

It made sense, but why adopt archaic dress and turn your children into beggars? He avoided the hall and took us down a road behind the cottages, into a larger clearing where seven immense greenhouses stood glittering in the sun.

"I'll show you a little bit of what we're all about," he said. I thought of the St. Harold's chapel and its tanks of bloated fish. Some part of me actually hoped to be impressed, so as not to feel embarrassed for him. And we had to listen, not to panic, if we were to find Chloe or escape unharmed.

He opened the door to the greenhouse with a key from a ring crowded with dozens of others. There were many locks in this utopia. Inside, it was foggy; a fine mist filled the air. From unseen pipes, the mist was seeping everywhere, soaking things growing in trays and on tables throughout the building. There was produce everywhere, even grander and glossier than those thriving in the earth outside the cottages: beans in pods longer than yardsticks, strawberries red as the plastic of beach balls, boulder-like canta-loupes. It was at once artificial and a kind of produce jungle where the edible things of the dinner table reclaimed their wildness, became, in this literal hothouse, like something man had yet to domesticate. There was a brutality to their sheer size.

"Year-round," our host boasted, "year-round harvesting com-parable only with the greenhouses of Iceland." Yes, I thought, I'd heard of those greenhouses, which tapped thermal springs to trick bananas into growing on sub-arctic lava wastes. The genius of a Nordic nation—he would reference that. To be polite, I had to admire something, which wasn't hard. It would've been hard *not* to be impressed. I'd complimented Jason on their strawberry preserves, so, to be consistent, I singled out a particularly spec-tacular strawberry plant, touching one of its swollen fruits.

It felt alive, in an almost animal sense. Our host picked it, and, gently, with the deft gestures of a magician, pulled it apart so that its hollow, whitish center was exposed. There was some-thing womb-like about its center, something like the yoni, the Tibetan symbol of the vulva, as though a fetus, a foreign cell, might be growing inside. Engineering, genetic engineering, that was why these vegetable things were growing so large, as outlandishly large as animals. They were doctoring genes, these people dressed like Charlemagne.

He offered us each half of the berry. "I'm allergic," Roberto said, although I was sure that was an excuse. So he presented the entire berry to me. Would they blatantly drug us, I wondered? I'd singled out the strawberries myself, but *he* had picked this particular one, and if they succeeded in drugging me, at least Roberto could come to my aid.

The berry was delicious, like some archetype, the first man tasted, far too large to consume in one bite or even two. "It's wonderful!" I was being perfectly honest, while our host grinned.

Something in the mist was making the air difficult to breathe, and, for a moment, I thought of Edward and his asthma and Clark, his mad brother, and their whole family ruined by these people. As our host explained the intricacies of their irrigation system, the pipes and pumps that coaxed water from the pond and the aquifer involved in all of this, I thought too of the stoned youngsters in Provincetown, and of the Giant abusing Helga. Some people "earned" their Nordic names, I thought, Helga, for instance, but not, apparently, Jason. There was a hierarchy here, layers of authority as calcified as India's ancient castes.

"You're using modern technology," I said, "yet—"

"Yet our appearance strikes you as part of another time."

"And another place," I said.

"A man without spirit, a man without knowledge of something higher, is like a person lying in a coma. He is no more than a collection of connected organs, heart, liver, stomach, intestines, kept functioning by artificial means." He said, "We live in a civilization hooked to a respirator."

He was locking the greenhouse we'd just seen. Through the murky glass of another, I could see blurry forms, bent amid the plants. The glass transformed them into colored smudges, like reflections perverted by funhouse mirrors. They seemed short, like dwarfs in Velázquez paintings. "What's in there?" I asked, wanting to see something other than just plants.

Not answering, he continued, "Our lives here are modeled on the Golden Age of Norse Exploration. Our outward appearance is actually unimportant, a reminder, like a string tied around one's finger. We honor our Master's Norse heritage, the age when the Northmen first touched these shores."

A claim refuted by most archaeologists. And I didn't picture the Vikings as particularly spiritual: burning monasteries, sacking towns. But I didn't argue.

"Our Master is from your part of the world." Our host scrutinized my reaction, which I kept minimal. This information could have come from Mrs. Mikkonen or from Jason, circulating at Ian's funeral.

In the greenhouse we were passing, with the opaque, misty glass, one of the small figures ran, ran down the center of the aisle between the plants. The figure ran behind glass so cloudy that it disappeared.

We were conducted away, to other greenhouses where more fruit, more vegetables were flourishing, even a collection of bonsai, little bits of Kyoto, cypresses and cherry trees centuries old. With care, with tenderness, they thrived. Restricted to their limited dishes, pruned, pampered, fed, they lasted centuries longer than their brethren outdoors.

The truncated trees reminded me of the bound feet of Chinese concubines, beautiful in embroidered slippers, but hideous when exposed, like hands brutalized by arthritis, like fetuses gone wrong. Here, our host said, bonsai were valued as "living ambassadors, emissaries from the botanical past." They were studied "at the cellular level" to see what they could teach about plant longevity. I wondered whether the metaphor with their pot-bound community was deliberate.

Our host continued, speaking complex agricultural jargon. He could talk forever about the beauty, the efficiency of their system, and make it all sound sane and even superior. He was boasting about their community avoiding the drought when the long-silent Roberto broke in. "Who does all this work?"

Our host maintained a beatific exterior. "We're a community, a family. Everything is shared."

"The woman we drove here," Roberto said, "she looked like a street person. She was dirty, she looked hungry."

"There is no hunger here, only abundance." The man nodded at the produce prospering in the greenhouse, at the raspberries, red as sores. "Just look around you. The hunger is outside, a spiritual famine. That compelled you to come here—perhaps." His "perhaps" was confrontational.

I knew, then, that I'd been crazy not to share Edward's story with the police. If these people were responsible for killing Ian, for causing Clark to go mad and die, for abducting Chloe, for all sorts of crimes, Almeida was right—it was best for the authorities to handle them. Leaving the humidity of our last greenhouse, I was about to thank him for our tour and ask for the keys to my Volvo, when he said, "Our people are fixing your car."

"What's wrong with it?"

"Only a flat tire, a small puncture."

Of course we'd taken some difficult roads, getting here, virtual gullies, winding through the woods. A rock, a nail could've damaged a tire. No, that was ridiculous; I was making excuses to absolve them, to stay calm, when I knew perfectly well what had happened—they had vandalized my car to prevent our escape.

Roberto was about to erupt, so I placed my hand flat against his chest.

"The Master is anxious to meet you," our host said.

Chapter Thirty-six

Some called him the Master, others, the Golden One. Was this the same person? Was this Mikkonen from Rockport, or some other authority? Everything was all so formal and ritualistic. We could've been Commodore Perry and his American crew negotiating entry into a long-closed Japan, trying to penetrate the paper screens of the shogun's palace.

"First, you must be purified," our host said to me, "before you enter his presence." "You may stay here," he told Roberto. "Someone will be along for you in a moment."

They wanted to separate us. "We'd both be honored to meet the Master. But I can't go without Roberto, I won't."

"Of course." He smiled as if indulging us. "Of course. The two of you."

I realized now I'd ensnared Roberto in my fate. And I'd been the one they'd targeted, caught probing.

Roberto sensed my fears, saying, "I wouldn't miss this for the world."

Our host ushered us toward a grove of birches, then into woods, past cairns of stones, and, standing in an expanse of muck, a fantastic lantern, a kind of iron spider, like the bristling Victorian lamps on the old section of the Boston Public Library. Surely this was a relic of Royall's community, disintegrating amid the skunk cabbage.

"That lantern," I said.

"It sheds no light," he laughed. "It's left over from Mr. Royall's Great Mistake, as we call it."

He disparaged Royall, just like Jason.

We crossed a small bridge of peeling logs, over a brook the drought had downgraded to a muddy hollow. Before us, in the woods, a kind of hut had been built into a brushy hillock. On either side of the structure's low entrance, granite troughs held water vivid with sunlight. A eucalyptus odor bit through the air. Of course, this was some sort of sauna or steam bath.

Was he going to purify us, seduce us, or both? The KGB had schooled Soviet agents in love-making of all varieties to compromise useful foreign visitors. But Roberto and I were openly gay, onstage, for God's sake, we couldn't be blackmailed.

"Loki will assist you," our host told us.

From the entrance to the bath, our first guide, the dazzling silent man with the sun tattooed on his back, came smiling, with fawn-colored cloth draped over his arm.

Our older host retreated up the path we'd just taken. At least Loki had the keys to my Volvo, I thought. Or hoped.

He actually spoke. "For you." The fawn-colored bolts of cloth were, we saw, clothing, shirts and pants with pewter clasps embellished with whorls like labyrinths.

Does telepathy work? Can thought travel from person to person without voice or modems or fiberoptic cable? At that moment, I sincerely hoped so. With a glance and a nod, I tried to rally Roberto to act the part, to improvise with the greatest intelligence and caution possible, to comply with these people's requests, however odd. If their leader wanted to see us, I reasoned, they wouldn't harm us, if they wished to, until we'd satisfied his sense of curiosity. They, after all, had engineered the meeting, right down to the "small puncture" in our tire.

Loki draped the extra clothing on the branch of an oak. Then, shy as a boy in his first gym class, he undid the clasp fastening his kilt and allowed the garment to slip down past his legs, past his ankles. Beneath the kilt, he wore a loincloth, glaring white as adobe against his tan. "You too," he said, and laughed. "The two of you."

Hard and smooth, he had shaved himself hairless, like a swimmer competing in the Olympics. Bending, he pulled open the low door to the steam bath, which you bowed to enter, like a shrine.

I stripped quickly. Roberto was slower, but he too removed his clothes, hanging them with mine and Loki's kilt and the fawn-colored items presumably meant for us.

Loki held the small heavy door, waiting for us to enter first. Steam billowed out, sharp with eucalyptus. "I don't like it too hot," Roberto said, fright and irritation affecting his voice. "Not too hot," Loki said, and, for the first time, I speculated that our companion was not haughty, mute, or foreign, but "slow."

Roberto balked at going first, so, naked, I slipped inside. I found myself in a long room, twelve by fifteen feet, gorgeous with tile and well-lit. Bulbs which Thomas Edison might have manufactured, big, with prominent filaments, like the stamens of lilies, were burning in brass lamps shaped like clusters of antlers. The walls were covered in murals, figures from Norse mythology: Thor, with his hammer; trolls with the wide, panicked eyes of trout; a spectral horse white as frost; and warriors with blond braids and blood-brightened axes. Spongy wooden benches rimmed the room, and, built into one wall was an altar, a block of granite inscribed with runes. Stacked in front of it were earthenware pots and iron instruments, pokers and tongs.

Roberto, now next to me, also gaped. Mist streaming down the walls seemed to animate the figures, making this seem less like a bunker dug in a Truro hillside and more like a dream or the underworld. But it smelled rank, like the St. Harold's gym, of bodies and the odor of plumbers' chemicals.

Loki came inside, then banged the door shut. He retained his loincloth. His buttocks were naked, heavily tattooed with abstract symbols.

I ran my hands over the tiles, over the ogres, gods, and warriors, now fading as the stream intensified. "Royall did this?" I asked Loki, instinctively simplifying my speech. "The artists in Royall's colony?"

"Not good. Royall—not good." Loki laughed then worked busily at the altar, scattering a spray of dried herbs that he'd retrieved from a ceramic jar on the floor. The herbs sizzled on the stone, filling the room with a welcome musky fragrance.

"Excuse me," Roberto said to Loki. "I'm not being disrespectful. I'd just like to know what's going on."

I was just as puzzled, unsure whether we were supposed to copy Loki's actions or observe.

"What does all of this mean?" Roberto said to Loki and to me. He was referring, I was sure, to our entire experience in Truro, to everything in this mad little fiefdom.

Loki dipped his fingertips into an earthenware jar on the floor by the altar. "Oils, oils for cleansing."

Laughing, he seized Roberto in a bear hug. "If you don't mind," Roberto protested, but Loki laughed and rocked Roberto back and forth, then gently wrestled him to the bench by the altar.

I kept glancing at the tongs by the altar, iron tongs, heavy enough to knock a man unconscious. I was about to grab them and attack Loki when he released Roberto and instructed him, "Lie flat. Just relax."

Roberto obeyed. Loki rubbed his hands together and repeated, "Oils, oils for cleansing," then began massaging Roberto's chest, in wide circles around his nipples, then in quick, rough strokes down his belly.

Roberto lay rigid, shaking his head. Loki continued massaging him, concentrating on his task like a third-grader concentrating on a test, earnest and serious. And harmless, I thought; if someone harms us here, it won't be him, but someone with greater authority.

Roberto cringed. Loki was working on his belly, his palms flat as he rubbed the taut flesh. Was this strapping man gay; was that why he'd been assigned to take us to this place? Roberto was too frightened to respond.

Loki kneaded Roberto's upper thighs. He was no longer pinning Roberto to the bench, so Roberto began to struggle to sit upright. "I've had enough," he said.

To distract Loki into giving Roberto a reprieve, I placed my hands on Loki's shoulders. I was shaking as badly as the night I'd found Ian on the breakwater. I was terrified he would feel me shaking, that I'd communicate my terror, flesh to flesh. "My friend is shy. He's a wonderful actor, much better than me, but you know the cliché, all actors are shy."

I was rubbing Loki's shoulders as he knelt by Roberto. His shoulders were wide as a yoke long-dead peasants might have used harnessing oxen. His skin, despite his size and tattoos, was baby-soft. I had to lift his long hair to massage his back. I thought of other people who had to mimic lust to save their lives, like Scheherazade amusing her sultan. But I had the advantage of being an actor, so, as Loki's long golden hair brushed against my body, I told Roberto, "Relax," and found myself becoming aroused.

Roberto seemed riveted to the bench, watching, letting me orchestrate the scene. Murmuring, Loki stood, still facing Roberto. He trusted me enough to turn his back to me when potential weapons like tongs and jars of herbs and oil were nearby, near the altar.

I began rubbing his lower back, where the loincloth knotted near his waist. I had taken my advice to Roberto and was beginning to relax, to focus on the moment and ignore the dangers beyond, so, playfully, I tugged at Loki's loincloth.

Loki faced me, took my hand, and dipped my fingers into the jar of oil he'd been using to massage Roberto. "Oil for cleansing." "Yes," I said, then surprised myself by laughing.

I rubbed the oil into my hands. Warm and runny, it exuded no discernable fragrance. Loki smiled, handsome and stupid. His loincloth gave no clue as to his state of arousal; the fabric was too puzzling, too thick. To gauge whether I should continue my seduction, I again playfully tugged at his loincloth.

Loki laughed. He mimed removing the loincloth, but kept it on. "I'm clean," he said, still smiling. Unsure what he meant, unsure what to do, I decided to act on my own, without glancing at the nervous Roberto.

As I massaged the oil onto Loki's chest, my erection knocked against his thigh. If this offended him, he'd let me know soon, I was sure.

Instead, he bent his knees and pushed the loincloth past his hips. Then he stood before me naked, for the first time. Wringing the loincloth in his hands, he repeated, "I'm clean."

Then a pulse traveled through me, not desire or fright, but nausea. Where his testicles belonged was a line of scabs, a line of scabs bright with infection, oozing pus.

Someone had used a knife on him. Loki had been castrated.

Chapter Thirty-seven

Roberto was rising from the bench, pointing through the steam to something beyond Loki. It was a young girl in ragged, archaic clothing. She crossed the room until she came to the altar. Then she sprinkled more herbs across the hot granite slab, with no more reverence or mysticism than a Mexican housewife setting down tortillas on her stove. Our nudity did not seem to embarrass her, although Loki quickly covered himself, as if she somehow threatened him.

"Are you done?" the girl asked Loki, superior despite her youth. "All done," he answered, as the herbs deposited on the altar filled the room with minty coolness. She walked toward us and Roberto positioned his legs to cover himself.

"If you're done," the girl told Loki, "get them dressed. The Master will see them now."

We washed, we three men, in the troughs of spring water by the entrance to the steam bath. While we were in the steam, someone had left towels in the branches of the tree containing our clothes. I found the thick towels, ordinary cotton with the manufacturers' labels still attached, comforting objects from the rational world.

"Leave them here," Loki commanded, when we attempted to retrieve our own clothing. "Yours," Loki said, of the fawn-colored shirts and pants.

Loki seemed to have rinsed off his playfulness in the trough of water. Stern and intent, he refused to interact with us beyond telling us to follow him deeper into the woods, along dirt paths crumbly from the drought, until we came to a building unlike any we'd yet seen—circular, of chalky concrete, with Bauhaus lines and slits of windows, like a bunker.

This was not the building where Jason had brought me, but he was here, part of a small crowd lazing on the grass in front of the building: a woman nursing a naked newborn; adolescent boys whittling something with bright knives; the Giant who'd guarded the entrance to their world, listening to a sputtering walkie-talkie. Jason's charcoal suit, his tie as red and narrow as a tongue, and his loafers with brass buckles looked absurd in the woods, in this heat. All these people, handsome thanks to genes or surgery, directed their attention toward us.

Jason smiled, a broad transforming smile directed at me, a smile of conquest, I thought. He whispered something to an older woman whose golden hair was becoming silver, a woman busy with a lap full of loose-leaf binders whose plastic covers were another welcome souvenir of our own century.

Would Jason doom us or help us or do neither? It was the woman who rose and picked her way through her compatriots. "The Master will see you now," she told us. Her soft face seemed motherly and sincere. "It's a beautiful day." But she spoke with rehearsed enthusiasm, like the receptionist in an oncologist's office, used to distracting patients. Her shift was richer than others I'd seen today, blue with acorns stylized in metallic threads. "I feel as though I know you," she said, voicing my own thoughts. Then she punched in some code, some combination into the panel of rubber buttons doing duty for a doorknob.

Inside, we entered a hall, frigidly air-conditioned and lined with shut doors, like some dangerous corridor in a dream. Everything was white—the concrete of the walls, the terrazzo of the floors— with no windows or furniture to break the bleakness.

I shivered in the skimpy clothing; Roberto hugged himself. The woman chose one of the identical doors and punched another code into a panel of buttons. Then, cautiously, the door glided aside—and we saw him.

He was immense; he must have weighed four-hundred pounds. He had a soft, doughy face and golden hair that went on indefinitely. It was the most beautiful hair imaginable, like the substance composing saints' haloes in paintings, but no Giotto or Cimbaue had ever captured a being such as this.

He was dressed in a robe the color of his hair, rich as a reliquary enshrining the bones of an apostle. Images and motifs, suns and serpents and runes, flickered into sight on his robe then vanished, like figures in a hologram. His toes, like fat slugs, protruded from gilded sandals. He sat on a dais, on a leather and steel chair, tapping at the keyboard of a laptop computer. In front of him, on a folding metal table adorned with paint-by-numbers roses—surely from his mother's home in Rockport—rested a large calabash filled with thick liquid the color of grape bubble gum.

The compulsive neatness so evident in the community outside was absent here. All flat surfaces in the room, desks, chairs, the tops of tables and cabinets, were burdened with stacks of papers, magazines, and books. And what books! Huge texts with leather covers soft as the spoors bursting from puffballs; books written by men sure the human body was governed by the four humors. Interspersed with these were magazines from Silicon Valley, and, chillingly, issues of *Janes,* the British armaments journal.

There were no windows in the room, and no chairs other than his. Roberto began to kneel, but I squeezed his arm to stop him. We had to stand, to retain as much of our power as possible.

His eyes were the pale blue penetrating sort. From this huge man came a tiny voice, a voice accustomed to obedience, with no need to be loud. "Why have you sought to sabotage me?"

"Don't be ridiculous," Roberto piped up, but the Master channeled his hostility toward me.

Wearing their clothing made me literally uncomfortable in my own skin, but I treated my answer as an actor's challenge, to sound as clear and confident as possible. "I've *never* tried to sabotage you."

He dipped two fingers into the calabash of liquid, then licked them clean. I remembered this gesture from a luau in Waikiki. It was poi in the calabash, the taro root paste esteemed in ancient Hawaii. In his girth, the Master resembled some Polynesian king whose shadow was so sacred that to cross it was to invite execution.

"Friendship seldom comes in disguise. You were observed, photographed, actually, in Stark, in Rockport, and twice on our property here in Truro. Not counting today."

We could hardly be blamed for our presence here today, I said. We'd come here by accident, we'd met a random hitchhiker who happened to be heading for their community.

"There are no accidents," he said, as though he'd coined this cliché, grown it in one of his greenhouses.

"Then that explains what happened to my car," I said, "the flat tire I got here. It was no accident."

I knew then that I had overplayed my hand. A hardness in his eyes lent strength to his moon face. He shifted slightly so that his laptop computer almost fell to the floor. "Your friend was an evil man!" he snapped, and a flush discolored his pallid skin the way sediment, shaken, discolors a beaker of liquid. He wasn't referring to Roberto, but I wanted him to speak the name first, to divulge as much as possible without my prompting him.

"You told Jason lies, about starting a small business. Your business is subterfuge." He straightened his laptop and resumed typing; it seemed an automatic gesture, like our hitchhiker fingering her knife.

I said the first thing that came to my mind: "I had to see you."

"He said the same thing."

"Who?" I asked, knowing the answer.

"Your desperate friend." His smile was at war with his eyes.

"You'll have to excuse me," Roberto said. "I'm not feeling well."

It was evident that he was telling the truth; he'd gone white. The older woman fetched a big silk pillow from a pile of junk mail and placed it on the floor. Roberto sank down, cradling his head in his hands.

We'd had a difficult day, I told our hosts, exhausting, what with the heat then the steam bath, the cleansing with Loki. Shuddering inside, I remembered the sores where his testicles had been. "We've had nothing to eat since morning."

"Of course," the Master said, brightening. He disrupted a stack of chaotic papers on a filing cabinet next to his chair, revealing a speaker. Cupping his hand as if whispering to a child, he mumbled something into the speaker, and, in a matter of seconds, another young girl, the smallest I'd seen here, came in, bearing a tray of fresh cut fruit, strawberries and peaches and plums.

I'd been daring enough to eat the strawberry Roberto refused in the greenhouse, but this tray of fruit—cold, fragrant, gleaming—had appeared all too quickly. But before we could make a decision about its safety, the Master frowned, and, indicating Roberto, scolded the little girl: "He's allergic to strawberries, he said so in the greenhouse." She curtsied, holding her grubby dress like a countess dancing the minuet, but the gesture was pitiful, coming from someone so fearful and so young. She scurried away with the plate.

"What I'm talking about is evolution," the Master said.

"Excuse me?" I said. I'd sat on the floor next to Roberto, who seemed a bit better. The subservience implied in our position bothered me, but I thought it flattered the Master and brought forth what passed for benevolence on his part.

"Have you heard of the brown tree snake?" he asked us, shifting so that new deities or demons flickered then vanished, temporary as mirages, in the folds of his robe. "The brown tree snake is native to southeast Asia, and to New Guinea and Australia. In its native habitat, predators keep it in check. But it fares quite well as a stowaway, slipping into packing crates, even winding around the wheels of jet aircraft, thus managing to cross oceans."

He made a feminine gesture; he gathered a handful of his hair and began stroking it. Then, from a plastic box, he drew a paper towel moistened with alcohol and rubbed his plump hands, afraid, apparently, of contaminating himself with his own hair. I thought of Loki's definition of being "clean"—castration—and of our "cleansing" with steam, oils, and herbs. Females here—abused women, neglected children—formed some sort of servant class, some of them. Was this Chloe's fate? Was she here, in some greenhouse or cell? How terrified a little child—or anyone—would be. I kept thinking of Miriam's crying, of how Chloe was afraid of the dark. We must find her, somehow, if she was here.

The Master resumed his zoology lesson. "This snake, the brown tree snake, has made its way to Guam, the tiny island of Guam in the South Pacific. There, it has no natural enemies. It is free to multiply rapturously." He enjoyed pronouncing the last word, smiling to reveal miniature teeth, juvenile as the milk teeth of a young boy. "The brown tree snake has infested Guam, at densities as high as ten thousand snakes per acre. It has been known to exist in sewers and emerge from pipes and drains into people's homes. It has bitten small babies in their cradles. It is immune to pesticides, and, because of its habitat and appetite for eggs, it has rendered the songbirds of Guam, the native songbirds, extinct in the wild. The songbirds of Guam exist only in captivity."

"I would like to go now," Roberto announced. "I'm sure that by now your very capable colleagues have fixed our flat tire, our puncture, the 'no accident.' Or are we in captivity, like the songbirds of Guam?"

Just then, the little girl returned, wheeling a rickety aluminum cart on which wobbled three steaming plates of something thick and vegetarian, turnip-colored. Again, the girl curtsied. Her legs were peppered with insect bites and scratches.

"Choose whichever plate you wish," the Master commanded. "I shall take the third."

He was giving us this choice to challenge us to trust him; everything couldn't be poisoned if he was to eat it too. "Shall," he had said, like a character from *Masterpiece Theatre,* yet the overall impression he conveyed, despite his robe and sandals and long golden hair, was of power and an alien masculinity, like the mountain of power that is a sumo wrestler.

Roberto chose first, then I did. The Master took the remaining plate. He was the first to eat, attacking the food with a golden spoon which he cleaned with paper towels before using. The food was very hot; it singed the roof of my mouth, but it tasted good, like yam with a barrage of spices, as if all the herbs in Scents of Being had been included in this one particular recipe. The Master was a noisy eater, smacking his enlightened lips, noisy as an adopted puppy at its first meal out of the pound.

The young girl remained in the room, along with the older woman, kneeling on the chill terrazzo. They kept their attention fixed on the Master as the three of us ate. The room, like the building where I'd been grilled by Jason, was air-conditioned bitingly cold. The little girl, in particular, seemed to be minding it, and she was so thin, so I said, "If you like, have some of my food."

"NO!" The Master's word filled the room, as the little girl recoiled in terror.

"It was delicious, but I've had plenty."

"She is not the right level!" the Master bellowed. "She has not evolved, she is not suitable!" He dabbed his mouth with a moistened towel. I'd angered him; his robe rose and fell unevenly while he caught his breath. For a moment, something akin to fear disturbed his expression as he said, "How did you first meet Ian Drummond?"

Chapter Thirty-eight

It startled me, his suddenly saying my half-brother's name, his bringing murder into our meal, into this engineered Valhalla. But wasn't that exactly where it belonged, where all of the events of this year originated—from Ian's death to the museum assaults to Chloe's kidnapping? So, when he asked the question, I felt a strange sense of relief verging on hope.

The little girl, in her dress bright with grease, took away our plates on her rickety cart. How could someone so fastidious tolerate someone so dirty serving him food? There was no logic to it. But expecting logic here was illogical. She was not the right "level," so perhaps her presence didn't count; Roman matrons went naked in front of their slaves, whose stares were no more embarrassing than those of the pet monkeys they'd imported from Africa.

His question was direct; so was my answer. "I knew Ian all my life."

"And all his too? Right up to the end?" Smiling, he exposed his stunted teeth.

"I didn't kill Ian," I said.

"Somebody did." He resumed typing on his laptop.

"How did *you* know Ian?" I boldly asked.

He set his laptop computer aside, on the tray with the paint-by-numbers roses and calabash of poi. "Ian came to me for nourishment," he said, this most well-nourished of men. "Ian came to me for spiritual nourishment, he was a seeker." The priest had used that word, "seeker," at Ian's funeral. "At least that was his initial guise."

"He was a lawyer too," I said.

The Master's voice, once small, became large enough to fit his frame. "Ian was a swindler, a thief!" he bellowed.

"Master, are you all right?" the middle-aged woman asked him.

He ignored her. "Your Ian, your wretched Ian, knew the end was near."

Loki had mentioned "the Fall," while the Master spoke of "the end."

"He negotiated the sale of your miserable school. He insinuated his way into the trustees' confidence just as St. Harold's was going bankrupt. Then he handled the sale to us, mishandled the sale, I should say. He cheated us blind—he sold land he'd promised us to a developer—and the land we bought by Lake Chiccataubett was useless! Useless—protected by the Endangered Species Act. Because some plant, some useless plant, the Berkshire bog orchid, was already growing there!"

I didn't argue with his hypocrisy about biodiversity, why the Berkshire bog orchid didn't merit preservation while the songbirds of Guam certainly did.

"I didn't kill your friend Ian Drummond, but whoever performed that deed, whoever stabbed him through the heart, did a great service for a small multitude."

The Master referenced only Ian's chest wound, ignoring his throat, cut ear-to-ear. Like the media. Was it possible he didn't know? Was it possible he was telling the truth?

"Whoever stabbed him only completed the work nature had begun. Nature, in her infinite wisdom."

"About the tax matter, Master," the middle-aged woman said.

"'Completed the work nature had begun'—what do you mean?" I asked as the woman approached him using a series of small bows, quick like spasms, then placed her bundle of binders and folders onto the metal tray, next to the calabash of poi.

"Ian sought my help because he was dying. He'd developed lymphoma due to a history of steroid usage."

Lymphoma—was that possible?

"I met him through my mother's business. His father visited my mother's place of business. Ian had been using steroids for years. In larger and larger amounts. The result was a cancer, a lymphoma. So whoever killed Ian wasted their energy. Nature had already taken that assignment."

Ian had certainly become muscular, very abruptly, and there *was* something unnatural about his body—it was swollen like the produce cultivated here. He'd changed during his time away from Boston. Yet he smoked and drank like someone from *film noir*. He'd littered his P-town bedroom with exercise equipment, which suggested an interest in bodybuilding, but whether that interest manifested itself through workouts or steroids, that was difficult to tell. No one had spoken of cancer—not his family and not the police—but the police had kept his throat wounds secret, so they might have kept his lymphoma secret too.

The Master drank from a pitcher of water with crescent moons of lemon floating through it. He seemed exhausted, spent by his anger or outburst, and his soft, wide face was covered in droplets of sweat. He clutched the pitcher with both of his hands, as if for comfort. "So we have met at last. And you have learned something, even you. About your insufferable classmate and the agricultural breakthroughs we've made here."

Then the Master and the woman exchanged nods—all but simultaneously. I couldn't tell who'd nodded first.

"I'll show our visitors out," the woman said.

This woman might have been encountered bringing bread to a bake sale or sons to a soccer match. Her normalcy was putting us at ease. Ushering us outside the bunker-like building, she said, "There's so much to see before you're gone."

The crowd on the grass had dispersed, Jason with them. It was a humid afternoon, the air thick and warm like felt. The woman introduced herself as Freya, so she'd earned her Nordic name—without falling out of favor, like the castrated Loki and

battered Helga. "Your automobile is fixed," Freya said. How she
knew this, it was hard to tell. She had been with us the entire
time during our audience with the Master or the Golden One,
whatever that creature was called.

We were standing outside the bunker-like building, on a
lawn so perfect it had no more weeds than the cellophane grass
of Easter baskets.

"We can start with the history of this place," Freya said. "Cape
Cod has been occupied since Paleoindian times."

Then, in the stillness, something shrieked—shrill and desperate. The sound stamped Roberto's face with fear, and mine as
well, I'm sure. Overlapping, we both asked, "What was that?"

Freya's smile remained intact. "It must have been a bird."

It had come from something larger than a bird.

"It sounded like *a child*," Roberto said.

I thought of Chloe, of course, and of the frightened girl
who'd served us food.

"It must've been an animal in the woods," Freya said.

It was hard to tell where the scream had originated, back
of the bunker-like building or elsewhere. Freya expanded her
account, with a digression about the Native American diet and
its archaeological evidence on their property: shell middens, the
scorched bones of deer…The cry we had heard was human, I
was certain—the girl who'd brought us fruit by mistake, being
punished.

"…The Native Americans roasted lobsters, smoked them or
put them in stews," Freya was saying, taking us away from the
Master's bunker and any further disturbance. "But you're interested in Royall, in his little experiment. At least you mentioned
that on your first excursion."

They knew everything, remembered everything, my exchange
with the Giant in the road, for example, but at least Royall was
a relatively benign subject, a means of diverting the discussion
from my past probing—as we sought to talk our way out of
this Hades.

She led us downhill. We did nothing more about the cry we had heard; fear kept us furious but silent. We went through woods with foliage dulled by dust.

"Most of the buildings from Royall's time are intact. After his experiment failed so swiftly, so pathetically, the grounds became a series of summer camps, but Royall's buildings were preserved."

She was admitting they'd lied to me earlier; the Giant had claimed Royall's buildings were destroyed.

Roberto, I sensed, was about to erupt. I prevented him by saying groups of artists had always intrigued me with the way they collaborated and cross-fertilized. "I worked with a group of actors in our comedy troupe."

"Yes, Jason mentioned that," she said.

I had more than enough material to approach the police—their link to Ian, the Master's anger over Ian selling the property at St. Harold's, and the sinister culture of this place. Yet the story of Ian's cancer had jolted me. Those malignant cells were a wild card I hadn't imagined.

"It strikes me as odd," I said, "since you mentioned Jason, it's odd that he's African-American—"

"It strikes you odd that he's African-American?" Freya said. "You are quite the Eurocentric." With her gold and silver hair and her dress embroidered with acorns in metallic threads, she actually laughed, then, with seriousness, said, "Are you a racist?"

"It's just that your emphasis here is on Norse culture, Norse names, these buildings inspired by the Viking age…And many of your people, like Jason, dye their hair."

"Women in pre-contact Hawaii bleached their hair. Aboriginals in Australia have naturally blond hair, and they're much darker than Jason. Dark skin and light hair are quite culturally compatible. Are you a racist?"

"Of course not."

Her actions of putting us at ease had thinned, just as the woods had thinned out into a huge sunlit meadow containing four squat stone buildings resembling the hall with the sun disk we'd seen earlier. Beyond these—gray and flat, like an elephant shot on safari—was a glacial boulder. Shading this was a tree, a beech so ancient cables connected its branches to brace them. A pond glittered back of these, its surface rippled like chain mail.

"Jason was in a great deal of trouble when he came to us," Freya volunteered. "In trouble with the law, in trouble with drugs. The Master saved his life. We're not concerned with race per se, we're concerned with preserving quality, the best of all life, animal and botanical, from the coming climactic disasters."

She detailed the evidence that things already were awry: alien species crowding out native life, tropical diseases like dengue fever creeping north. Glaciers were melting like unplugged freezers, the ozone layer was rupturing. Why these verified concerns should excuse child abuse and a Hitlerian fringe of eugenics, she didn't specify. She ran her fingers through her hair, so that her head moved and her sea glass earrings tinkled like wind chimes on a country porch. "Our hair is an expression of unity—and respect for our Master's heritage."

Freya unlocked the door to one of the low buildings. As she turned the iron key, rust crunched in the lock. Inside, the room smelled of decay, of wood rotting and metal corroding. There were windows in the room, but any light they might have shed was censored by heavy shutters.

Beds lined the long room. They were without mattresses; ropes sagged where cushions or mattresses once belonged. What were their lives like, the men who'd used these beds, these sons of Civil War veterans, who'd worn condoms made from animals' skins, who'd ridden so many horses and never heard of a virus? What was it like sleeping in these stone dormitories on these beds Leif Ericsson would have found familiar? And what charisma, what force, made artists from the Appalachians to the Cascades forsake their known lives for Thomas Royall's regimen? Mikkonen too possessed this power, the ability to inspire, to compel others to heed his wishes. Shamans and inventors had this too; they could expunge doubt from their personalities, squeeze it out like splinters.

The starkness of the artists' beds contrasted with the majesty of one chair, carved with gods and gnomes in never-ending battle.

"The beds were used by the artists. This throne was used by Royall when he paid them a visit. Royall was very hierarchical," she said, as if their community was as democratic as a New England town meeting.

"The metal-workers slept in this dormitory." On a table, through the murk, I could see an array of swords, axes, a pike, even an iron bird, all vulnerable with rust.

"Why did they come here? What attracted them to this land?" I asked, remembering the museum exhibit and assuming the stone just ahead was the same one in the old photographs.

"They passed nothing on," Freya said.

Roberto picked up an axe. Rust dropped from its blade onto the table.

"They passed nothing on," Freya repeated. But of course. The Master was concerned with procreation, the begetting of cells, not art, so Royall's community, and Roberto and I, met with pious disapproval.

Their ecological doomsday festered in their imagination as vividly as any revelation John experienced on Patmos. It was a wonder these people sent their low-caste children to panhandle among us in Provincetown; it was a wonder they hadn't teamed with the fundamentalists against us. But perhaps Royall's all-male enclave—dead by Harding's inauguration—was scapegoat enough.

Freya now spoke in the singsong tone of a docent at a historic house: how the men were divided "by muse and material," how the metal-workers' forge had been struck by lightning and now lay in ruins under poison ivy, how local anti-German sentiment flared up after the Kaiser's submarine shelled Chatham. "And then, in all the ruckus, Gilbert Dyer killed Royall."

Gilbert Dyer—the model for *The Fisher Boy* in the Provincetown Municipal Museum. "What?" I said.

"Dyer killed Royall," Freya said.

History, the authorities, the media of the day, had said Royall had disappeared. His clothing and car had been found in Truro, on the town's Atlantic coast, at Skusset Beach. She laughed. As my eyes adjusted to the dark, I could see the stone walls had been plastered then whitewashed and painted with figures, with naked blond men wrestling and swimming in some vague summer landscape all conifers and fiords. Except for the absence of women, this display of Teutonic flesh might have suited the Master and his followers just fine.

"They found Royall's grave in the woods," Freya said, "while they were gathering mushrooms." She shooed us out and was about to lock the door. "My sons found him," she said, and her voice broke.

Then I knew—who they were and who she was. Of course, she handled the community's finances—and she'd had two children, both of them sons.

"It got to my older son," she said, banging shut the door, as if shutting out the memory of her older mad son, shutting out the memory of both sons...

As we neared the rock, I could see it was a boulder, scoured by a glacier from some place further north—the tundra of Canada, the mountains of New Hampshire—then transported here by that grinding sheet of ice. Scratched into its sides were graffiti of sorts, something patterned on the script of a dead people, a dead culture. Were they Norse? Probably not. But the markings on this rock had lured Royall to this land, and, in a sense, exerted significance for these people.

The tree, the beech, next caught my attention. It had bark the gray of varicose veins and was thick, surely thriving when the crew from the *Mayflower* stole ashore to raid baskets of corn local tribes were stockpiling for winter. Hanging from the limbs of the ancient beech, among its reddish-bronze leaves, were dozens of tiny golden bells—and pieces of what might be beef jerky, buzzing with flies.

"What are these?" I asked.

"Cause for celebration," Freya said brightly. "Offerings from births. We've had three this month."

Hanging in the tree, rotting in the sun, the umbilical cords twisted in the hot August wind. This was their Tree of Life—the tree connecting heaven and earth—Yggdrasill, the Norse had called it, but the umbilical cords smelled like roadkill. Like the rest of this place, their Tree of Life emanated the stink of death.

Freya touched the umbilical cords, her fingers lingering on their scabby surfaces.

"We should go now," Roberto said.

Something stirred in the shade of the tree. On the grass by the pond, half hidden by the rock, something moved with the awkwardness of exhaustion. I thought it was a dog, but then saw the gleam of naked flesh and the links of a chain connecting a human ankle to the tree.

Roberto hadn't seen this. He was trying to disengage from Freya. "Thank you for everything," he was saying, using all of his skills. "This whole day has been fascinating."

It was a girl. Her head had been shaved and her back was shining with welts swollen fat like maggots. She was naked, so that the mud mingled with her wounds. She'd been chained by her ankle to the tree with its rotting umbilical cords.

Seeing me, she cringed, like a dog from a puppy mill that associates human contact with brutality. She wasn't the girl from the Provincetown Public Library or the girl I'd encountered in the road in the woods or the child who'd served our food; it was someone else. She was crawling toward a bowl of water, which the chain prevented her from reaching. I gave her the bowl and she snatched it and rolled away, like a starving dog defending a hunk of gristle.

"How dare you?!" Freya was suddenly beside me. She'd bumped against a branch, jingling its golden bells.

"This girl needs a doctor!" I shouted. "Can't you see that?"

The girl cringed, holding the bowl of water.

"Look how you've frightened her," Freya said.

"She's frightened of you, of whoever did this!" I said. "What did she do wrong? Do something inappropriate for her level?"

Roberto now saw her, saw the welts and the wound where the chain had grated away flesh. "Oh, God!"

They might be doing this to Chloe, I realized. Anyone who did this was capable of anything. "Undo that chain!" I said. "Undo it right now!"

"I think it's time you went on your way," Freya said.

"Not without her, not without taking her to the hospital," I said.

"She is being healed right here," Freya said, "by the air and sunlight, by the stone and the tree and the power of the Master."

"That stone is a hoax!" I yelled. "The Norse never reached Massachusetts."

"Now!" Freya called to a figure beyond Royall's buildings.

From a distance, he looked like a welcoming sight, dressed in our century's clothing, wearing a T-shirt, denim jeans, and orange work boots.

"He'll show you out," Freya coldly stated, and, as her colleague came closer, I saw that our argument was ended by what he carried in his hand—a very contemporary piece of metal, a gun.

His reflecting sunglasses made twin duplicates of my frightened face. He was swarthy, Mediterranean. Grit from a boat or garage had lodged permanently beneath his fingernails. He was missing his van with its backrest of wood beads and synthetic fur sheathing its steering wheel, and he was missing his soundtrack—the classical tapes he'd played louder and louder—after picking up a hitchhiker, a young man he knew, at the Orleans traffic circle earlier this year. The assault might have been fantasy, but the "assailant" from Edward's story was here, exactly as described.

To see a gun pointed at your gut is to see a gun for the very first time. In a movie, it's a prop; mounted on a wall, it's a trophy; in a shop, it's merchandise. But, loaded and aimed at your body, at the vulnerability of your flesh, it is something entirely different—the instrument of your destruction. Suddenly, your worrying about AIDS and finances and the loneliness of age falls away.

"We have treated you as guests, but you have not responded in kind," Freya said.

I heard the flies buzzing on the umbilical cords.

"Please see them out," Freya said to the gunman. There was a gentle sadness to her voice.

Chapter Thirty-nine

We could've run, I suppose, but the weapon made us obedient, tethered us to this man, their Enforcer, the way the naked girl was tethered to their tree.

"The car is the other way," Roberto said.

Him saying that flooded me with guilt, guilt at my involving him in craziness I should have left to the police.

"Your things are at the steam bath," the Enforcer told Roberto, forcing us into the forest.

Were we really headed for the steam bath, or was he taking us deep into the woods to be shot? Or stabbed, like Ian, our throats cut ear-to-ear?

Now, like the night on the breakwater, everything became vivid—the sharpness of the briars, the gleam of the poison ivy, the corrugated texture of the bark on the oaks and pines, and the smell of heat and dry brush. The forest fire danger was "off the charts," the radio had reported. I wondered, at this moment, was my mother painting? The thought of my mother painting brought tears to my eyes; it seemed like the saddest thing in the world.

We reached the steam bath. It was still fired up; genies of steam were seeping from its door. Our clothes, like rescuers, lay snagged on the same tree.

Roberto seized his.

"No," someone said.

Beside the entrance to the steam bath stood Jason—and Edward, Arthur's treacherous treasure. Edward was wearing his tie-dyed shirt and the gym shorts made of that icy-blue fabric, the clothing he'd chosen for Arthur's party that grotesque Memorial Day weekend weeks ago. So he had abandoned the fundamentalists, just as he had abandoned Arthur—and his mother and these people in the past. It was part of his character, abandonment. Edward shifted from season to season, like the sandbars, like the shoals, of Cape Cod.

"No," Edward repeated.

"What do you mean, No?" Roberto asked.

With the last courage in my system, I blurted, "Is Chloe here, Edward? Is Chloe Hilliard here? What in God's name do you want with that little girl?"

"There is no Chloe here," Edward stated.

"We just want to leave," Roberto said.

"You must be cleansed first," Edward said. He nodded toward the steam bath. "Go inside."

They weren't going to shoot us, they were going to scald us to death, they were going to scald us to death in the steam.

"Go inside," Edward repeated, his voice the only cold thing at that moment. Then, lightly, he touched my shoulder—tentatively, as if to make sure that I was real. It was eerily like my gesture at St. Harold's years ago, my touching Ian Drummond in the chapel.

"You're a fool doing this," I told Edward. "After what happened to your brother."

He smiled, in his self-effacing way, the geisha's smile he'd used at Herring Cove to beckon men to his blanket so he could rebuff them. Then he walked briskly up the trail until the vegetation closed over him and he was gone.

"Gentlemen," someone said, "we don't have all day." It was Jason, in his Armani. But it was the Enforcer and his gun coming closer that made Roberto and me obey when the Enforcer commanded, "Give back our clothing."

Naked, I felt that much more defenseless. There were two of us and two of them, but we stood still as the dolls in Mrs. Mikkonen's shop. Was the Enforcer's the last face Ian had seen? Would I die at the hands of the man who'd killed my brother?

Jason opened the door to the steam bath.

"Cleansing," the Enforcer said.

As if we needed to be cleansed to *leave* their property.

Steam rushed from the door, in scalding, lethal billows.

We'd been allowed to eat the same food as the Master not because we were on his level, but because we'd been sentenced to die. We'd been sentenced to die before I'd derided their stone or demanded they free the chained girl. The Enforcer was waiting for Freya's signal. They had meant to kill us all along.

"We just want to leave," Roberto said. "We'll leave you alone, we won't say a word."

The Enforcer advanced toward us, pointing the gun. In desperation, I remembered he had let Edward go. If Edward's story was true, he had assaulted him, raped him, *but* ultimately he had let Edward go, let him flee to Provincetown, where Arthur found him, sleeping on the sand on the beach.

The Enforcer jabbed the gun into my ribs so that my heartbeat amplified, filling my chest.

Roberto ducked into the steam bath and I followed.

Steam scalded my skin, made my whole body sting like a fresh cut.

"It hurts to breathe!" Roberto yelled.

We heard a bolt fall outside and lock the door.

I felt the skin around my nostrils begin scorching. "Get down, *get close to the floor!*"

I thought the floor might be spared the rising heat, but the tile seared my hands and knees.

I found the altar through the thickening steam, but the potential weapons I'd seen during our "cleansing"—the iron tongs, the pokers, the jars of oils and herbs—had been confiscated.

"They're going to kill us!" Roberto was yelling. "They're going to kill us!"

I pulled him through the steam toward the entrance. I struggled to open to steam bath door, but the bolt defeated me. Scratching at the spongy wood got me nothing but splinters for my efforts. I could feel the arteries in my head pounding. In desperation, I threw my weight against the door again and again until something in my shoulder snapped.

Then, suddenly, coolness slapped my face. I wasn't even aware the door was yielding; that was obliterated by the injury to my shoulder, a white-hot searing that made me urinate.

Someone seized my wrists, saying, "Hurry up, damnit!" and pulled me upright. It was Jason. He yanked out a gasping Roberto.

My chest and arms were, red, scarlet, as though I'd sustained a hideous sunburn. My eyes were runny, but, once they cleared, I could see the Enforcer sprawled still on the ground, next to his sunglasses and some tongs from the altar.

"Get dressed and hurry the fuck up!" Jason told us.

Baffled, stinging, grateful, we complied.

"He's unconscious," Jason said. "I just hit him."

He was helping us, God knows why. He hadn't pulled us from the steam to stab or shoot us. We pulled on our clothes. He showed us a trail that led to Old Barn Road. "There a gap in the fence there."

"My car—"

"They abandoned it in Welfleet hours ago," Jason said. "You were considered dead meat as soon as you drove onto the grounds. You've caused me enough trouble, now get the hell out of here!"

"What about Chloe? Have you got the little girl?"

"Get out of here!" screamed Jason.

We ran. My clothing chafed my scalded skin. The trail was confusing—overgrown, blocked by fallen branches, and, once, by a rotting possum, swollen with death. How close we'd come, I thought, how close we'd come to losing our lives.

At least water was not a factor interfering with our escape. The brooks we crossed were mere gullies of muddy stones; swamps, expanses of muck and straw. My calves cramped, I felt awful. "Rest, just a minute," I begged Roberto, but, with his legs strengthened by bicycling as a courier, he refused. "Not yet. In a while."

So, visualizing the Enforcer regaining consciousness, I ran. Why had Jason helped us? I kept wondering. Had the Master changed his mind and decided to spare us? No, of course not; Jason had stopped the Enforcer by force, by attacking him with the tongs, by risking his own life.

I was faltering again when Roberto plunged through a field of ragweed to call out, "Here's the fence!"

Chapter Forty

But where in God's name was the gap in the fence Jason had mentioned? We'd forged our own route from the woods through the ragweed. We traced our steps back to the woods then saw the answer. To the left, the ragweed was matted flat by foot traffic, matted like the hair of a dog with mange. We followed this path then located the gap in the fence, low, close to the ground, used by youngsters from the cult, I guessed. We had to squirm beneath the fence—worried that it might be electrified, which it wasn't—tearing our shirts on the talons of metal, on the vandalized chain-mail guarding the Master's kingdom.

But then we were free! We had reached Old Barn Road. I could've kissed its asphalt.

I wanted to contact the police the way someone stranded in the Sahara wants greenery and water. We saw a house a short distance away, and, aware of our bedraggled state, asked to wait in the back yard, under a pear tree with the hornets, while the baffled owner telephoned the police.

◇◇◇

Roberto sat in the station, drinking cup after cup of spring water while I recounted our story and my theories about our day, Ian's death, and the probability the Master had kidnapped little Chloe. One policeman, Sergeant Colby, summed up, "So you're saying that these people tried to kill you?"

"That's a fact." Roberto channeled his impatience into crushing his paper cup.

"Why were you visiting these people in the first place?" Sergeant Colby asked me.

"They killed my brother, Ian Drummond—"

"And you visited them? Believing that?"

"The man with the gun, their Enforcer, killed Ian. Clark, the schizophrenic, couldn't have done it, he was too incompetent."

Sergeant Colby, who had also been drinking a Dixie cup of water, began scraping the wax from its rim. He chose his words with equal care. "There are some solid leads in the Drummond murder and Hilliard kidnapping. In regard to the situation at the former Royall property, that is a very volatile group of people, with a history—"

"They tried to scald us to death!" I shouted. My head was throbbing as though I was still in that hellish steam. "There are children being abused—"

"We know," Colby said, "we've heard these allegations. Yet you say this African American—"

"Saved our lives," Roberto said.

Sergeant Colby stopped his scraping. "Isn't that a bit contradictory?"

"What about Chloe?" I asked.

"We hope that case will be resolved shortly," Colby said.

"Resolved" sounded grim.

Did the police believe us? They advised us to avoid the cultists at all costs. It would be best, in fact, if we could lie low a few days, stay clear of our customary Provincetown haunts in case the Master's protégés tried to pursue us. My Volvo, ditched in Welfleet, according to Jason, had yet to be found, but the police would give us a ride anywhere in Truro.

Barton Daggett, the rotund St. Harold's alumnus who'd been at Ian's party, owned property in Truro. It was ten-ten, a bit late, but I phoned him from the police station and told him quite truthfully that my car had been stolen and asked to spend the night at his house and bring a friend.

He was most hospitable, picking us up in his Alfa Romeo. He'd shed a few pounds since our last meeting and developed a teak-dark tan. I withheld the exact circumstances of my Volvo's abduction until I was deep into a vodka Collins, on Barton's back porch. Like Ian, Barton was an amateur military historian. The walls of his porch were a virtual armory of swords with gleaming blades and degenerating tassels. Insects, moths and mosquitoes, clung to the exterior of the porch's fine black screens, unable to reach the light or flesh they craved.

As the vodka worked to loosen my tongue, I felt compelled to confess what had happened to us earlier. We were, after all, in hiding under Barton's roof, possibly luring killers to these premises. Draining the last of my drink, I told our tale. Barton registered no more reaction than Ulysses S. Grant and Robert E. Lee, on the cover of the book of Matthew Brady photographs on the coffee table in front of us, next to a pipe, an ashtray, and a pewter lighter shaped like the battleship *Maine*.

"…So we barely escaped with our lives," I concluded. Then I remembered: "At Ian's party, weren't you complaining about these people being disruptive?" And, looking at the insects clinging to the fragile black screens separating the porch from the outdoors and the dark woods crowding the yard, I remembered, with fright, that this house abutted the Master's fiefdom.

"Indeed I was complaining and I was *wrong*," Barton stated.

Roberto, exhausted, was sleeping in a big Eastlake rocker.

"I spoke in haste when I characterized them as 'hippies.' A good number of their company are crackerjack scientists, including their leader." Barton lit his pipe with the battleship *Maine*. His next thought seemed inspired by the lighter. "Once, I would have said they weren't worth the powder to blow them up with, but a month ago, I changed my mind." Barton certainly had his Gothic touches; that might allow him to excuse some of the Master's behavior.

The screens on the porch were soft; they belled in the hot wind and could easily be cut. And we could easily be watched, from the woods. I couldn't believe Barton as he puffed his pipe and speculated that our experience with the Master was "probably some sort of misunderstanding." He'd had words with a man named Badr, "a fellow about seven feet tall," the Giant, surely; they'd argued about noise, about their shooting in the woods, culling deer what with the Lyme disease outbreak. "Of course, I agreed with their constitutional right to bear arms. It was their firing them in proximity to my house I objected to, but we settled things amicably enough."

Barton had to admit he'd been as prejudiced as we were before he'd been invited for a tour of their compound by a lovely woman about his age, Freya. Had I seen their greenhouses and the laboratories in the concrete, modern building? They were growing Inca corn from kernels found frozen with a mummy, a child sacrifice in the Andes.

"Yes, they're keeping up the tradition. They sacrifice children today—and castrate adults."

"I didn't get that intimate—"

"How did this tour of yours come about?" I asked, not having found these people initially welcoming.

"Oh, I'd threatened to sue the pants off them," Barton said. "I mean, they'd caused a godawful racket, all that gunfire, but Ian told me they were essentially harmless. We discussed them at his St. Harold's bash."

But the Master claimed Ian had swindled him, I said, on the deal about selling St. Harold's.

"Oh, yes," Barton said. "They'd thought Ian concealed the fact that the meadow adjoining Lake Chiccataubett couldn't be developed because the bunny-huggers had snooped around and found some damn endangered plant. But Ian claimed it was all a misunderstanding. He hadn't known that plant even existed."

"They killed him," I said.

"No." Barton kept smoking his pipe. "They're hardly killers, just a band of idealists who take *Prince Valiant* too seriously. Why Ian and their leader, Mr. Big, go way back."

"Mikkonen."

"Enormous man. Very brilliant."

"Did you meet him?"

"Very briefly, in his lab. He was engrossed in some problem about their aquaculture business, raising tilapia."

The tanks of rotting fish in our old chapel.

"Ian knew Mikkonen from his mother's shop in…what's that tourist trap?"

"Rockport."

Roberto snored peacefully. More and more insects were collecting on the outsides of the screens.

"Correct, Rockport. I ate some bluefish there that was out of this world."

"Ian knew Mikkonen—"

"Because of Papa's sticky fingers. Papa Drummond would come strolling into Mrs. Mikkonen's shop and clip things, forget to pay for things. Bad form."

"Dementia, Alzheimer's."

"Well, one day, a few years back, Mikkonen and Ian crossed paths when Ian stopped by to return a Cossack doll Daddy had lifted…" Barton seemed to consider this whole history a string of amusing *faux pas*. "But it wasn't real estate or kleptomania that brought Ian and Mikkonen together. It was God."

He was relishing my skepticism.

"I know spiritual is about the last adjective you'd couple with the Drummond clan, but Ian came to me, he sat right in that chair—" He pointed to where Roberto was now snoring.

"When? This year?"

"Last year, last June."

When Ian allegedly was in San Francisco. Had the Master's story about Ian seeking spiritual nourishment been true?

Barton blew smoke from his pipe on a mosquito that had breached the screens and was circling his arm. "Ian told me he found Mikkonen poised to make a killing in biotechnology. But Mikkonen offered Ian something more."

"Like what?"

"Something he'd never found in that competitive family where everyone was always chasing some cup or blue ribbon. A sense of peace." Barton stated it as a kind of challenge. Barton said Ian had been "instructed in meditation" by Mikkonen, that he'd even attended retreats at the Truro compound.

"Before or after their quarrel about the land, about St. Harold's?"

"Before, I believe. Sorry, I didn't offer you a refill—"

"Did you tell any of this to the police?"

"Heavens, yes!" Barton said. "I hightailed my way to the Provincetown police the morning poor Ian was found! But they seemed preoccupied with those Christian Soldiers, they thought Ian's murder was some sort of 'hate crime.'"

I couldn't believe what Barton was telling me, confirming Ian's links to the Master, and, incredibly, confirming that the police knew all about these links all along. So why hadn't they arrested Mikkonen, or connected Clark to Mikkonen and confirmed who he was, linked their John Doe in the pauper's grave with the panhandlers and that massive man who'd ordered us scalded? Barton showed no reaction when I'd quoted Mikkonen claiming Ian was seriously ill. I mentioned it again: "Did Ian have cancer?"

He slapped a mosquito on his arm. "Ian was as healthy as a horse," Barton said. "Look how he'd built himself up. He was what your generation calls buffed."

"That might have been steroids."

"Ian never mentioned any health problems to me."

"Did he mention knowing an Edward Babineaux? Before this summer?"

Barton was flicking the battleship *Maine* lighter, but it had run out of fluid and was failing to produce a flame. "He didn't mention any Edward at all."

"How about a Paul?"

Barton shook his head, just as Roberto was blinking awake. "What time is it? I think I may have dozed off."

I was sure I would spend the night awake, but fatigue overpowered me and I got nine hours of deep, dreamless sleep, in a four-poster bed with mahogany pineapples and a thermal blanket. I actually needed the blanket due to the aggressive air-conditioning. Roberto, beside me, claimed the cold kept him awake, his San Juan blood felt frozen.

Barton offered to let us remain with him, but I refused. "Where else can we go?" Roberto asked, using one of Barton's disposable razors, standing at the bathroom sink wearing nothing but a foamy beard of shaving cream.

"What's the least likely place we could go?" I wondered aloud, rubbing my showered body with one of Barton's heavy towels, which could absorb a monsoon.

Just then a loud rap on the bathroom door made me jump. "The police are here, they've found your missing car!" Barton reported.

I'd braced myself for vandalism, for slashed upholstery and the radio ripped from the car, but my Volvo, found on Orcutt Road, Welfleet, was in pristine condition. In fact, it had been washed, in defiance of the ban due to the drought. And the theoretical puncture was, of course, invisible.

We agreed to leave Cape Cod. My apartment, Arthur's house, the White Gull were all known to people like Edward, in league with Mikkonen. Yet I also felt responsible to tell Arthur all that we'd learned, for his safety and "for the record"—should anything happen to us.

We decided to phone Arthur later that morning, after first driving directly to Boston. I was doing sixty on Route 6, in Suicide Alley, that section of highway where you're requested to keep your lights on even during the day, where the road is so narrow, one lane in each direction, a slot banked by high sandy hills. We were listening to music then the Boston news, ragged with static: "...A hiker in Provincetown made a grim discovery early this morning. He found the body of a young girl in the Province Lands..." Then the sound crackled off, as I pounded the radio and went numb then alert with panic. "...not known at this point whether the body is that of little Chloe Hilliard..."

I almost steered into the oncoming traffic, but Roberto yelled, so I braked, sending a pile of roadmaps from the dashboard into his lap. Instinctively, I turned the up volume of the radio, but the story already was over, succeeded by a commercial about a water park.

We turned around at the first opportunity, then roared back toward Provincetown. "There must be some mistake," Roberto said.

"The mistake was the police not raiding those crazies." I surged past a Chevy with Utah plates. I wasn't even seeing the road ahead, I was bombarded by images of Chloe—dipping her mermaid into Arthur's fishpond, collecting pebbles by the harbor, rubbing against Roberto's legs…And I fought awful images—the young girl chained to the tree in Truro and the body in the woods in the Province Lands.

Finally we took the left into Provincetown proper so that dunes and ponds gave way to shingle houses with clotheslines and trellises of roses. Double-parking, blocking Commercial Street, I banged on Miriam's front door until my knuckles hurt.

"She's away!" I became aware of somebody calling. It was a woman with red braids, sanding something in the front yard of the house across the street. "You're not a reporter, are you?"

"Of course not."

"Miriam is at Arthur's, the poor thing. What kind of monster—"

People in cars blocked by mine leaned on their horns. I responded by raising my middle finger.

Near MacMillan Wharf, we were delayed when a drag-queen, bulky and masculine as the Statue of Liberty, complete with silver lamé robe and tinfoil torch, crossed the street. She was followed by Superman and Mr. Peanut. Of course, I'd forgotten! Roberto pre-empted me by explaining, "Carnival."

The weeklong, late-August extravaganza, our own Mardi Gras, a time when the spirit of Provincetown, sometimes summed up by Speedos and a Corona with lime, made room for some gender-bending whimsy, for rhinestones and rouge. A man in enough leather to have skinned a roundup of steers was escorting his partner in full geisha drag, face ghostly with rice powder, lips painted red and compact as a cat's anus.

I noticed a scattering of fundamentalists, but nothing like their numbers in early- and mid-June, and their office looked closed. But Provincetown was mobbed. Carnival's end-of-summer bacchanal, the last before Labor Day, filled the guest houses, bars, and shops with riotous crowds.

Edging into Arthur's driveway, I scraped his picket fence and swore. To encourage me, Roberto squeezed my shoulder, the one I'd injured on the steam room door, so I winced.

"Thank God you're here, we're beside ourselves," said Arthur, spent and trembling as he poured himself a Campari. Miriam was upstairs. He'd given her a sedative. "Will this nightmare ever end?" The phone was ringing constantly, media people making a nuisance of themselves. Arthur seemed vulnerable amid his material treasures, the Sandwich glass, the ormolu, the highboy Duncan Phyfe himself had constructed. He had been Chloe's surrogate father, filling that absence to his benefit and hers. Now, the vision the busyness of driving had fended off asserted itself—a child dead in the underbrush, murdered and left to the elements.

"Is it…definite?" Roberto asked.

Arthur was making no attempt to hide the tears streaking his face. "Nothing is definite. The clothes on the girl don't sound familiar, but she's been held two weeks, so these butchers could have given her…" I thought of the killers in Truro, insisting we change into their garb.

Then the stairs began creaking just as the telephone—loud as a stone shattering plate glass—began ringing. "Don't answer it, I forbid you to answer it!" Miriam said, gripping the banister with both hands for support as she descended the stairs, one slow and heavy step at a time. "The police said they'd come, not call. This has nothing to do with my daughter." She began sobbing silently, as if her finite supply of tears for this lifetime had been expended.

She wore one of Arthur's terrycloth robes, its pockets brimming with tissues. She was barefoot, like some desperate pilgrim on the loneliest of holy roads. "I saw Chloe in a dream." She knotted the cord of the robe. "She told me she was fine and she's never lied."

"Thank God for the sedative, I'm so glad you slept," Arthur said.

"What on earth do I have to be thankful for?" Miriam snapped. "Thankful some other girl was found dead in a ditch? What kind of monster would do such a thing?"

We all froze when we heard the sirens in the distance, knifing through the air. Was this the police coming with awful news? The room—the people, the furniture, our thoughts, the atoms comprising everything—seemed to pause on their journey through time. Then the sirens grew more faint, moved away.

"They sound like fire engines," Roberto said. "They're not coming here."

It was nearing noon, so Arthur urged Miriam to join him in the kitchen for some curried chicken on a fresh baguette. Roberto followed. Alone in the living room, I punched on the television, keeping the volume low. Even though the police had promised they would visit, not phone, and be sure Miriam heard the first estimate of the dead child's age, a sense of fear rippled through me as the picture bloomed on the screen. It was a bit before twelve, so I'd expected the cheers and bells of a game show. Instead, I saw reporter Doug Doherty, handsome with concern, against a burning hillside. Bat-like ashes flickered through the air as he spoke.

"There are fires now throughout the lower Cape. All of them started at approximately ten o'clock this morning, and the worst are in Truro. Police don't think that is a coincidence. Two suspected arsonists have been apprehended by the Provincetown police. They have refused to answer questions, and, when asked about their identity, gave numbers instead of names in response. The suspects were discovered running through the woods of Cape Cod National Seashore, not far from the location where the child's body was found. They tried to escape using this old van..." Footage of a Volkswagen, rusted through like a useless old muffler, was broadcast. The van's steering wheel was sheathed in fake fur. "…The Provincetown police who arrested the pair were shocked to discover that their van was packed with explosives as well as what may be containers of deadly bacteria. Both suspects were tattooed with emblems of Norse mythology—and both men had been castrated."

Then the camera cut to an anchorwoman at a desk, Marcia Haight, remarking how dry conditions were throughout Cape Cod, calling the fires "a disaster waiting to happen, with or without help from some very disturbed people." Then she shifted so that her body moved but her jacket's padded shoulders remained still. "Are there any new developments at the compound, Doug?"

The screen changed to a helicopter shot of woods, with a pond and greenhouses glinting like mica in the sun. In a voice-over, Doug Doherty said, "What we know at this moment is that the Provincetown arsonists were part of a cult centered around this commune and a mysterious leader called the Master. At eleven-fifteen this morning, after the arson suspects were arrested, two Truro policemen, Sergeant Reginald Colby and Officer Paul Driscoll, entered the compound grounds with a search warrant and were shot. Sergeant Colby, an eight-year veteran of the department and father of five, was killed. Officer Driscoll remains in critical condition."

We had spoken to them just last night.

Doherty returned onscreen as the hillside back of him erupted in flames. Some fireman gestured for him to move. The camera panned a traffic jam as Doherty said, "Route Six is impassible. Provincetown, in fact, is now cut off from the rest of the world." Behind him, cars shimmered in the heat, then a curtain of smoke obliterated the scene. "This just in, Marcia," Doherty said, "I've just been informed that Officer Paul Driscoll of the Truro police department has just died."

I ran into the kitchen, shaking. Roberto was eating some bread. Arthur was persuading Miriam to try his curried chicken. "You can eat *around* the meat. There are apples and raisins and walnuts in it too."

"There's trouble," I said, there in the kitchen where Edward had concocted his bouillabaisse. "Hurry up, come into the living room!"

We stared at the television, at a still photograph of a chubby blond boy holding a basketball, then at scenes of Rockport, Bearskin Neck, and Motif Number One. "The cult leader, Lucas Mikkonen, grew up in Rockport," Marcia Haight was saying.

I was next to the telephone when it rang, and, automatically, picked it up. I remembered we weren't supposed to answer it, but, holding the receiver, I said, "Hello. Hello?" Then the caller hung up.

Doug Doherty, now away from the fire, spoke against a backdrop of a motorist tending to his overheated car, a casualty of the massive traffic jam. He said, "All summer long, residents of Truro, Welfleet, and Provincetown have complained about strange things happening in their communities, about hitch-hikers, panhandlers, and shoplifters in odd clothing. When confronted these people claimed they were Scandinavian tourists, but it turns out they were just plain trouble."

"In my shop," Miriam said, "they'd steal anything that wasn't bolted down."

I had to ask her: "Did you ever meet them in Truro, Miriam?"

"Never," she said emphatically, picking a slice of apple from her curry then eating it.

"We were *there*," Roberto said, as the helicopter shot of the compound filled the screen.

"You were what?" Arthur said.

"We were there, just yesterday," I said.

Miriam and Arthur gave us quizzical looks, as if we were news groupies who were lying or at least exaggerating.

I thought of Jason, who'd saved our lives and of the girl they'd chained to the tree, I thought of Edward. But what about Chloe? Was she really the little girl they'd found in the woods, or was she still alive, under siege, at the compound? Of course, a motive for her kidnapping still eluded me, eluded everyone. If Ian had been killed over a real estate deal, over the St. Harold's land by

Lake Chiccataubett, why was Chloe targeted by the Master? Or Miriam? Surely it wasn't revenge for catching street kids in her shop, catching them pocketing cheap amethyst beads. Yet the Master's people were abusing children, and female children fared especially badly.

Doug Doherty was speaking again: "While purporting to be involved in organic farming, the group, police say, was amassing an arsenal of chemicals, for use in agriculture and in an Armageddon they refer to as the Fall.

"Police believe the community was divided by a rigid caste system, and that those at the bottom were sterilized, forced to submit to genetic experimentation and take part in tests involving biological weaponry."

Marcia Haight took a turn: "Police believe today's tragedy was triggered by the cult believing authorities were about to link them with the death of a young girl whose body was discovered in the woods of Cape Cod National Seashore early this morning. The young girl's identity is not being released pending notification of next of kin…"

Arthur spoke up. "You can see the fires from the terrace. Truro is burning." Miriam and Roberto ran to look.

"This could be a long stalemate," Marcia Haight was saying, in a voice-over with the helicopter shot of the compound. "Police have cordoned off the property and are asking the Master and his followers to surrender peacefully, but their only response so far has been additional gunfire. A SWAT team is standing by or on its way, so we are told."

But the stalemate died young. What happened next seemed to take place in slow motion. There was a choreography to it, like an exercise performed by masses of athletes in a stadium in some totalitarian country. Smoke began issuing from points around the compound, spirals of smoke. Then the smoke became flames, gray smoke bursting with sparks like some Fourth of July spectacle gone horridly wrong, until the compound was surrounded by a seething ring of fire. You could see it from the air, from the helicopter, this ring of fire that *seemed to burn inward,* as if following some pre-arranged route, devouring the woods and raging toward the compound, toward the greenhouses and the pond, which was like an eye gray with cataracts, blinking through the smoke and the heat.

"We're outta here!" somebody said, apparently one of the helicopter crew.

"What on earth is going on?" Marcia Haight was asking. "What do you hear on the ground? Doug? Doug?"

The helicopter edged away from the conflagration.

"Marcia?" Doug was saying, as flames tore through the woods of Master's world. "Marcia, we understand that the fire now raging on the compound grounds was started by people from their community. I'm some distance away, on Route 6, but I can see the smoke, there's a virtual thunderhead of smoke."

The helicopter view, the gray smoke with sparks and flames rupturing through it, resembled the shroud of ashes Edward's lost brother Clark had prophesied before his death.

"Perhaps this is the Fall these fanatics have anticipated for so long," Marcia Haight was saying.

I couldn't watch any longer, I just couldn't. I felt dizzy, sickened. Chloe was there, in all that horror, Chloe who'd worried about her sandcastle and doll's broken arm.

I joined Arthur, Miriam, and Roberto on the terrace. I rubbed my hand against the wood, against the side of the house, to make sure this was real and not a nightmare. Through the big silver maple, across the water, you could see hills of Truro blazing, not the compound, of course, that was too far away, but one of the fires these Dark Age arsonists had ignited.

The sight mesmerized my friends. They kept shaking their heads, muttering to themselves. I thought back to the party on this terrace that inaugurated this summer.

"It's all burned," I whispered to Roberto.

"I can see," he said, staring at the hills, not realizing I meant the Master's compound. He moved off to join the others.

If Chloe had been unharmed, if Chloe had been being held by those demonic people, there was little chance that she was alive after this. For me, the flowers in Arthur's garden suddenly had the dead smell of floral arrangements at a funeral.

The television was on, just out of earshot in the house, so the others would learn the news as soon as they returned to the living room. I was lacking the strength to tell them, I didn't have the courage or heart now that I believed Chloe's last chance was gone, incinerated, so instead of staying on the terrace or returning to the house to face the television, I decided to check the damage I'd done with my car, scraping against Arthur's picket fence.

Walking the gravel of the driveway, I found that I was crying. Stale tears, long unshed, stored from earlier losses, were leaking from my eyes. Examining my front bumper, I saw that it was streaked with white paint, and that the post of Arthur's fence was askew, battered by the impact of my car. I felt similarly battered, exhausted, spent with tension and grief.

I was trying to right the broken post when I saw someone at the edge of my vision. My back stiffened as my system went on alert. The police, after all, the Truro police, had warned us to lie low, to avoid our regular haunts. And those very officers were now dead, killed by the Master's operatives in a shootout. But I had seen the conflagration in Truro; surely the Master's followers were dead in their biotech Valhalla, or else in custody of the authorities. Of course their other community, at St. Harold's, hadn't been mentioned, but surely the police in Stark had those people under control; something had to be coordinated out there.

"Why Mark, hello!" the familiar voice said. "You're still in Provincetown, I'm surprised!"

At first, I didn't recognize the woman greeting me. Dressed in black denim pants and a white cotton blouse with tulips embroidered along its collar, she wore sunglasses obscuring half her face. Her hair was shorn short, like a boy ready for Little League, and a diamond dominated her wide tanned hand. "It's Sallie, Mark, Sallie Drummond!"

I was happier to see her than I'd ever been in my life, happy to see someone from my Gloucester past. I hugged her, gathered her in my arms; I could tell she'd lost weight. "How are you doing?" I asked—and it was more than just a casual phrase.

"I guess it's just beginning to sink in," Sallie said, "that my brother is really gone, and that my father is…fading away too." As she spoke, she began slowly walking toward downtown. "I don't think my father even knows who I am," Sallie sighed.

Though still dazed from the news from Truro, from our day with the Master, I felt compelled to walk with Sallie, just for a few minutes, to confirm or deny the bizarre things Barton and the Master had told me about Ian—about the rumors of his dealings with the Truro community, about lymphoma and his spiritual quests. Of course, I had to broach the subject of his murder gently, gradually, so I began with its origins on Cape Ann: "Your father…sometimes went to Rockport, didn't he?"

Sallie nodded.

We rounded the corner by the old Coast Guard station, with its white buildings and weedy parking lot. I would walk with her just a minute.

"…Did he ever visit a shop called Doll World?"

"Doll World? He visited them all."

Beyond Provincetown Harbor, an orange glow interrupted the smoke above the Truro hills. I thought of Chloe now as lost, as lost as Royall's youths, whose ghosts swam through Provincetown Harbor.

"Did he ever mention a Mrs. Mikkonen?"

The chill Sallie returned. "My father has advanced Alzheimer's disease. His short-term memory has been shot for years. He doesn't mention much of anything that makes sense."

We were reaching the part of town where Commercial Street begins living up to its name. The old houses with their gardens and colors varying like salt water taffy were yielding to shops, hair salons, and restaurants. This part of Commercial Street was clogged with traffic. I knew Roberto and the others would be wondering where I'd gone, but I had to question Sallie and thought asking her to stop might irritate her ever-volatile temper.

I asked, "Do you remember Ian visiting a shop in Rockport to return a doll your father took by mistake?"

Before Sallie could answer, a giant gold scallop shell, the size of a satellite dish dispensing limitless channels, came rolling onto Commercial Street from the hill below the monument. Spilling from it, among ropes of blue tinsel seaweed, were mermaids with five-o'clock shadows, with fishtails of vivid sea-green sequins. King Neptune, in a conch-shell crown and a loincloth of plaster starfish, was asking, "Are we sure we have enough beads to throw?" and "Are we sure the parade isn't cancelled because of the fires?" King Neptune was sipping a margarita, blue as automobile windshield fluid, its rim glittering with salt.

"What on earth is that?" Sallie asked.

"It's a float for Carnival. See? The name of the bar sponsoring it is written on its side."

Carnival was happening, in spite of Chloe, in spite of Truro. The liquor, the sex, the costumes, it all continued. To some degree grief was always private.

Further down Commercial Street another float was stalled in the traffic, a flatbed truck bearing cages of men in chaps and chains, grinding their hips to a stereo system that kept catching and going silent, making everyone feel embarrassed.

"This is still such a culture shock, but if my brother was happy here…" Sallie hooked her arm into mine.

"Was…Ian in good health this past year?" I asked her.

"My brother was not HIV-positive," Sallie said.

"He'd built himself up—"

"Through a lot of hard work. He worked hard at everything he did."

Some Christian Soldiers were watching the parade, standing outside their office. The men wore half-bewildered smiles. One of their female companions had caught a string of beads thrown from one of the floats; she was holding it her hand, unsure what to do with it. I thought of Edward, their former colleague, dead, no doubt, in the Truro inferno…

"Did Ian have lymphoma, or any kind of cancer?"

"Of course not!" Sallie acted furious, but kept her arm hooked in mine.

"Are you sure?"

"Of course I'm sure, he would've told his family! My God, Mark, you don't keep a thing like that secret!" She seemed genuinely stunned. "Where did you hear such nonsense?"

"Just a rumor. Bar talk."

As we neared the town hall, the crowds became thicker, louder and more agitated. A greater number of people were in costume, mostly men, in finery mocking their masculinity, like the boy in a hoop skirt busy with ruffles and bows, like a flirtatious Confederate spy. Men wore iridescent wings like dragonflies, the miters of Renaissance popes, the tights of pages from the court of Lorenzo de Medici. The twins from Arthur's party were dressed as sisters, with tanks of Siamese fighting fish secured by wicker daisies to their hats.

Other men favored hyper-masculine attire, promenading as football players and as the police who'd harassed them at rest stops. One man posed as the Czar, in a uniform with epaulets and medals from some production of *The King and I.*

Anyone here, I realized abruptly, could be a refugee from the Master's scorched kingdom, *if* they'd been away at the time of the fire...

"Did Ian even mention a Lucas Mikkonen?" I asked, noting that all the public telephones next to the Unitarian/Universalist meetinghouse were taken, so I couldn't call the others to tell them I was walking with Sallie. Then again, they weren't answering the telephone.

"That name is so odd," Sallie said. "McEwan."

We were distracted by an argument in the street, between one man dressed as Icarus and another dressed as an angel. Icarus, in a Porsche, had rear-ended the angel's vintage Cadillac. "I can smell your breath from here, you're drunk!" the angel was shouting.

"Mikkonen is his name," I said, knowing I should speak of him in the past tense. "His family is Finnish, from Rockport."

Sallie brightened. "Lucas from MIT? An engineer? Heavy-set?"

We were almost to MacMillan Wharf. There were public phones there, but none was free. "I've got to make a call," I said. "I've got to tell my friends where I am."

"You can use the phone on our boat," Sallie said. "Alexander is docked at the wharf."

Chapter Forty-one

His boat was a fiberglass dream, forty feet long, vivid with chrome and sunlight, like the fin of a fish Thomas Royall might have painted in this very harbor eighty years ago. Sallie's fiancé shouted from the boat's bridge, as he saw us. "Heeey!" He elongated the word, scrambling down to pump my hand.

Alexander certainly had the looks to fit his boat. He could've been a model in some haughty clothing ad, on the porch of a white-columned plantation, on the lawn of a house in the Hamptons, some place where everyone oozes breeding and ease. Today, his eyes were a blue so dark they could be mistaken for chips of lapis lazuli. He wore a rugby shirt striped red and black, its collar open to display the hair on his chest.

"Hey, bro'!" he said, jabbing my shoulder. "Great to see you!" He had the boundless confidence of a jock so secure he has no need to bully. He seemed at home on a boat; he was, after all, a marine biologist.

"You know," Sallie remembered, "that Mikkonen came to our house once, in Gloucester. He drove a horrible old van, like something left over from Woodstock. His weight gave him problems, trouble with his back, so he used one of those seat rests made from wooden beads. It looked about as comfortable as a bed of nails…He was very overbearing."

She'd mentioned the seat rest, the clue that linked Jason and the Enforcer and Mikkonen. I wondered, had she seen the coverage of today's catastrophe in Truro, the news about the shootings and conflagration? A pall of smoke from the fires in Truro was metastasizing into the sky above Provincetown Harbor, like the warning Mt. Vesuvius gave Pompeii.

"Sallie," I said, "I'd like to talk more, but I've got to find a phone to tell my friends where I am."

"Look no further," Alexander said. "Honey, where did you put our cell phone?" He rifled through some things on the deck, a poncho, a jumble of paperbacks, some glass jars that made Sallie scowl.

"You promised you'd dump those specimens overboard!" Sallie complained. To me, she said, "Most people put fish on the grill or in a pan. Alexander puts them in formaldehyde."

"Honey," Alexander said, "you've got to be a tad more organized. The cell phone must be down in the cabin."

"In the cabin?" Sallie sounded a little surprised.

"In your cabin," Alexander said.

"Come on, Mark," Sallie said, "you can make your call from our boat."

Climbing aboard, I'd concentrated on acting as comfortable with nautical matters as possible. I'd grown up in Gloucester, but my boating experience was certainly less extensive than the Drummonds'; we'd never owned anything like this. And Sallie—half-sister or not—still made me self-conscious, and she was watching me intently.

"Excuse the turmoil." Sallie stepped over a Seattle Mariners sweatshirt. "Follow me, Mark."

She led me into the salon, which was paneled in beige laminated wood that a salesman might describe as "champagne." Built into the starboard wall were a sink, stove, refrigerator, microwave, and television, and a counter of bright aqua faux stone. To port, were a table topped with the same faux stone, benches, and a couch of fine-grained cream vinyl.

Toward the bow, stairs descended to two cabins and the head. The first cabin Sallie tried was locked. "He said my room, didn't he?" Sallie said. It was odd, I thought, their having separate cabins. For a large boat, the cabins were cramped; hers was mostly bed. Curtains covered the slits of windows, compounding the sense of claustrophobia.

Sallie rummaged through some books among the chaotic bedding—books about sea vents and plankton and the bleaching of Caribbean coral reefs—but she kept shaking her head in frustration. Inside some sour sweatpants, too big to be hers, she found something that made her say "Eureka!"

She handed me the black cell phone and stood staring in the doorway while I fumbled with the instrument in search of the "on" button. The phone's surface was sticky with some sort of gruel, and the boat, I thought, was somewhat messy to belong to a scientist, but that was stereotyping.

After finally finding the "on" button, I almost lost my balance when the boat shifted as the dull rumbling of its motor activated. "I can't go out sailing," I said. "I don't have time."

"This is a *motor*boat." Sallie was ever-pedantic.

Did I feel anything for her? Any brotherly affection, any tenderness, any warmth, any sense of a shared family history, even shared DNA? No, nothing. I knew then and there that I would never be a Drummond, never feel for any of them what I felt for a close friend or lover, for, say, Chloe or Roberto or Arthur.

"Can't you even turn on the phone?"

I'd tried, but it wasn't working.

"Alexander is just getting fuel," Sallie said, "on the other side of the wharf. When there's a line at the pump, he just circles the harbor."

I think I said it then to assert my power; I felt lost on this boat, with this quirky cell phone—and the Drummonds had always intimidated me, the whole family. I told her, there, in the messy cabin: "I know who did it, I know killed Ian."

She was shocked, of course. Her jaw dropped open, then a strange kind of smile began then died on her lips. I thought her smile might be relief that justice at last was imminent.

"What?!" she said.

"It was Lucas Mikkonen," I said, "or his orders, anyway. A man called the Enforcer actually did the killing. He drives that junky old van you mentioned. The van with the backrest. A hustler named Edward Babineaux was somehow involved. It's all connected to the land deal at St. Harold's."

I blurted out the story of my day at Truro. "Oh, my God," Sallie kept saying. I kept pressing buttons, but the cell phone seemed dead. I was beginning to feel faint from lack of food and dizzy from the boat's motion.

"Give me the phone, Mark." Sallie was very calm. "I guess it needs re-charging."

Sallie led me back onto the deck to discover, to my amazement, that Alexander had steered the boat away from MacMillan Wharf, far into Provincetown Harbor. "I thought he was getting fuel, damnit!" I said.

Sallie shouted to her fiancé at the helm, on the bridge. "Alexander! Mark has some amazing news! He says that Mikkonen creature—the cult leader—was responsible for Ian's death!" She stripped off her sunglasses, and the skin around her eyes looked slack and discolored, bruised, as though she'd gone sleepless for days. "Alexander!" she shouted, but the wind and the argument of the seagulls absorbed her speech and the boat plowed seaward so that the spires and piers of Provincetown were becoming miniature.

The seas were slightly choppy. Hurricane Felix was churning through the mid-Atlantic, endangering the lily fields and pink stone cottages of Bermuda, and whipping up whitecaps even here. My stomach was developing its own private storm and my thoughts were whirling, bright but shapeless, like Carnival confetti.

"Damnit, Alexander, answer me!" yelled Sallie.

A whale watch boat was rounding the tip of Long Point, close to shore. The wake from our speeding craft sent it rocking gently so that its passengers, collectively, let out a thrilled "Ahhh!" But when its captain sounded his horn, there was anger in his series of short blasts.

Sallie bounded up the ladder to the bridge, with me behind her. Alexander sat in one of two chrome and vinyl chairs, his tanned hands gripping the wheel.

"Mark has proof Lucas Mikkonen killed my brother," Sallie snapped.

Unlike Sallie, Alexander didn't smile at this news. He said, "That's extraordinary," and kept staring straight ahead.

It was actually cold at sea. Sallie was now wiggling into a cinnamon-colored sweater she'd harvested from a tangle of clothing on the bridge. This looked like a party boat, I thought, like something chartered in Miami for spring break. My mother had always described the Drummonds as reckless, so perhaps they sought reckless people to marry, to continue their tradition, the way Lucas Mikkonen sought ways to preserve strains of lost Inca corn.

"My brother-in-law—brother-in-law-to-be—had a first-rate legal mind," Alexander was saying, "he had the theory down pat…"

Long Point was now a blurry horizon of dunes, something Lawrence of Arabia might have seen in the Great War, the war that undid Royall and his artists' utopia. In those very dunes, farther toward the bath house, I'd last seen Ian Drummond alive. *"Vaya con Dios,"* he'd called, then, later, he'd done just that—gone with God.

"…He had the theory down pat, old Ian did, but his execution was a major fuck-up. And people don't like that. Not one bit."

He was disparaging Ian, which didn't seem to faze Sallie at all. Was that because she was used to it?

Sallie said, "It sounds perfectly reasonable to me. My brother made the mistake of befriending that monster. Things went bad about the land deal at the school, so people from the cult—"

"Are toast." Alexander completed her sentence.

"In the fire," I said.

"I'll go re-charge the phone, Mark," Sallie told me.

"No you won't," Alexander commanded.

"What Mark found out changes everything!" Sallie insisted. She repeated my story about the community in Truro while the sun ricocheted on her engagement ring and the diamonds comprising her tennis bracelet. Clasping my hand, she said, "Come on, Mark, you can make your call now."

"That phone is no good!" Alexander said.

Sallie said, "You promised—"

"I was mistaken," he said.

"So was I!" Sallie shouted. She yanked the diamond tennis bracelet until it ripped from her wrist, fell in two segments onto the mats at our feet and down through the ladder to the lower deck. "If you don't let him call, I'll call the police, Alexander, I'll call them, I swear it, damnit, I swear it!"

That was when I saw it, after first looking at Sallie, scarlet with frustration, then at the diamonds glittering on the mats at our feet. It was lying on the deck of the bridge, kicked into a corner by a pair of binoculars and a bottle of India pale ale. It was a mermaid stamped from plastic in some Asian factory, distributed as a promotion for a fast-food chain. Picking it up, I saw that it was missing one arm and was sticky with the gruel that had adhered to their cellular phone.

"Mark is perfectly comfortable reporting Mikkonen to the authorities, aren't you, Mark?" Sallie's voice was jagged with pain. "Those people in Truro did everything. Those fanatics who all died this morning."

But she was wrong and she knew it. And *I* had been wrong.

Alexander eased the boat to a halt. We were far out at sea. A fog was gradually collecting around us, so that we were enveloped in a silvery grayness. The water was gray and there was a heaviness in the air, as if, after weeks of punishing drought, it might rain.

"The phone is dead, honey. I busted it this morning, remember?" He stooped to pick up a segment of the bracelet. "Women," he said to me, laughing, "maybe you and—who is it, Antonio?—have the right idea."

He smiled when he saw me with the broken mermaid. From a towel on the second vinyl chair, he drew a knife that shone even in the thickening fog, a *diver's* knife with a thick serrated blade.

"This is nothing personal, Mark. Some things are done out of necessity."

I had no understanding of the perverse equation governing his actions, but I knew that it somehow included kidnapping and murder.

"He's seen the doll, honey, so it's over, it's history. I told you old Mark was the curious type."

The knife had a rubber handle, strong enough to cut barnacles from rock or cut open abalone—or a man's throat.

"Is Chloe safe?" I said. "Why did you take Chloe? What's she to you? I don't get the connection, Alexander."

He was calm as a counselor. "That's family business."

"Well, I'm family, too!" I said, "I'm Sallie's half-brother!"

"That," he said, "is unfortunate."

I found myself laughing a crazy, desperate laugh at ever wanting to belong to that family, at ever being in awe of their grandeur.

Neither of them said a thing. He rose, pointing the knife in my direction. With a sailor's grace, he leapt down the ladder from the bridge to the main deck. "Follow me," he told me.

I was alone on the bridge with Sallie. For an instant, I considered manning the controls but they baffled me, the compass in its bubble, the dozen gauges and dials, the switches for the bilge pumps, for the searchlight, the horn…

"Are you coming down or do I have to get you?"

"This is not going to happen, Alexander!" Sallie said.

I had to buy time, had to keep him talking. As I climbed down the ladder, he pressed the tip of the knife against the nape of my neck. I felt the sharpness that had ended Ian's life. Facing him, all pulse and sweat, I asked, "Why did you do it, Alexander? Why did you kill Ian?"

"You too, honey," Alexander said. "Come down."

She said, "I'm sorry, Mark. I thought he just wanted to speak with you at the wharf. To make sure you weren't on his trail." Climbing down, she began crying.

"You're still an accessory," Alexander told her. "In this and in covering up your brother's accident."

"Accident?" I said. I scanned the sea around us, but there was no one else in sight. The chaos in Provincetown and Truro—the fires, the gridlock—had reduced the number of recreational boaters. There was no one else to turn to—Sallie was my only hope, this half-sister who'd shunned me as family, this spoiled heiress complicit in her own brother's death.

Alexander threw her some keys. "Sallie, go to my cabin and get a blue nylon jacket in the top drawer. Don't be alarmed if it seems a bit heavy, I've sewn weights into the pockets. Mark, I've got to ask you to disrobe. You're going for a swim, and I don't want to leave the cops any clues."

"How was Ian's death an accident?" I asked him.

His expression was handsomeness untroubled. "I don't owe you any explanations."

"You owe it to her—to your fiancé!" I shouted. "You owe her an explanation why you killed her brother!"

Sallie's eyes were bright, like the diamond ring that dominated her hand the way this psychopath dominated her life.

"It was an accident, Mark," Sallie said. "It was really Ian's fault. He'd been drinking at the beach then back at his house. Ian was so jealous by nature. Jealous that I was getting engaged. Jealous of Alexander's success."

All along, I'd assumed Ian had been killed returning from the beach, returning from his hollow in the dunes in Herring Cove. But he'd gone home first, to his house on the hill, to that spaceship of a house overlooking the breakwater. If he had been killed returning directly from the beach, from meeting me, from our sex in the dunes, he would have been found.

"They went for a walk on the breakwater, after dark, Ian and Alexander, after dinner," Sallie said. "Ian got mad and pulled a knife on Alexander. They scuffled and lost their balance—the rocks were very loose. They fell and Ian accidentally got stabbed."

"That is a lie," I told Sallie. "Ian didn't pull a knife on Alexander—Alexander pulled a knife on *him*. The only knife Ian carried was his Swiss Army knife, with the little collapsible blades. That was much too small to slit Ian's throat—ear-to-ear, *almost to the bone."* I shouted at Sallie, "I know because I saw him, *I saw Ian dead on the breakwater that night!"*

"What?!" Sallie again began crying.

"He's lying," Alexander said.

"I was at the beach, all day," I said. "I saw Ian there, at Herring Cove. We shared a bottle of vodka. We talked in the dunes."

The boat was rocking. The waves had swollen and the white-caps sent spray that occasionally wet our faces. Sallie, lost in the immensity of a sweater that was obviously his, was sobbing.

"Why did you take Chloe?" I yelled at Alexander.

"Take your clothes off, you prick," Alexander ordered me. "You're going overboard, naked, with no identifying clothing, no wounds, no marks—" To Sallie, he said, "He knows about Chloe, so he's got to go."

"He'll kill Chloe too, if he hasn't already," I said. "He cut your brother's throat, he cut his throat!"

"He was wounded in the chest, honey," Alexander stated. "Just like the newspapers said. And that was an accident."

Alexander advanced toward me, readying the knife.

I had always thought of the sea as my ally; I'd grown up in Gloucester, which drew its living from the sea. I saw myself at five on Good Harbor Beach, by the rust-colored rocks in the eelgrass of the estuary, and I saw myself with Ian, off Ten Pound Island, in a sea that seemed eager to claim my life. It might do that today, I thought.

Unless I decided to fight.

I could fight only by remaining calm, calm as on stage. I was doing a scene, I told myself. And fighting for Chloe and my life.

Unlike the Master's Enforcer, Alexander wasn't armed with a gun. He couldn't kill me from a distance, he had to get close enough to stab me, and, unlike Ian, I couldn't be taken by surprise. This time, I wouldn't let fear shut me down, freeze me the way it froze me in Truro at the steam bath, when we'd filed in, obedient as schoolchildren during fire drills.

"A Swiss Army knife isn't something you use suddenly, it's too slow. You have to take it out, choose the right blade, unfold the blade…" I pointed to the divers' knife Alexander had the bravado, the gall, to use again. "Look at that knife closely, Sallie, that's the knife he used to kill your brother, our brother—"

"He's right, the papers said—"

"The part about the throat wound wasn't published in the papers. Sometimes the police withhold details of a crime, it helps them to weed out false confessions! Remember, Ian's casket was closed. That was because of the wounds to his throat. That wouldn't have been necessary if he'd only sustained chest wounds."

"It's all lies," Alexander said. "He'd fought with Ian, he'd assaulted him in public. Ian told us all about it, remember, Sallie? He didn't speak with Ian the day Ian died because he and Ian weren't on speaking terms!"

"Sallie, please, I'm your brother!"

Sallie's crying seemed to provoke the seagulls, which were circling the boat like a Greek chorus. That passing simile, that theater cliché, called to mind a detail of my encounter with Ian that might convince Sallie I was telling the truth, about seeing Ian dead and alive.

I said, *"Chorus Against Fascism: The Greek Resistance."*

"What?" Alexander laughed.

"By Stavros Zarefes," I said. I repeated the title and author as the gulls kept squawking in their chorus. "That was the book Ian was reading the day he died. He showed it to me when we talked in the dunes. He left, then I fell asleep on the beach. I found him coming back, on the breakwater, dead. With his throat slit open, ear-to-ear."

"It's true, Alexander." Sallie was speaking as softly as I'd ever heard her. "I remember us talking about that book that evening. You mentioned being in Greece, in Symi, at the sponge diving museum—"

He lunged toward me, grappling my shoulders, the knife in his right hand. The shoulder I'd injured in Truro, throwing myself against the steam room door, sent a current of pain coursing through my system that made me buckle and drag us both down. He'd been clutching the segments of Sallie's broken diamond bracelet, and, as we struggled, these dropped to the deck.

He was readying the knife, his plan about a body with no wounds now abandoned. With desperate effort, I punched at his face and pushed him so that he stumbled and I stood.

It was strange that at that moment that time did not stop but seemed to stretch, like the endless seconds before an inevitable collision. I saw, on the deck, between the segments of the bracelet, three possible weapons to save my life—some rope, a bait bucket, and a jar of something dead from the sea, floating in something murky, in formaldehyde.

I seized the jar of marine specimens and struck the crown of his head so that the jar broke and glass, fish entrails, and poison went streaming down into his eyes. "My God!" he gasped. "I can't see!"

Blood from his scalp went running down his face. Blindly, he bumped against the bait bucket, still clutching his knife. "Sallie!" he screamed. "Get me water to rinse—"

Would she help him? Would she switch sides at last?

She pushed me aside, crunching through the broken glass as she stepped toward Alexander to place her hands against his chest—her dark hands with the diamond ring sparkling against the blood-red stripes of his rugby shirt. She picked shards of glass from his rugby shirt as he bellowed, "Get me water to rinse my eyes, *Sallie. NOW!*"

Then she shoved him.

"Cunt!" The blood from his scalp in his eyes went streaming down his face to his neck so that it mimicked Ian's wounds. He raised his knife to slash at her, but missed. She shoved him and he fell against the low side of the boat, slipped in the fish entrails, then righted himself. Then she shoved him again and he lost his balance, and, flailing his arms, he fell overboard.

He screamed. A wave, gray and massive as the side of a whale, washed over him. He seemed dazed by his wound, unable to swim. I saw his hand, then the top of his bleeding scalp.

There was a life preserver within easy reach, but neither of us made any move to throw it.

Alexander's face rose briefly above the water before he sank for the last time, and the only sounds were the heaving of the waves and the chorus of gulls arguing and arguing...

Sallie began sobbing, staring at Atlantic.

"Where are the keys to the cabin that's locked? Chloe's in there, isn't she?" I shouted.

"...Above the sink," she said. "...Marked '1.'"

I found them, suspended from a small brass rack shaped like an octopus. I had to coax the lock, wiggling the key in and out, but finally it gave.

They were side by side on the bed, bound with plastic restraints on their wrists and ankles—the little girl and the old man—Chloe and Duncan Drummond.

"Chloe!" I hugged her.

There was no acknowledgement in her eyes, only fright. Her mouth was smeared with that gruel that had stuck to the cell phone.

She seemed exhausted, stunned. Duncan Drummond stared out from his ruined mind.

"You'll be fine," I told Chloe, almost believing it.

Chapter Forty-two

"Ian Drummond was killed by Alexander Nash to inherit the Drummond family fortune. Alexander had the perfect opportunity to commit the murder and be fairly confident it would be pinned on someone else. Given the craziness that was happening here this summer." So said Sergeant Almeida, at breakfast with Roberto and me, on the back porch of the White Gull. The summer-long drought had at last broken. Dumpling-like clouds monopolized the sky, and a hard rain was drilling down onto the guest house garden, and, beyond, onto the water of Provincetown Harbor, which looked pitted, like metal.

Almeida would explain what he'd learned from the various investigations, from the West Coast authorities, from the survivors of the Truro inferno—and from Sallie, my pitiful and treacherous half-sister.

They'd met in a wine bar, Sallie and Alexander, amid the exposed brick and easy-listening music. She claimed she'd gone west to experience the mountains, but the lure of the Cascades hadn't brought her to Seattle; her family had driven her from the east, that nonstop drive for competition, chasing the blue ribbon, being number one, in sports, in business, in life.

"She was a vulnerable girl," Sergeant Almeida said, "beneath the image of the steely equestrienne. Alexander knew an easy mark when he saw one. He wasn't a marine biologist, by the way. That's why he brought those props onto that boat, the books on oceanography, the jars of specimens in formaldehyde.

He wasn't in the east doing research at Woods Hole, the story he'd sold Sallie and the Drummonds. The closest he came to being a marine biologist was working one summer in a salmon cannery. In Alaska.

"That's where he came from, from a military family. He grew up on the big air base at Caribou Bight. He moved to San Diego, Coronado, when he was ten. He tried junior college for a couple of years, taking courses in economics and political science."

"No acting?" I asked.

"He hardly needed instruction in that. Alexander had joined the Army but got booted out during basic training, for injuring another soldier during a fistfight. That ticked his old man off once and for all. The old man cut Alexander out of his will and told him to get lost, which he certainly did. In more ways than one.

"That was very traumatic for Alexander. He'd been raised to think of family as very important, with his Mormon roots and so on. The old man was an ancestry nut; he'd traced his family back to Norman lords, or so he told his kids and anyone who'd listen. He made all of his kids carve their coat of arms as soon as they turned twelve as a kind of rite of passage. Alexander was one of nine children in a litter that included an Annapolis graduate and the mayor of San Clemente, so he probably felt like a spare tire at best even before his first real bad screw-ups.

"After breaking with his family, Alexander bounced from scam to scam, in everything from a chain of steakhouses to a greyhound racetrack. He was a first-class con man, great at pitching an idea, closing the deal, then bailing with the cash just before it all went sour. Not the way to win many friends. By the time he showed up at the Potlatch, the wine bar where he zeroed in on Sallie, he'd burned his bridges throughout the west coast.

"The image he presented was a house of cards. A house of credit cards, to be precise. He seemed prosperous, even prominent. He had a loft full of Native American art. He knew vintages of wine and hot tips on stocks. He was active in libertarian politics and the right-to-life movement, of all things.

But the veneer was beginning to crack. He'd beaten up a couple of girlfriends, fractured a woman's skull in Portland. His chief attraction to Sallie was, ironically, her family. Her traditional, moneyed family from the east—the exact life Sallie yearned to escape.

"Alexander was after Sallie's family's money. Which was all the more tempting since so few heirs were on hand to inherit it. Sallie and Ian were change-of-life babies, so their brothers, Fulton and George, were much older—and sterile, unable to father children. They'd caught mumps in their late teens at Exeter. Prep schools were bad news for that family.

"So Alexander, with his outsized ego and big family hang-ups, decides he and Sallie will found their own dynasty. He'll become an instant Boston Brahmin, to thumb his nose at his old man in Coronado.

"Alexander moves east with Sallie. And right away, Ian gets on his case. Unlike Fulton or George, he's local, in Massachusetts. And he's got an inquiring mind and a combative personality. He's very curious about his sister's fiancé.

"He catches some BS in Alexander's marine biology and figures his whole story is bogus. He phones the Woods Hole lab where Alexander allegedly works and asks for his title for correspondence. And of course the lab people say he hasn't ever worked there, not fishing, not cutting bait, nothing. —Sallie admits Ian told her all this, but love is blind, right?"

I hadn't seen Sallie since she'd lured me onto that boat, into that cruise to nowhere, and I didn't want to ever see her again, or any of that sorry, sordid family, whose blood in my veins now felt like some kind of infection.

"So Ian keeps needling Alexander, who gets madder and madder. Who is this rich lout to sabotage his plans, his pipe-dream of the good life?

"Alexander gets obsessed with shutting him up at all costs, and soon. The cult dumps the dead dog on Arthur Hilliard's doorstep and Alexander, ever the entrepreneur, sees a golden opportunity, pardon the pun. Provincetown is in turmoil—between the Christian Soldiers and the street people's invasion, so when Alexander kills Ian, everyone assumes it's a hate crime. All should be well. Another young Drummond heir is dead. Alexander can establish his dynasty in peace, funded, in the long-term, by Sallie's family." Then Almeida smiled, savoring the moment like a replay of a Red Sox home run in Fenway Park. "But there was just one catch—the issue of Ian."

"But Ian was dead," Roberto said.

Almeida cracked his knuckles, pausing. His timing was good, good enough for improv. "Ian was dead, but he hadn't been sterile. *He was the father of a three-year-old daughter, Chloe Hilliard.*"

Roberto and I sat stunned. There was nothing Drummond in Chloe's features, not the line of her jaw or the color of her hair, not her eyes or her ears or her smile. There was no more Drummond in Chloe than in me; Miriam's genes had prevailed completely. And Chloe being Ian's daughter made her my blood relation, my niece, in fact. I had saved my own niece from death in the Atlantic.

Miriam had confessed to the police. She'd been truthful about her Peruvian tragedy, about the diplomat's son and the car crash in Lima. And she'd been truthful about Martin, the stranger from the sketching class she'd seduced in hopes of fathering her child. She had indeed gotten pregnant, but miscarried during her first trimester.

"So she asked an old friend to be a sperm donor, and he was willing and able. He'd been an equal-opportunity Casanova in his youth. Ian Drummond fathered Chloe, and then ruined his relationship with Miriam by scorning the child once she was born. Ian had told Sallie about Chloe just before Sallie moved west. He felt safe confiding in her because she was leaving Boston, less likely to tell the family whom she was hell-bent on avoiding.

"Now remember, with Alexander we're dealing with a whacko obsessed on founding his own blueblood dynasty. And he's almost there, things are humming along. Then you come waltzing into the picture. And call on the happy couple at Ian's house."

"Because Sallie asked me to," I said, a bit defensive. "She tried to pawn off this junk Ian collected at St. Harold's."

"Right, and that's all she really wanted at that point," Almeida said. "But you tried to talk family, you claimed you were Duncan Drummond's son. Sallie, ironically, didn't believe you. Duncan hadn't told his kids he was your dad: he'd told his wife and their lawyer, that was it. Sallie thought you were nuts, but she told Alexander. And he believed you, with every paranoid brain cell in his head. And you repeated the story to Alexander in Gloucester, so Sallie claims he told her. You were the last thing Alexander needed—another young Drummond heir—and investigating Ian's murder to boot."

I remembered Sallie, half naked in her bikini bottom and diamond tennis bracelet, the one that came undone on that awful boat. "How could Sallie…how could she stay with that psychopath after she knew he'd butchered her brother?"

"Her equestrian training may have come in handy. That concentration, that way of focusing. Alexander admitted he'd caused Ian's death, so she willed herself to believe it was an accident, to believe his story. That Ian was jealous of her relationship with Alexander, so Alexander suggested a private talk. Then they'd gone for a walk on the breakwater after dinner, Ian and Alexander together, and Ian pulled a knife then got stabbed when they'd struggled.

"It was a risk for Alexander to sell Sallie that story because the wounds to Ian's throat could have been mentioned by the media. But Alexander was lucky—the throat wounds were known only to us—and to you. We told the funeral home not to mention them to the family, that they were part of the murder investigation.

"Once Sallie helped Alexander cover all that up, she became a kind of accessory after the fact. As he was helpful enough to remind her, day in and day out. Sallie can, legitimately, claim she feared for her life, feared Alexander's physical violence. He'd beaten her badly after Ian's murder."

Of course, I remembered her bruised face when I'd met her at Adams Pharmacy. She'd claimed her father, in his dementia, had hit her.

"Alexander kidnapped Chloe without thinking his plan through. Sallie, meanwhile, was desperate—"

"But not desperate enough to call the police," I said. "She lured me onto that boat—"

"Correct. It was Sallie who'd phoned Arthur's to be sure you were there, after trying your apartment and the White Gull. Sallie was the hang-up call you got while watching the news, the fire at the Truro compound, the police raid. Sallie knew it might be necessary for you to be silenced, if you got suspicious of Alexander—he'd hinted this might mean roughing you up at most. Then, out at sea, when you blamed Lucas Mikkonen for Ian's death, that was music to Sallie's ears. She wanted to drop you back at the wharf, but Alexander wanted something a bit more permanent. He was probably bent on killing you both, you and Chloe, the last Drummond heirs in his way. So when you saw her toy, when you saw Chloe's mermaid, you played right into his hands, it was perfect. That was just the excuse to pitch both of you overboard.

"If you hadn't come along, I think Sallie might've snapped. She might've fought Alexander over harming the little girl. Chloe was the last link to her brother, after all. Ian had told Sallie—and Sallie alone—that he was the little girl's father. And she foolishly told Alexander."

He would explain Ian's ties with Lucas Mikkonen, the Master. I'd been right, Ian and Mikkonen had met at the doll shop when Ian's father, Duncan, in his dementia, took a doll without paying. When Ian returned the doll to Mrs. Mikkonen's shop, her son was there, visiting Rockport with his entourage to bully a printer about a bill, the printer I'd questioned in my "inquiry," as Almeida put it.

"They were kindred spirits, Ian and Mikkonen, both seekers with the need to know what lies beyond. And now, presumably, their questions have been answered."

So, amid the blackened buildings and dead Tree of Life, a body had been identified as Lucas Mikkonen's.

"Ian was ill with lymphoma," Almedia said.

"Ill or dying?" I said.

"Very ill. Which was probably tied to steroid abuse. Fuelled, of course, by the Drummond family mania in sports."

Roberto said, "So if Alexander had just bided his time…"

"Alexander wasn't good at biding," Almeida said. "And he didn't know Ian was sick because Ian never mentioned his cancer to his family. In the Drummond household, physical weakness was a disgrace. So Ian shared his illness with only two people in the world—the Episcopal priest at the family church in Gloucester and his other spiritual advisor, Lucas Mikkonen."

"What will happen to Sallie?"

"Well, shoving Alexander overboard was perfectly within the realm of self-defense. He was wielding a knife and ready to use it on anyone thwarting his plans."

I hesitated, but curiosity got the better of me. "I'd heard the killer left something behind. On the breakwater." That I'd worried was the broken vodka bottle, covered with my incriminating fingerprints.

"Oh, that was a false lead," Almeida said, "a wallet we traced to a tourist from North Carolina."

"How did you first suspect Alexander was Ian's killer?" Roberto said.

"Mrs. Drummond tipped us off, Ian's mother. He'd lied to her about playing varsity tennis in college. She could tell he was new to the game, so that got her suspicious."

Then he arrived—he blurted his name and title in the Federal Bureau of Investigation, but, for me, he would always be Jason. His hair was shorn, but he'd retained his Italian suit and tart manner. "I don't have much time." He checked his onyx-faced watch with no numbers. He pulled up a wicker chair, blocking our view of Sergeant Almeida as naturally as the moon eclipses the sun. "I hope I'm not interrupting anything."

"Not at all." Almeida rose so fast that he almost grazed a hanging pot of fuschia. "I was just going to leave."

Jason called the Truro community "a biotech firm turned hit squad." If a god was involved, it was surely Mars; theirs was a religion based on war. There was little being accomplished involving farming and genetic research. They were successful at growing one crop, tobacco, which they gave to certain children to stunt their appetites, to save on groceries for the lower castes. But the dazzling produce the community hawked, including the jams Jason supplied to Scents of Being, was a mere cover. Jason said, "Their produce was grown through the inordinate use of fertilizers and pesticides, some illegal, actually. But their biological dabbling was even worse. We found outer buildings, not burnt, thank God, with stocks of biological weaponry. Plague, botulism, even some rare tropical pathogens."

"What happened to Edward," I asked. "Edward Babineaux?"

"Ah, yes, the family Babineaux. Edward survived a few hours at Cape Cod Hospital, before dying of smoke inhalation. But his mother is doing just fine, she's in custody."

I saw the pitiful image of Edward, connected to tubes and blinking machines, in an intensive care unit all bone-white tile. Arthur's treasure, with his hard body and fragile lungs—of course the smoke had overwhelmed him. Despite his treachery and deception, I felt pity for Edward and guilt for my hitting him that day in my apartment.

"I accused him of ransacking my apartment," I said. "Someone had searched it. Moved all my furniture."

"Yes, the street children, the panhandlers. Sent to Provincetown to spy on you. Since you'd been asking so many questions. They found a mysterious towel, hidden under your bureau. Covered with a substance resembling blood, so they stole it to be tested in their lab. The substance turned out to be tar, tar from the beach."

After all my worry that that stain was Ian's blood, blood from the horror on the breakwater. "Did any of those children survive? Those children they'd turned into slaves?"

"There are a small number of survivors, mostly children, ironically, of the lowest caste. They were locked in Royall's old ice house, in the woods. There are fifteen survivors, out of a total of ninety-four residents of the Truro compound. That figure includes the two arsonists captured in the National Seashore. Twenty-six people were arrested in Stark, at the prep school, St. Harold's."

"Edward Babineaux warned me about the Golden One," I said. "He warned me I was in some sort of danger."

"At that point, he was probably projecting," Jason said. "He knew he was in danger himself."

"Why did the Enforcer let Edward go? The Enforcer—the man you knocked out to free us—"

"Emmanuel Costa. He survived. He's talking now, talking a lot."

"Did he really rape Edward, then let him go?"

"Oh, yes, Edward's rape story was true. Costa confirmed it. It was a friendly reminder of how Edward should accommodate their target, Arthur Hilliard. Edward had tried to run away from Truro, but Costa caught him, hitchhiking. Edward's assignment, given after his capture and assault, was to find a moneyed gay man to somehow blackmail. That's why he showed up on Arthur's beach; he'd probably gotten wind of his big party. But Arthur had no dark side, no secrets, he was just too respectable to blackmail. And Edward took a liking to life at Arthur's, so he resisted Costa's pressure to move on. That's when Costa dropped Eberhardt on Arthur's doorstep."

"Eberhardt?" I said.

"The racing driver?" said Roberto.

"Edward's dog, named for the racing driver," Jason said. "Tied with a ribbon—not red, by the way. Costa killed the dog to remind Edward how he could end up. If he didn't toe the line. Costa was the phantom phone caller, too, calling for Edward to shake down Arthur or come back. Those calls Edward answered nights at Arthur's."

"The cult was so desperate that blackmail became a potential as a source of revenue?" Roberto asked.

"Sure, the cult was in trouble with the IRS, so the street children's spare change and other small scams got to become fairly important." Jason inspected one of the White Gull's singed muffins, then put it back on the china plate. "Edward was afraid to return to Truro empty-handed, so he fled to the Christian Soldiers. In the end, though, he went back to the fold."

"And left us to die at that steam bath," I said. "If you hadn't come along—"

Jason cut short my compliment. "Saving you two blew my cover. I had to leave the compound that very evening. Had to haul my ass out of there because of you." He picked up the same charred muffin he'd just rejected, then set it down. "Fools rush in."

We blushed, Roberto and I. No wonder Almeida avoided this guy.

"But I rescued a girl they'd tied to their Tree of Life. There were others I couldn't help, that girl they found dead in the Province Lands the next morning. Killed by pesticide poisoning." He shook his head. "They kept the worst things hidden. Even from their followers, even from me."

I remembered the blurry figures running behind the misty glass in the greenhouses.

I said, "Despite all he saw, despite all he knew, Edward went back."

"When the chips were down, his first loyalty was to the cult. It was really…all he had."

"But it had driven his brother, Clark, insane."

"Wrong," Jason said. "Clark was ill long before the family became involved with the cult. Their refusal to allow him access to his medication for schizophrenia undoubtedly contributed to his death, in that when he was expelled from the compound, he wandered into Provincetown, and, confronting the exhibit on Royall—with its photographs of familiar landmarks like the buildings and the pond and the rune stone—he went berserk.

And the title of one picture didn't help. He attacked the art and the museum staff, then he was arrested and killed himself in jail."

"Did you see Clark that day, the day I saw you going to Scents of Being, the day Clark went crazy at the museum?"

"No," Jason said. "I didn't see Clark, and, as far as I know, he didn't see me. Of course, Commercial Street, all of Provincetown, is awfully cozy."

"Did Edward know Ian before this summer?" I asked.

"Possibly. Through the cult."

So Edward being in Ian's bedroom might actually have been planned. At the St. Harold's memoriam party. They might have arranged some sort of meeting that I'd unknowingly sabotaged.

"You went to Ian's funeral," I said to Jason. "I saw you." Thanks to Gaston, Suki Weatherbee's Senegalese husband, outraged by Jason's hair.

"I was sent by the cult," Jason explained. "They were worried about the Drummonds. They wanted me to listen, to see if the family connected the cult to Ian's death. Given the bad blood between them."

"It was you at our show, too. Wasn't it?" I said. "You were the guy posing as an agent. At our second show at Quahog. With just the two of us."

"Negative."

"So who was it? The Provincetown police?"

"Not that I know of."

"You're got a fan, Mark. Deal with it," Roberto said.

"And the fundamentalists had nothing to do with anything that happened here this summer?" I said.

"Not directly," Jason said, "other than sheltering Edward. But they set the stage for Alexander to murder Ian and be confident everyone would label it a hate crime. They shook things up, put everyone on edge. As did the street people, of course." He smiled. "By the way, old Thomas Royall got his revenge of sorts. Against those pseudo-Vikings who despised him."

It was thanks to the brothers Babineaux and their mother's penchant for wild mushrooms. Last year, Edward and Clark had been collecting wild mushrooms when they uncovered human remains in the woods, on the grounds of the Truro compound. The remains were skeletal, buried without clothing or belongings of any kind except for a small animal's tusk set in silver on a chain. Foul play was obviously involved; the victim's skull had been crushed. The cult instructed the Babineaux brothers to keep this secret, because, with an IRS audit and past troubles with the police about gunfire and shoplifting and so forth—a body on the premises was the last thing they needed. But Clark was always more rebellious than his younger brother: he telephoned the police, who kept his identity secret. The discovery of the body was the perfect pretext to get authorities into the compound and then invite the FBI to infiltrate the cult, via Jason posing as a drug dealer in search of enlightenment. "They were racist enough to buy the stereotype. Of course, the dreadlocks helped. We, the Bureau, were also investigating the group on kidnapping charges involving an Ohio girl. And there were allegations of child abuse long before, in those toxic dumps they had the nerve to call greenhouses."

It was ironic that DNA testing proved the skeleton had nothing to do with the site's current residents. The victim had been murdered long before the Master was even born. "The skeleton was Thomas Royall's," Jason stated.

I stopped drinking my orange juice. Mrs. Babineaux had mentioned this murder during our tour; I'd assumed it was slander, nonsense. I said, "But Royall supposedly drowned." He'd become the target of anti-German hysteria on the Cape after the Kaiser's U-boat had shelled Chatham. He'd supposedly killed himself because his colony was collapsing; his clothing—sandals, a robe embroidered with runes—had been found on a beach in Truro.

It was planted there, they now believed. Jason said Royall's utopia had been seething with resentment over the special treatment accorded their leader's favorite, Gilbert Dyer, the model for *The Fisher Boy*.

Eventually, Dyer became Royall's companion in the physical sense, violating Royall's own rule that the colony remain celibate. Dissension flared in the ranks, resulting in fights and acts of vandalism. Royall and Dyer clashed when Dyer seduced a sculptor. Royall clawed Dyer so severely he grew whiskers to hide the scars.

Then the Chatham shelling occurred on July 21, 1918, and local thugs attacked the colony, destroying some kilns and looms. The next day, both Royall and Dyer vanished. It appeared that Royall had drowned himself, despondent that his utopia was unraveling. Dyer was discovered three weeks later, dead of a morphine overdose, in a flophouse in Boston. "Lost, it was thought, without his mentor. We now know better. Re-reading Dyer's suicide note in light of discovering Royall's body makes it plain that Dyer bludgeoned Royall to death.

Pathologists were able to certify the skeleton belonged to Royall by matching DNA extracted from the bones with a blood sample taken from a relative of the painter in Wisconsin. The authorities had kept this information quiet so as not to alert the media and jeopardize their case against the cult. Jason added, "History repeated itself on that property. The theme of internecine warfare."

So why had he mentioned that body to me, that night at the Truro compound, in the chill room with the fire in the fireplace? Abruptly Jason lost his hipster cool, his FBI hubris. Like an actor losing concentration on stage. He mumbled something about "unfortunate" and "procedure" and "these things happen," then at last bit into the burnt muffin he'd been toying with yet again. I gathered his confiding about the body had been an error. He changed the subject: "You remember when my beeper went off? That was the Provincetown police. With the news of Chloe Hilliard being kidnapped. At first we thought she was in Truro, in an outer building, hidden away. The cult had such an awful record with small girls."

"Why would anyone get involved with such crazies?" Roberto asked.

"The cult offered answers to the lost, a sense of belonging, spirituality of a sort. Its message of eco-reverence coupled with Norse flavorings was not totally ridiculous. Not totally. Unfortunately, with its pesticides and stores of TB and Ebola, it violated its own theology. And creating that serf caste of abused female children, that was unconscionable, unconscionable."

"Some men in the cult were castrated," I said.

"And some women sterilized," Jason said. "Anyone who'd earned a Nordic name who subsequently lapsed by breaking the rules forfeited the right to propagate by going under the knife. They were all made 'clean.'

"The cult had benign beginnings, in a yoga group in western Massachusetts called the Circle of Harmonic Peace. That's what Theo Babineaux, Edward's father, joined.

"Lucas Mikkonen sought out the Circle after a nervous breakdown at MIT. He stayed involved with them right through earning his doctorate and starting a biotech firm with four of his classmates.

"Mikkonen was fired from that company when he admitted he'd been falsifying data. Then the Circle became his life. He sank more and more money into the organization, eventually assuming total control.

"When he chanced upon the old Royall property, it appealed to his Norse heritage, hoax of a rune stone and all. It was the perfect place to become the Master—to isolate his followers and scheme against his classmates, now millionaires, biotech's big *wunderkinds*.

"Then Mikkonen met Ian at his mother's shop, returning a doll Duncan Drummond had stolen. For Ian, ill with lymphoma, Mikkonen was a confidant spiritual mentor—and a convenient customer to buy some land at his old prep school. So Mikkonen bought the property, then discovered the bog lily prevented his bringing in the bulldozers. He felt cheated, he felt had. Ian probably had made an honest mistake. It doesn't appear he knew about the plant.

"Then things in the cult were going woefully wrong. Mikkonen's health was breaking down due to diabetes and obesity. The IRS was auditing him, the red ink was flowing. Gradually, Emily Babineaux, his accountant, and Emmanuel Costa, her lover, took control of the cult in very elegant, very quiet palace coup. All but invisible to the Master's flock.

"By that time, Mikkonen was a virtual prisoner. Revered but imprisoned. Indispensable but immobile. Like the queen in a termite colony."

"Emily Babineaux began targeting a new enemy—not Lucas Mikkonen's biotech rivals, but the HMO she blamed for her husband's death. For misdiagnosing his pancreatic cancer. She earmarked the same germs for new enemies, on the date Master had chosen for his debacle, the autumnal equinox—the beginning of fall."

The Fall, of course, the day they all talked of.

"Emily Babineaux was not known as the treasurer within the cult, although that was certainly what she became—and more. She'd been given a new nickname for her way with the dollar. And with the IRS agents conducting the audit. Before her marriage, she'd studied art education, so she could have suggested the nickname herself.

"Her subjects in Truro called her the Golden One."

Chapter Forty-three

Arthur Hilliard's garden was flourishing. Thanks to his defying the ban on outdoor watering, it was thick with daisies, hollyhocks, and chrysanthemums, all competing for our attention. On the terrace overlooking the flowers and Provincetown Harbor, Arthur was grilling tuna steaks bloody as any beef while Roberto and I stood watching.

"I don't like chrysanthemums," Roberto announced. "They're too September."

"Labor Day happens," Arthur said. He was elated, and with good reason. His Swim for Scholars, held yesterday and dedicated to Ian's memory, had gone…swimmingly, raising $80,000 toward college scholarships for deserving students at Provincetown's high school. Roger Morton was absent, a patient at Ashdown Farms, the exclusive Connecticut clinic, being treated for an eating disorder. It was this and not something organic that had been wasting his body all these months.

"I'm donating my reward money for your finding Chloe to our Swim for Scholars Program, Mark," Arthur informed me. "Didn't think you'd mind."

Arthur wasn't observant enough to know that I'd welcome his check. He just assumed everyone had money, that it was something you're born with, like ears. So my reward that summer was staying alive, my new life with Roberto, and, eventually, recognition on stage. Reward enough.

Standing in Arthur's garden, I recalled his earlier parties, especially the one this past Memorial Day weekend, beginning a summer that would fill so many graves. I remembered the unlucky *Vasa*, the bone-white Swedish tall ship in the harbor, and Ian swilling his Heineken and Edward serving his fragrant tureens of bouillabaisse. Ian had been right about one thing: we live in an imperfect world, "full of mosquitoes and people who dump trash in national parks." But that shouldn't stop the rest of us from attempting to improve it, in our persistent, incremental ways.

"When are they coming?" Arthur was asking. "They're late."

Minutes later, "they" appeared: Miriam, Chloe, and, of course, Alicia. The anxiety of the summer had chiseled away Miriam's weight so that she looked spare, rationed, even more intense—and she was choosing more conservative clothing, like this mauve silk dress. She gripped Chloe's hand so tightly the little girl winced. You're my niece, more or less, I kept thinking of saying; you're the only Drummond I'll ever love. But I left those words until much, much later.

The greatest change the summer had wrought was in Alicia. Gone were the mohair sweaters and barrettes. She was wearing a dust-gray jogging suit for our little celebration, although she'd retained her mustard seed charm. She had left the Christian Soldiers, "left but not renounced." With Miriam's help, she'd recognized her relationship with Karl, the manager of their Provincetown office, as abusive and co-dependent, so, when he'd resigned his position to work for a conservative think tank, she'd used the occasion to cancel their engagement, deciding to think about becoming Unitarian. Or Catholic or Church of the Nazarene. The Christian Soldiers would linger in Provincetown until Thanksgiving, dispensing abstinence literature and Hollings Fair's book on parenthood, *Spare the Rod*; then they would depart, having garnered as much publicity as possible, overshadowed as they were by Ian's slaying and the maelstrom that followed. Hollings Fair decided to concentrate on anti-evolution crusades in the West. He sold his office on

Commercial Street, which was occupied successively by businesses selling Cuban food, hemp hammocks, and pewter knick-knacks—knights, Merlins, dragons. No business would last there longer than six months. Rumors persisted about supernatural phenomena driving tenants away, but a cable TV crew that staked out the building with psychics, cameras, and bugging devices came up empty.

"Chloe!" I called to her. "It's so nice to see you!"

She didn't answer. Like her mother, she'd lost a good deal of weight. Being woeful cooks, her kidnappers had fed her little but Ritalin-spiked Cream of Wheat, to keep her quiet.

Miriam hugged me, whispering, "Thank you again," as Chloe broke away to hide in a hibiscus bush. "Chloe," Miriam called to her, "Mark is the good man from the boat, you know that. The bad man is gone and the police have arrested the bad woman." Sallie was actually out on bail, under sedation herself, with her family in Gloucester.

"Chloe, all my goldfish have been asking for you," Arthur told her, as she peered between the stalks of the hibiscus bush like some frightened forest creature.

"I owe you all the biggest apology in the world." Miriam directed her attention toward Chloe, as if her gaze itself sustained the child's very existence. "I just couldn't tell the truth about…Chloe's father because Ian was so dismissive after she was born. He'd just laugh and belittle the whole situation. 'My little transgression,' he called her. Empathic as always…The police told me they had the kidnap suspects under surveillance without specifying who they were. They were watching Sallie and Alexander for two days, the whole time they were living on that boat. The police were about to move when the Truro thing broke." Miriam squeezed my shoulder, the sore shoulder, of course, and said, "Thank you for saving my little girl's life…Uncle Mark."

A bee shopping through the hibiscus drove Chloe back toward her mother. She buried her head in the folds of Miriam's dress. Then Arthur produced Chloe's favorite beverage, a bottle of cold cream soda. Refusing it twice, she gave in the third time but didn't want her Krazy Straw: "That's for little kids," she asserted. "She's grown up a lot," Miriam said. "She's had to. But the psychiatrist says she's coping as well as can be expected."

"No tall ship for this party," I remarked to Arthur as I scanned the choppy water of Provincetown Harbor.

"The Scandinavians have gone. All of them," said Arthur.

"I'm going too," Miriam announced.

"What?" several of us said.

"I'm selling," Miriam said, "my shop, my house. Everything I own in Provincetown." It wasn't just the traumas of this summer; it was that "Augustitis" was hitting her Junes, year after year. "And Chloe won't go near my shop, and I don't blame her. She thinks every customer has come to take her away."

I pulled my present for Chloe from its recycled paper bag. "Look, Chloe," I said. I tested the title: "Look what Uncle Mark has brought you." It was a rubber crab that emitted wheezy squeaks.

"Oh, honey, isn't that crab adorable?" Miriam said.

"It came from the ecology store," I said.

"I've seen those," said Alicia, newly environmentally aware. "Those toys are manufactured from old bottles and wrecked cars."

Which did not endear the crab to Chloe at all, who took it gingerly, as if wary it might pinch…

…The last guest didn't come until after we'd eaten. She arrived in her "experienced" Cadillac, her "one bourgeois indulgence," she always called it. Its battered bumper was adorned with a new sticker. "I'm a friend of Bill W.," it read.

My mother wore a shift the color of orangeade and a hat of matching Italian straw. To my surprise, she was not alone. "This is Subash," she said of her solemn companion. "Subash Malik."

"From the meetings," Subash said, as if all of us should know what that meant. He was a rotund man, probably from the subcontinent, with gray hair and a Wild West moustache waxed into ends as sharp as dental pics. "Your mother is a one-in-a-million lady," he told me, pumping my hand exactly three times.

It wasn't really a statement I could repudiate, so I just nodded.

"Subash teaches at the Kennedy School of Government at Harvard," my mother said. "He just got tenure."

Subash beamed. "And what talent your mother has. Between her artwork and her musicianship, she's just amazing, just incredible." Lightly, he touched my mother's arm, and I felt ludicrously possessive, like a jealous toddler. "What a view," Subash said, loosening his Harvard tie. "It's straight out of Joel Meyerowitz."

"One of the few straight things around here," Roberto said.

Subash laughed then shook hands with the rest of my companions, concluding with Chloe. "…And I'm pleased to meet you, young lady. What is the name of your pretty spider doll?"

Chloe giggled and squeezed the crab so that it squeaked.

I introduced my mother to my friends. Roberto I left for last: "And this is my partner, Roberto Schreiber."

"Oh, I'm so happy to meet you!" my mother said. It had been Roberto's idea to invite her to this barbecue specifically to jump-start our relationship. "You've both been through so much. Yet you look so placid and domestic."

Arthur again became the host. "You used to sing here, a while back," he said to my mother. Chloe was dipping her crab into the little fishpond.

"'A while back,' you're being awfully kind," she laughed. "I sang in a little dive called Jubilee's. Dark, smoky, and terribly authentic."

"Jazz," Arthur said.

"She was very good." I said that because it was true, and at that moment, I needed truth more than anything on the planet.

Roberto was staring at my mother, the way I must have stared at his father.

"I'd gone to the New England Conservatory," my mother told Arthur. "But I was a little racy for them."

"And you brought Mark to Provincetown when he was all of…ten?" Arthur asked.

"Eight," my mother said. "And when we visited the museum, Mark was just *entranced* by *The Fisher Boy.*"

"They found Royall's bones in Truro," I said. "Buried on the grounds of that awful commune."

"Good heavens," my mother said. "Years ago, people used to joke that Truro considered Provincetown very scandalous. But now Truro is making up for lost time." She turned toward me. "We should do the same. Do you mind," she asked the others, "if I borrow my son for a few minutes?"

"We're just friends for now, Subash and me," my mother said, out on Commercial Street. "You know, it's silly, but, years ago, I worried about getting married because I thought you might be jealous."

"Never."

"He's a wonderful man. Erudite, brilliant, cheerful as all get out. His wife died of a heart attack five years ago. That's when he began having a problem." Then she said it: "Drinking. Like me. He has a summer place in Annisquam. I met him at AA in Gloucester."

Which explained his "meetings" reference and the bumper sticker on her car. Saying congratulations didn't seem to fit, but I hugged her, there on Commercial Street. I was able to do that.

"Joining AA was my prayer of thanks. For your making it through this nightmare of a summer. It's the closest I'll ever get to being holy."

We walked toward the dunes, away from the crowds and restaurants and shops because my mother said she needed a little privacy. "That's no reflection on your friends—especially on your wonderful young man. Another wonderful young man."

Between the houses and trees, we could catch glimpses of the ocean, of the water that had almost received my corpse. I thought of Alexander Nash, whose body, partially devoured by bottom dwellers, had washed up on Nemasket Beach, where it was found by clam diggers at low tide. I would think of Alexander—dead instead of me—for the rest of my life.

"I remember staying here at the Wharf," I said. "That time you sang at the club."

"You used to look out to sea. From that pier." She was folding her big sun hat in her hands, squeezing it so roughly I thought she might damage the straw. "I shouldn't have encouraged you to look out to sea. It was wrong, it was dishonest. Duncan Drummond offered to marry me. He offered to leave Janet and more or less elope. But by then I'd seen the kind of husband he was, the indifferent kind of father he'd become, and I didn't want to be more indebted to him than I was. His children—Fulton and George—seemed pretty damaged, and poor Janet had just had Ian. A clean break…just seemed preferable. The irony is—one reason I refused to marry Duncan was his drinking. That and his compulsive philandering."

I had to say it. Was that my Drummond recklessness? "But you let them buy your silence. And you told me those lies—"

"I guess I thought…a good lie was better than the bad truth. Sometimes people just make mistakes."

We had come to the place where the street met the water.

"You've turned out fine, Mark," my mother said. "God knows this summer was a test. Saving that little girl—"

"The Talmud says that if you save one man, you save the world. According to Roberto."

"You saved me, too," my mother said. "That talk in the kitchen was my wake-up call. To get it together, to get sober."

Momentarily, we glanced at the breakwater, at the line of granite snaking toward the dunes of Herring Cove Beach. A cold wind, full of autumn and football and encroaching winter darkness, blew goose-bumps onto our skin. The wind seemed to scour the sky of sea birds, and the water assumed a cobalt-blue cast.

She said, "Let's take a different route back," and we turned away.

To receive a free catalog of Poisoned Pen Press titles, please contact us in one of the following ways:

Phone: 1-800-421-3976
Facsimile: 1-480-949-1707
Email: info@poisonedpenpress.com
Website: www.poisonedpenpress.com

Poisoned Pen Press
6962 E. First Ave. Ste. 103
Scottsdale, AZ 85251

ANA   Anable, Stephen.

           The Fisher Boy.

$24.95

DATE			
JUN 1 8 2008			